There was only one Johnny.

A last name wasn't necessary to clarify this guy. I kept the numbers of all the wærewolves who kenneled at my place for full moons, though I'd never yet needed to announce a change in plans.

I dialed Johnny's number. It rang twice. "Johnny, it's Persephone Alcmedi. I—"

"Hey, Red."

That threw me. My hair's dark, dark brown.

"Red?" I aked.

"I've decided I'm going to call you Red from now on."

"All right. I'll bite—no pun intended. Why?"

He snickered in a very masculine way and lowered his voice. " 'Cause I like the idea of the big bad wolf visiting you and Grandma."

Vicious Circle

Linda Robertson

Juno Books
New York London Toronto Sydney

Pocket Books
A Division of Simon & Schuster, Inc.
1230 Avenue of the Americas
New York, NY 10020

First Juno Books/Pocket Books paperback edition July 2009

Cover design by John Vairo Jr.
Cover art by Don Sipley

Manufactured in the United States of America

10 9 8 7 6 5 4 3 2 1

ISBN: 978-1-4391-5428-1

This book is dedicated to . . .

my parents, of course.
Mom, thanks for being an avid reader yourself,
and for keeping imaginative little me supplied with books.
More moms should be like you.
Dad, I know you're proud of me.

And to my boys.
See? Dreams *can* come true
with hard work and perseverance.

Thank Yous:

Red-Caped Hero Thanks

to Mr. Thomas Grandy, my high school creative writing teacher. Because of you, I kept on believing in myself all these many long years.

and to Linda Partlow. Not *all* friends are created equal, but writing friends are the best kind. You not only read but offered support, critiques, sarcasm, witty ridicule (whether or not I deserved it), and the occasional *"now-I-really-think-you're-weird"* shrugs. How cool is that?

Java-n-Chocolate Thanks

to my writing group, the Ohio Writers Network. Michelle, Laura, Melissa, Rachel, Emily, Faith, and Lisa. This bunch is so cool they even have a mascot. . . .

Margarita Thanks

to my editor, Paula Guran.
"Where's my thimbleful? Jose!

Howling Thanks

to Jim Lewis.
You love me exactly as I am. Wow.

Reverent Gratitude

to my Muse who has many names.

CHAPTER ONE

Half past six A.M. A ruggedly handsome man . . . Arthur, yes, *Arthur* . . . held me in his strong arms, gazing into my eyes with sensitivity and understanding and desire, and he was about to kiss me, and—

The sound of the garage door opening ruined my perfectly romantic dream. Blissful slumber broken, I shot out of bed ready to defend my home.

With a baseball bat in my white-knuckled grip, I eased an erratic path—to avoid the squeaky spots—down the stairs. I crept toward the kitchen; the eastern windows were still dark. Ahead, a door on the right connected the house to the garage. I could hear someone starting up the steps out there.

Holding my breath, I hefted the bat.

The door opened.

"Damn wærewolves dumping Krispy Kreme boxes on the lawn."

"Nana." I sighed, relaxing and lowering the bat. I slipped it behind the door.

She didn't even glance my way as she stepped in with the newspaper and a ragged-looking pastry box. Grass blades clung to her pink fuzzy slippers. The paperboy must have missed the driveway again.

She'd just moved in yesterday, so I wasn't used to her being here yet. Clearly, an eighty-four-year-old woman didn't need as much sleep as I expected.

With a Marlboro pinched in the corner of her mouth, she shuffled across the kitchen and asked, "So you get up early nowadays, Persephone?"

I snorted. "No. And I didn't know that you stopped sleeping in."

"Well, as a matter of fact, the crack of dawn is my new alarm clock."

"You're still early."

"Blame the nurses," Nana said. Then she muttered, "They act like it's a boarding school. Get up. Take your medicine. Eat. *Exercise.* Play bingo. I'm paying for it, I should get to sleep and smoke whenever I want." She grumbled all the way to the trash can, where she shook the doughnut box hard enough to make its cellophane top crackle. "This sat out there for at least two goddamned days, you know." This time she spoke louder, so I knew she was talking to me.

"I've been busy," I said, "moving *your* things from Woodhaven." Mentioning the moving reminded me my muscles were sore. The rude awakening and my tense acts of stealth hadn't helped.

She looked at me and frowned, but I wasn't sure if her dour expression was due to my words or my choice of pajamas—lavender panties and a cutoff purple tank top with the words *Round Table Groupie* in ancient-style letters on a shield. It's an accurate description. I've seen every movie and documentary ever made about Arthur Pendragon and amassed a collection of books and artwork based on Arthurian legends. No artist or actor has ever come close to capturing Arthur the way my dreams have, though. Funny that.

Nana tsk-tsked. "Where's your nightgown?"

I had a flashback of the long flannel gowns she'd made me to sleep in as a child. They were straight out of " 'Twas the Night Before Christmas." I wondered if, in her youth, she'd won a lifetime membership to a secret club called Clothiers for the Frumpy Woman. "These *are* my pajamas."

"That's all you sleep in?"

"I lived alone until yesterday, Nana, so what I sleep in hasn't been an issue." Still, the cold October air swirling in made me wish I were wearing my robe. I shut the door she'd left open.

Nana shoved the pastry box into the trash. Little pieces of cut grass cascaded to the kitchen floor. "Damn filthy animals anyway." As she shuffled back to me, her hand smoothed priggishly up and over her mound of white hair. I knew what was coming next. I would have mocked her as she said it, but she was looking right at me. "Witches and wolves aren't meant to mingle." Nana still held to the old adage from long before the public emergence of other-than-human communities.

"Stop it," I said. "They're my friends."

She took the cigarette from her lips and blew smoke up at the ceiling, then pointed the ash-end at the box in the trash can. "Some friends."

I gave her an apathetic look and put my hands on my hips. I *had* started this day ready for a fight.

"They obviously don't think much of you," Nana added. She turned down the hallway.

That wasn't true. "I can't help that you don't like wæres. You're entitled to your own opinions, but don't expect me to feel the same way."

She snorted.

I suddenly realized that I had picked up that rude response from her.

Nana shuffled from the kitchen into the dining room, then into the living room, newspaper still folded under her arm. "To them, you're just some weirdo version of a confessional priest."

Despite being fully aware I was being baited, I followed her. Not because I wanted a fight; I really didn't. But I also didn't back down when someone picked a fight with me. I felt compelled to stop this now, before it became a routine. I'd been forced to listen to her spout her anti-wære opinion repeatedly during my years growing up in her house. Now, well, this was *my* house.

I stopped in the doorway. My old saltbox farmhouse was decorated in an eclectic attempt at Victorian. The living room—with its deep-red walls, stone hearth, and bookshelves filled with everything I own on Arthur—was my sanctuary. Posters of Camelot-themed paintings by John William Waterhouse, Sir Frank Dicksee, and other artists hung in big black-and-gold frames. This was usually a soothing room for me, but not this morning. "Confessional priest? What's that supposed to mean?"

She waved me off, then answered anyway. "You kennel them, alleviating their consciences so they can 'go on.'" Despite the pseudo-drama she added to the last two words, she might have sounded somewhat sage-like but for her verbal stumbling over the word "consciences"—adding a few more syllables than needed. In an attempt to recover, she quickly added, "Besides, friends don't leave garbage on your lawn. Real friends are more respectful than that."

Nana's slippers had tracked cut grass through my house. Sore muscles made me cranky. I snarled, "I'd have thought that family, more so than friends, should be respectful."

"They should."

"You're not."

She turned. "What?"

I pointed at the floor. "You're dropping grass garbage all over my house."

"Where?" she demanded again, squinting at the floor.

There was nothing wrong with her eyes, but she wasn't above feigning elderly ailments when it benefited her.

I strode back to the kitchen and fetched the little broom and dustpan, thinking that at least I'd only have to mow for a few more weeks. Of course, I'd be spending the next few months mopping up melted-snow tracks instead.

After I dumped the debris in the trash can, I shot a glare through the dining room and into the living room where Nana sat. Nana was safe from my glare, hidden behind the newspaper. She had parked herself in *my* cozy chair. It didn't help my mood to realize that it would now be *her* cozy chair.

"You have a valid point," I said, returning to the living room, "but I don't mind if my friends are negligent with a doughnut box. They're responsible enough to kennel themselves on full moons. That matters more to me, and it should count for something to you."

"Right. It counts for something. It counts for them being stupid. Wolves change on full moons; witches raise energies and cast spells on full moons. Why they would want to be anywhere near you during a full moon is beyond comprehension."

"That's the only time it's safe! They're *already* going to change!"

The phone rang. I jumped, then hurried to the kitchen to answer it. A glance at the clock above the old olive-colored stove told me it wasn't even seven yet. Calls this early usually weren't good news. "Hello?"

A formal female voice said, "Persephone Alcmedi, please."

I was immediately worried: the caller pronounced both of my names right the first time. A rare thing. I hoped it wasn't the administrator from the nursing home. They had told me to expect a delay and several headaches getting Nana's Social Security routed back to her and, before coffee, I just wasn't ready to think as hard as the admin was going to want me to. "Who, may I ask, is calling me at six-forty-three in the morning?"

"Vivian Diamond."

I knew of her—definitely not someone affiliated with the nursing home. She was the high priestess of the only Cleveland coven officially endorsed by the Witch Elders Council, or WEC. Vivian's name-dropping social style didn't impress me, and her manner of leadership tended to snub true practitioners in favor of schmoozing the deep-pocketed wannabes. Consequently, I didn't attend the meet-ups or open rituals she held. I did just fine out here in Ohio's farmlands as a solitary.

"I apologize for calling so early," she said, her voice just a bit nasal, "but I need your help. Your name was recommended."

"Recommended by whom?"

She paused. "Lorrie Kordell."

Lorrie used to kennel here on full moons, but had moved closer to Cleveland for work. She was raising her daughter, Beverley, single-handed and single-incomed. I wondered how they were doing. Since Lorrie had found a place in the city to kennel, I missed the popcorn and Disney nights with Beverley. (Crunchy food and musical comedies covered up the sounds of the kenneled wæres nicely.) "How are you acquainted with Lorrie?"

"Who is it, Seph?" Nana called.

I hit the mute button and yelled back, "It's for me, Nana!" Was she going to pry into everything?

"She recently joined my coven," Vivian said.

Shocked, I didn't answer. *This* was what Nana had meant. Wærewolves avoided magic rituals at all costs. The energies raised could cause partial body-shifts—usually of the head and arms—but the mind suffered more than the body. During a partial shift, the wære-mind could devour the human-mind, leaving only a maddened, murderous beast. By law, police could kill on sight any wære in a non-full moon partial transformation.

"Miss Alcmedi?"

"I'm here."

"Miss Alcmedi?"

I undid the mute. "I'm here."

"I'd like to meet with you. Today. Early, if possible."

"Let me check my calendar." Pulling my John William Waterhouse day planner from my purse under the phone stand, I flipped through the pages. It took effort not to fall into daydreaming over the artwork, but I dutifully scanned the appointment lines. The only notation was *column due 3 P.M.* on yesterday's date. I'd met the deadline a day early. A few Tarot readings for regular customers were penciled in for later in the week, but no appointments had been formalized, so my schedule was clear. Reading a high priestess's cards could lead to a larger Tarot clientele. The extra money would help me offset the cost of a live-in Nana.

"What would be a good time and place for you?" I asked. Keeping Nana from crossing paths with clients would be better for all concerned.

"The coffee shop on East Ninth, about four blocks from the Rock and Roll Hall of Fame. Say, one hour?"

Damn. She was seriously urgent. "I can just make it, unless traffic turns into a nightmare." I knew *of* her, but not what she looked like. "How will I know you?"

"Oh, don't worry. I'll know you." She hung up.

I hated it when people didn't say a closing before hanging up. And she'd *know* me? How? I returned the phone to the cradle charger. When I turned, Nana stood in the wide doorway staring at me.

Her wrinkled face was expressionless. If I hadn't known she'd always been that way, I might have thought all the wrinkles were hiding a reaction. "Who's dead?" she asked.

"Nobody's dead."

"People don't call this early unless someone died in

the night." She paused. "Or do your 'friends' do that crap too?"

"The phone rings, Nana, and I answer it. Sometimes it's my friends and sometimes—"

"Fine."

Having her here was going to be like raising a spoiled teenager. She was going to roll her eyes, cut me off, and act like I was inferior.

She shoved a folded section of newspaper at me. "I'm done with this part." She turned and shuffled past the big oak dining table, pudgy hands rising to smooth over her dome of white hair.

The gesture reminded me I hadn't written her weekly hair appointment in my datebook. She insisted on keeping her hair in a beehive style, so it was more like maintenance than hairdressing. (For a good portion of my childhood I thought her head was shaped funny. When I eventually realized it was all done with curlers and hairspray, it diminished her scariness.) I put the newspaper down, grabbed a pen, and jotted the appointment in.

As I finished writing, the paper's front-page headline jumped out at me: *Woman Found Dead.* Underneath, in smaller letters: *Authorities suspect cult involvement.* Scanning the picture, I recognized the face of a crying young girl being restrained by medics, hands reaching toward the sheet-covered body on a stretcher. The girl was Beverley Kordell, Lorrie's daughter.

CHAPTER TWO

Vivian was late.

I'd opted to keep myself from crying by being angry. Transforming any other emotion quickly into anger might not be my best quality, but it could be useful. The nervous energy it stirred up, however, had to be expended somehow. So, as I sat in the coffee shop waiting, my knees took turns bouncing in irritation and impatience. The soles of my burgundy suede flats were getting quite a workout.

Wearing blue jeans, a maroon blazer, and a black tank top, with my dark hair secured in a loose braid, I'd somehow managed a business-casual look, though my mind was reeling as I dressed. I didn't care if Vivian thought I appeared professional or not.

Hunched over the article about Lorrie's murder, I reread it for the fifth time, wishing the news were anything but this. Lorrie had been found in the bedroom of her apartment by the police acting on an anonymous tip. Beverley had been asleep in her own room when the police arrived. The article said nothing about the cause of death, only that Lorrie's body had been "allegedly arranged in a ritualistic manner" and that "symbols were drawn on the walls with what authorities believed was her blood."

Despite the fact that this October morning came with more than the usual amount of Ohio fall chill in the air, I sipped on an iced mocha. My stomach was churning hot. The coffee's flavor was much too strong. I wasn't sure if the barista had made it wrong or if the bitterness was a projection of my present mental state.

Trying to find something good in the situation, the only positive I could see was that Lorrie had known a secret of mine I hadn't wanted to share. Now I didn't have to worry about it ever coming back to haunt me. The rest was all bad. I'd never see Lorrie again. And poor Beverley! So young—her tenth birthday was next month—and now alone.

I knew how rough that was. At about her same age, I ended up with Nana. Beverley didn't have any living grandparents, aunts, or uncles. Poor kid. With whom would she live?

My eyes burned. I had to stop thinking about her or I'd start sobbing again like I had in the shower.

By now, blood tests would have revealed Lorrie's affliction, and the murder would make tomorrow's headlines again. Another notch in the belt of those trying to prove the violence and danger of wæres in the community. Bad press like this made it harder for the good, responsible wære-folk trying to blend into society. I could imagine a terrible version of how this would play out: witchcraft symbols at the murder scene would spark an investigation of the local coven; then the news would break that Lorrie had been infected. Some journalist itching for a Pulitzer would do an exposé and reveal that Lorrie and Vivian were connected, leading to negative public outcry and, worse, Vivian and her coven enduring an inquest by the Elders Council. It had potential to become a witch- and wærebashing media circus.

That was probably why Vivian had called me. She wanted someone uninvolved to do a more objective Tarot reading.

Not that my current state could be termed "objective."

I'd been eyeballing every woman who walked in for the last fifteen minutes. Downtown Cleveland at eight A.M. was a hub of hurrying businesspeople. Many women came and went, tidy in their office wear and comfort-pumps. I expected Vivian to be among them, incognito with a secretarial-type day job and a real life. But when I was finally approached at eight-fifteen, it wasn't by an executive assistant.

"Miss Alcmedi?"

She'd been here all along. As soon as the crowd thinned, she came to my little table and called me by name. Her name badge read *Vivian, Manager.*

With her blond curls fastened up and the ends wildly spraying out, she reminded me of a doll from my childhood; I'd dunked the doll's head in the toilet whenever I wanted to "wash" her hair. It had taken a toll. Vivian's hair, however, looked soft, and the style suited her much better than it had my doll. Her makeup was flawless and, as she bit her lip, her too-white smile glistened. No way she actually drank what she served unless she had those teeth professionally bleached.

My knee stopped bouncing. "Hello."

Under her apron, Vivian wore a pretty cream-colored blouse with long sleeves and sensible cuffs. Combined with tan corduroy slacks and trendy shoes, the outfit made her look like one of her more businesslike customers. Her jewelry, though, was overdone: Diamond stud earrings, a matching necklace and bracelet set in gold, and at least one ring on each finger. Apparently, Vivian took her last name as an accessorizing decree.

"Sorry I couldn't get to you sooner. One of the girls didn't show up. I'd have said something to you, but you went through Mandy's line."

What I knew of Vivian Diamond had come secondhand from Lydia, an elderly witch from whom I'd bought my house and land and who still lived about ten minutes from her former home. Lydia attended every meet-up and coven ritual without fail, then always found a reason to call or stop by and give me a report. Not that I asked her to; Lydia wanted me to get involved. She told me once that I'd make a better high priestess than Vivian. It was flattering, but I'd never been interested in the role or the exposure that came with it. Lydia was one of those sweet old ladies who were nearly impossible to say no to, but I managed, citing my youth as a disadvantage.

Still, here Vivian was, and she didn't seem *that* much older than me if I was correct in gauging her at thirty-ish. And she led the WEC-endorsed coven? Had been leading it for maybe eight years? From Lydia's reports, I'd assumed Vivian would be fifty-plus.

Though most witches in the big cities aren't as secretive about their path as their counterparts in smaller towns, Vivian wasn't wearing any pentacles or goddess-symbol jewelry. I thought speaking quietly in code would be prudent. With a quick, room-sweeping glance, I lowered my voice and asked, "You wear the garter in the group?"

"Yes, but only when we're doing a specifically Stregan ritual."

I frowned; she'd taken my question literally. Strega is the Italian Wiccan tradition; in it, the high priestess wears a garter to show her status, the way kings wear crowns.

Vivian's expression darkened then, as she seemed to understand why I had asked. "I started young," she snapped. Questioning her authority must have hit a touchy spot.

A small, sad smile curved her lips a fraction as she noticed my newspaper. "Let's go to my office, shall we?" She turned without waiting for my reply.

I gathered my purse, newspaper, and velvet Tarot bag and followed her through a door marked *Employees Only*. She removed her apron, placed it on a wall hook, and slid into a standard office chair behind a desk so neat it didn't seem used. The small space was well organized, with oak filing cabinets and shelves adorned with bookends bearing the shop's logo. On the highest shelf was perched the only thing that seemed out of place: a wooden box. It had rust-speckled iron workings and an old lock. I liked it; it seemed very Arthurian, like a cross between a suitcase and a pirate's treasure chest. If I'd had to guess, I'd have said it probably held some kind of successful-business-spell items. Or maybe a charm that kept her rent from rising beyond a point that allowed for profitability.

I lowered myself into the folding chair positioned

opposite her. The newspaper and purse went underneath the chair; the Tarot bag stayed on my lap.

"Obviously you know about Lorrie's death," she said.

"Yes." I smoothed the fringe on the velvet bag.

"I know who did it."

My head snapped up. I hadn't expected *that.*

Vivian's chin dropped. Her fingers came up and fluttered about as if her shaking hands could wipe away the words she'd just said. Trying to cover the awkwardness, she shifted and almost put her face in her hands, but seemed to decide against it. Doing so would have messed up her impeccably applied cosmetics.

I waited for her to go on, but she remained silent. I didn't need the cards to tell me what to say. "You have to go to the police."

"I can't." She opened a drawer and pulled a tissue from a pocket pack. She dabbed at her perfectly lined blue eyes. "Look, if I start butting into police business, the police will start butting into coven business. I know how that game works, and my coven is far too important to me."

I was right. Her ability to be impartial and objective had totally evaporated. "You could call in an anonymous tip," I suggested. The police had already had one of those. If she wouldn't be talked into it, I was confident that the cards would convince her to do the right thing in the interest of justice.

Vivian exhaled a trembling breath. "This is not an issue for the police, Miss Alcmedi."

"I beg to differ. Lorrie's dead. She was *murdered*!"

"Even if I told them everything," she said, "the police

would never find the killer. It will go unsolved. They think it's random because it looks random."

"Random? Occult symbols were scrawled on her walls with her own blood!"

Her voice came small and scared. "I know."

No more excuses. "Would you like me to do a reading and see what input the cards have as you make your decision?" I was careful to word it that way. People always have to make their own choices.

"Oh, please!" She threw the soiled tissue into a wastebasket. Then she started to laugh. "You think I asked you here to read my cards?"

My knee started bouncing again. "That *is* what I'm best known for among witches." A coldness was forming in my stomach that had nothing to do with the iced mocha. "Ms. Diamond, I'm not into gossip. If you don't want your cards read, then I don't see what any of this has to do with me."

Vivian assessed me, her blue eyes icy. "Lorrie told me how you helped her last year. Help her again."

I froze. My heart leapt to my throat.

Had Lorrie told my dark secret? She'd vowed to never speak of it! And she'd told Vivian?

I'd done some Tarot readings for Lorrie last year. A real creep had been stalking her, and his dangerous intentions were clear in the cards. She didn't have time or the grounds to get a restraining order so, to protect her and her daughter, I resolved to help. I confronted him. The situation with him got out of hand, though, and . . . I accidentally killed him. It wasn't intentional or premeditated. The police never solved the case. I suspected they hadn't tried too hard. The guy turned out to be a druggie and a convicted rapist, released from the pen on a legal technicality. Still, he was a human being, and I'd taken his life.

I put on a confused smile. "I'm sorry; I don't understand. How is helping her move to Cleveland relevant?"

"Miss Alcmedi, I'm not talking about you moving her knickknacks."

"Then what did Lorrie tell you I helped her with?"

"She told me enough to know that your interpretation of the Rede is, shall we say, looser than most witches'."

The Witches' Rede is a code of ethics written in the twentieth century but based on older documents and traditions. Due to my lineage—traceable back to ancient Greece—I considered myself more of a pagan, but I generally accepted the Rede's standard.

I stood. "That's not true."

"Well, you're obviously not as concerned about your karma as I am about mine. Besides, Lorrie's murderer would anticipate me taking action. I'd be burning myself at the stake to even think about trying to confront him. But you . . . you, he'd never suspect." She smiled confidently. "You're only a name on the rosters, someone who won't even attend local meet-ups. An inactive solitary." The last sounded demeaning.

I wanted to retort something nasty, but I didn't. First, what I had done *would* cost me, karma-wise. Second, I chose to be solitary and refused to let her make me feel like it was a bad thing. A slow breath escaped me. Vivian knew about a very criminal action of mine, an action never publicly known or prosecuted. That made me extremely nervous. In fact, my legs felt weak. I wanted to sit down, but sitting might indicate I was interested and wanted to hear more.

"Her killer must be stopped," Vivian stated.

"I'm sure the police will see to that if you go to them." I said it confidently, but I knew it was a lie. Lorrie had been a wære. Out of fear, and probably power envy, otherwise fine police officers conveniently forgot their "Serve and Protect" oaths when a wære was involved. They even had a shoot-first policy. The police were protected by self-defense claims, and frightened human juries—suspiciously, such cases were all scheduled so a full moon would expose jury members who were wæres—readily and regularly agreed with the police.

When officers refused to investigate a crime involving a wære, it was tolerated by their superiors and supported through "paperwork" claims. This meant that until the insurance companies, currently in litigation, reached an agreement with the individual states about police coverage, the officers could refuse wære-related duties because the risks were "higher than normal." The legal battles were spearheaded by lawyers for families of deceased officers who had been left without financial compensation due to carefully worded loopholes.

I'd written in my column about the insurance companies wanting premium payments from a specialized task force created for crimes involving wæres and vampires. Likewise, the states were accusing the insurance companies of taking advantage of the times. Both sides argued vehemently because the coverage reached too deeply into their financial pockets.

Privately, I feared both sides would find a mutually agreeable solution: declare open hunting season on all wæres.

I didn't blame people for being fearful of something they didn't understand. After a couple of decades, humanity as a whole was still adjusting to the fact that vampires, witches, wæres, fairies, and other supernaturals had lived among them for thousands of years. They would probably never have known if it hadn't been for a freak mutation of wære genes or, some said, a military experiment that had gone bad. Up until then, if anyone heard a tale of someone being bitten by a "werewolf," they assumed it was fiction. After the wære "virus" appeared, it became a fact to fear.

When things changed, all kinds of other-than-humans had to come out of the paranormal closet. Just like all downtrodden minorities, they had to organize to protect themselves. For the wæres, the extermination threat was immediate. They reacted with a wære-enforced responsibility policy. They broadened their kenneling approach and developed a local-level system that identified all wæres to an area pack leader. The system went through some restructuring and refining processes, but it was all handled by their own kind, and proven sympathetic folks like me, so they could trust the security of their identities. It was working. In the last few years, instances of wære attacks had become rare.

Vampires, thanks to their magnificent and well-funded propaganda machine, had a head start: humans bought into their alluring image long before the virus. The fairies convinced citizens they were benign in a brilliant-if-utterly-false public relations campaign and weren't considered as threatening as wæres. Neither were witches, for the most part.

But with the change of a word or two in certain laws, we'd all be lumped into a single "shoot on sight" category. Large portions of every group organization's dues went to cover costs for political lobbyists and legal eagles trying to keep that from happening.

That complex cycle of legal logic was just the human side. WEC's machinations were infinitely more intricate and ambiguous. That was why I stayed away from them.

"No," Vivian said. "If the American justice system decided to deal with the murderer, influential people would find a way to free him. But we both know what a joke that idea is. The laws won't touch him. We're on a precipice here, Miss Alcmedi. If we don't show people that we witches will police our own like the rest of the unnatural population, this world is going to get very ugly very soon."

I agreed with that theory, but I didn't intend to tell her that.

Carefully, she said, "The murderer needs to be stopped immediately and permanently."

"And you want *me* to stop him 'immediately and permanently'?"

"Yes."

"Lord and Lady!" I continued, feigning confusion. "I don't think we're on the same page here."

"Don't be coy, Miss Alcmedi. It doesn't become you."

I wanted to smack that smug smile off her smirking face. "I don't know what you're talking about."

"Of course you do. As a solitary, perhaps you don't realize how information and details sometimes come out during spiritual discovery. It can be like hypnosis and therapy and confession all rolled into one. And you're not a good liar."

I stared. My meditations were like confessional therapy, but they were private.

"I know what you did to Lorrie's stalker. Simply do it again." She shrugged. "This guy deserves it even more. He didn't just threaten her; he murdered her."

I could not believe what she was proposing or the gall it took to propose it. "Who the hell are you to be pushing for this? You're not an Elder. You're just a high priestess in Cleveland."

"A high priestess with goals, Miss Alcmedi. And a plan. WEC can't deny me a seat if I save their asses, now can they?"

Still I would not acknowledge anything to her. "Contrary to whatever Lorrie may have told you—"

"I pay well. Say . . . a hundred thousand?"

I tried to keep my eyes from bugging out of my head. This witchy coffee-shop manager had a hundred grand of disposable income? What the fuck was in the coffee here?

The mention of the dollars jazzed me and cooled the heat of her earlier insult. Nana had very little money—enough, basically, to keep her in cigarettes and blood-pressure pills. Since college, I'd made a fluctuating income as a freelance writer. After landing a few well-paying magazine articles and doing some sporadic technical writing, and through constant frugal living, I had managed to buy a house on twenty very rural acres. I could keep it only because farmers rented the acreage and my little column was running in multiple newspapers now. It had been nine papers until last week; now it was six. A certain newspaper conglomerate had been acquired by another, whose owner had lost family to a wære attack a decade ago and had no intention of running a column designed to create sympathy for those afflicted with the virus. I could've handled the resulting decrease of income, but now that I would be providing for Nana too, it would hurt.

Vivian's money would be a welcome financial cushion—but no. I wasn't a killer for hire, nor did I want Vivian to have leverage of any kind on me. Lorrie's story was hearsay, and Vivian had no proof. If I admitted it, she might try to blackmail me. If I didn't, she had nothing. I wondered if her office was bugged or if I was being filmed by a hidden camera.

I slung my purse and velvet bag over my shoulder. "I'm sorry, Ms. Diamond. I think you clearly misunderstood Lorrie."

"Two hundred thousand?"

After giving her a nasty look, I turned to leave.

She didn't let me get far. "What about poor Beverley?"

I stopped with my back to her, my hand hovering over the knob. *Grab it, turn, and stay out of this.* My conscience was torn. *You have to help Beverley! No one else will!*

I turned back to Vivian. "If you were Lorrie's friend, you'd tell the police what you know. But you're a coward who's chosen to hide instead."

"I'm not hiding!" Vivian stood. "Lorrie's will names me as guardian for Beverley. I have an appointment with the Department of Social Services at ten." She sank back into her chair. It rolled a few inches, though she didn't seem to notice. "Granted, it indicates more of a connection to her than I'd like the public to be aware of, but . . . I never thought I'd get custody. Nobody ever thinks the worst will actually happen."

I wasn't willing to sympathize with her. In fact, I was wondering how Lorrie could have come to think so much of Vivian as to make her Beverley's guardian. I felt a stab of jealousy that Lorrie hadn't picked me.

"You don't understand." Vivian sniffled and wiped her nose with another tissue. "I can't raise Beverley like this. Not with me being the reason her mother's dead!"

CHAPTER THREE

You're the reason Lorrie's dead? Explain."

Vivian returned my stone-cold stare with a steady, self-satisfied look that said she knew she had me now. That really ticked me off. "You already understand what danger I put her in, Miss Alcmedi."

"Yeah, I do. But when did you know?"

"From the start." She glanced down. "I knew she was a wære from the start."

"Then why? Why would you let her risk it? Why risk it yourself? 'An' it harm none.'" I quoted the Rede's first phrase.

Vivian hit the desktop. Her glare blazed. "Don't you dare quote the Rede to me as if I don't know it! You have no right to quote that to me, hypocrite."

I admit it *was* rude; as high priestess, she had to know the Rede and all the various codes and laws backwards and forwards. But calling me a hypocrite? "You're not spotless either."

Vivian looked me up and down, then squinted at me, thinking so hard I almost expected to smell smoking brain cells. But her heated anger eased, slowly. Drawing little circles with her finger on the top of her desk, she finally said, "My interaction with Lorrie wasn't risky. We met privately at her home once a week. We never did energy- or spell-work. It was just a faith and prayer Goddess thing for her. She needed it." Vivian paused, swallowed, and continued piously: "Lorrie continued to kennel for her monthly security, but she came to me for her soul's solace. She needed spiritual guidance in her life as she dealt with what she'd become. She feared hurting Beverley or, worse, that Beverley would come to fear her and run away."

Her self-righteous tone did nothing to endear her to me. "Did you warn her of the danger?"

"Lorrie wasn't ignorant! She knew the dangers and, yes, of course, we discussed them. As I said, I simply counseled her on issues of faith." Her gaze strayed along the edge of my newspaper. "I didn't know the bill for guiding her spirituality would be this high. I didn't think the council would find out."

"Wait a minute. The council? You mean the Witch Elders Council?"

Vivian nodded grimly. "WEC *did* this."

"Wait, wait, wait." I sat in the folding chair again. "Are you saying they knew you were spiritually counseling a wære and because of it they—as a group—violated the Rede to have her murdered?" Me breaking the "An' it harm none, do as ye will" law was bad, but I'd done it unintentionally. For the council to sanction law-breaking knowingly was a different matter.

Vivian re-situated herself in her chair. "Not WEC exactly, but . . ."

"But?"

My tone was harsher than I had meant it to be. Vivian latched onto it with a snotty little smile. "Am I ruining your perfectly naive concept of the world?"

I really, really didn't like her. "I'm *not* naive." *Am I?*

She sat back in her chair, exuding arrogant confidence. "The Elders aren't above the temptation of corruption, deary girl. And they've never had a deep love for PAW."

PAW was the acronym for Packs and Allied Wæres. The wæres' version of WEC, they administered the "responsibility policy." I copied Vivian's position as best I could, right down to the impassive expression. "You better start explaining why WEC would feel it necessary to take such actions."

"The less you know, the better."

"I disagree."

"Too bad."

"Then the answer is no. I'm not buying you an Elders seat and I'm not getting involved in a WEC versus PAW pissing contest." I got up and left her office without looking back. This time, it was easy.

As I crossed the wide seating area, however, my steps grew sluggish. I felt so sorry for Beverley. Her devoted mother was dead, and nobody was going to do anything about it. Not one governmental agency would do a damn thing to help her or solve the case. There would be no justice for Beverley unless I did something . . .

But this was madness. I couldn't do *this.* What was I thinking? Entertaining the idea was just plain stupid.

Some of my anger was vented on the coffee shop door; I shoved it open so hard, it rattled. I half-stomped to the crosswalk that led to the parking area where I'd left my car.

"Miss Alcmedi, wait!"

Vivian's voice came just as I arrived at the crosswalk. I crossed my arms and waited, letting her come to me. I told myself if the light changed, I was crossing. Vivian arrived first. Before she could speak, I held up my hand, and then I did the talking.

"WEC may not like you counseling a wære, but they wouldn't act against the Rede. Not like this. A verbal or written first warning would have been logical, and if you didn't comply, then they could renounce you and strip you of your position." If she wanted one of their seats so badly, why would she risk it this way? "This whole story stinks, and I don't believe you."

Her chin lifted somewhat. "If you bothered to come to a few of the local meet-ups," she retorted, "you'd know that WEC isn't as lofty as they'd like everyone to believe."

I didn't budge. Lydia never mentioned anything about the meet-ups' discussing WEC for good or for bad.

"Look." Vivian bowed her head and rubbed it wearily. "I know about your column, and I'm concerned about giving you details. I have to make sure that nothing I say to you is in any way considered an interview. And you have no right to scold me for 'hiding' when you won't even use your real name for your column." She crossed her arms, mimicking me. "Who are you hiding from, I wonder?"

So she knew I was the writer behind my byline: Circe Muirwood. I was surprised, but not much. All the wæres who kenneled at my home knew that. If Lorrie spilled my secrets to her, that was the smallest of them. I ignored the dig. "Did you get a verbal or written warning? Did you know Lorrie was in danger?"

"No!" Vivian stomped her foot and dropped her arms to her sides to emphasize the word, then leaned closer to whisper. "That's why he must be stopped. Lorrie never knew. She never had a chance! And hers was not a simple, isolated incident. At first, WEC used him discreetly, but now . . ." She glanced furtively at some people approaching from up the street.

"Sounds like you need to get the support of several coven leaders and confront the Council. Sounds like 'they' need to be stopped, not 'him.' "

"No. They've lost control. He's become a rabid watchdog. He's taking it upon himself to act like surveillance and security, and he's begun to act whenever he feels it is necessary. He's out of control."

The people were close, and the fact that their presence bothered Vivian made me resolve not to let it bother me. I said, "They should tighten their grip and restore control."

"They can't tighten their grip on him!"

"Why not?"

Vivian waited until the pedestrians had passed us before answering. "He knows too much now. If they try to stop him, he'll use what he knows against them."

"Maybe he should. If things are so bad, a restructuring might be therapeutic."

Vivian clenched her hands into fists. "You can't possibly understand what you're saying. If you were active in your community, your opinions might be worth something to me."

"How do you know all this?" I asked. "You're not a Council member."

"I have close friends seated in WEC." She said it with

an arrogant toss of her head. "I've made no secret of my ambitions to be voted in, Miss Alcmedi, but I have to wait two more years to finish my decade of coven service to be eligible. By then, he may have destroyed the council and, like I said, if I save their asses, they have to give me a seat immediately. With him gone, they will have to revert to the old ways. The time-honored ways. He knows I intend to change things; that's why he did this. To stop me. That's why I am the reason she's dead." She gave me an imploring look. "If he isn't stopped, if we don't show we will take care of our own problems, the government will legislate our annihilation. There is no other way."

"There's always another way."

"A way that stops a killer, avenges your friend, saves the council, *and* stops the government from wanting us all dead to make life easier? You have something that accomplishes more than that?"

She had me there.

"He's already created countless orphans, Miss Alcmedi. And Beverley will not be the last. Beverley herself might be in danger." Vivian edged closer. "Are you willing to take the job, or aren't you?"

My stomach churned. The roof of my mouth turned pasty. Sweat dampened my neck and palms.

I had acted to keep Beverley's mother alive once before, to keep Beverley from becoming an orphan. In the guilt I'd suffered after what had happened, I consoled myself with the knowledge that Lorrie and Beverley were safe.

Had I scarred my karma for nothing?

Karma-wise, I couldn't abandon Lorrie's spirit now as if she hadn't mattered. I had *killed* for her. Accidentally, yes, but I had blood on my hands. If I didn't avenge her now, well, stuff like that makes ghosts go insane. Her spirit might refuse to cross over and lash out in frustration as a phantom. This was a wrong I had to make right.

Then there was the matter of Beverley. How could I live with myself if something happened to her, if I had the opportunity to do something to save her from further harm and refused?

"I'll take care of it." I was glad my voice sounded confident.

Vivian smiled. "Good."

"I'll have to know where to start. And I'll need a contact number for you. One that will reach you at any hour." I handed her one of my business cards and a pen; she wrote her cell phone number on the back.

As she handed the card to me, she said, "His name is Goliath Kline."

I repeated it in my head a few times, though I doubted I could forget that name. "Your 'donation' will be in cash."

"Half now. Half afterward."

"Agreed." I dropped the card into my purse. "Tomorrow at four, at the coffee shop."

The gleam in Vivian's eyes disturbed me enough that I found myself wondering if the coffee shop had security cameras. I decided I should have someone else pick up the money for me. Someone who'd smell a trap if Vivian had one in mind. "A friend of mine will collect it. And, Vivian?"

"Yes?" she asked with a condescending grin. It made me happy that some of her lipstick had smeared on her teeth.

"As for your meeting with Children's Services concerning Beverley, you have some rather lofty parental shoes to fill. I'll be watching you."

Her smile disappeared. She knew a challenge when she heard it. She blinked, clearly shifting gears. "How will I know your bounty collector?"

"Trust me. When he walks through your door at four, you'll know exactly what he's come for." I hoped Johnny didn't have plans for tomorrow afternoon. He was the only one I could think of who might be able to handle this and not ask a billion questions.

CHAPTER FOUR

I sat in my silver Avalon, a car bought more because of the Arthurian reference than the gas mileage, and gently banged the back of my skull against the headrest. *What are you doing? An' it harm none, you witch! An' it harm none!*

In addition to following the Rede, witches and pagans believe that what you do comes back to you "threefold." If you shoplift and harm a store financially, the Fates will see that you're harmed back in triplicate. If you're kind and good, you get kindness and goodness back in triplicate. "Pay it forward" isn't a new idea at all.

I groaned. I was so screwed.

How could I have just agreed to kill someone for money? My next life was going to be a bitch. Talk about karmic suicide.

With trembling hands, I started the car and cracked the windows open. Fresh air helped me think, but the city air stank like a tire shop. I cranked up the radio and drove until the air smelled cleaner and deep breaths helped me feel calmer. By then I was halfway home and had pondered—yet again—the "wære problem."

The conspiracy theorists were probably right—some top secret military experiment to create super-soldiers using wære DNA had run amok—but no one had come close to proving it. I doubted they ever would. How could the government admit responsibility for the chaos that had followed?

It wasn't as bad for witches. Outside of fairy tales and the minds of religious fanatics, we were usually seen—accurately—as humans with a different sort of knowledge and the skill to use it. A great deal of what we did was no different than what other humans did—like meditation.

The crisp air had cleared my head. I'd made it a point to know the locations of all the area parks, and I proceeded to the closest one. Taking the blanket and a bottle of water from my backseat, I walked to a spot where I'd meditated before and spread out my blanket. I stepped into the middle, sat, and closed my eyes in the soothing presence of old trees. The sun was warm, though the breeze remained chilly. I listened to the branches rustling, the leaves dropping. Cleansing breath in, out. Center and ground.

Focusing on the music of shade crickets and the lyrics of birds, I popped the flip top on the water bottle and gave a flick of my wrist, squirting a circle of water around me.

"Mother, seal my circle and give me a sacred space.
I need to think clearly to solve the troubles I face."

Meditation was second nature to me. I could slip into an alpha state as easily as changing channels with a remote. It was just like breaking into the chorus of a song you'd known all your life: you took a deep breath and you sang.

What I visualized, when I meditated, was a grove of old ash trees beside a swift, clear river. My totem animals and spirit guides visited me there. A buckskin mustang frolicked in the fields, but she never came close. I didn't know her name or why she let me glimpse her, but I knew she was there, and I guessed I'd find out why when I was ready. That was how this place, this meditation of mine, worked.

Today I visualized myself sitting and putting my feet in the so-clear river water. I cleansed my chakras and imagined all my worries and doubts sinking down through me and flowing out of my toes, released into the rushing water.

"Mother, guide every step that I'm about to take.
Direct every thought and deed, every choice I make."

A flock of geese flew overhead, honking. I wasn't sure if it was a real sound from the world around my body or just a sound within my meditation.

"Your heart is heavy."

I turned in the meditation, pulling my feet from the water. A gray-and-tan jackal stood three feet away from me. My current totem animal, his name was Amenemhab. Before he had taken up the role, a lizard named Shoko had been my totem. They changed when I'd learned what they had to teach. Amenemhab had introduced himself a few weeks ago. I knew a life change was coming when the totems changed, so I'd consulted my Tarot. The cards concurred about the change and warned me that it had something to do with Nana. Silly me, I'd been afraid she'd die. Somehow, her moving in with me was almost as bad. "Yes. My heart is heavy."

After glancing upriver, then downriver, the jackal sat. "You appear relaxed on the outside, although inside you are not."

"That is true." Agreeing with totem animals kept the meditations smooth and quick. Denial wasn't something they let you get away with. I reclined on the soft grass of the grove, feeling my feet drying in the warm air.

The jackal lay down too, his muzzle on his paws, nose pointed toward my head. "What is it that worries you?"

I told him about Lorrie being murdered and about meeting with Vivian.

"Why do you think you agreed?"

"I have a justice streak a mile wide. Even as a kid, I stood up to bullies on behalf of smaller kids and protected kittens from cruel little boys. Convinced by a school counselor that all this was due to my mother leaving me, I found it logical that in some mental way, every time I opposed someone, I was confronting my mother. But teen angst fades, and I've gotten over her betrayal."

Amenemhab gave me an unconvinced look.

"Truly, I have. And now, with the desire to 'right the wrongs' still evident, I believe I was born with this programming."

"Righting wrongs is not a bad thing," he said.

"I know. I like helping people fix things, especially if I can help them fix things for themselves."

"Tarot is perfect for that."

"Right. But people aren't perfect. Even with the answer staring them in the face, they often can't take action, or at least they can't take the *right* action. Or just won't. That gets frustrating."

"Then there are the people who've been wronged without provocation."

He meant Lorrie, but I also thought of another friend, Celia, my college roommate. I had started college determined to earn a law degree. After Celia and her boyfriend, Erik, had been attacked during a camping trip, nearly died, and ended up turning wære, I had seen firsthand just how ineffectual lawyers could be. Nothing was done about it. When the newspapers picked up the story, though, people took action. A campus group was formed to provide valid information about wæres. It helped promote awareness of the dangers of the marauding wæres and publicize facts about the conscientious majority. I realized then that journalists sometimes had more power than lawyers and changed my major from pre-law to journalism.

"Has this desire to right wrongs diminished as you've grown up?"

"No. If anything, it's grown stronger. For instance, last week, some teenage thug cut the grocery line, stepping in front of an elderly couple I was standing behind. I tapped him on the shoulder and told him that cutting wasn't nice and that the line started behind me. I'm only five-six, and he was like six feet tall and three feet wide. He looked at me like I was a maggot, sneered, and said, 'Sucks to be you.'"

"What did you do?"

"I calmly put down my half-gallon of skim milk and loaf of whole-grain bread. Hands on hips, I smiled sweetly. I said, 'Last chance.' He smirked and asked what I was gonna do." I stopped, grinning at the memory. "Maybe it was because I'd caught the end of a Stooges show that morning, but in a flash I had him by both the ear and the nose. I walked him beyond the end of the line. He didn't say another word, though he did a lot of sniffling trying to resettle his sinuses."

Amenemhab laughed.

"Granted, this trait has gotten me into trouble most of my life. I know this, and still I can't help but act when I know I can make a difference. That being the case, I should've known to offer Vivian my condolences on her situation and get the hell out of her office. But I couldn't. I'd felt the nudge to act on Beverley's behalf already, and . . ."

"Go on."

"She's such a great kid. It's so awful that this has happened, and more so because it happened to *her.*" It was easier to keep from crying in meditation. "The picture of her from the front page keeps floating up in my mind. The anguish in her expression, the fear and loss, moved me. I have no idea how to get in touch with her, yet I want to call her."

"What would you say?"

I swore quietly. "I knew you were going to ask me that."

He laughed, ears perking. "And still you came." He cocked his head. "So. What would you say?"

I took a deep breath and imagined it. "'Uh. Hi, Beverley. It's me, Seph. I miss watching movies and eating popcorn with you. I heard about your mom.' No. Maybe, 'I saw the newspaper' would be better. No, maybe she'd feel all embarrassed and put a wall up before I started—"

Amenemhab cleared his throat. It was a signal. I put myself back on track.

" 'I know how you feel, Beverley. Really, I do. I was . . .' " I stopped. I felt tears pushing at the corners of my eyes and fought them by grinding my teeth until I'd mastered myself.

"Say it."

" 'I was left by my mama too. No, no, my mama wasn't murdered. She left. Literally. But I wish she'd died. It would have been easier to take her absence if I hadn't known she'd chosen to leave me behind.' " The bitterness of my voice startled me. I stopped talking until I felt control return. I thought I was over all this. It made me angry to realize I wasn't. " 'I'm left hating her. At least you can always remember loving your mom.' "

Amenemhab did not respond at first, then asked, "What does that tell you?"

"It tells me that I'm drawn to Beverley's pain and loss because I've shared it. I think I can offer her some guidance through this awful time. I want to offer it."

"And?"

I knew he wouldn't let me go without admitting it, so I stopped fighting it and blurted, "And I'm not done hating my mother for leaving me." Damn it.

"Good," the jackal said. "Now that we have an understanding about the burden on your heart, tell me about this other weight that's heavy on your conscience."

The light on the river glowed; the sun was setting here because I wanted to go, to avoid this conversation. My gut was twisting with guilt and realizations I didn't want. Realizations I had to face, regardless. "I agreed to take Vivian's money and dole out the justice that other humans won't."

Silence. Then, "Your hands are shaking."

"I think my victim may be a Council member. A High Elder or maybe someone protected by one."

Amenemhab cocked his head. "Victim? Don't you mean 'target' or 'mark'?"

Wasn't he going to lecture me about the Rede? "Whatever. I may be writing my own death warrant."

"Your fear, at least, is justified. Your pain, however, confuses me. It is not all pain for Lorrie's death and Beverley's loss. You also feel pain for yourself."

I stood, wiped my damp palms on my jeans, and wrapped my arms around myself. "Nana has a saying: 'Once is a mistake, but twice is a habit.' I've never had much use for most of her sayings, but this one . . . this one hurts."

"Why?"

I stared across the field, not wanting to face him as I said, "I'm mentally trying to justify this, but I know that worming my way around the Rede is wrong."

"Persephone."

His tone drew my attention to him.

"You are overthinking. If all this is true, if he has killed, then he has already broken the Rede."

"Me breaking it back in retaliation isn't right."

"And what if you are not acting out of vengeance, as

the word 'retaliate' suggests, but as an instrument of justice?"

I squinted. "Mind-set does not change the action."

"It doesn't?" he asked.

"No matter how much I validate this situation, no matter how much this guy deserves it, I've allowed myself to become an assassin. Even before the deed is done, the intent to do it brands me." After a pause, my hands fell limp and empty at my sides. "That's not who I ever wanted to be."

The jackal rose too. "The flower sprouts up from the ground when the sun and the rain give the seeds cause to grow. In the right environment, the stem will grow strong and produce a bud that will bloom when the time is right. A rose is a rose, Persephone, and a lily is a lily. They do not choose what color they are or what their petals will look like; they are what their roots have made them. And they can be nothing else."

A chill crawled up my spine.

The jackal turned and loped away.

CHAPTER FIVE

When I got home, Nana's old Buick sat in front of the garage instead of in the turnaround, thus blocking me from parking my car inside. She'd gone somewhere, probably to get cigarettes, and not considered where she was parking when she returned. If I'd given her a door remote, she'd likely have parked in my garage. But parking was the least of my worries. Thc thought of that old woman on the road, endangering other unsuspecting people, terrified me.

I pulled in behind the Buick and got out. I pushed the remote button, the door opened, and I walked in through the garage. When I stepped into the kitchen, I heard a high-pitched whining.

I dropped everything on the counter and ran to the living room.

Nana was fine. In fact, she was sitting on the brown-slipcovered couch, grinning. Beside her on my already abused sofa was a big, dark-furred puppy. He had a deep wrinkle above his eyes, as if he had too much skin. It made him look worried. I didn't blame him; my anger was mounting.

Cautious of my tone, I asked, "What's this?"

"This is a doggie. Named him Poopsie," she said proudly.

"Poopsie?" I hoped it wasn't going to turn out that he was named for an overactive attribute. I stepped over to see him better but only got halfway before he leapt from the couch and came at me, barking and wagging his tail so hard his whole butt wiggled. "He's doing the Twist. You should've named him Chubby Checker." His legs were extremely long. Tentatively, I reached out to pat him. He turned and shot back to Nana.

"It's a wonder people ever sell anything through the classifieds," she said. "You know? Only a few people really know how to advertise. But your owners knew what to say, didn't they, Poopsie?" The old smoker's rendition of the silly voice people use when they talk to babies or pets made me want to vomit. She scratched the pup's head. "No other ad claimed their animals were super, but your owner did. How could they *not* say that about you?"

Suddenly suspicious, I asked, "What did they say about him?"

"The ad said he was a super Dane. And well, I figured he was perfect for me, 'cause I never met a Danish I didn't like." She laughed hard. It sounded like she was going to hack up a lung.

I didn't even break a smile. "Can I see the ad?"

Nana pulled off her pink slipper, exposing her misshapen hammertoe. Seeing it always made me wince. That had to hurt, didn't it? How did she balance properly with that? She held the slipper out to the pup and enticed him into snapping at it. He lunged and sank his teeth into it.

"Paper's on the table. I circled it." I left the two of them playing tug-of-war.

Making a mental note never to leave Nana alone with the classifieds again, I picked up the paper and read the ad circled in blue ink. The only thing encouraging about it was the word *paper-trained.* The "free to good home" part had some merit, but not much. I knew there was no such thing as a "free" puppy. I went back to the living room, pointing at the ad. "This . . . this . . . is a *Great* Dane puppy?"

"I told you that, Seph."

My voice tightened. "Nana."

The puppy yanked the slipper from Nana's grip, and she laughed and slapped her knee. "My stars! What a strong little doggie!"

"Nana, your 'little doggie' is going to turn into a two-hundred-pound behemoth in the next six months. He'll be this tall at the shoulder." I indicated with my hand. "He'll eat like a teenage boy." I thought of my high school prom date, Gregory Newberry. We had gone to a fast-food restaurant before the dance, and I watched him scarf down a pair of triple-patty burgers and a large order of fries. Shocked me at the time, but I guessed it prepared me for seeing the way wærewolves ate. And that reminded me of what had happened to the tables I'd left holding sweets too close to their kennels. "Not to mention what's going to happen to my furniture!" I could imagine the gnaw marks on my coffee table from a teething puppy.

"I knew it." Nana stood and pointed at me. "I knew you'd throw a fit! He's *my* doggie. If you can have your unnatural wærewolf friends over all the time, then you can deal with one *natural* canine. He'll protect me from your vicious, so-called 'friends.'"

I threw my arms up, tossing the paper dramatically. "Nana. My friends wouldn't hurt you, and they're here overnight only once a month! Lord and Lady, they don't even come in the house! They go straight to the storm cellar." I paused to get a breath and redirect my thoughts away from the defensive. "You're bringing an animal into my home and you didn't so much as ask me if you could!"

Voice soft with remorse, she said, "I thought it was my home now too."

My every memory of her had a tough-as-nails overtone to it; she simply couldn't inspire me to pity her by offering me a pout.

Sensing the defeat, she resumed arguing. "He'll keep me company when you're out gallivanting with your so-called friends. Isn't that right—oh!" She began to laugh.

I followed her gaze to discover Poopsie pissing on the newspaper where it had landed, in the corner on top of my picture album.

I screamed. He dropped his leg but pissed a stream across the wood floor as he squatted and whined his way back to Nana.

An hour later, with Nana sulking in her room and the dog in one of the cages in the storm cellar, I'd dried the pictures in danger and removed all the unharmed pages. I'd get another binder; this one had to go. After scrubbing the corner of the living room twice, I promptly went for a drive. She had been here less than twenty-four hours and had already managed to drive me from my own home in search of serenity.

There were a few scenic fields I knew of. A bridge over a fast stream. A woodland grove—the leaves were crimson and burnt gold and palest yellow, their branches full of the season's glorious color. A few more weeks, and those same branches would be bare. By the time I'd seen all that, I'd made it nearly back into the civilized world. I saw a gas station and stopped.

I pulled the Waterhouse day planner from my purse and flipped to the back, where I kept phone numbers. I knew I should join the twenty-first century and get a cell phone, but I was resisting. I knew if I got one, it'd be a ball and chain—and a bill—I'd never be rid of. Besides, where I lived, it wouldn't get much of a signal.

A Post-it note was stuck to the page. It read: *School Brunch* and had this Saturday's date under it. Had it been six months already? In high school, Olivia, Betsy, Nancy, and I had been the "not-so-in" crowd. Afterward, Nancy had stayed in Halesville—which was weird, because she was the most intellectual one. The rest of us had parted for separate colleges and separate lives. We all ended up within a few hours' drive of one another so, twice a year, we got together in the central location of Columbus for a brunch or dinner. We chatted on the phone from time to time when there was a problem among us that I, of course, was needed to fix, but lately I couldn't help feeling as if the separate directions we'd all grown in had left us on different life maps. Having nothing in common anymore made for tedious gatherings. Keeping in touch had become a vain attempt to hold on to the past. There was very little in my past I thought was worth that much effort. Hell, it was too much trouble just keeping the present in line.

I moved the Post-it and searched the list for the name "Johnny." A last name wasn't necessary to clarify this guy. There was only one Johnny. I kept the numbers of all the wærewolves who kenneled at my place for full moons, though I'd never yet needed to announce a change in plans.

I put quarters into the pay phone and dialed Johnny's number. It rang twice.

"'Lo?"

"Johnny, it's Persephone Alcmedi. I—"

"Hey, Red."

That threw me. My hair's dark, dark brown. I tried going blond in my late teens. A week later, all the prissy cheerleaders at school started saying things like, "Your Greek roots are showing." I dyed it back to brown; blond hadn't been me anyway. I was a darkling. "Red?" I asked.

"I've decided I'm going to call you Red from now on."

"All right. I'll bite—no pun intended. Why?"

He snickered in a very masculine way and lowered his voice. "'Cause I like the idea of the big bad wolf visiting you and Grandma."

I laughed so hard, people pumping gas turned to stare at me. Johnny's sigh made me imagine the satisfied smile he surely wore. He loved attention.

"I knew you'd call me eventually," he said.

"Sorry to disappoint you, but this isn't what you think it is."

"Damn." He breathed the word more than said it.

Quickly, I asked, "Busy tomorrow?"

"Never too busy for you, Red."

"Stop it. And don't read into the words." On full moons, the wæres let themselves into my storm cellar and locked themselves into the cages they wanted with whomever they wanted to share them with—an important choice, since these caged animals passed the time by mating, and furious mating by the sounds of it. (Wæres differed from natural wolves in that they didn't have to be in heat for such activity.) When I went to unlock the cages at dawn, Johnny was always alone. He teased me and howled at me—the pack clown, so to speak.

"Aw, c'mon, Red. Go out with me just once. I won't bite. I won't even lick if you don't want me to."

I grinned, but softly said, "No."

He sighed. "Hey . . . you know about Lorrie, right?" His voice had gone soft too, and serious.

"Yeah," I said. A heavy, sad silence filled the line between us. I wanted to say something else, but everything that came to mind was a statement of the obvious. And I couldn't say, *Don't worry, I'm taking care of it.* "I don't know what to say."

"I hope they get the bastard." Johnny knew better than most what a crock the justice system was to wæres. Maybe he didn't know what to say either.

"Me too." I paused, then asked, "Um . . . Busy or not?"

"I said I wasn't."

"Perfect. Would you please go to Cleveland and pick up something for me in, uh, well . . . your stage clothes." He fronted an awesome techno-metal-Goth band. My friend Celia was now married to Erik, who was the drummer.

"In daylight hours?"

"Mm-hmmm. At four o'clock."

"Awesome. I love scaring the white-collared types. What'm I picking up?"

"Probably a briefcase or something like that."

He paused. "You don't know?"

"Long story."

"Sounds like perfect dinner conversation to me."

I rolled my eyes. "Johnny."

"Okay, okay. Where?"

"From the manager of a coffee shop near the Rock and Roll Hall of Fame. On East Ninth."

"No way! The place they roast their own beans?"

I had to smile. His enthusiasm never waned. I didn't mean to be cruel, but if any man would make a good wærewolf, as in cousin to man's best friend, it was Johnny. He had the personality of a tail-wagging leg-humper that had just gotten its treat. "Yep."

"Cool. Wait—what's in it for me?"

Going with the thought I'd just had, I said, "Treats."

"Oooo baby."

"Not those kinds of treats, Johnny. I'm talking steaks."

"Don't blame me for trying, do ya?"

"Never." I had to admit, his interest in me was flattering—and his voice seemed sexier to me on the phone than it ever had in person—but my personal rule was direct: don't flirt with the wæres you kennel. Kind of like no office dating. Of course I'd only adopted that rule *after* he started flirting with me. But I couldn't date him. He . . . he had these tattoos that were just . . . ominous.

"So . . ." he drew it out. "Am I keeping this briefcase or whatever until the moonrise, or do I get to make a special trip to see you and Grandma?"

In a mocking, childlike voice, I teased, "What big ideas you have."

He growled low. "I got other things bigger than my ideas, little girl."

My cheeks flushed red enough to suit the nickname. Johnny was different. The other wæres, in human form, were just people. Johnny had such presence!

I'd always thought he just flat-out scared me, but talking to him now—more than we ever talked when he kenneled—I had to wonder. He was funny. He was witty. Was it different now because I needed him to do something for me? Was I that shallow?

No, it had to be because this was the first time I was on the phone with him . . . hearing him without seeing him.

I realized it was *all* about his appearance. That made me feel bad. I didn't judge people on looks. Not usually, anyway. And though I'd not thought Johnny was a bad person based on his looks, I'd definitely judged him as "not boyfriend material" because of them.

"I'll be home; bring it to me there." I'd have to test my theory and see if he still intimidated me.

He hesitated. "I'm not complaining, Red. I'll play fetch with you. But why aren't you doing it, if you're just going to be home?"

"I'll explain when you arrive. Okay?"

"Okay," he said brightly. "It'll be about five-thirty or six by the time I make it through traffic and get to your place, so I'll just go ahead and pick up something for us to eat. See you then." He hung up before I could protest.

CHAPTER SIX

After I dug more change out of my purse, I checked the planner again and dialed up another wære. "Good afternoon," a warm, alto voice said in a formal business tone. "You've reached Revelations. I'm Theodora. How may I help you?"

"Theo, it's Persephone."

Silence, then: "I know about Lorrie," she said.

"Yeah. I heard too." I couldn't rush into the reason for my call; it would be too callous. "Did Celia call you?"

"She called every wære in the county, I think."

"Is there reason to think more wæres will be targeted?" According to Vivian, that was a no, but how were the wæres taking this?

"It does appear to be a hate crime, so I guess, but . . ."

"But what?"

"I know people, Seph. Wæres take care of their own, and they've already hit dead ends on the info trail. I don't think they'll be able to do much with this one, and it really makes me mad. Lorrie was . . . my friend." She sounded like she was going to cry and, for tough Theo, that meant something. "Thanks for calling, Seph."

I knew she wanted to end the conversation and dry her eyes, but I had a reason for calling other than what she thought. "Theo, actually, I called to hire you." She co-owned a business that performed background checks on people.

"Oh? What can I do for you?" She'd relaxed into the friend voice.

"I need you to check the name 'Goliath Kline' for me. Whatever you can find. Address, history, membership in clubs, anything at all."

I heard her typing in the background. "Is that a *K* or a *C*?"

"Not sure." Vivian had spoken it, not written it.

"Any aka's?"

"Not that I'm aware of."

"Birthday?"

"Not a clue."

"Hmmm. I usually need a birth date to clarify that I have the right person, but I'm willing to bet there's not many guys named Goliath running around."

"I'm with you on that one."

"Soooo . . . should I tell Johnny to watch out 'cause he's got some competition?"

"No! It's nothing like that. It's . . . it's for work."

"You dropping names in your column now?" she teased.

"No. I just need some info on this guy . . . for another, uh, job."

"Is he a local fella?"

An assassin wouldn't root himself anywhere long enough to be a local, would he? But this guy was connected to WEC. Since there were only five U.S. groves (they officially call their groups "groves" as opposed to "covens" because they like to think of their authority as lofty, like tree branches), and Ohio was part of the Chicago grove, I answered, "I doubt it. Probably has connections in Chicago." What was I going to say if she got enough info to guess at his profession? Damn, I didn't want to start having to make up lies. "Bill me?"

"Sure. I know where you live." Her throaty laugh came in a series of little barks.

"How long does this take, usually?"

"Mmmm, well, since I'm such an overachiever," she said sarcastically, because I had accused her of such on more than one occasion, "my afternoon work was done this morning, so I'll probably have it tonight or tomorrow. Depends on whether his non-localness gives me problems. What's your time frame for this? You want me to snail-mail it, e-mail it, or bring it out next moon?"

"Can you call me with details as soon as you can? If you have time, that is."

"Well, since you're my friend and all, I suppose I can make an exception." We both giggled.

I considered the wæres my friends, but I didn't feel truly close to any of them except Celia, because she and I had roomed together in college. To hear Theo call me her friend gave me a warm feeling inside. This day was making me feel quite fragile when it came to personal relationships. "Thanks, Theo."

"Any time."

Back in the Avalon with a newly filled tank, I drove on to a little strip mall. I took my time picking out some bread and cheese in the mini-mart, then added a can of tomato soup. Dinner for both Nana and me was easy *and* cost less than six bucks.

While cooking, I started thinking about my meditation. Totems were always giving cryptic answers. It was important not to think too intensely about it right away; I tended to "read into" it if I didn't get a little distance and reflect on the information slowly. The longer I stood there considering what Amenemhab had said, the more I realized that he'd left me with questions I hadn't had before I meditated. I mean, hell, was he saying I had a Redebreaker in my family tree, or an assassin? Or both?

That thought caused me to burn the first toasted cheese sandwich.

"I hate the smell of burnt toast," Nana said, coming into the kitchen fanning at the smoke and coughing. She never coughed from cigarette smoke.

Of course when I saw her and that beehive hairdo, I almost laughed. Despite the totem's allusion, there was no assassin blood in me. Had to be a Rede-breaker. But I wondered what Nana could have done to break the Rede. My nana was many things, but she took her witchcraft very seriously. I doubted she had ever broken the Rede. Though my ancestry boasted a long, traceable line of impressive witch heritage, I didn't know much about any specific ancestors. I might have to investigate. The Redebreaker was probably my mother.

Through the Styrofoam sound insulation that Celia and I had inexpertly installed in the cellar ceiling, I could hear the pup barking.

"Sorry," I said to Nana.

"Just make another." She reached for the loaf of bread.

"No, Nana. I'm sorry I got angry about Poopsie."

Hope filled her eyes. "I can keep him?"

"I guess. He has to take obedience training, though. He's going to be huge."

She sighed dramatically. "I'm sure he's almost fully grown."

"Nana." I put the spatula down. "He's a Great Dane. He'll be this high at the shoulder." I showed her again.

Her eyes widened. "You're not exaggerating, are you?"

"No."

"As big as a wærewolf?"

I nodded. "But a little leaner and with sleeker fur."

She went to the dinette table and backed into the chair she'd decided was hers. "I thought you were exaggerating. Before, in the living room." Her old fingers curled the place mat. "I didn't realize he'd be so big, Seph. I . . . I can't take him back. They're moving away."

"I didn't ask you to take him back." "They" must've been desperate to let an old lady take such a soon-to-be-behemoth dog.

The toasted cheese sandwiches got made in silence, except for the sound of the microwave dinging when the tomato soup finished heating. I sat on the bench across from Nana, and we ate. She flipped through the mail I'd brought in. "This one's for you. You had classes with her, didn't you?"

I checked the return address. My high school friend Nancy Malcovich.

"Yeah. Great." My lack of enthusiasm made my sarcasm glisten.

"What?"

"This means she doesn't trust a live phone conversation." I put the envelope down, determined to let it wait until I'd had my dinner. It's easy to decide to ignore letters when you're sure they're bad, like bills you don't have the funds to pay. But, as with bills you don't have the funds to pay, you can't resist opening a letter and seeing how bad it is. I ripped the envelope and pulled out the smooth, slightly marbled tan paper. The cross design printed on the letterhead didn't surprise me. Nancy had found Jesus and been "saved" a year ago.

> *Dear Persephone,*
>
> *I'm writing to you because I think you, more than Olivia and Betsy, are capable of understanding me, of appreciating what I'm trying to do even if you don't agree with me. I've truly changed. It's not an act like Olivia says. I realized today, after Olivia called me, that no one else in this group has changed since high school. I don't think they ever will.*

At least I wasn't alone in thinking that.

> *That is ludicrous too. The whole world has changed so much, but our little clique of girls hasn't? Do you remember when we were kids? Before all the nightmares decided to let the world know they were real? Do you remember what it was like before the horrors became real?*

I hadn't known she was so scared. Her getting saved suddenly made sense.

> *Sometimes I just want to grab Olivia and shake her and demand that she wake up, that she acknowledge how much her words hurt me. How much her stagnation hurts her. But I think it would take more than shaking to get through to her.*

Definitely, I thought. Like a decade of hypnotherapy . . . though a bottle of Smirnoff might work in the short term.

I kept reading.

> *She hates me, I'm sure of it. I represent something she fears, so she tries to hurt me to keep dominion over me and subdue me.*

And of course Nancy couldn't see that she was having exactly the same unjustified reaction where wæres were concerned.

> *Maintaining a friendship with you and Betsy exclusive of her would be unfair to ask, and likely impossible. I hope you don't hate me. You're the one who listened to me, who didn't snub me immediately when I announced that I'd gotten saved. But I saw the snubbing in Olivia's eyes. I heard her words encourage Betsy's snubbing. You've always stood alone. I've always admired you for that.*
>
> *I'm coming to our luncheon this weekend, but I'm afraid it will be the last time. I can't deny who*

I've become just to ease Olivia's conscience. Or yours, my friend. The world has become a frightening place. Inhumanity is everywhere! Who can be trusted any-more? There should be required testing for everyone. The public has a right to know. God didn't make those abominations.

But I digress. I don't know why I think you can do something about this dying quartet of ours. I'm not even sure I want you to. But maybe you can. Maybe we can all stay friends if you do. If I knew what words to say to Olivia, I would say them. But I don't. You're the editor-person. If any of us knows the right words, it's you.

Nancy

I was supposed to try to save her from *Olivia's* opinions? Her own were pretty harsh. And scattered. But of course, she wouldn't see it that way. Her way, similar to so many on her path, was the only right way. And I was so tired of being in the middle.

"Must be bad news," Nana mumbled.

"Hmmm?"

"You're frowning hard enough to make your hair grow."

I snorted an awkward laugh. It was better than crying. Losing friends sucked, no matter how the death of friend-ship came about. So I went the other direction, toward a new friend. "Let's go get Poopsie some food and a new collar." I stood and cleared the table. "When we get back, we'll bring him up out of the cellar."

Nana's grin could have lit up the night, but then sud-denly it faded like a bright idea shorting out. "Your wolf friends don't leave their fleas in the cellar, do they?"

• • •

Poopsie had all a puppy could want, including a cushy dog bed in Nana's room. It wouldn't fit him for long, but I hoped it would get him through the whining stage.

After locking the doors for the night, I stood perfectly still just inside my door and concentrated. Closing my eyes and flicking that switch to hit alpha, I reached out with a part of me that was not tangible. Stretching across the acreage as if it were no more than a coffee table, my spirit self could touch the power of the ley line that ran across the rear of my property.

Ley lines are a pure "source" of power. As I understand it, if you visualize the planet's surface lined with geodesic triangles with all the lines carrying flowing power, the intersecting points are like power stations. An intersection, called a nucleus, has power that is available in increased amounts, like water in a deep aquifer.

As a witch, I can tap into a ley line and draw on that power, but it can be very dangerous. Ley lines are volatile. As power flows—affected by moon phases and astrological correspondences—it can swirl and eddy dangerously.

My line ran from the Serpent Mound to Indian Point Park. I was relatively close to a nucleus, so the current stayed strong here. Putting my metaphysical hand near it, I sensed its speed and level in the thrumming pulse of its flow. Using just my fingertips, I redirected a minuscule portion along the path I chose, guiding it to refill the wards that kept my windows and entries safe. Problem was, even the tiny touch of power was like sticking my hand in boiling water and, as it gushed through me, every nerve felt scalded. I quickly released the line and emptied all of it into the wards, retaining none for myself.

No electronic security system on the market could rival my metaphysical one.

That done, I flicked off the last light and headed up the creaky oak steps, deciding halfway up that I'd be stuffing cotton into my ears to block the dog noise out.

The phone rang.

I turned and went back down to find the cordless phone ringing on the coffee table. I picked it up and hit the button even as I turned back for the steps. "Hello?"

"Boy, do you know how to pick 'em." It was Theo.

"What do you mean?"

"This Goliath guy. Better than a drama on Lifetime."

"What'd you find?"

"Well, I just dropped the printouts and photocopies in the mail to you. There's way too much to go over this time of night but, in a nutshell, he was born in Texas, seemed to have a normal life for a while, then became a sensation when he got a perfect score on the SAT at age ten. Forty-eight hours later, he was kidnapped. Taken from his bed in the night."

My stomach tightened. I didn't watch Lifetime because of stuff like this.

"And now he's what?" I asked. "Twenty? Thirty?"

"Now he's undead."

"What?" I froze at the top of the steps. "A child vampire?"

"No. They let him grow up before they turned him. And coincidentally, his younger brother, who witnessed the kidnapping, grew up to be the now-notorious Reverend Samson D. Kline." She paused. "Do I hear whining?"

Wæres have such good hearing. "Yeah. Nana got a puppy."

Her throaty laugh erupted again. "You could've asked Johnny to move in. He doesn't whine or shit on the floor."

"Are you sure?" I asked.

She cackled.

I sat down on the bed in my room and changed the subject back. "Samson D. Kline. You mean that guy videotaped in the hotel room with—"

"That's the one."

The soft glow of my bedside lamp on the pale butter-yellow walls could not soothe away the panic starting to form inside me. My target wasn't a rogue council Elder. He was a damned vampire. Vivian hadn't mentioned *that*.

I hate vampires. Anal retentive know-it-alls, the lot of them. They smell like the bottom of a pile of raked leaves after a three-day rain and are probably just as buggy. I suppressed a shiver. Every vampire I'd ever met spiked my creep-o-meter.

I would just call Vivian and tell her the deal was off. Another call would stop Johnny—or stop him from making the trip, anyway. Nothing short of a strong chastity spell would stop his flirtatious personality.

"Persephone? You got quiet on me."

"I just didn't expect that."

"What? That his brother is a fundamentalist hypocrite?"

"No, that Goliath Kline is a vampire." I stood, slipped

out of my jeans, and tossed them onto the wicker chair in the corner. "Any idea where he keeps his dirt bag?" Vampires really did have to sleep on a pillow of their home earth. I always envisioned it as a place for the worms to go when they'd eaten their fill from the inside. Yuck.

"The word on the street is that he's got a major position with a master vampire."

"'Word on the street.' Listen to you." The implications of what she'd just said didn't matter to me. I was not messing with vampires. A creepy human stalker was one thing. This was totally another. One: The undead aren't easily tricked—stupid people aren't allowed in their exclusive club. Two: You can't sneak up on the undead—unless they're distracted by, like, a hundred automatic machine guns firing at them at once or something equally bad like, say, the *sun.* And three: The undead aren't easily . . . *stopped.* I say "stopped" instead of "killed" because they're technically already dead.

"You're the journalist. You have contacts of the lying-low kind, don't you?"

"Of course, but you're like a human resources specialist in a well-decorated office uptown. Not where the lowlifes tend to come to gossip."

"I said lying-low, not lowlife. Big difference. All work and no play sucks." Her voice dropped low. "My contacts and I play in the same hidden sandbox. I like it. And speaking of that, I'm going to be late."

I walked to the bathroom and started prepping my toothbrush. "Hey, I didn't mean any insult."

"None taken."

"Thanks, Theo . . . don't get sand in your undies."

She cackled again. "Okay. I'll make sure to take them off first."

I rolled my eyes. "Good-bye, Theo." I put the phone down, did my dental duties, then found some cotton balls and stuffed them into my ears.

Back in my room, I opened the pajama drawer on the big white dresser and chose a tank top with the Lady of Shalott silk-screened on it. After changing, I jerked the covers down and sat on the bed, reaching automatically for the little chain to click off the light on the bedside table. My hand, however, stopped, and I stared at one of my prized possessions, a three-by-five photo of the man my mother had claimed was my father. The picture had once been a five-by-seven, but I'd trashed the half with Mom in it.

I didn't touch the crystal frame; the hinge on the back was loose. Only the fact that it sat perfectly balanced on a doily kept it from sliding down.

He was Egyptian—his skin was dark, his hair black, and his eyes bright brown. Handsome features like high cheekbones and a well-formed mouth over a dimpled chin gave him an air of refined masculinity. The arched brows made him mysterious, a bit dangerous. His expression here was serious, but I'd always imagined that if he smiled, it would come easily to him, and that his teeth would be straight and glossy white.

Around his neck he wore an amulet of Anubis, jackal-headed god of ancient Egyptian afterlife. Seeing it had been what stopped me from clicking off the light. Though his picture sat on this table for as long as I'd lived here—the dust on it was proof—I didn't look at it every day. I'd forgotten about his amulet, hadn't put together my totem jackal and my father.

Amenemhab had said of the flowers, ". . . they are what their roots have made them. And they can be nothing else." I'd laughed off the family tree issue, thinking only of Nana and my mother. I hadn't considered the unknown other side of my family.

Now that I knew the killer was a vampire, though, everything had changed. I jerked the little string on the lamp and pulled the quilts up tight around my neck, peering at the dark through the skylights overhead. "Instrument of justice" or not, I wouldn't even begin to consider going after a vampire.

CHAPTER SEVEN

"Hello?"

I could barely hear Vivian's voice over the sobbing and screaming in the background. Though muffled as if her hand was covering the mouthpiece of the phone, Vivian's exasperated scream—"Just shut up!"—came through anyway.

I hadn't even gone downstairs yet; I was sitting on the end of my bed in the glow of an up-slanting sunbeam, watching dust float in the air. My ears itched from having cotton in them all night. Not that I'd slept much. The thick wads had successfully blocked out Poopsie's whining, but my own thoughts couldn't be stopped. Still, I had a speech ready for Vivian. A good one.

The sobbing grew more distant, and I heard a door slam. "Hello?" Vivian said again, trying to sound calm and collected.

"Vivian? It's Persephone."

"What do you want?"

I switched sides with the phone to rub the other ear. The background sobbing had caught me off guard, but then I guessed its source. "Is that Beverley?"

"Of course it's Beverley . . . the little tyrant."

Tyrant? I couldn't keep the anger from creeping into my voice: "Is something wrong?"

"No. What do you want, Miss Alcmedi? Please keep it quick. Thanks to Beverley, I'm already late for work."

Beverley's screaming rose again, and various muffled sounds followed. Initially, I'd thought that Beverley had run off and slammed a door behind her, but now I realized Vivian had left Beverley and was fighting to keep the door shut to separate herself from the little girl who was repeating, "I want my mom" in a desperate chant.

It made my heart ache. My prepared speech faded away. "Do you need some help?" I asked.

"I can't hear you, Miss Alcmedi, but don't worry, your money will be ready at four." She hung up.

The phone was still in my hand when Nana ambled into my sunny room.

"Aren't you fixing breakfast?" I heard the lighter click as she lit a cigarette.

Numbly, I said, "No." I couldn't tear my eyes from the blank digital display of the phone. The words still seemed to echo dully: "I want my mom, I want my mom . . ."

I remembered feeling that wretched and misplaced. I remembered running through a cornfield, blasting through stalks and spiderwebs and crying so hard I couldn't see. I'd collapsed when I had fallen into a muddy ditch between fields and sobbed myself to sleep. My first real experience with the Goddess had been in that cornfield.

"Persephone?" Nana prompted.

"There's cornflakes. Or toaster waffles."

Poopsie bounded in and pulled up short, somehow managing to skid despite the carpet. He thumped down on his backside. Everything in the upstairs of my house shook. The crystal frame beside my bed clunked down on its back, the loose hinge having given way despite the doily.

I twisted to right it and paused, looking again at my father, at his Anubis amulet. I studied the sport coat he wore, searching for telltale signs of a pistol underneath. I tried to, but couldn't, detect where a shoulder holster might be hidden.

"Fine." Nana walked away. "Hope you don't expect me to eat boxed food every morning. Even the nursing home fixed real food."

Poopsie sat where he'd landed, panting. "You have to be more careful if you're going to stay here," I said. He gave a little bark and was up bounding after Nana and, from the sound of it, crowding past her on the stairs.

I grabbed last year's phone book from the low drawer on the bedside table; I kept the newer book on my desk downstairs by the kitchen phone. Flipping through the yellow pages' "Churches & Places of Worship" section, I found what I was looking for in a sizeable, poorly designed ad: *The Church of God Almighty, Reverend Samson D. Kline, Pastor.*

That poor little girl deserved justice. "For Beverley," I whispered as I dialed.

"They wanted it and they got it. Damn them all!"

In a Hooters booth, sitting across from Samson D.

Kline, I couldn't help staring at him. The fundamentalist preacher and local televangelist wore a light blue polyester suit with a white shirt. A Donald Trump comb-over sat like a thin gray dollop atop his head. Drooping jowls wiggled on either side of a bulging double chin from which his boring black tie descended. His piggish dark eyes gave him the look of someone constantly attempting to cry, but never succeeding.

"Them homosexuals"—he pronounced it *hom-o-sect-shuls* in precise syllables inflected with a deep-rooted southern drawl—"they wanted equality. Tolerance. Just one homo with clout in Hollywood, and the right words licked into the right ears, and everyone obeyed, eagerly climbin' on the butt-fuckin' bandwagon. That modern Babylon made sitcoms about them. *Humanized* them, as if their practices weren't profane abominations of God's holy plan! They taught all the boobs watching the boob tube to react with pity and understanding for these destroyers of the Western world."

Since we were sitting in Hooters, the word "boob" attracted more attention than it would have if we'd been elsewhere. Men at other tables were starting to stare at him—it took something as downright bizarre as Reverend Kline to get men to look at anything but the waitresses in this place.

"Made daytime talk show hosts of them to make sure that American housewives would be converted to this new tolerance—" His voice started to rise again.

"*Mis*-ter Kline." I cut him off with a sharp tone. "This is Hooters." I gestured around the restaurant. "When you suggested that we meet here, I assumed you knew—"

"You know what they say about assuming."

"—I assumed you knew it was a restaurant, but obviously you don't, so let me clarify: that side of the table is not a pulpit, and I didn't ask for an interview in order to be converted." I thought, but didn't add, *you hypocritical bastard.*

"But that's my new campaign. Isn't that what this interview's all about?"

I smiled. "I apologize if you *assumed* it was."

My round-bellied guest let out a Scotch-laced sigh, and his eyes followed a waitress carrying a tray across the room. "You want to hear about how I lost my network broadcast, don't you?" His expression became pained. "About the video. Won't you people ever stop? It was research! I swear! I wanted to understand them perverts, in order to convert them!" His pasty skin started to get blotchy as the passion of his words grew. He thumped the table. "I was used, made a spectacle of . . . became part of that whole *humanizing* scheme. The devil's revenge is cruel against those who do the good work." He sucked the last of the Scotch off the melting ice cubes in his glass. "What kind of story are you writing?"

It took me a heartbeat to recover from the well-practiced tirade and respond to his question. "I'm not writing a story."

"You said you was a journalist and wanted to ask me some questions." It came out *quest-yuns.*

"I am a journalist, but this is not an interview."

He squinted. "Then what do you want?"

I wanted answers, so I had to put up with his bigoted crap to some extent. *For Beverley's sake,* I told myself again.

If I was going after a vampire, I had to know everything I could, gain every advantage I could.

I took a hundred-dollar bill from the little purse on my lap. If not for the promise of Vivian's cash coming this afternoon, this would have really hurt my budget—especially after providing for all of Poopsie's canine needs. Nonchalantly, I laid it on the table. It was crisp and flat, a new bill. I pushed it toward him, but kept my finger on my end of it.

His eyes lit up, then darkened. On the phone I'd only offered him a fifty-dollar "donation." Seeing the Benjamin, he knew this was going to be bad. "Tell me about . . . Goliath."

One eye squinted up suspiciously, but his blotched skin paled. "You're a devil, young lady." His mouth twitched. "And you offer too little for my soul."

"Mr. Kline—"

He leaned forward and snatched the bill away, crumpling it into his chubby fist. His face pinched, and his eyes squeezed shut. He took a deep breath and released the Scotch fumes in my direction again. But this time the smell had a hint of antiseptic to it, like that of a hospital about to burst into flames.

"The shrink my parents took me to, years after the abduction, did a regression on me. Menessos, that . . . that . . . *bastard* was there. As he is now. Unchanged. Fucking vampire. Worse than the perverts, the undead! And any of them in power of others, so much worse. . . ." His voice went all little-boy scared; then he recovered. "He lured my brother away with false promises. Lured him right out the window. His words were like candy to Goliath." His pious look faltered; he snorted and sat back.

Menessos? Who was Menessos? "What did he say?"

"He promised to teach my brother, tutor him. To make him powerful and . . . immortal." His eyes darted up; his expression instantly became an angry stare. "You'd love to be one of those freaks, wouldn't you? That's what this is about."

"No, I wouldn't and no, it isn't. Absolutely not." Of course I thought people who watched his show and followed his bizarre beliefs were almost as freakish as vampires. Most of his followers would have done better with regular doses of lithium than regular doses of him.

"The gleam in your eyes says different." He paused. "You're walking into the garden, little girl, with your belly just rumblin' for an apple."

"My beliefs happen to be other than your own, but I've always thought the Garden of Eden story would have been much better if Eve wasn't portrayed as such a mindless character manipulated by suggestion. I mean, if she were a little bolder, more resourceful and confident, why, she and Adam might've had snake for dinner instead."

He stared at me, seemingly confused. I'd spoken just fast enough to keep him from interrupting. Perhaps he'd never entertained the thought that Eve could have been bold. He said, "So you don't want to become a vampire?"

"No. My purpose is other than that, Mr. Kline. I assure you."

"Oh." He drew out the sound like a discovery. He tucked the wadded hundred-dollar bill into the pocket of his unironed shirt. "Revenge, then, is it?" His face went devoid of emotion. "I know what the creature that was once my brother does for him."

He assessed my expression carefully, then continued with neither bombast nor drawl, "Take my advice: drop it. Whatever he did, let it go and get on with your life and be happy you've still got it. Because I guarantee you, if the genius bastard who once was my brother has reason to think you're of interest in any way, then you're already being watched. There'll be no surprising him. If you act against him, he'll be ready, and he'll retaliate. And if Menessos gets involved . . . he will destroy you, destroy your spirit, and leave you wishing Goliath had killed you." Miserably, he added, "Who do you think arranged and leaked the video of me? A human servant set me up from the start. With all my good intentions for the soul of my brother, with all the power of my God backing me, if *I* didn't have the strength of mind and character to defeat Menessos, you're a fool if you think *you* can, missy."

When he pushed his chair back and stood, I knew I was getting the check for his drink. At least his loud tirade had kept the waitresses at bay long enough to keep us from having ordered any food. "I suggest you keep your head down," he said, "and forget whatever it is you think you know. Goliath will only take so much nosing around. Take that bit of advice seriously." He pointed his sausage-like finger at me. "It'll keep you from scrounging through McDonald's Dumpsters to soothe your hungers."

CHAPTER EIGHT

Nana stood in the doorway between the dining room and the kitchen. She had been there for not quite a minute. She'd shifted her weight and sighed heavily four times already. At my dining room desk, I sat typing out my recent activities and thoughts on my laptop. Writing it all down helped me keep it straight in my head, and suddenly there were so many threads in my life that I needed a visual. This kind of exercise had blossomed into the column that now provided my income.

Pointedly, Nana cleared her throat, but I didn't stop typing.

"Aren't you going to cook any dinner?" she finally said.

I glanced up from my computer screen and, even though I didn't intend to stop typing, I couldn't help it. Nana wore a white sweatshirt and white sweatpants. Her irritated, hands-on-hips pose accentuated her snowman body shape. Her white beehive was still ruffled in the back from an afternoon nap she insisted was only a few minutes of resting her eyes. I knew better—her snoring had greeted me when I arrived home from meeting Mr. Kline. It was a struggle not to let my amusement show.

"Well?"

"Not today."

"Do you know what time it is?"

"Nope." I paused to rethink how to spell "discipline." Nana always said it *dis-li-pline.* A lifetime of hearing that pronunciation made me have to stop and think when I had to write that particular word; otherwise I'd put an extra *l* in it.

"Well, for your information, it's after six. It's dinnertime."

"So?" A smile slipped onto my face. For all the hang-ups my childhood had provided, teasing her equaled the mildest retribution.

"So? I'm hungry! Poopsie's hungry." He loped in when she said his name. "I'm not eating out of a box again."

"Chubby's dog food is in the garage. And don't you dare start feeding him table food!"

"His name is *Poopsie,"* she said defiantly, patting his head.

I saved my document, closed the laptop, and got up. "All right. I'll feed him. But he's going to be too big to be called 'Poopsie.'" He followed me eagerly into the garage and across the cracked cement floor to his metal crate. I scooped his puppy chow into the bowl and placed it deep inside the cage, just like the puppy book said to do. "There you go."

He didn't move from his spot by the garage door.

"Go on. Your dinner's in there."

He sat and gave a whine.

"Okay. I'll make her get you a cooler name."

Another whine.

"And it won't be Chubby."

He barked and leapt into the cage and started to eat just as a motorcycle roared up my driveway, throwing gravel. I stepped back to the kitchen in time to see Nana slam the cupboard door in disgust and shuffle out. I announced, "Dinner's here."

"Delivery?" she asked, turning.

"Yup. You should smooth your hair down in the back."

Her hands shot up self-consciously. "Who delivers out here," she grumbled, heading for the living room as she spoke, "besides that grumpy paperboy who couldn't hit a driveway if it were the size of Texas?"

"That paperboy isn't tossing out papers while riding a bicycle, Nana. This is the country, not the suburbia you're accustomed to. Out here, paperboys are grown-ups driving cars, and usually they're going about sixty. If the paper's on the property at all, he didn't miss."

From the living room, she'd have a good view of our guest coming in. Wanting to avoid her having a conniption, I started my warning as I jogged down the hall to the door. "His name's Johnny."

"The paperboy?"

"No, Nana. The man bringing dinner. Now Nana, don't freak. He's—"

Nana was already peering out the window. "By the lunar crone's eyes, would you look at that!"

"Nana—"

"I thought they quit making handsome deliverymen back in the sixties!"

I stopped. She thought Johnny was handsome? Her inflection hadn't been sarcastic; her words hadn't been confirmation of a suspicion, but a surprised observation.

His tattoos made him seem disturbingly scary to me. I stared at her as she stood at the window with the curtains parted, smiling out at the porch. Johnny's boots thumped across the wooden boards. He was knocking before I could open the front door.

"Hello, Red." Johnny smiled, his low voice warm and rich. His tone said so much more than "hello." Behind him, the golden leaves rained down from my pair of oaks. Wind whipped over the porch and through the screen to chill me as I stood staring up at him, ensnared like a cat in a cage.

Johnny wasn't the kind of guy I flirted with. Remembering how we'd talked on the phone, embarrassment clenched my stomach. I forced my attention to neutral space—the floor—catching details of his jacket and black T-shirt beneath, the leather pants he wore. Where did guys over six feet find leather pants? Johnny was at least six foot two. His motorcycle boots, with silver-plated chains clinking, oozed utter bad-boy coolness that no red-blooded female could deny—and added another inch to his height. His presence screamed power and danger.

Everything he wore enhanced his dangerous look, and all of it was on purpose. Didn't that justify my fear? Did that mean I didn't have to beat myself up for being shallow, since I was only reacting the way he wanted people to react to him?

My hand shook as I tucked my hair behind my ear, bit my bottom lip, and looked up again.

He wore his black hair pulled back as usual, leaving the tattoos on his face strikingly exposed. Black lines surrounded and decorated his eyes like the Eye of Horus or Wedjat. My heart beat more slowly and my blood felt colder in my veins. Multiple tiny, white-gold loops adorned each brow, each ear. Little diamond studs glistened on either side of his nose.

He smiled and, strangely, it was as fearsome as it was friendly. "Food's getting cold, Red."

"Oh. Yeah." *You can do this,* I told myself. *He just* seems *scary. Ask him in.*

I swallowed and put on a fake smile of certainty as I reached for the latch. "Come in."

Johnny stepped inside. This was my personal space; allowing him in here felt completely different than opening the cellar, which wasn't accessible from the house.

"I got Chinese. Might have to nuke it a bit. It stays hot pretty good except when it's on the back of a bike in October. There's nothing out here, you know. Not even a gas station. I got this in Cleveland, at one of my favorite spots."

He paused, taking in the living room's deep red walls, the chocolate-brown-corduroy-slipcovered furniture, the worn tan pillows. I felt my insides shrinking. I hoped he wouldn't say anything cocky about all the Arthurian artwork and books being inside an old saltbox farmhouse.

"I've never seen your inner sanctuary before," he said. "You've got style, Red."

I managed to say, "Thanks." He wasn't too choosy if he approved of an aging farmhouse with creaky floors and little in the way of modern decor. I hoped we would make it through the evening without him catching on and cracking jokes about my weakness for Arthur.

He sniffed. "Did you get a dog?"

"I did," Nana said as if she were sharing a secret. She stepped away from the window and was actually smiling. It made her look like someone I didn't know.

"Really?" He turned to Nana. "What kind?"

"A Great Dane puppy," I said unenthusiastically. "He's huge."

Over his shoulder, Johnny said, "Me too," disguised in a cough. He did it so quickly that I almost didn't catch it. Silently, I prayed that Nana had missed it. "I brought these especially for you." He held a picnic basket out to Nana, complete with red-and-white-checkered cloth. He was going all out for the Red Riding Hood thing. I couldn't imagine sinister-looking Johnny going into a basket-and-candle shop, but I guessed he had.

Across the basket's top, wedged under the handles, was a carton of Marlboros. "For me?" Nana asked sheepishly.

He placed it into her hands. "Check inside the basket."

Nana removed the carton and stuck it under her arm so she could open the hinged lid. "Cookies!" she exclaimed. With a deep breath, she took in the scent of them. "Oh. They smell divine! What kind are they?"

"Macadamia nut and white chocolate chip," Johnny said. "Made 'em myself just today." He offered her his hand. "I'm Johnny."

Nana shifted the basket and accepted his hand readily. His tattoos didn't faze her at all. It made me wonder why they disturbed me so much.

"I'm Demeter. Demeter Alcmedi."

"It's a pleasure to meet you, Demeter." He properly put the emphasis on the first syllable, as she had in introducing herself. She always hated it when people made her name sound like a Frenchman asking for a yardstick, *duh-ME-tur.* He was definitely racking up brownie points with her. Didn't she know he was a wærewolf? She could usually tell right away. "The cookies are for after dinner, though. I hope you like General Tso's Chicken."

"My favorite! Did you tell him, Seph?"

"No." I didn't eat meat, so I began to wonder what he'd gotten for me. "Kitchen's all the way back." I pointed down the hallway.

He carried the bag on to the kitchen, boots thumping and chains clinking. Nana was smoothing her hair again. "Did I get it?" she asked.

"Yeah." I laughed quietly.

"What?" she asked.

"He brought Chinese. I guess you're eating out of a box anyway."

"This is different." She patted her basket happily and carried it down the hall.

When I joined them, Johnny had put his leather jacket on the back of a chair and started taking out the white paper cartons at the dinette table with two chairs on one side, a bench on the other. I got down the mismatched kitchen plates and grabbed some flatware from the drawer. "Uh-uh," Johnny said, wagging a finger at me. "You have to eat with chopsticks."

I gave him a dubious look; he countered with a defiant one. "Okay," I conceded, "just don't be too harsh when I'm wearing my dinner."

He glanced sidelong at Nana placing her basket out of the way on the countertop by the sink and whispered to me, "If you get messy, I promise, I'll clean you up personally."

In the instant it took for my cheeks to warm, the image of him licking sweet-and-sour sauce off my cheek filled the cinema in my head. I couldn't move.

Johnny took a plate from my hands and began dumping one of the cartons onto it. "You're vegetarian, aren't you?" he asked in normal tones, as if to cover up that he'd whispered to me.

I swallowed and wished I could pull the heat from my face as easily. "Yeah."

"I couldn't stand not having a couple of thick and juicy filet mignons, rare, with lots of peppercorns. Mmmm. Love it."

Having figured him as a porterhouse type, I made a mental note. I'd promised him treats.

"Here you are, Demeter." He sat the plate before her and came back to serve up another little box. He noticed the big oak dining set in the room beyond. "Oh, you have a dining room. Should we eat in there?"

"No. I never use it," I said.

He shrugged. "Okay."

"How'd you know I was vegetarian?"

His eyebrows jumped up and down, and he acted like he was locking his lips shut with a key. Then he quipped, "Celia told me."

Celia was the first wære I ever knew. After the attack, I thought she and Erik were going to die—everyone did—but they both made it. Then we found out about their lunar furriness. I helped them find a safe house to spend their full moons in. When I bought this place, we fixed the cellar for them. At first it was just the band, but as she met more wolves and brought them along, we kept adding kennels. It was practically a pack now.

Celia was filling the cages as fast as we could renovate the space for them. The wæres brought pizza and beer and pretty much partied in the storm cellar until the change happened. Listening to them talk about the ups and downs of wæredom shaped my column topics. They each paid me twenty bucks a night for kenneling services and a continental breakfast of Krispy Kremes. Since that seemed to be the doughnut of choice for all wære-creatures, I'd bet the company's sales always spiked before full moons. "Celia," I repeated.

Johnny stopped serving and faced me squarely. "I asked her a lot of things about you." He was very close. Though he'd kenneled here for six months—meaning I'd seen him six times, and then only when opening the cages in the mornings and leaving the doughnuts—I'd never been this close. He smelled like cedar and sage.

For the first time, I really looked at him. Not with furtive embarrassment. Not even with fear. I looked and paid attention. All the things I feared faded for an instant, and I saw Johnny beneath the tattoos. He had steely, blue-gray eyes.

"You two come and sit down to eat," Nana ordered us.

Taking my plate of steamed vegetables on rice, I went to the table and deliberated about where to sit. If I sat across from Nana, Johnny could choose which of us to sit next to, but if I sat beside her, he would have to sit across from us both. That seemed the best plan. So I sat and tried to figure out the chopsticks, but I couldn't get anything to my mouth. By the time Johnny had filled his plate with some kind of chicken dish and sat with us, I'd tried, without success, to pick up a bite of food a dozen times. Nana laughed at me. I felt terribly foolish, but I laughed too.

"I'm going to starve if you won't concede to letting me use a fork."

"You're using them like a shovel and holding them wrong," he said. "They're delicate, but they won't break. Hold them like this. Firmly." He indicated how he was holding his, and I noticed he had more rings on his fingers than I did. "Pinch the food."

I moved one stick, then the other, and held the chopsticks up for inspection. "No." He put his chopsticks down. Reaching across the table, he took my hand in his before I could protest. Gently, deftly, his warm hands repositioned the sticks and molded my fingers into position. "There. Now try it. Pinch."

I did, and actually got a bite. The vegetables needed half a minute in the microwave, but to warm them up, I'd have to set the chopsticks down. Then he'd have another chance to "help" me position them properly. I decided to eat the food just as it was and avoid further hand-holding. "Oh," I said, chewing. "So that's how you do it."

"I thought you already knew how to do it," Johnny said brightly, as if there was no innuendo in the statement at all. "Next time, we'll try French. Or Thai. Some Thai can be really hot. I like it hot."

Next time?

"Oh?" Nana said conversationally. "What about Greek?"

Johnny grinned and, despite the Wedjat tattoos, it was mischievous in a very little-boy way. Nothing scary there at all—until his smile decreased and he focused hard on me while he answered her, "I don't think I've ever tasted anything Greek. But I'd love to."

I'm not accustomed to being mildly flirted with, let alone blatantly flirted with. A little is one thing; it lets you know somebody's interested. It's flattering. But Johnny never did anything on a small scale. The sexual-tension thing—which he clearly thrived on—rose to an overwhelming peak for me with Nana sitting there, her old ears hearing every word and not catching a single innuendo. I was scared that she'd catch on. Scared she'd start cussing and go all indignant on us. Scared she'd laugh like a banshee and proceed to bring him up in conversation every morning at the breakfast table.

He had to stop.

When we were all nearly finished, I asked Johnny, "What's that you're having?"

"Bo Lo Gai Pan. It's chicken and water chestnuts, pea-pods, mushrooms, vegetables, and pineapple." He lowered his tone and continued. "On your tongue the pineapple just—"

I cleared my throat loudly and interrupted him. "You picked up the package?" I didn't want to know what the pineapple did on his tongue. I just knew it'd be another innuendo.

Clearly amused but unoffended, he said, "Of course."

I asked, "Briefcase?"

"More like a little overnight duffel. It's on my bike." He pushed his plate away.

Except for a few grains of rice clinging to a patch of sauce, the plate was empty. The man knew how to pinch with his sticks. There was a joke there, and I was glad I hadn't voiced my thought aloud.

"That manager. She a friend of yours?" Johnny asked.

Nana stood up and cleared our plates away. I stared after her as she carried them to the sink. I don't think she would have helped if it had just been the two of us for dinner. Clearing the table and doing the dishes had been my chores since age eight. But I was the roomie in *her* home then. Now, despite the situational reversal, I had to wonder what she was up to.

"More like an acquaintance. How'd she react?"

"She was cool." He sounded disappointed.

"What about the customers?"

"The place was empty except for a little girl sleeping in the corner."

I muttered, "Damn her," my voice barely above a whisper.

"Her kid?"

"No. You didn't recognize her?"

"Should I have?"

"It was Lorrie's daughter, Beverley."

"Beverley! Oh, she was facing away. If I'd known . . ." He paused. "What's she doing there?"

"Lorrie knew that manager, made her Beverley's guardian in her will, so Child Services has given her temporary custody."

"I can't believe what happened," he said. "Heard about any arrangements yet?"

"I don't think anything can be done until they release the body. I'm sure Celia will stay on top of it and let us know."

Nana came over and patted Johnny on the shoulder. "Thanks for dinner."

"So where's this pup of yours, Demeter?"

"In the garage. Would you like to meet him?"

"Sure."

The two of them went out, and a swirl of cooler air wafted in as they left. The cool air helped refocus my thoughts. Vivian was simply not up to parenting a grieving child. I doubted Vivian would abuse her physically, but Beverley needed mental support and understanding, not the rejection clear in Vivian's tone and actions. In an effort to calm my instincts, I reasoned that I shouldn't get involved in Beverley's care. I was already way too involved in settling up with her mother's killer. Social Services would check up on Beverley —

Shit. No they wouldn't. Her mother had been a wærewolf. Though Beverley was clear of the virus, they'd conveniently lose her file and forget she was out there. Damn it, wasn't there anyone else who cared?

"Yes. You do," Nana said, opening the door to the garage.

My eyes widened at the thought that she'd suddenly become a mind reader.

"You have as much right to voice an opinion as anyone else," she continued, over her shoulder to Johnny. "And, actually, I agree with you. I think 'Ares' is much better than 'Poopsie.'"

I was relieved: at least Nana wasn't a mind reader. "Ares?" I asked.

"Johnny said he thought it suited him better. So 'Ares' it is."

The pup yipped happily from the garage.

Mystified by her agreeableness to Johnny, I went and stood beside her as she leaned on the door frame, fondly smiling out the door she hadn't shut. After checking her face, I had the distinct impression that she was admiring our guest's backside. Johnny and Ares were playing tug-of-war with a big rope toy I'd bought in the hope that it would save my couch. Both were growling merrily.

Nana turned and shuffled a few steps away, then stopped and faced me. "If you were smart, you'd make a mess of yourself and let him clean you up." She disappeared into the hall.

My mouth was still hanging open when Johnny suddenly let the pup have the rope. He took his cell phone from its belt clip and opened it. "Hello?"

I was surprised he could get a signal out here.

"Yeah . . . shit. How bad? Do they know? I'm on my way." He shut the phone. "Sorry, Red, I gotta go." He leapt up the steps to the landing and passed me in a rush, headed for the front door. I grabbed his leather jacket from the chair and followed.

"What's going on?"

He didn't pause; he just opened the door and went out, talking as he walked. "Theo's in the ICU. Car accident."

"Johnny wait—" I was jogging to keep up.

"When they find out she's got the virus, they'll pull the plug! I gotta go." He slipped a leg over the motorcycle. He took the jacket from me and slipped it on.

"You mean Theodora Hennessey, right?"

He nodded tersely; his face had hardened. He started the bike.

"I'm coming with you." Awkwardly, I threw a leg over the seat behind him. It'd been a long time since I'd ridden on a motorcycle. Hands on the big black saddlebags, I situated myself so I wasn't right up against him. He looked over his shoulder at me, curious. His mouth opened; then he clamped it shut and shrugged out of his coat. "Put this on."

I did.

"I'm getting there ASAP, so hold on tight," he said, and for once I didn't think he was just being smug.

CHAPTER NINE

After about ten stoic minutes, I gave in and wrapped my arms tight around Johnny's waist and let my body nestle against his. Without a helmet or goggles or even sunglasses, my eyes were forced shut. All I could do was *feel*. . . . Feel Johnny's hard, lean body, tense with urgency, muscles moving with the bike as he swerved around, and I believe on a few instances *between,* cars. It was like dancing to the rev and hum of the engine, swaying together, except we didn't use our feet.

It takes me an hour to get downtown; longer if I have to fight rush-hour traffic. Johnny got us to the Cleveland Clinic in forty minutes flat. By then, of course, I needed a hairbrush in the worst way.

I felt like the little Chihuahua trying to keep up with the boss dog in those cartoons as we entered the hospital. Johnny's long legs took him smoothly and swiftly inside while I half ran to keep up, finger-combing my hair in an effort not to look like the witch stereotype.

"Johnny!" Celia's voice. We turned. "Persephone!"

We hurried toward her, but she moved reluctantly, like someone with bad news he or she doesn't want to share. Celia was a beautiful woman, pale and petite and slender with golden-blond hair in a stylish, short cut. She always wore something fashionable but kept to soft and muted colors. In tan corduroy trousers and a khaki turtleneck adorned with a sheer, gold-tone scarf, she could have passed for a chic doctor's wife. I'd always thought she carried herself like an approachable princess: highborn, but not high-minded. When we neared, however, I could see that her swollen red eyes barely held her fear in check, adding a feral warning to her demeanor. Her arms spread wide for me. "Didn't expect *you,*" she said, choking up as she grabbed me in a hug.

"How bad is she?"

Celia's hair tickled my skin as she buried her face against my neck. She squeezed me so tight I couldn't breathe. There's nothing like wære strength. "First Lorrie, and now this." She let out a sob. I hugged her back, her sweet-orchid cologne mixing with the sanitized hospital smell as she cried into my windblown hair.

"They're running the tests now," she whispered. "They suspect already."

"How is that?" I asked, looking up to catch Johnny's reaction.

"She ripped the dashboard apart with her bare hands."

"She what?" Johnny demanded.

Celia pushed out of the hug, but immediately wrapped her arms about herself as if she were cold. "What I was told . . . and overheard . . . was that her SUV went over the abutment of a bridge. The paramedic said it looked like it had landed on its nose, then fallen back onto the tires. She was conscious when they arrived, the steering wheel pressing against her chest—the air bags didn't go off. She was screaming and coughing up blood. They tried to calm her, told her they'd get the jaws of life and have her out in fifteen minutes. She said, 'Fuck that' and tore the steering column off, dragged herself out the front window, then collapsed."

"Shit," Johnny said.

"She pulled herself out of the wreckage! Can you imagine?" She wiped her eyes with her hands. "Her right leg is broken." She shivered. "Both ankles are broken. Five ribs. One punctured a lung!" She put a hand on her stomach. "They did a CT scan. The nurse told me the good news was, aside from the punctured lung, her internal organs looked good. The bad news was she had a fractured pelvis. The trauma surgeon was going to put in a chest tube to drain fluid from the lung, and put her leg back together."

"Excuse me."

We all turned. Two police officers stood three feet away from us. I detected Johnny's spine stiffening and shoulders squaring from the corner of my eye. "Yes?" he said, voice low and taut.

One of the officers was older, I'd have guessed fifty. The other was half that, and he shrank back a step when Johnny spoke. "You're acquaintances of Ms. Hennessey's?" the older man asked, unflinching as he assessed Johnny.

"We are," Johnny said.

"We don't anticipate Ms. Hennessey will be able to answer questions right away; could we get your names and contact information? Perhaps you could answer some questions."

"Sure," I said. "What questions?"

"We've received eyewitness reports that Ms. Hennessey's vehicle was forced over the edge of the bridge by a black Hummer. Do you know anyone with such a vehicle?"

We all said no.

"Do any of you know why anyone would want to tamper with Ms. Hennessey's vehicle?"

Before either Johnny or I could react, Celia interrupted. "Oh God, there's the nurse."

We all turned to the plump woman with a face like a stone cliff full of crags and crevices. Recognition of Celia brought her to us, but she clearly disapproved of Johnny in a glance. "Are you family of the patient Hennessey?" she asked.

"They are," Celia lied.

"Yes," I lied too.

"Bet this won't surprise you, then. Her test is positive for the wære-virus," she said distastefully, with a sharp glance at Johnny. "We're discharging her now. If you would—"

"What? Discharging her? The full moon isn't for another . . ." I stopped to think.

"Twenty-five days," Johnny said.

"By then we'll have her moved elsewhere," I added. "No one will be at risk."

"We are not properly set up to care for wæres, and several of our employees here feel caring for wæres violates their moral conscience, and"—she held up a hand to ward off a protest—"federal law allows them to refuse. However, the State Shelter Facility is fully staffed with folks who will treat wæres. For this reason, as well as for her own well-being, she is being discharged *now.*"

"State Shelter?" Celia echoed, her voice hollow. She and Johnny shared a look of defeat.

The State Shelters were like human dog pounds. Their idea of health care was ridiculous. Unwanted pound animals got better treatment. I couldn't let Theodora go there.

"This is so fucked up!" Johnny shouted.

Anybody who wasn't already staring at him did then. The police had disappeared, probably fled as soon as they heard the test was positive.

My stomach was a chunk of ice. "We'll take her."

"What?" the nurse asked, incredulous.

Johnny and Celia were staring at me.

"Are you saying that you want to sign an AMA waiver—Against Medical Advice—and take the patient with you?" She laughed.

I swallowed. "Yes."

"Persephone, think about this," Celia said.

"No, it's perfect," Johnny said to her.

"You'll have to go to the registration area to arrange for payment," the nurse interrupted.

I ran a hand over my windblown hair. I didn't have my purse or checkbook—not that I thought I had enough money to cover what they were going to charge. Then I remembered Vivian's money. "Johnny. Is the duffel still in your saddlebag?"

He did a double take at me, between glares at the nurse, and said, "Yeah."

"Get it." I pushed up the sleeves of his oversized jacket and said to the nurse, whose smug grin had disappeared, "I want an itemized bill. Whatever IVs are in her, stay in her. Whatever fluids, medicine, blood, or plasma is currently being given to her. I'm paying for those too." I turned to Celia. "Did you drive here in your CX7?" We had to transport Theo, and I wasn't sure I wanted anyone from here to take us and know where we went.

"Erik brought me. His Infiniti." Celia's eyes widened as she understood. "The seats fold down. He's waiting outside the ICU room now. I'll get the keys and tell him what you said."

The nurse scanned me up and down. "You know your friend is as good as dead if you take her away from professional care?"

"I know she's as good as dead at the State Shelter."

"We'll take our chances," Johnny affirmed.

The nurse walked away.

I shouted after her, "I want the stretcher or backboard or whatever she's on too." She didn't respond. "You hear me?" I shouted. She waved her hand up over her head. From where I was, it looked a lot like she flipped me off.

I sat in the back corner of Erik's black Infiniti FX45 beside Theo, who lay crosswise in the space on a backboard. She looked like hell. Neck brace, dark circles around her eyes. Weird casts on her leg and ankles. Her toes were dark, greenish, swollen, and shiny. I held the IV bag up to keep the fluids moving into her. The tube poking from her side was the size of a garden hose; it didn't seem like too much was coming out just now.

I had a healing chant on the tip of my tongue, but I didn't dare call the energy and use it on a wære. Erik and Celia were silent in the front seat; Johnny was on his motorcycle, ahead of the Infiniti, leading the way. He'd said he knew where to go, promised it'd take less than thirty minutes.

I smoothed hair off her brow. Why would someone tamper with her car or run her off the road? As I sat there, I gave my first thought to the fact there would be people who would ask those same questions if I killed Goliath Kline. Surely he had friends or lovers or someone in his life . . . or, rather, undeath . . . who would mourn him. If I, by some miracle, did manage to kill him, that wouldn't be the end of it. *An' it harm none . . .*

Being an assassin meant harming far more than just the target.

We hit a bump in the road; Theodora moaned.

"Theo." I took her hand in mine. "It's Persephone. I'm here. I'm with you."

Another bump; she moaned again. "Hurt."

"Don't try to talk right now. We're taking you to get help." I didn't want to say "we're taking you to a veterinarian." It didn't sound right or inspire hope. Though going through the change would cure just about anything wrong with a wære, the full moon was weeks away, and keeping her alive until then would be a miracle. But Johnny had said he knew a vet who'd treat wæres, as long as they paid in cash. It was the best we could do for her. "You're going to make it, Theo. I promise. Hang in there." Though I had no idea if it was true, I added, "We'll be there any minute."

"Seffffff," she whispered.

I leaned close. "Shhh. Theo. Save your strength."

"Wasss him. Ran me off . . . off th' rrroooad." She squeezed my hand. *"Go-li-ith."* Her grip went slack.

Checking for a heartbeat, I found the strong beat hammering against my fingertips.

I should've felt relief, but I couldn't. She'd said Goliath had run her off the road! She'd recognized him . . . her sources for background checking must have included photos. More importantly, Goliath knew she'd checked him out and—just like the reverend had said—he had taken deadly offense to it.

And that meant this was my fault.

"She's stabilizing." Dr. Geoffrey Lincoln, D.V.M., slipped his hands into his lab-coat pockets. He was an average-sized man, about five-nine and around 190 pounds. Receding short brown hair, brown eyes, glasses. His jaw had a nice shape to it, but his lips were thin like smokers' lips. When he concentrated, he made a flat line of his mouth. At Johnny's growled insistence, the doc had been kind enough to meet us at his facility despite the fact it was well after midnight.

"I will loan you the equipment and check on her, but"—he continued with a sincerely apologetic expression—"she can't stay here. I have people in and out of here every day with their pets, people who love their furry animals but feel completely threatened by the portion of our population who *become* furry animals. If just one person saw her, the feds would shut me down within an hour."

Celia crossed her arms. "This is like the Trail of Tears, what the government did to the Native Americans. They can't just slaughter us, but they can deny us every basic human right to encourage genocide."

I went wide-eyed, remembering her college paper on Native Americans. Though it had been a good report on a cause she had felt passionately about even before she became a wære, I feared if she started on that subject, we'd be here forever.

Fortunately, the magnitude of the situation must have left her speechless, because the room was silent except for the sounds of the blood pressure machine starting its cycle. The veterinarian's office had previously been the site of an urgent-care facility, and Dr. Lincoln had inherited several pieces of equipment left behind in a storage closet. Now, in addition to the BP cuff, Theo had an EKG monitor, some kind of suction device attached to her chest tube, and an IV machine.

Between Johnny's and Dr. Lincoln's shoulders, I could see Theo's face. Unconscious, heavily medicated. Almost dead, because I had asked questions and she had searched for the answers.

"My house," I said. "We'll take her there."

Everyone helped. Even the doctor pitched in. He allowed us to transport her in a horse trailer and then carried the monitors behind Johnny and Erik, who had the difficult task of keeping the backboard level as they took Theo upstairs. Preceding them, I wished I'd changed my sheets this morning, but there was no time to change them now.

"Do you have extra pillows? You'll want to keep her legs elevated, especially the right one." Dr. Lincoln checked Theo's toes as he spoke.

"Why are her casts soft?" Erik asked.

"They're temporary," the doctor answered. "When the swelling goes down, I can get regular casts on her."

Nana finally emerged from her bedroom in her nightgown and robe, got in the middle of the throng of people, and demanded, "What the hell is going on here?"

Johnny stepped toward her. "Red, you've got to shuffle some things around in your room so the doc can plug in the monitors. Why don't I explain this to Demeter while you go do that?"

"Perfect." I was grateful for something to do and even more grateful to have someone else to deal with Nana.

Dr. Lincoln arranged syringes, medicines, and bandages for Theo on my dresser top. He stressed that we must not exceed the dosages he marked on the bottles. "If she wakes and is in so much pain she's begging for more, call me," he said. He plugged in the machines and told Celia and me what beeps were good, and what beeps were bad and what to do about them.

"I'll stop back tomorrow evening—or, I mean, later tonight—and bring a feeding tube and change the catheter bag. I can't guarantee what time, but you should have enough supplies."

When Dr. Lincoln left, Celia came to me. "We're going to go home," she said, "but we are coming right back."

"Celia, you don't have to do that."

"Yes, we do. Three weeks is a long time, and you can't do it alone."

I suddenly realized what an enormous commitment I'd made in offering my place to Theo. I wasn't a nurse, let alone a full-time caregiver. The idea of getting help was suddenly a very welcome one. If they helped for a day or two, that would be great; if they helped for a week, even better. I'd open my home to them for the duration, if they were willing. With Nana, a puppy, a column to write, and a vampire to assassinate, I was going to need help with Theo. "Okay."

"We're going to get some clothes and our sleeping bags, and we will be back. We'll use our camping gear and take the third floor."

After what had happened to them while camping, I always marveled that they continued to find any fun in it. "Celia, it's a floored attic! Take the empty bedroom."

"You take it."

"I'll sleep on the couch."

She leaned in closer and said quietly, "Johnny wouldn't miss an opportunity to spend more time with you, so of course he says he's staying too. He can have the sofa. You better have your own room. We have an air mattress at home for guests. We'll bring that for you."

"But—"

"No 'buts.'" She hugged me and I smelled her orchid perfume again.

"I'm so grateful that you guys want to help. I know Theo is too."

"With four of us, the shifts will be easy. We can make Johnny cook."

"Johnny cooks?"

She pulled away. "Fantastically."

"Will my kitchen survive?"

Celia pointed her finger at me. "Be careful, or you won't want him to leave. I often come home to find the band having a songwriting bash in my kitchen. Stage equipment on one side, simmering pots of scrumptious soups or a roast on the other—well, *you* wouldn't want a roast, but believe me, you won't go hungry."

Johnny was much more than I had given him credit for possibly being.

"We'll be back soon," she said, and left.

Alone, I stood at the end of the bed watching Theodora, and the weight of my actions hit home like a stake in my heart. Here was a life before me, and the thread of this life was in the Fates' hands. Were they twining it thicker, or were their scissors ready to sever it? I stared at my hands. Could I intentionally sever such a thread?

I shut my eyes and let the tears fall.

All I could do was cry for Theo and pray for her. With careful attention not to invoke any power that might affect Theo, I said,

"Goddess hear my humble appeal,
Grant Theo strength enough to heal.
Restore her body; give grace to her.
Make her aches and pains fewer.
With perfect love, make her new.
Right this wrong, I beseech you."

After repeating it thrice, I ended with the standard, "As I will, so mote it be."

Johnny's boots sounded on the steps; a soft creak came as he leaned on the door frame.

"Your grandma is such a cool old lady."

I snorted. "I never knew she had a split personality."

"Huh?"

"She likes you. I've always been a burden."

He came forward a step. "But *she's* staying with *you,* right? Not vice versa."

"Tables have turned, I guess, but she doesn't want to acknowledge it."

"Old people never like things to change. It's like when they can't move fast anymore, they can feel the world moving past them more and more. They're afraid of being left behind." He paused, easing further into the room. "I want to stay and help too, if you'll let me." He put his hands up innocently. "I'll behave. I swear."

"Of course." I shifted to face Theo.

He stepped closer. "Red? What's with the cash?"

I turned back with my eyebrows high and my mouth open. No words came out, though. Just a sigh that thought about turning into a maniacal giggle.

I couldn't just casually say, "Oh, it's money for an assassination hit on a vampire." He'd never believe me. He'd laugh and ask for the truth. I shut my mouth and turned back to Theo without answering. My arms folded over my chest.

All threads and all guilt aside, what had I been thinking, agreeing to a hit on a vampire? I'd decided to do it for Beverley, for that sweet little suffering girl, but noble ideas weren't good enough here. *I am an idiot.* Goliath had tried to kill someone who had only researched him a little.

My gut was so cold and I was so mad at myself.

"I guess I shouldn't have left it on the bike," Johnny said, joining me at the foot of the bed. "I figured it was like Avon or something."

It took me a heartbeat to grasp that he was still talking about the duffel.

"I thought if I left it out there, you'd walk me out to the bike to get it when I left. I was hoping to steal a good-night kiss while we were out there."

I spun around, ready to give him a big-worded lecture about unacceptable times for come-on lines. With his lupine speed, though, he grabbed my arms and moved in. "If you're in trouble, Red, be honest with me," he said. "I *will* help you."

"I'm not in trouble, J-Johnny," I stammered, wondering what he would categorize under the heading of "In Trouble." The cedar and sage smell of him was strong. His grip was tight. I wanted to feel his arms around me and hear him tell me everything would be okay, that I hadn't fucked everything up. But in order to take any comfort, I'd have to tell him everything. That was a risk I wasn't willing to take.

"If you're laundering it, and you've spent more than your take, that'll get you in serious trouble."

I laughed nervously. As I looked up at him—this close—his stern, fearsome eyes peered right through me. "I'm not laundering money." That would have been so much easier and safer than what I *was* doing.

"Then what?"

I wanted him to let go of me. And I didn't. "I can't tell you."

He snorted. "I knew you'd say that." He released me and brusquely turned to leave. He stopped at the door. "If things change, my offer stands."

CHAPTER TEN

Sitting at my dining room desk, the unused oak dining set behind me, I typed the title of my column—*Wære Are You.* I wondered how many people got the pun. Probably not as many as I hoped. I should ask the editors how many letters and emails they were getting from furious English teachers thinking I couldn't spell.

By Circe Muirwood. My pen name. To protect the innocent me.

> *Profile of a Wære-parent: Part One*
>
> It's a well-known and well publicized fact that wæres cannot have children. However, there's a segment of this once-human populace made up of people who were already parents when infected. Yes—normal, everyday people with real jobs and families can be wæres in secret. Maybe that's why your best friend and her husband didn't double-date with you and your honey last weekend—your best friend's husband was furry and kenneled securely.
>
> What I'm getting at is this: They're

> people. Furry or fanged, they were once normal human beings like you. If you're a single mom with an ex-husband who is a deadbeat dad who ran and pays no child support, think what it'd be like if you added the concern of monthly furriness to your list of worries. It's not just painful in the physical sense of changing bodily, it's painful because you find out so many things . . . who your friends are, who you can and can't trust, who will ridicule and harass you, who will help you hide . . .

I saved it and shut the laptop down. I began massaging my temples, not sure I could use any of it. Maybe it was stupid to think I could write a lucid column with all this going on.

I heard Celia and Erik come in the front door. Erik started quietly up the steps, but Celia stepped into the living room and followed the light to where I sat, still rubbing my temples.

"Headache?" Celia asked, coming in. "I'll get your ibuprofen."

"No. Thanks." I stretched as she passed me en route to the kitchen. "Just had to get some thoughts out. You get all your stuff?"

"Yeah." She'd traded her New England-chic outfit for a more relaxed jogging suit. It was sage green and matched her eyes. "Erik's setting up your air mattress in the spare bedroom now." She paused. "He wants to take the late watch with her tonight, so if I stay on watch until ten in the morning, and then Johnny is on watch until four—

that'll clear him up for cooking dinner. If you'll take four until ten at night, Erik will take over after you."

"Glad someone among us can think up a workable shift plan." I hadn't given it any thought and would've just winged it.

She smoothed her hair, obviously tired. "I brought a clipboard and made up a medicine schedule so we know when she gets what and how much and who gave it. We have to be organized. We can't afford a mistake." Her eyes welled up with tears.

That she was unsure made me unsure. I didn't like it. In denial of that thought, I said, "She's gonna make it."

"I don't know, Seph," she said softly, leaning against the door frame. "Twenty-five days is a long time in this little half-assed hospital we've had to construct."

Firming my voice, I said, "She's a wærewolf and—like you did, Celia—she'll pull through. We just need to keep her as comfortable as possible for now."

Celia wiped her eyes.

"So what's this about Johnny cooking?" I asked.

A laugh burst from her, as I'd hoped it would. "I can't figure him out. Looks like this Goth prince, sings like a siren"—she came in and sat in a chair so she was across from me—"and there's nothing he can't do . . . except, apparently, woo you."

"Hold on, there," I said.

"He asks me about you all the time. Like he's a teenage boy with a crush. Can't you go out with him just once and get me out of the middle here?"

"He had dinner here today."

"Dinner?" She sat straighter.

"Yeah. Before all this started, of course."

"That's why you two came together! Oooo, and a clingy motorcycle ride. Well, that's something." She paused. "What'd Nana say about him?"

"She actually liked him!"

"No way!"

I giggled. "Listen to us! Now *we* sound like teenagers."

Celia teased, "Well, forgive me for thinking you're lying! Your nana never liked any guy, let alone one with tattoos and piercings who rides a motorcycle."

"No others walked in with a carton of Marlboros, mac-nut cookies, and General Tso's Chicken."

Celia chuckled. "Wait till I tell Erik that! No wonder Nana let him talk her down when she was set to protest. No offense to your witch abilities, but that man's got magic, I tell you. Voodoo stuff or something. He just knows the combination to unlock any door barring his way."

"He told me he'd had a plan to steal a good-night kiss from me."

"Duh. He's been nuts about you since he started kenneling here."

What was I supposed to say? The truth, I guess.

"Look, Celia, I've been really . . . stupid. I let the tattoos intimidate me until I saw only them, not him. It took me this long to realize I was being stupid about that, but still, he's frontman for a techno-metal-Goth band. That's awesome, but realistically, as far as relationships go, that lifestyle seems ill-suited to monogamy, y'know?" I studied the floor. "You and Erik are an exception to every rule that's ever tried to apply to you, but how often can that kind of dream partnership come true?"

"Erik's known him for three years now, Seph." Celia had told me about how Johnny left Darkling Dose, a Detroit-based hard-rock band, to start his own. Erik had asked to audition for the drummer position but, she'd said, it was more like an interview. Johnny wanted people of similar ideas and ideals. Erik fit the bill, as did bassist and programmer Philip "Feral" Jones. "In all that time, nobody has interested him—not that the former band lacked groupies who wanted his attention. Nobody caught his eye. Until you."

For an instant, I wondered if that meant he slept with the groupies and just didn't get attached. Was that a jealous pang I felt? I counseled myself sternly to stop it. "Celia. Please don't make me feel obligated."

"I'm not trying to. You know that. It's just that everything's coming together now." As a trio, called Lycanthropia, they were the hottest band in the tristate area. "You ought to hook him while he's still available," Celia said.

"I'm sooo not fishing." I leaned my chair back on two legs to stretch again. "I don't have time."

Celia smiled wistfully. "Seph [illegible] I know Michael hurt you."

My heart seemed to stop when she said the name of my old boyfriend.

"And I know that you're going to take care of yourself," she went on. "But you don't have to be alone."

Denying the old pain, I went for humor. "I'm not. Nana's here."

"That's not what I meant, though you *are* busy being invaded right now, huh?" She stretched and yawned. "I'll ask Johnny to make a brunch tomorrow—"

"Damn!" I slapped the desk.

"What?"

"I'm supposed to go to Columbus tomorrow. High school friends gathering for a brunch." I paused. "I'll cancel. They'll understand." I wasn't sure Nancy would understand, but Olivia and Betsy wouldn't likely even notice.

"No. I think you should go. We can hold the fort. If it's a brunch, you'll be back by four, right?"

This was going to be a big deal for Nancy; I knew it. "Yeah. Earlier, probably."

"Then go, Seph." She put a hand on my arm. "That's why we're all here. Tending Theo has to be done, but if we all pitch in, it doesn't have to totally interrupt anybody's whole life."

Celia stood up. "I'm going to check on Erik and Theo, but I want to know one thing before I go." She stopped at the doorway.

I stiffened, afraid she was going to ask about the duffel. "What's that?"

"Would Johnny have gotten that kiss he was after?"

I put my head down on the desk and groaned.

Celia giggled all the way down the hall.

"What is the devil, really?"

Betsy and I exchanged a quick glance when Olivia asked the question of Nancy.

Nancy, in a very conservative navy-blue turtleneck and sweater, blinked at Olivia, clearly stunned by the question. She looked so pale since she'd stopped wearing makeup, and her dark hair was in a bun under a little lace doily—her look was positively severe. At the realization that the question was meant derisively and not seriously, Nancy set her after-brunch coffee down with a harsh *chink* of china on china. She didn't answer.

"Well. Apparently you've memorized only a portion of the witnessing methods. No doubt you'll read up on unbelievers with this question tonight, right?" Olivia tossed her head, a motion that would've flung her long peroxide-blond hair bouncing over her shoulder if it hadn't been so overprocessed that it hung flat and lifeless around her face. She wore a bright red T-shirt with an acid-washed denim shirt over it. Her fire-engine–red lipstick had worn away while she'd eaten, and now she seemed haggard with it missing.

Nancy swallowed hard and gazed at me imploringly. She was wrong to trust me to know what to say, because I didn't.

"German chocolate cake," Betsy said, adjusting her glasses. "German chocolate cake is the devil."

Olivia laughed.

I'd always thought of Betsy as Velma from *Scooby-Doo*. She'd had the same hairdo, a short bob, for as long as I'd known her. She wore round-framed glasses and couldn't see a thing without them. Though she did wear short skirts, she'd never been a fan of orange like Velma—thank goodness. With her carrot-colored hair, it would have been a disaster.

I leaned forward, pointing a finger at Betsy. "I knew it. I *knew* coconut was evil. Anything that comes from something that looks like a shrunken head has to be." I glanced at Nancy. *Play along,* I willed her mentally. But there was only reproach in her tight and sharp expression. It was entirely accusing.

"Go on, Seph. Make fun of me too. *Persecute* me. Disregard the past we've built."

"Seems to me the only one disregarding the past is you." Olivia was not being diplomatic.

"Wait a minute." I didn't like how this was going. "Your choice is yours, Nance. I've always respected your choices. I still do, but you're not respecting ours. We all have different callings." And how. "Aren't you allowed to have friends who aren't of your faith?"

Nancy's eyes teared up.

"Of course not," Olivia snapped. "She must socialize with her own and cut ties to all the nonbelievers, for they will weaken her. Sounds like a cult to me."

I glared at Olivia. She glared back, daring me to defend Nancy. It was clear she could cut her ties with both Nancy and me because she had all of the friends she needed in one: Betsy. They worked at the same factory, and they both had bar stools at their local dive that had been molded over the years to fit their backsides perfectly. I would have said that aloud, but they had become the kind of women who would think it was a compliment, the kind of women we had used to mock in high school.

"Well? Doesn't it?" Olivia pressed.

"You take everything so personal, Nance. You've become a real downer," Betsy said gently. "Stop judging us and let things be how they used to be."

"Things will never be how they were." Nancy reached for her purse.

Olivia sighed as if she were the one being slighted. "Can't you just be one of those people who gets saved and only acts different on Sundays?"

"Olivia—" I started.

Nancy stood. "I believe in it! That's why." Nancy tossed her napkin to the table and proceeded to the coffee shop door with confident steps, but she hesitated at the door and looked back. At me. I couldn't tell if the look was hostile or remorseful. I was watching her go—letting her go, but watching. I didn't want it to end this way, but it was her choice. Who was I to stop her? My gaze fell away.

These people were the reason I had a pen name. In school, I'd kept my beliefs secret. Every other time I had trusted someone with the truth, it had been used against me, so I took no chances with this group. Without them, I'd have been a complete social pariah. For a long time I'd known that if Nancy learned that I sympathized with wæres, she'd hate me; moreover, if she knew I was a pagan, because of her new beliefs she'd have to hate me more than she hated Olivia and Betsy.

I respected her for walking out. I knew how she felt all too well.

"I believe in java," Olivia said loudly, raising her cup to Nancy in salute.

Betsy couldn't hold in her giggle. Nancy had always been melodramatic, always said things like "persecute me," but it could have ended some other way. This was . . . snotty. We could have parted without Olivia's belittling manner. But that was Olivia. If you weren't with her, you were against her.

The bells on the door jingled loudly. Nancy had left.

I stared into my flavored espresso. I was Nancy's friend. I'd just failed the biggest friend test ever because I hadn't gone after her. My inaction meant I didn't care about her. But I *did* care about her. That was why I'd let a good friend just walk out of my life on her own terms. I hoped she held her head high.

And I—I who hid my pagan roots like a vain woman with a bottle of peroxide—my religion wasn't something I put out there to get a reaction with, like some of my peers did. That wasn't the point. But fear of rejection, rejection like Nancy had just experienced, had kept me from it for years. If I'd ever told Olivia and Betsy, they would have reacted with "Ooooo" and would have thought it was all fun like the sitcoms made it out to be. They were the types who would see "An' it harm none" as a free license.

But not Nancy. She cared. She would have tried to talk me out of it as if I were merely a confused little girl with the wrong directions to the candy store. She would never have understood. My comfort with it would have tweaked all her taboos and set her on a righteous indignation trip.

Betsy sniggered, pushed her glasses back up her nose. "What's with her? She on the rag or something?" She looked at me for the answer.

I considered asking Betsy if she was truly that brainless, but I didn't. If she worshipped anything, it was Olivia. So, yeah, I guessed she was brainless. "We gave her no reason to stay," I said.

"She found her 'faith,'" Olivia said, making quotations in the air with her fingers.

"No," I said. "She lost it. Her faith in us, I mean."

"What?"

"Nancy will be better off without feeling indebted to us for something even as small as a twice-yearly meal."

Hell, so would I.

I was ready to let go of my past, of the friends I had grown up with and knew well. I was ready to embrace the future alone, because they could not go where I had to go. They'd let various fears fence them inside their comfort zones. Not a bad thing, but a limiting thing. I wasn't that different, really.

I guessed I'd just grown up enough to know when to let go.

I said, "I gotta go."

"You gonna be next?" Olivia asked, her tone accusing. Betsy peered at me curiously.

"To walk Nancy's path?" I laughed softly. "No. I'm in for a different kind of trial by fire."

"Oh? Have another coffee. Do tell."

My leg started bouncing impatiently. "No, Olivia." Give her nuggets of information and she'd chew them up and spit them out like high-powered bullets, wounding me. "I have to go." I pushed my chair back.

"No, you don't. You're rejecting us like Nance did."

"Did you ever think that maybe you've got it backwards, Olivia? Maybe Nancy kept coming back because she *didn't* reject you. She just wanted to share something with you that gave her great peace. And isn't that what friends should do? You, however, wouldn't let her breathe without making a snide comment to her. Maybe things could have been different if you hadn't pushed so damn hard. If you ask me, you rejected *her.*"

"Well, I didn't ask you."

In high school, kids become friends because they have the same classes or ride the same bus. Because they like the same band or they play a sport together. The four of us had become friends because no other cliques would have us. "What we knew of one another stopped being relevant years ago," I said. "We've all changed. Our brunches are like strolls in the past. Nice, but meaningful only to us." I paused, looked at Betsy, then looked back to Olivia. "Somehow, I know you two will still be hanging out a decade from now, retelling stories about the same stupid things we did at prom or at the homecoming game. And it won't matter. Your future is being halted, dragged back toward a false glory in the past. You're using Betsy to uphold the importance of it. Neither of you has any goals anymore. Opportunities stagnate around you. And I'm glad it's not me." At least the wæres in my life all seemed to be progressing in a positive manner, despite their lunar affliction.

I opened my purse as I stood. I tossed down a hundred-dollar bill like I did it all the time. Olivia's eyes almost bugged out of her head. "This last brunch is on me. Have a nice life, ladies. And *don't* call me."

With the bridge to my old life in flames, I left.

CHAPTER ELEVEN

Since Beverley didn't visit anymore, my TV was used only for news and weather. With all the people in my house, however, a little entertainment seemed wise. So, before leaving Columbus, I dared the traffic nightmare known as Polaris Parkway. In the DVD section of the Best Buy, I tried to decide on some titles. After the breakup with my high school sisters, I was not in the mood for a chick flick and picked up a handful of action movies in utter defiance of emotional mushy stuff. I steered clear of monster flicks for the obvious reasons and headed for the checkout. As I waited, however, the screens in the television section caught my attention. It was a local newsbreak between shows, and as they showed clips of the upcoming news for the night, there was Beverley's face. She was crying "No, no, no . . ." and shaking her head. It was like footage shot yesterday at school.

Where the hell was Vivian? Why wasn't she protecting Beverley from this? Why was Beverley even at school?

In the Avalon, with my purchases in the passenger seat, I stopped at the next gas station and pulled up to the phone. I didn't have enough coins, so I had to run in and buy a can of Pepsi and get change.

"Hello?"

"Vivian, it's Persephone Alcmedi."

"Miss Alcmedi," she said. "Have you completed your work already?"

"We have to talk."

"I'll take that as a 'no.'"

"Where's Beverley?"

"Asleep. Thank the Goddess. I couldn't take one more minute of her incessant crying."

"She's mourning!"

"Of course she is. But she doesn't have to do it so loudly."

Bitch. "She was on the news."

"Okay."

"Okay? That's all you have to say? It looked like reporters were mobbing her!"

"Her mother was killed. Of course they want her on camera. It makes people tune in."

"Vivian," I said through gritted teeth.

"Oh I get it! You're calling to give me *parental* advice! How many pups have you squeezed out for your pack friends? That's right. None."

All the way to the gas station I'd thought about how to say what needed saying without being judgmentally "you should this" and "you should that."

"Ignoring her won't work," I said bitterly. "Grief doesn't just go away after a certain amount of tears have been shed. She needs help. Being her guardian obligates you to see that she gets it. And letting reporters mob her at school isn't going to cut it."

"You're so responsible, Miss Alcmedi. What with all your commendable hobbies, column-writing, kenneling, killing. This is just one little girl. I think I'll manage."

"It doesn't look like it."

"Looks can be deceiving."

"I *know* Beverley. And I know grief."

"Thank you for your advice. If that's all—"

"It's not. You didn't tell me my mark was a vampire."

Vivian laughed condescendingly. "Goddess, you *are* a novice if you think I'd offer you two hundred thousand for a mortal."

"You could have warned me. I had someone gather background info for me and that person nearly paid for it with her life." Vivian didn't need all the details.

"That's so sad. You don't even know how to do your own work and friends are paying for it. You must feel awful."

Why had I agreed to help this bitch?

"I clearly made a mistake in hiring you," Vivian whispered. "I realize that now. You can back out of our deal, Miss Alcmedi. Because I, too, have erred; I will allow it. Just return the cash—"

"Shut up." She was pissing me off. And I didn't want to talk about the cash because I'd spent a tenth of it on Theo, who was out a vehicle as well. Not that she'd be driving any time soon, but I owed her. "I'm calling because of Beverley. I told you I'd be watching you. Now I'm telling you: you're fucking up. If you like, you may think of me as Social Services, without laws to restrain me . . . but then, you know how loose my interpretation of the Rede is."

"Don't threaten me, Miss Alcmedi." There was a thin thread of fear in her tone.

"Then do the right thing by that child and don't give me cause to feel another face-to-face meeting is in order."

"Nana, are you even listening to me?"

She sat in her rocking chair and listened to my brief description of what I had said to Vivian about Beverley. Her rocking never sped up or slowed, and her attention remained focused on the wooden hoops that had locked together the fabrics of the quilt she was sewing. Though I'd closed the door behind me, lest the wæres hear and ask questions I didn't want to answer, I was now unsure she even knew I'd come in. Could her hearing have gone that fast?

"What business is that of yours?"

I rose from her bed and paced. I didn't want Nana to know details. "I saw Beverley bombarded by reporters on the news. Vivian's not helping that little girl, and she needed a wake-up call."

"Again, what business is that of yours?"

I stammered, "I care. I seem to be the only one who does." I had to get Beverley out of Vivian's house.

"Leave it to the authorities."

"You mean the same system that would have sent Theo to a State Shelter to die? I can't do that." I snorted. "I won't do that."

"You called and threatened this Vivian, didn't you?"

I didn't answer.

Nana stopped rocking and let the hoops rest in her lap, and only then did she glance up at me. "I've raised a bully. How in the name of Athena's sweet justice did I do that?"

I could've given her a list. She had been a hard-as-nails authority figure in my youth. If I reminded her of that now, though, she'd just deny it. I stopped and crossed my arms. "I'm not a bully."

"I suppose you have another name for it? Like Public Attitude Manager. You young people make everything so difficult."

Where had *that* come from? My anger slipped a little toward worry. What had Nana done now? "Make what difficult?"

Nana put her quilting aside and picked up her cigarette case. "You're either overanalyzing or overemphasizing. Can't you ever over*simplify* anything?" She put a cigarette to her lips and readied the lighter.

I eased down on the bed, rubbing my forehead. "What are you talking about?"

She took a long draw off the cigarette and released it slowly. She crossed her legs and started rocking again. "You know, you probably wouldn't be so rash and dramatic if you put your passions where they were supposed to be and let that young man smooth you out a little."

"What?" The shriek leapt out of me as I stood.

"It would do you good, you know. Goddess knows he wants to."

"Nana! I'm trying to talk to you about the safety of a little girl I was getting rather attached to before her mother moved to the city! What Vivian's done is totally against the Rede—damn! I wish I'd thought of that when I was on the phone!"

"Go cleanse your chakras and meditate. You've got it so bad you can't think straight."

"Got what? What do you think I've got, besides the insanity in my gene pool?"

She just rocked and stared at me. Her usually expressionless face had changed. Her cheeks rounded just a little, narrowing her eyes in the scariest way—she was amused. At me. At the thought of me having a boyfriend. It made me feel embarrassed and small.

"He's a wære, Nana. He's probably the one who tossed the trash you griped about on my lawn. What happened to the 'witches and wolves aren't meant to mingle' bit you always preach at me?"

"They *don't* make good friends, but it's my understanding that for an occasional tryst they're all right."

I walked out. Nana encouraging me to have a *tryst* with a wærewolf caused my creep-o-meter needle to spike.

CHAPTER TWELVE

I was on watch with Theo.

The regular creak of Nana's rocker told me she was still quilting. Celia and Johnny were in town getting groceries. Erik was sleeping on the third floor—I could hear his regular snores faintly through the ceiling.

The wæres had the IV bag–changing down pat; I wouldn't have to do it on my watch. I checked Theo's toes. They were cold, and the greenish color now had some yellow to it. Still swollen.

She was damn lucky to be alive at all. And very *un*lucky to be my friend.

I washed her face and cleaned dried blood from between her fingers and from the cuticles of her nails. The professional shaping and painting of them had been ruined in tearing her dashboard apart.

Guilt overwhelming me, I sat in the window seat, as far from Theo as I could be while still being in the room. I drew a small circle around me in the air and meditated. Cleansing my chakras, as Nana had suggested, would have entailed energy work, and that wasn't safe around Theo. A full transformation would cure her and save her life, but a partial transformation would doom her irreparably. So I kept this meditation to a mental exercise and refrained from sticking my toes in the stream. I didn't need to wash the negative energy away immediately; I could do that later. Besides, my guilt over Theo's condition was tightly wound up in that energy, as it should be. I deserved to bear that guilt.

"Let it go." Amenemhab padded to the water's edge, a few yards upstream, and began to drink. After a moment, his ears pricked forward and his head came up. Water dripped from his muzzle. His attention focused across the stream.

The buckskin mustang galloped through the woodland. Sunbeams shining through the branches flashed on her hide, making the dun glow golden. Her thick black mane and tail flounced, accentuating her graceful and majestic strides—fast but unhurried, or at least not urgent. As evidenced by every flexion of her sinewy limbs and sleek form, she ran for the joy of running.

"Who is she?" I asked.

Amenemhab stared after her so long I wasn't sure he'd heard me. Then he said, "She is the One who called to you. Who comforted you in the cornfield."

"The Goddess? Is a horse? In my meditation?"

"She can be anything, anywhere. Today, in this hour, She is here and She has taken the form of a horse. Today She feels the current of energy and moves with it, perhaps stirs it and guides it along the proper paths as She guides us all."

"I must have lost my way, then."

The jackal cocked his head at me. "Why do you say this?"

"I don't feel like I'm treading a path, but a rocky mountainside that isn't supposed to be traveled. I have taken steps away from the Rede, away from Her guidance. And away from common sense. That's why She was there," I pointed, "and not here."

"Just because you cannot see the path beneath your feet does not mean it isn't there. It is simply a road less traveled, as it were."

"Ah. A bumpy road designed to tame the more stubborn, no doubt."

"Or a path meant to show the more resilient that they are capable of more than the average task." When I didn't respond, he continued: "She relishes what She can do and takes the form that accomplishes Her task with the most efficient grace. Shouldn't all living things relish what they are, what they can do and be and create? Wouldn't happiness and peace be attained if everyone did?"

"Of course."

"Then why do you try to limit what She can call you to do?"

"I'm not."

"You are."

Knowing what he was getting at, I disagreed emphatically. "She wouldn't want me to be an assassin. To break the Rede."

"Those who choose not to abide by the laws of the Rede, those who subscribe to no laws that would censure them, will not be stopped by any laws. Justice may come in the afterlife, but sometimes they need to be stopped in their present life, stopped before they interfere with greater plans."

I hoped that didn't mean the Goddess wanted Vivian on the Elders Council. "You're saying She *would* want me to be a killer?"

"Is that so inconceivable?"

I smirked. "So I'm the lucky one who gets to fuck up my karma, right?"

The jackal opened his mouth in what had to be a smile. "Perhaps you have it backwards. Perhaps this charge is the opportunity to exculpate trespasses in the past."

"Karma doesn't work that way."

"Doesn't it?"

This was like braiding thorny branches; every twist had painful possibilities.

"She wasn't here as a brilliantly white unicorn or a midnight mare," he said. "She showed Herself to you in the colors of mild tarnish, in the wilder form of a mustang."

The stream trickled by, the only sound between us for many minutes. I thought Amenemhab would lope off and leave me with that thought, but he didn't. He sat and watched the play of light on the water, patiently waiting for me to figure it out. Fine.

This was bigger than me, my easily bruised ego, or my karmic future. Still, I did not have to like any of it. And the weight on my shoulders felt impossibly burdensome. How could I be *that* important? I never stood out anywhere else in my life; I wasn't ready to think there was any place that I should. So I said the words he probably knew were coming: "I don't want to be a killer."

"You've already accepted the money. Spent some."

"I can pay it back."

"Or you can do the job."

"A vampire is too much for me."

"Are you afraid?"

"No." I paused. "Yes."

"Fear isn't weakness, you know."

I looked at him sharply.

"Giving in to fear is. But then you are not likely to give in to it, because you are not alone."

Was he dropping notes to Celia? "Neither is my intended target." The Reverend Kline had said his brother worked for another vampire. I made a face; last year the vampires had come out with another public relations campaign, trying to further soften their image. They thought changing all the "master vampires" into "executive vampires" made them seem less like evil slavers and more like reasonable businessmen.

"You're right; Goliath is not alone. But you know someone breaking the Rede who is very alone."

"Vivian." Of course. "Will she hurt Beverley more to get at me?"

"Do not worry about this. The child is not leverage in her eyes, but a burden she wants to be rid of."

I frowned at him. "Why would Lorrie have wanted her as Beverley's guardian anyway?"

"Financially, Lorrie struggled; Vivian doesn't. What mother doesn't want to see her child have everything she could want?"

"But it isn't working out that way!"

"No. Lorrie saw a false side of the high priestess."

"I'm beginning to think my first meeting with her was the same." She'd been grumpy with me even then, but I'd given her several reasons. "What's up with her?"

"You should ponder that."

"I mean, I get it that she's using me to clear the path for her entrance to the Elders Council. I'm just a tool to her. And yeah, I hate being used, but achieving something good is worth swallowing my pride a little. Just . . . is this really 'something good'?"

"You should ponder that," Amenemhab insisted.

I gave him a wry look.

He lay down as if settling in for a long rest. "Ponder what you know; the answers to what you don't know are there. It is an equation you must solve to see."

Closing my eyes in the meditation, I thought back, reviewing our meeting. What did I know about Vivian? What could I see and add up? Being high priestess equaled knowledge of magic and energy as well as people-management skills. Overdone accessories equaled vanity, money, or just a penchant for diamonds. Neat office equaled neat freak at best and obsessive-compulsive disorder at worst. Spiffy wooden box equaled a carrying case for some cool magical thing. Too much cash for a coffee-shop owner equaled, well, there's money again. I'd guessed the box held something to do with the business, but I didn't think she had a goose in it laying golden eggs. What if its contents had nothing to do with the business and everything to do with her?

She was younger than I thought and had been offended at me expecting her to be older. That, as well as her vanity over accessories and perfect makeup, suggested the box could be holding a glamour spell. Perhaps she had charmed, literally, the wings off a fairy. Maybe the WEC induction was as much about vanity to her as everything else. Still, all that money came from somewhere, and fairies weren't known for their cash supplies. Vampires, however, were notorious for the liquidity of their assets, no pun intended. Wait—

If Vivian was connected to a vampire—some people call it "marked," but I always say "stained" because it denotes shame, and a vampire's mark is worse than being forced to wear a scarlet letter—it would make her age more slowly, simply due to supernatural residual effects. I said, "She's stained by a vampire."

Amenemhab bowed his head. "See? Equation solved."

"Solved? Nothing's solved! This whole thing makes no sense anymore. Wait—"

The jackal grinned.

"She can't sit on the Council if she bears a stain."

"And how would she get rid of it?" he asked.

"Kill the vampire who gave it to her . . ." My eyes went to slits

"But?"

"But she can't act against him herself because, as I understand it, the bonds inherent in the binding stain create a kind of compulsive protectiveness and devotion between all those linked. But again, if I'm right, Goliath's death would hurt her. His pain and grief would seep down to her, maybe even kill her. Why would she do that to herself?"

"I doubt a roundabout suicide is her motive. It's simply an inherent risk—and one she's ready to accept, so she's likely prepared to counter it by some means."

"She's getting me to do the dirty work she can't do, so she can have a shot at being an 'Elder.'" I was seriously pissed. "I'm just a small part of her plan."

He gestured with his head in the direction the mustang had gone. "But you're a big part of *Her* plan." He winked. "She may have been there and not here"—he pawed the ground—"but a long time ago, Persephone, in a field of corn, She chose you. You. Take heart, for today, in the midst of your turmoil, She showed Herself to remind you that She is nearby."

Leaving the meditation, I took up my protective circle, stretched and checked on Theo. Then I returned to the window seat and stared out the window.

Vivian was using me. I knew that. But she was using me more than she wanted me to realize. I had agreed to be used, I thought, in order to protect Beverley and, I had to admit, attain vengeance for Lorrie's murder. Did Vivian's further use of me make a difference? Now that Theo had been harmed, did I have more reason to kill? But if I hadn't agreed to do harm myself, would Theo have been hurt?

I thought of the mustang. Did She have a hand in all this? Was the totem correct? Was I somehow meant to be Her tool?

Whatever I had originally thought, whatever my motivations or Vivian's, it was time to accept what either my own human foolishness had gotten me into or what the Fates had inexorably willed: I had a vampire to assassinate.

Deep breath. That thought made my shoulders heavy.

My ears detected a knocking sound and I stilled, listening. It didn't repeat, so I figured it must be something banging around in the dryer. Who knew what kinds of sounds Johnny's clothes made, with all the studs and zippers and chains. I'd seen him stuffing things into separate mesh laundry bags. It was surreal seeing him washing clothes. At my house.

Then the knocking came again. A quiet, meek knocking. It stopped. But I knew I wasn't hearing things this time. Going out in the hall, I peered down the stairs. A shadow darkened the window of my front door. A short shadow.

I hurried down and opened the door. Beverley stood there with her face in her hands, her dark hair in crooked ponytails, and her shoulders jerking rapidly in sobs. "Beverley!" I exclaimed, unlocking the screen.

Her face was splotched with pink; her usually bright blue eyes were swollen from crying. "She left me," she said, shaking all over. "She drove here. Screamed at me all the way. Told me to get out." She pointed at the driveway, where a box sat behind my Avalon, the flaps shuddering in the breeze.

I had the greatest urge to hunt Vivian Diamond down and slap her around. I guess it showed on my face; Beverley started sobbing again. "I'm sorry! I'm sorry!" she cried.

"Honey!" I went down on my knees and touched her arms. She had always been a spindly kid, but she looked waiflike just now. "I'm not angry with you. I'm angry with how Vivian's treated you. Come inside."

Her expression was unsure. "My stuff."

"We'll get it in a minute."

"Somebody'll steal it. I won't have anything and I got the—"

"There's nobody out here. For miles," I said gently. "But I'll get it. Okay?" It was important to her.

She waited on the porch until I came back with the box. She held the door open for me as I went in. "Thanks. I'll set this over here for now." I placed it at the end of the couch. "How about you and I have some milk and cookies?" I asked, hoping Nana hadn't eaten all of Johnny's cookies.

We sat at the table with glasses of milk and a few of Johnny's white chocolate macadamia nut cookies. Beverley didn't touch hers. She seemed to be staring at a spot on the table between the cookies. So I picked up a cookie, broke it in half, dunked it in my glass, and held it there for a few seconds. I "mmmm"-ed when I ate it; Beverley glanced my way. I dunked the rest of that half. "Don't you dunk your cookies anymore?"

She shook her head "no" in timid motions.

"Want me to warm them a little in the microwave?" Same response. "Beverley."

"You don't have to pretend like you want me here." She spoke with such weariness and resigned sadness that I could have cried. "Vivian tried to be nice at first too. But I know you don't want me either. Nobody wants me. Only my mom. . . ."

"Beverley," I said firmly. Reaching across the table, I took her hand. "That's not true. I *do* want you here. I've missed watching movies with you. Eating popcorn." Tears rolled out of her eyes, but she didn't say anything. "But I want *you* to want to be here, too, and I should warn you: things are kind of crazy here right now." I stood.

Since Vivian had left her here, I'd guess that'd be considered abandonment. That might help if this got nasty legal-wise . . .

What was I thinking? I was going to kill a vampire, and I was worrying about the legal ramifications of custody? I rubbed my brow. I was becoming paradox incarnate.

"Since you were last here, my grandmother has moved in with me. She's got the room you usually slept in, but I'll show you the other room, where you can stay. Okay?" She needed to sleep, and to wake up feeling safe and wanted.

"What did you mean, it's crazy here?" She held my hand tight as I led her up the stairs. "I've always liked it here. It's quiet, and you have such pretty paintings."

"Well, a friend got hurt really bad. You remember Theo? One of your mom's . . . friends? She needed a place to stay. A few other friends are staying here to help look after her. She's in my room, and we have to go past there to get to the other room. She has monitors and stuff hooked up to her—don't let it alarm you."

As I expected, Beverley stopped in front of my open door. "What happened to her?"

"She had a car accident. You remember Celia and Johnny and Erik, right? They are helping out with taking care of her until she gets better. Erik's upstairs sleeping because he gets the late shift. The other two went into town to get some groceries, but they'll be back later." If I had a chance, I'd call Johnny's cell phone and tell him to pick up some kid stuff—like cartoon-character cereals or something.

"Do you always take care of people?"

The thread of hope in her voice made me want to hug her tight and tell her it would all be okay. But Nana had done that to me, and things still weren't okay. "I do the best I can."

I led her across the hall to the third bedroom. There were a few stacked boxes of my things, a laundry basket, and a twin-size air mattress on the floor along one wall. "I've been staying in here, since Theo's in my room. Would you mind sharing the room with me for now?" Hands on hips, I looked the room over. "Once Theo's better, we could make it into your room and paint it and decorate it however you want."

"Do you really want me to stay with you?"

"Yes, of course. If you don't mind staying with me, that is. For now, we'll get another mattress and put it on that side for you." I smiled. "It isn't much, I know. But it'll get better."

"I like it." She peered out the window.

"Good. I'll go get your box."

In the kitchen, I dialed Johnny's cell phone.

" 'Lo, Red."

"Hey. Still shopping?"

"At the checkout now."

I heard Celia's voice ask, "Who's Red?"

He whispered, "Persephone is."

"Her hair's not red," Celia protested.

"You two save it for later. This is important. Get out of line—"

"I'm always out of line," he laughed.

"I need you to get some other things."

"Like what?" I heard him whisper to Celia, "No, don't unload the cart yet. Red needs something."

"Some kind of fun kid cereal," I said.

"I already got Lucky Charms. That okay?"

I should have known. "Only if you can share them."

"Right. *Another* box of Lucky Charms."

"And get another of those air mattresses, and some sheets for it. Like some soft pink flannel ones." Nana had brought her stock of quilts and was constantly making more, so we didn't need blankets. "And get cookies too. Oreos. Some microwave popcorn." I knew Beverley liked those snacks.

"Ooooo. And I had you pegged for satin sheets and champagne and strawberries, but I didn't think our big night would come so soon. You know, Oreo crumbs are gonna show big-time on pink."

"They're not for . . . *us*." I was so embarrassed and frustrated, I could hardly get the words out.

"Okay, okay. I'm wiping the image of you in pink flannel sheets and cereal in Oreo crumbs from my mind."

Blinking as if that would remove the stunned roadblock on the tracks of my train of thought, I managed to awkwardly reply, "You gotta stop, Johnny. You said you'd be good."

"While I was there. But I'm not there. I'm here," he declared proudly, raising his voice like a superhero. "At the superstore!"

I could imagine all the leery patrons staring at the crazy man now. "Right." Celia's laughter drifted through the phone too.

"Who's moving in now?" he asked, more seriously.

"I'll explain when you get here. Don't forget: air mattress and sheets, popcorn, and cookies."

"How about I make cookies? I can make 'em way better than Oreos."

"I know. But my new guest would prefer Oreos. Trust me."

"Asking for my trust. This is getting better all the time, Red. Buh-bye."

I hesitated. "Bye." It was an awkward closing, and I stared at the receiver before hanging it up. I took the box from the living room and started up the stairs with it. Beverley sat halfway up; she startled me. "I didn't see you there."

"Thank you."

Shifting the box to my hip, I said, "Huh?"

"For asking them to get things for me."

"Pink is okay, right?"

"Yeah."

"I haven't been a . . . a young woman"—I didn't want to say "little girl"—"in a long time, and I'm sure things are different now. I'll get up to speed if you give me a little time. I promise."

Feeling totally lame, I put her box in the room. I didn't even have a dresser for her to use. I couldn't say, "Well, I'll leave you to settle in," because it was a box and the floor. There was no "settling" to it. I wondered if we could get her things from the apartment she and her mother had shared or if there was some police procedure to go through. Vivian wouldn't have bothered to take her there, I was sure. Ms. Diamond seemed content to let this girl suffer and live out of a box. It hurt my heart. "They won't be back for an hour or so. If you want to rest, you can use my bed." It was all I had to offer.

"Okay."

"I've got to check on Theo, but, um . . . I just wanted to say that whenever you want to talk—if you want to talk to me—about, well, about things . . . that'll be okay. Or not. You don't have to. I thought I should make sure you knew that." I bit my lip, knowing I sounded so uncool and nervous.

I left.

Theo's monitors remained steady; her fluid bag was still more than half full. Good for a while. I stepped back to peek into the spare bedroom. Beverley had moved her box right beside my stack of boxes. She was curled up on my bed with one of Lorrie's sweaters, on a stuffed cat with its arms around her neck as if it were hugging her. She looked up at me. "If you need me," I said, "I'll be in the kitchen for a few minutes. Remember, it's a big, old house. With creaky floors. I figured I should let you know where I'll be." A quick, apologetic smile flashed across my face.

Beverley put her nose down to the sweater, breathing deeply of the scent of someone who could never again comfort her. Someone who should never have been taken away.

CHAPTER THIRTEEN

When the intrepid wolves returned from the superstore, I gave them a quiet rundown on Beverley. Johnny made lasagna while Celia and I went off to get the air mattress set up.

Dr. Lincoln was a no-show so far, and he didn't answer his phone. Theo moaned despite the morphine that was supposed to keep her sedated. "If only she could change," Celia said. "All this damage would mend in the transition."

Celia traced a finger down Theo's arm. I thought about skin, about how superficial it is, yet how it holds all our parts together. People's personalities, their souls, are in there too, but something more than skin held *those* in.

For too long I'd allowed myself to see only the surface of so many people around me. Maybe I was that shallow.

No, that wasn't true. Ever since college, though, I'd tried to keep everyone from seeing anything other than my surface. My skin was a wall, a shield, protecting me. Protecting my heart. But that protection came, I now realized, with a cost. If I didn't let people see inside me, see past my surface, then I couldn't see deeper into them.

I wanted to think I was doing better. I was seeing the man inside Johnny. The man who cared, the man who kenneled alone.

Celia touched my arm. She was a touchy-feely person. More so now, as a wære, than ever before, but her hands were warm and comforting even in that small gesture. "You okay?"

Relaxing, I said, "Yeah. If we can just buy her some time, she'll change and she'll be fine." We crossed the hall to the bathroom to wash our hands before dinner.

"Three weeks is a long time," she said, "but we're going to do everything we can. With all of us here, I do feel more hopeful." She exhaled as we dried our hands. "I could use a drink, though."

"There's some beer hidden in the garage."

"Hidden?"

It was my turn to shrug. "I didn't want to listen to Nana gripe about it."

"Gripe about what?" Nana asked, stepping into the doorway.

"All these people in the house," Celia said quickly. "But you don't mind us, do you? We really are trying to be respectful."

Nana pursed her lips. "The noises you and that man were making upstairs last night weren't very respectful."

Celia's eyes went wide and her face flushed instantly crimson.

"Nana!"

"It wasn't." She waved her hand at us. "Move. I have to use the toilet."

Celia and I made a hasty exit, but paused at the top of

the stairs to share a glance that turned into a laugh as we went down to the kitchen. Beverley was having Oreos and being entertained by Johnny, who was currently balancing an antique bud vase on his chin.

"Is that how you got that adorable cleft?" Celia asked.

He jerked, caught the vase as it fell, and grinned as he rubbed the little dimple in his chin, almost hidden in the stubble. "Nope. I think I was born with this angel kiss." He put the bud vase back on the window ledge. When he turned back, his expression and manner were serious. "Theo?"

"Moaning a little," Celia said. "Morphine may be wearing off a little early."

"Did you ever get through to the doc?" I asked him.

"Still no answer. But Feral called." His expression was grim.

"Feral" Jones, the bassist in Johnny's band, had once been Theo's boyfriend and had initially brought her here to kennel. They'd separated as friends, but they still shared a cage in the storm cellar on full moons. I'd have thought that the arrangement made him still her boyfriend, but they didn't act as if it did. "What'd he say?"

"Someone sacked both Theo's condo and Revelations."

"When?" Celia asked.

"This morning for the condo. Neighbors heard things falling and breaking and called 911. They trashed everything and left before police could arrive. It seems that they got to Revelations right after she left yesterday and broke in there. A lawyer from the office across the hall came back to catch up on some work. Saw the door standing open and the mess when she arrived. Called it in."

We were speechless.

Hands fisted at his sides, Johnny said, "That's why the cops were at the hospital. They knew. They'd already connected the break-in and the accident."

"It was *her* phone that rang," Celia said. "I heard a phone ring when they were prepping her for surgery. I was in the hall . . . thought it was a nurse taking her own call, but what they said . . . I thought it was weird at the time, but I bet the police were trying to locate her about the break-in. Her cell phone must have been in her purse, and I know they kept those things with her in the room . . ."

Johnny's right fist smacked into his left palm. "Someone did this to her purposely. The cops were digging for who and why, but when they found out she was a wære, they split. Crimes don't matter if the victim is infected."

My insides sank. *I* had done this to her. *My* questions. If they had sacked Revelations, did they know about me? Had Theo left a note on her bill for me: *Background on Goliath Kline?*

"Is that true?" Beverley asked softly. "About wæres?"

We adults threw glances at one another like hot potatoes.

"Yeah," Johnny said, then added, "I'm sorry."

Beverley shot out of her chair. As she passed me, her brimming tears fell.

Johnny looked at me, face pained. "Aw, shit. I didn't mean to . . ." Johnny said.

"I know." I went after her. "Beverley."

She darted up the steps and nearly ran into Nana coming from the bathroom. "Sorry," she cried as she ran into the room she'd be sharing with me.

Nana asked, startled, "What's going on now?"

"Don't worry, I've got it." I slipped past Nana and entered the bedroom, shutting the door behind me. "Beverley."

She stood facing the corner with her arms wrapped tightly around herself, shoulders jumping as she cried. "Whoever killed my mom will get away with it, won't they? The police won't do anything because she was . . . was *infected*."

"Beverley." I realized I didn't have a clue what to say. Of all the people in the house, she was the last one I would tell what I'd agreed to do in order to try to right this wrong.

Beverley turned and threw herself against me, hugging me and crying. "It's not fair! It's not fair! My mom was a good person and I loved her and I want her back!"

Holding her tight was all I could do. I said, "I know you do. I know."

After dinner, I tucked Beverly in.

"How is she?" Johnny asked when I came back to the kitchen. He'd been cleaning up, and he flipped the dish towel over his shoulder.

"Sleeping."

"I wasn't thinking. I feel like an ass."

Sliding onto the bench at the table, I said, "It's a harsh truth, but one she'd have to learn about sooner or later anyway. Dancing around it won't help her." I paused. "Celia with Theo? I'm shirking my shift."

"No. I gave her a glass of wine and sent her out on the front porch."

"Wine?"

"Can't cook Italian without wine."

There wasn't anything drinkable here. "You gave her cooking sherry?"

"No. I got some good stuff." He shifted the dish towel over his forearm and took a bottle from the cabinet. Holding it over his arm like a waiter, he asked in a French accent, "Would Mademoiselle care for a drink?"

I couldn't help smiling. "Sure." He poured from the fancily labeled bottle and brought it to me. It was rich and smooth. "Mmmm. Why didn't you serve us this with dinner?"

"Aw, with the kid present, I wasn't sure it would be right."

Some guys make references to children in derogatory terms, but Johnny's tone made his words affectionate. He was so sensitive to Beverley's situation that it made me soften a little more toward him. I could almost feel it physically. Warmth spread over me, and I quickly said, "I'm going to take this glass up to Theo's room, where I should be anyway, and relax in my window seat with a book. Thanks."

I turned to leave. After a few steps I glanced back and, sure enough, he was staring at my behind. His eyebrows jerked, and he flopped the dish towel over his shoulder and went back to cleaning up the kitchen.

I climbed the stairs slowly, not because I was tired, but because I was thinking about what Nana seemed to be telling me about him, and then her complaining about the noise Celia and Erik had made. She didn't like wæres, didn't like my wolf friends, but she was pushing me to screw around with one. I wasn't the Queen of Paradoxes—she was. Maybe I was in line for the throne, but at least I came by it honestly.

In the window seat, I sipped the wine. The night was full, and the stars were out. I glanced up through the skylights, then returned to studying the glistening dots through the west-facing window beside me. This dark was the only world the vampires knew—*shit!*

I had to get some extra protection into my wards, and pronto. Grabbing my Book of Shadows from the bottom dresser drawer, I returned to the window seat and flipped to the section about wards.

I heard footsteps on the stairs, and Celia came in. "I brought in your mail. Been out in the box all day."

"Thanks."

"This came," she said gravely, holding up a stuffed manila envelope. "It's from Theo. Mailed yesterday."

She'd checked the postmark. "Okay. . . ." I drew it out as if I didn't understand the significance of [illegible]. Theo had said she'd dropped the material about Kline in the mail when she had called the night before last. It would have gone out after midnight.

"Were you expecting this? I mean, do you think she might have known she was in danger and sent something pertinent to you?"

"Oh! No. I'd asked her to do some research about a guy for me."

"A guy? Anyone I know?" She grinned and slapped the envelope against her thigh; then her smile faded as another thought occurred to her. She lifted it back up. "This is a lot of info. Theo usually gets rap sheets, Seph."

I had to be careful, but I felt certain I knew what Celia was thinking. "It's for an article I'm writing. Not a candidate for boyfriend."

"Oh." She sounded disappointed. She handed over the envelope.

Erik came down the attic steps. At five foot eleven, he had to duck his head to traverse the attic stairs. His lean, muscular body, befitting a drummer and a wære, sauntered into my room as he moved to accept a hug from his wife. He never dressed as stylishly as Celia, but it wasn't from a lack of trying on her part. At least he accepted her advice on his hairstyle. His layered brown hair suited his face, though the thin beard made him look stern.

They went downstairs to get Erik some leftovers. I sat there with the envelope across my Book of Shadows. Did I open it now or later? Later, I decided, after I'd boosted the wards as best I could. Priorities.

Tucking the envelope under the Book of Shadows, I reviewed my options. I found notes on a technique a friend had shared with me not long after I moved in. I hadn't used this amplifier technique yet. It had never been necessary. The fact that I felt I had cause to now made me sad.

I was unable to resist opening Theo's envelope any longer.

Photocopies of newspaper and Internet articles slid into my hand. The first was the initial abduction article; whoever had written it had little info and just played up the tug-on-the-heartstrings angle. The article reproduced a school photo of a young boy with bright eyes and pale hair, nice-looking but awkward the way kids can be when they're growing fast. There were also numerous printed-out Web pages from an online e-zine, *Out of the Dark.* I'd heard of it, knew it to be full of conspiracy theories like the ones surrounding the wæres as well as articles on UFOs and vampires.

The printout pages were all about known and suspected vampire activity, including official-looking minutes from Vampire Parliament meetings with lists of who attended and who had been absent. Theo had highlighted some names on the "absent" roster. The next page showed more absentees, also highlighted. This time there was a note on the side that Theo had written: *Goliath suspected of assassinating these parliament members; they've not been seen since.*

I scanned the article. The author had a smug sense of self-importance and a good head for word usage. Most *Out of the Dark* articles were written in succinct Web style or on a tenth-grade reading level like newspapers, but this one had polysyllabic words and deep metaphors. I'd have bet a vampire had written it. Who else would have access [illegible] guage? Why tell on one's own, though? Maybe the author copied the style to avoid suspicion.

When I got over critiquing the article, I reread it to evaluate what it meant in relation to my situation. Goliath was clearly a highly trained and experienced assassin.

This Goliath guy—thank the Goddess—had, so far, left Beverley untouched and alive. If he found out I was the one who had asked Theo to check into his background, if he came here, would he leave anyone in my house alive?

My stomach knotted. I had endangered not just Theo, but everyone I cared about. I had to amplify my house wards *now.*

"Celia," I said, entering the kitchen, "I need to—" I almost said "boost my house wards," but thought she might wonder why I thought it necessary. Wait, that was okay. "I need to boost my house wards. If someone is after Theo and didn't finish, I don't want them getting in here. Would you cover for me for about fifteen minutes?" I hated having to think and rethink before I spoke. Goddess help me, I preferred honesty. *How do habitual liars deal with all this?*

She agreed, and I gathered the necessary items and hurried into the backyard with my Book of Shadows under my arm and a broom in hand. A set of old skeleton keys dangled from a big ring around my wrist like an awkward bracelet. In seconds, Johnny, who had been taking out the trash, was at my heels, following.

"Whatcha doing?" The childlike inquisitiveness in his voice made me smile.

"I'm going to increase the power on my home security system."

"Wouldn't a screwdriver work better than old keys and a broom?" The last word was dragged out, surely because he realized the nature of what was transpiring.

I stopped and turned. He saw the book in my arms and pulled up short.

"Oh. You're doing witchy stuff."

"Yeah."

In an instant, I understood how I had shown my fear to him for months. His expression turned fearful and he retreated a hasty step. "Home security system. Is that like, all around?" He gestured sweepingly with his arm.

"Yeah."

"Whoa—is that safe? For me and the other wæres, I mean?"

"I think so."

"Think?" His tone was just a bit higher.

"Yes, Johnny. It's safe for you. In the house, anyway. I stir up the energy and task it. After it is set, then it is like the latent energy in any rock or tree. It will alarm like any security system if someone crosses the threshold. It does not affect you or anyone else—it affects me, so the alarm stirs an energy reaction within me. It's perfectly safe inside the house. But not out here while I work."

"Right. I'll just be in the house, then." He smiled and left.

Johnny wasn't afraid of *me;* he was afraid of what I could do—raise energies—and how that could affect him. Rightly so.

When I reached the center of the back of the house, I put the book and keys on the ground at my feet. Facing north, I took three deep breaths to ground and center my being. I began, in a state between full consciousness and alpha—I call it "sub-alpha," and yeah, professional brain researchers probably use that same term for something else, so it's not a technical term coming from me, just personal slang.

Sweeping the broom in a complete clockwise circle all the way around my house, I repeatedly chanted:

"By sun and moon, intentions pure,
Isis make my home secure."

When I returned to the book and keys, I leaned my broom against the house and said, "As above, so below, my circle is sealed, so mote it be."

On my knees, with my hands on the ground, fingers curled in the grass, I called to the ley line. The nearby power thrummed softly in my fingertips—something like being near a stream you can hear, but not see. With the energy line, though, I "heard" it with all my being. Imagining my spirit self stretching across the distance, I held my hand near the flow. Strong, as usual. Vibrant. I cupped my hand and stuck it into the flow. My arm went numb up to the elbow. My every nerve sizzled as before, but the sensation quickly shifted from heated almost-pain to dull warmth, like being on the edge of drunk.

Yes, this could be very dangerous.

I pulled some of that power into me, feeling the thrumming grow strong, roiling and stretching through me as if trying me on for size. Quickly, I dumped it into my clockwise path around the house.

"Walls and windows, beams and boards,
Let no one unwanted through my doors.
Alarms resound and protect me
Should anyone try forced entry."

After I'd repeated it three times, I could feel the energy approaching from the other side of the circle. I pulled my cupped spirit-hand from the ley line and continued pouring the power out until the pathway was full. "So mote it be." With my spirit-hand empty, gooseflesh rose over my skin. I shivered.

Taking up the keys, I removed four from the ring. Making another clockwise circuit, I shoved one down into the ground, pushing it deep below the grass on the east side of the house.

> *"This energy now is keyed to this house, keyed to me.*
> *My wærewolf friends remain untouched and move freely."*

I repeated the process, placing keys at the south side under the porch, at the west side by the garage, and, back at the beginning, on the north side. With each key I placed, each repeat of the phrase, the flow of the energy increased. By the time I was done, it was swirling fast and powerful.

When my shift ended and Erik relieved me, my tired body had just enough energy to make it to my new room, where I changed into my pajamas and melted into a human puddle on the air mattress as quietly as I could so as not to disturb Beverley.

I awoke at two A.M., feeling uneasy, and it had nothing to do with the air mattress under me or the lasagna or the wine. The waning moon was a gibbous beacon outside, offering a night-light–level glow to this room. Lying still, ears perked, I listened. All I could hear was Johnny and Erik in the next room. Erik was on call with Theo, but he and Johnny were talking about the songs for the CD they were about to go into the studio to cut. I heard the words "Deep Lycanthropia" several times, as well as things like "got the lyrics, but not a chorus or title" and "maybe a bridge here."

Suddenly an alarm went off in my head like a slow police siren.

The unease was my new perimeter wards signaling—damn! I hadn't used this kind of spell before, so I hadn't realized the unease was the alarm. Now I knew. The siren in my head was definitely a break-in, but the sluggishness of its whine told me the culprit was aware of the wards, had tried to counter them, and probably thought he or she had been successful at it.

It couldn't be Goliath. As a vampire, he'd have to be invited in, but he could have witch friends who would try to counter a ward spell.

I threw back the covers and slipped from the bed, silently opened the door, and tiptoed across the hall, stepping on the sides where the boards didn't squeak. I couldn't just release the alarm throbbing in my head; if I did, whoever was breaking in would sense it and know I had been alerted and had shut it down. If I let the alarm continue, they would think that their counterspell had reduced it so much I wouldn't notice it as anything more than a ringing in the ears.

Pushing open the door to Theo's dimly lit room, I stepped in, and the men turned to me with wide eyes. Only then did it hit me that I was wearing only red panties and a red tank top with a stylized lion rampant.

"Red," Johnny said, his voice tellingly breathless.

"Damn it! Look at my face," I whispered harshly. "The

perimeter wards I placed earlier woke me up, and now my house wards are alarming. Someone's breaking in. And they're doing it in such a way that they think they're countering my wards." Both men stood immediately. "Wait! You have to step quietly and not let them know you're on to them."

"Them? How many?"

I made a face. "I can't tell. Might be just one, might be several."

"Do you have a gun?" Erik asked.

A strangled laugh tried to escape my mouth. "No." My baseball bat was still behind the door in the kitchen.

They shared a look, and Johnny whispered, "Follow me."

I grabbed his arm. "The boards squeak more in the middles. Try to stay to one side or the other."

He led Erik out into the hall. Beverley and Nana were sleeping. Celia, on the third floor, was also asleep. I stood in the doorway wondering what to do. I wanted to follow them, but if they were unsuccessful, I was all that stood between whomever was coming in and Theo. But it was me and Theo whom the intruder probably wanted most.

I couldn't stay *there.* I grabbed a black silk robe from the back of my door and knotted the belt. On my way out the door, I had a thought. I grabbed the syringe of morphine that had been readied for Theo's next dose and went down the steps.

After living here for more than two years, I knew this house well. But in the dark, with adrenaline pumping and my ears distracted from real sounds by the sirens in my head, every dark shadow held ominous possibilities.

When my foot hit the foyer floor, I heard a shout and a

thud from the kitchen. A scuffle ensued. In Nana's room, Poopsie—I mean Ares—began to bark. I released the wards, knowing the jig was up, and ran to the kitchen, ready to give an injection. Someone hit the light before I could get there, though, and blinded me for a second. I held back to let my eyes adjust.

A familiar voice growled, and I heard a splash of water followed by the thudding of two heavy bodies dropping to my floor, one snoring. I stepped deeper into the shadowed corner.

Vivian stepped past me. In a flash, I lunged forward, sank the needle into her neck above her coat collar, and pushed the plunger to release the morphine.

She screamed and twisted. I felt a jolt, but I stayed with her and rode her to the floor, hearing my silk robe rip. A pop-top water bottle skidded down the hall. I thought I had her pinned with my body, but she pushed off of the floor, rolling. The move flipped me off of her. Her strength confirmed to me that she was indeed "stained."

I pounced back onto her, hands grabbing her hair and using my weight to push her down and crack her head on the floor. She shouted again, jerking away. I felt some of her hair give, but my grasp stayed firm. Kicking at me, she connected with my shoulder, and the impact made my grip weaken enough that she rolled free and rose up before me. I could still see the syringe sticking out of her neck. She stretched back, reaching to remove it. I'd missed a vein, clearly, but it was in her. It had to have some effect, right?

"You bitch!" She threw the syringe to the floor and stepped forward, swaying.

Standing, I put my fists up before me. Breathing heavily but ready for a brawl, I snarled, "You're breaking into *my* house, and *I'm* the bitch?"

She staggered to the side. "It's mine. I'm not leaving without it."

"Without what?"

Her eyes rolled up, and her knees buckled. I don't think she felt her skull hit the floor.

CHAPTER FOURTEEN

Vivian had come in through a window in the mostly unused dining room and headed for the kitchen. The men had caught her there, and whatever she'd done put them to sleep. Luckily, it hadn't pulled energy and pushed them into a partial change. Hearing Ares pawing at the door upstairs, I knew that in a few minutes Nana would come to investigate. I closed the window, reinstated the wards, and tried to wake the men up. Shaking them didn't work, but I discovered that their shirts were wet and smelled like valerian.

Remembering the water bottle that had rolled down the hall when I'd surprised Vivian, I jerked the men's damp shirts off over their heads, Erik first. Johnny began rousing as soon as I lifted the fabric from his skin, revealing more tattoos. On my knees beside him, I hurried, ignoring the artful images on his skin and trying to pull his shirt off before he came fully awake, knowing he'd have a slew of innuendo-laden questions.

"Red," he said, grabbing my hands as the collar slipped over his face. He took in our positions and my exposed shoulder where the robe was ripped. His eyes glanced over my breasts, saw the rise and fall of my chest from heavy breathing. The look he gave me was all male and—

Erik groaned, waking, and suddenly Johnny was scrutinizing the room, surely remembering what had happened.

I gestured at Vivian. "Put her in a chair and tie her up." I opened my catchall drawer and found the bundle of "Braided Cotton Premium Clothesline No. 7" that Lydia had left along with other household odds and ends.

"What'd she do to us?" Erik asked, yawning. "Where're our shirts?"

"She used a natural, if magically boosted, sleep aid, I think." I handed Erik the rope and went down the hall to get the bottle. "I took your shirts off so you could wake up. Don't put them back on without washing them first."

When I came back, they had positioned Vivian in a dining room chair. I stared, mesmerized, at Johnny's bare back as he worked to tie her up. It was almost entirely covered by an intricate tattoo. A red Chinese lion-dog and a black dragon battled across his shoulder blades. The movement of Johnny's muscles made the creatures seem to fight or dance.

"What's with her?" he asked as he bound her feet together. "You think she came to steal the money back?"

"What money?" Erik asked.

I shrugged at Johnny and ignored Erik, turning to set the water bottle on the counter.

"Some kind of witch-fund thing," Johnny said.

This was going to be touchy; I was grateful he would try to cover for me. Caffeine might help me think clearly enough to avoid telling them the horrible truth. "I need coffee."

Just as I got the coffeepot going, Ares bounded in, and Nana followed. She assessed the shirtless men yawning contentedly and stretching like cats sunning themselves. Next she noted Vivian, bound to a chair with her head lobbed forward uncomfortably. The tied ends of a dishrag flipped up from her hair, revealing that we'd also gagged her. The rotten side of me had wanted to use the damp and soapy rag hanging over the faucet, but my conscience wouldn't hear of it, so I'd decided to use a clean one.

"What is going on down here?" Nana demanded, eyeballing my ripped robe and exposed undies. Her shocked expression made me tighten my robe properly around me. "Well, I can guess. This kind of debauchery is typical of wæres, but I'm ashamed of you, Persephone Isis! This isn't what I had in mind, and you know it. It's . . . it's even upset my Ares." His ears pricked at his name, and he licked her hand.

"Debauchery?" Johnny elbowed Erik. "Debauchery. That's what I'll call that song I wrote and couldn't think of a title or chorus for." He grinned broadly and said it again. "Debauchery."

Celia and Beverley came into the kitchen behind Nana. Apparently, bedhead was contagious. It was official: we'd awakened *everyone.*

"This isn't what you think it is, Nana. This is Vivian, the High Priestess. She broke into the house. We stopped her."

"Broke in?" Nana shuffled over to Vivian. "She doesn't

look like a burglar." Nana sank onto the bench across from Vivian and glowered at me. Ares sat beside her.

I shrugged. "She said, 'It's mine and I'm not leaving without it,' but I don't know what 'it' is."

Into the silence that followed, Beverley meekly said, "It's my fault."

Everyone turned to her, leaning in the doorway.

"You know what she came for?" I asked.

"Something I took from her house."

I winced. "You took something of hers?"

"She said such mean things! It made me mad. She stomped around shouting at me for so long, then she told me to pack all my stuff. She threw the box at me and told me to be quick, that she'd be waiting in the car and if I wasn't out there in ten minutes she'd make me walk." Beverley swallowed hard. "So I packed my stuff. And since she was in the car, I packed her spell book under my clothes. I wanted to get back at her. She must've figured out I took it." Her head dropped down. "I'm sorry, Seph. I shouldn't have taken it. I'll go get it." Beverley walked away.

"Gutsy kid," Johnny commented just as the coffeepot beeped to signal it was done brewing. "Java's ready. Who's drinking?"

A chorus of "me's" answered him, and he started getting out mugs.

My hand ran over my hair. Vivian would wake eventually. If we ungagged her, she'd tell them all about our contract. How much guilt could I take without snapping?

Beverley came back with the book held in her enfolded arms. It had a wooden back with iron workings like a very old book or one made to appear so. She laid it on the countertop and pushed it at me, her expression ashamed.

I knew how she felt; if Vivian started talking, I was going to feel shame too.

The cover of the book had a triskelion secured to it with iron nails that looked like horseshoe nails. It seemed like something Arthur might have found on a quest.

"Lunar crone!" Nana exclaimed. "That book! Where did you get it, child?"

Beverley leaned against the pantry door and pointed at Vivian. "From an altar table in her bedroom."

Nana rose, moving Ares out of the way, then grabbed a handful of Vivian's hair and jerked her head up to see her face. With her other hand she touched, tentatively, Vivian's forehead. With a shout, Nana jerked away as if burnt. Ares rushed to put himself between her and Vivian. She stumbled over the big pup; Erik caught her, steadied her.

"Nana?"

"Sit, Ares," she said. He did. Nana took a step past him and stumbled again, but this time it wasn't the pup's fault.

Again, only Erik's intervention kept her from going down. "Let's get you back on the bench, shall we?" he said.

When she was safely at the table, Nana stared at the book fearfully. "I tried to see into her mind. She has some protection wards about her person."

I remembered the jolt I felt. "I injected her with the morphine—I got a jolt too, but it wasn't that bad."

Nana asked, "Your wards connected to you?"

After thinking through the words I'd said, my answer was, "Yes."

"They absorbed the brunt of it for you, then." She gestured at Vivian. "It's probably jewelry."

Going around the counter to the dinette, I lifted Vivian's head by the hair. A chain hung around her neck, down into her shirt. With a nod toward the butcher-block knife set, I said, "Kitchen shears." Celia handed them to me. Lifting the chain with the edge of the scissors, I maneuvered it around, pulled it free, and cut it loose. The chain and the little wire-bound stones attached to various links tumbled to the floor. I kicked it away.

Nana gestured at Erik. "Help me." He gave her his arm and she returned to Vivian and repeated the forehead-touching maneuver, then returned to her chair. She said nothing as she moved, and when she sat she remained silent. The rest of us traded glances. The tension thickened the air in the room until breathing felt difficult.

"What did you see?" Johnny finally asked.

Still, my melodramatic Nana took her time answering, and the longer she was silent, the more worried I became. Could she have learned about Vivian's and my business deal that quickly?

"Demeter."

"She didn't write that book. And it's not even hers; she stole it from another. Let me see it."

I slid it from the counter and placed it on the table. Nana pulled the wooden binding closer to her. That surprised me because she'd seemed afraid of it just minutes before. She reverently opened the first page. "Ahh, Latin," she whispered.

Her melodrama made me weary.

"Do you know what this is, Persephone?"

I crossed my arms. "No."

"This is the Trivium Codex."

I shut my eyes to keep from rolling them. I had enough to worry about.

Nana caught my annoyance anyway. "I'm serious, Persephone." Ares sulked under the table to lie at her feet, probably because her tone had changed.

"What does she mean?" Celia asked.

Nana's head lifted. "It's a legend among witches." She turned back to the first page, ran her fingers over the page. "It is a Latin translation, of course . . ."

My arms lowered, slowly. She wasn't being melodramatic at all.

"The original would have been in Akkadian. The Akkadians used Sumerian as a religious language, you know. They called their goddess Ishtar, but their sacred writings were in Sumerian, so she was called Inanna in hymns and the like. But the author of this book was not writing a prayer. Not at all. She would call her goddess *Ishtar.*"

"Ishtar?" Celia asked.

"Goddess of love and war," I said, feeling a bit guilty.

"And fertility," Johnny added.

Nana said grimly, "This is no ordinary Book of Shadows."

I hesitated, trying to figure out why Vivian had this

legendary book and how she might have gotten it. "I know, Nana."

"You don't look like you believe me."

"I do, I just—" I didn't finish.

"Just what?"

"Are we going to have to safeguard it now too?"

She closed the cover again, caressed the triskelion. "We could learn much from this book, you and I." Her voice shook. She leaned in, then angled the book up to the light, moving her finger as she translated the words carved in a circle around the triskelion. "One cursed by the sun, one cursed by the moon, one cursed by her heart."

"What fun. Curses all around," I muttered sarcastically and turned to go back around the counter to my coffee.

As I sipped, Nana regarded Johnny, then Erik and Celia. "You carry the curse of the moon. Like your friend upstairs."

Celia grabbed Erik's arm. "Does that book have a cure?"

Erik took her hand, clearly surprised. "Would you want it if it did?"

A breath escaped her. "Of course! We could be normal and have babies, Erik. A family."

Celia turned back to Nana, her eyes glistening. "Does it?"

Nana's expression turned sad. It seemed that for the first time she saw my friend not as a "filthy wære" but as a woman who longed to be a mother. "There is no cure."

Celia's hand slipped from Erik's. It was clear in her eyes that in the instant it had taken for her to ask the question, years of hopes and dreams had sprouted, and Nana's words burnt them up just as fast. It hurt me to see Celia that hurt; it reminded me of Nancy. I asked, "Then what *is* in the book?"

"It's a compilation of spells, of course. I'll have to look through them to see exactly what they are."

"Then how do you know there *isn't* a cure in it?"

"Because of the legend of this book. If there were a cure, the writer would have used it."

"The writer was a witch, right?"

"The writer loved a wære." Nana faced Celia again. "And she would have wanted to have his babies."

Ares leapt up and ran to the front door, barking. "He probably needs to pee," Nana said. It was funny to hear an old woman say "pee," but the hour was too late and the moment too serious for any humor to be appreciated.

"I'll let him out," Johnny said, following after Ares.

A second passed and I called, "Wait, he's paper-trained. He should go in the garage." I started after them.

"You're paper-training a Great Dane?" Johnny called back, incredulous.

"Not me, his former owners." Ares was scratching at the door to get out. My first thought was to scold him; then another thought hit me. Johnny was just reaching for the knob. "Johnny, don't!"

He stopped. "What?"

"Ares knows to go in the garage. It's the only place we've taken him to"—I couldn't say "pee"—"to do his business." I finished quickly, "I don't think he has to go."

Johnny looked at Ares.

"Vivian wouldn't have walked here," I said. "Where's her car?"

"Would she have brought someone with her?" he asked.

I shrugged, peering out the window. Her car sat at the far end of my driveway.

"Got a leash?"

"Huh?"

I expected an innuendo in answer, but all he said was, "I'll take him out and see."

"Johnny."

He flashed a grin and tweaked my cheek. "Aw, you're worried about me."

I released an exasperated sigh and got him the leash. He looked it over appreciatively and wiggled his eyebrows at me.

"Erik," he called. "Come out with us." As soon as his feet hit the porch, Ares went to barking again and pulled for the end of the planking. Johnny held tight to a post, keeping the dog back as he sniffed the night air and surveyed the dark yard. Erik went out then, and he began smelling the air as well.

"What is it?" I asked from the doorway.

Johnny swiftly tied the leash around the pole and growled, "Beholders." He ran. Erik followed him. Both of them were fast, lean shadows in the dark.

"Beholders?" I called after them. Ares whined and strained against the collar and leash, trying to follow them. "What are beholders?"

It wasn't easy, but I dragged Ares back inside and crated him for his own good. Nana poured a second cup of coffee and parked herself right in front of the Codex. Beverley looked on with her. Vivian stirred, lifted her head slowly, and moaned. Blinking, she looked about, trying to focus and having trouble.

"Should she have come out of that so soon?" Celia asked. She'd brushed her hair and was presently working on Beverley's. "It was a full dose, right?"

"Full for Theo. Dr. Lincoln kept them small, since drugs affect wæres so readily."

"You'd think it'd be the opposite, that it'd take more to do anything to us," Celia said. She gestured at Vivian. "But she's not a wære."

"No, but she's stained," I said.

"Stained?" Celia asked, concern in her voice.

I approached Vivian. "That's right, isn't it?" I let my disgust show in my face. "You've got a vampire's mark." It seemed dirty in a contaminated way, like having lice or something.

Vivian squinted at me and tried to talk through the gag. Though garbled, her intended words were clear enough: "Fuck you."

Since most of her cheek was covered by the gag, I smacked her temple, hard. "Don't talk like that, even muffled, in front of my nana and Beverley. You understand me?"

Vivian glared.

"Do you understand me?" I asked again, this time with a handful of her hair pulled tight.

She shut her eyes.

"Where did you get the Codex?"

Having previously forgotten, she remembered it now

and foggily scrutinized the room until she spotted it on the table in front of Nana. She strained against the cords. I moved to stand behind her but didn't release the handful of her hair. With one finger against her cheek, I pushed the gag free of her mouth. "Where did you say you got it?"

"That book is mine."

"Not anymore."

She laughed. "You're an idiot. He'll take it from you, and he'll kill you just for having seen it."

"Who?" I asked, but I thought I knew. I mean, she was stained, yet free, living a good life, working at a coffee shop—which still made no sense to me. "The one who marked you?" Her glare turned positively malicious. "It's a good security blanket, huh?"

"The best," she said through gritted teeth. "And unless you've made good on my little contract, you-know-who will be coming for it."

"Little contract?" Celia asked.

I tightened my fist in Vivian's hair, a warning. I needed a minute to think of an answer that would avoid—

"She didn't tell you?" Vivian blurted. I jerked her head back, but before I could reach for the gag she said, "Not even after her friend's little car accident?"

I looked at Celia. She looked at me. A deer caught in car headlights must feel like I felt then.

Johnny and Erik came in the front door. Both were breathing like marathon runners after a race. It gave me reason to pause and an instant to think. After they closed and locked the door, the men came quickly to the kitchen. "They got away. But more are sure to come."

"What are beholders, anyway?" I asked, hoping the diversion would make everyone else forget what they'd just heard.

Johnny started to answer, but Vivian growled, "The beholders have been here already?"

"You knew?" he asked.

"Go to my car. Inside it is a wooden box—pray they haven't taken it already. Bring it into the house. Now." She barked orders as if she was going to be obeyed despite having been tied to a chair after breaking and entering. "Do it, or we'll all be killed!"

Johnny asked me, "What is she talking about?" His urgency and tone dropped as his attention flicked back and forth between me and Celia. He smelled the tension between us. "What did I miss?"

I jerked the gag up and into Vivian's mouth.

Everyone was staring at me except Vivian. I glanced around the room. My friends, Nana, and Beverley were all waiting for me to say something, to explain. The wolves shifted closer to each other, a pack trait for certain. I felt like I was standing at the wrong end of a loaded gun. My heart pounded in my chest.

They'd all put so much faith in me, come here to help me. Did I have enough faith in their friendship to tell them the truth?

I thought of Nancy. She'd had enough faith in friendship to tell me and Olivia and Betsy her truth, enough love for us to want us to have what she'd found. And we had helped her right out of our lives for it. I didn't want to lose the wærewolves—I realized then how much I valued them. And not for the money kenneling brought in either—I spent most of it on their treats anyway. They were the only outside connections I had to the world. I'd holed myself up, alone, in this saltbox farmhouse for two years. Just a computer and me, with me denying that I needed anyone or wanted anyone in my life. If not for the wærewolves, I'd have no one. Nana would be it. I didn't want Nana to be "it" for me.

I swallowed hard. The breath I took filled my lungs with the heaviest air.

"All of you have trusted me. Trusted me with your secrets, trusted me not to betray you in your mainstream life. Trusted me to keep you safe during the full moon, and to let you out when it's passed." I stared at the floor and licked my lips. "It's time I started trusting you back."

CHAPTER FIFTEEN

Vivian contacted me after"—I focused on Beverley—"after your mother's murder. You see, last year someone was stalking Lorrie." I looked around the room, meeting everyone's eyes in turn. If I was going to say this, I had to do it right. "A real sleaze. I did a spell using dirt from your father's grave, Beverley, a spell that's supposed to enlist the aid of those who've passed. But this stalker jerk was an addict of some kind, and the subtle influences from the other side must have gone unnoticed. Anyway, after a Tarot reading I did for Lorrie, it was clear his intentions were malicious and it seemed that someone would have to physically confront him. So . . . I did." I looked to Johnny last, and it seemed like I was making my confession to him. Somehow, that made it easier to continue.

"You?" Erik asked. "She was wære. Why didn't she just knock him around?"

"Erik." Celia took his hand. "Lorrie wasn't like that. She was afraid of her strength. She wouldn't hurt a fly before she was infected, and that didn't change afterward." She nodded at Beverley. "Your mom was the sweetest person I ever knew."

Beverley swallowed hard, fighting tears.

"This guy always seemed to be around when Beverley was, and Lorrie was afraid he'd hurt her. When I confronted him, he pulled a knife. We struggled. He was on something, maybe PCP, I don't know. It made him strong, but clumsy. We fell, and the knife went into him. He died."

Vivian started laughing through her gag.

"Shut up," Johnny said with such vehement sternness that she obeyed without hesitation. When he looked at me again, it was my cue to go on, but my boldness had seeped away.

"It was an accident," I said. "I didn't go there to kill him, but apparently Lorrie must have thought I had. She told Vivian, who obviously thought I was keen on being some kind of assassin." I felt so stupid and so ashamed I couldn't meet their eyes. "Vivian said she knew who'd killed Lorrie and asked me to . . . to retaliate. To kill him." I could feel my hands shaking, and I planted them firmly on my hips.

"And you agreed?" Nana asked, incredulous.

"I saved Lorrie's life once, and it was taken from her anyway. I thought of Beverley and I knew the police wouldn't pursue the case of a wære-victim."

So soft a whisper left my nana that I scarcely heard her. "But the Rede . . ."

I had to look at her, but I couldn't maintain eye contact. A heartbeat's worth was all I could stand. "I know, Nana. I know." I didn't want to get into the things Amenemhab had told me. Nana might understand my talking with a totem-jackal, but the others wouldn't.

"Did you . . . fulfill the contract?" Johnny asked, his tone very careful.

"No. I had a name. I asked Theo to check him out. She found out he was a vampire—and not just any regular bloodsucker either. He's the abducted brother of the Reverend Samson D. Kline. He was trained and allowed to grow up before he was turned; now he's at the right hand of a very dangerous master vampire, the one who took him. When I found that out, I called Vivian to tell her to forget the deal, but Beverley was there sobbing, and Vivian was treating her so badly."

"Are you saying that's why Theo was run off the road? Why her home and her business were sacked?" Celia asked.

Vivian nodded emphatically. I hated it that she was enjoying this so much.

"Yeah," I said. "In the truck ride to the doctor's, Theo whispered to me that it had been him who ran her off the road. It was probably him, or maybe those beholders if they do that kind of thing, who sacked her apartment and office." I forced my head up and met the eyes of everyone in turn. I'd done this, and I had to own it. "What happened to Theo is my fault." I saw a mixture of horror and surprise on their faces. All except Beverley's.

"Wait," Beverley said. Her dark hair was now loose, a little wave where the pigtails had been. With those big blue eyes looking up at me, she seemed so grown up. "You took on a vampire for my mom?" she asked.

She seemed impressed. But I didn't deserve her admiration.

"Beverley, I haven't even *seen* him. I took Vivian's

money, asked questions, and ended up spending some on Theo's hospital bill. I thought it would be helping everybody out all around. Get a killer off the streets, with justice served, and the money would help me take care of Nana." I smiled at her. "I wanted everything to be good. To work out. But . . . I can't do this. I can't defeat a vampire, especially not one of his caliber."

"Why not?" Johnny asked. Everybody turned to him, as stunned as if he'd just proclaimed himself Elvis.

"What do you mean 'why not?'" Celia interjected. "Seph's not an assassin."

He crossed his lean arms. "She's got all she needs to be the Lustrata."

"A lust-what?" Celia asked.

Despite my badly wanting to know what it was myself, lights had flashed in the hallway. "There's a car coming up the drive," I said.

Vivian went hysterical, straining against the cords and shaking her head and blabbering on though we couldn't understand any sound she made. But I remembered her saying we'd all get killed if we didn't get the wooden box from her car. Taking a handful of her hair to make her be still, I pulled the gag down. "Who is it?"

"It's *him,* you idiots. He'll rip through all of you and save me for last. You should've gotten it out of the car. I told you. I *told* you!" I jerked the gag back up.

"Kill the lights," Johnny said and started down the hall. Celia flipped the switch, and we fell into darkness again.

Vivian mumbled. I thumped her in the head. "Shhhh."

"It's cool," Johnny announced. "It's the doc." Celia

flipped the lights back on. I started to the door, then stopped and looked back at Vivian.

"I'll watch her," Erik said, crossing his arms bouncer-style.

"Thanks." I glanced at Nana, who was turning pages in the Codex; then I joined Johnny at the door.

"I'm gonna get that box from her car," he said.

"Wait. What is a lustra-whatever?" That seemed more important than finding out what beholders were.

He turned and regarded me with a sly, approving smile. "Tell you later."

Dr. Lincoln stepped up onto the porch. "Sorry I didn't make it out sooner," he said. "I got called out to treat a mare that had gotten herself stuck in a deep, cold mud-hole. My cell phone showed your number so, it being a Saturday night, and knowing how nocturnal wæres are, I drove by. Saw the lights and stopped."

That he had gone to the trouble impressed me. "You should be in bed, Doc."

"Yeah. So should the lot of you, I bet. And none of you have been saving the life of a little girl's pony, either. Being a hero like that makes me feel too good to sleep." He yawned. "Or it did. I guess the long drive and late hour sucked the adrenaline right out of me. Anyway, I thought I'd check in on her."

"Please, come on in."

"Sure." He paused. "Hey. I noticed the lights went out. If you're having power fluctuations, the machinery won't function properly and—"

"Oh! We're not having power fluctuations. We were just turning them out, then we noticed your lights in the drive." I didn't want to offer any more details, so I quickly herded him toward the steps, hoping he didn't see Vivian tied up in the kitchen.

"I'll take him up," Celia said, coming down the hall.

I stopped. Didn't she trust me with Theo anymore?

She must've seen the question in my eyes. "Beverley needs to talk to you," she whispered, and gestured toward the darkened living room.

"Oh."

Beverley sat on my couch with her knees pulled up under her chin and her arms tight around them. "You okay?" I asked.

"Yeah," she said, even as she was shaking her head *no.*

I sat beside her, close but not touching. "You know . . . my mom left me too."

Her head popped around, eyes wide in the dark.

"She's still alive; she just left me. I haven't seen her since I was about your age."

"Why'd she leave?"

"She kind of ran away to be with her boyfriend."

"What about your dad?"

"I never knew him," I said, knowing she could relate to that as well. Her dad had died trying to save Lorrie from the wærewolf that attacked them in a park after an anniversary dinner. Lorrie told me about it once. Beverley, six then, had been left with some close friends for the weekend. "We're alike in that way, Beverley. Our parents are gone. I'm so sorry I couldn't do a better job of protecting your mom. I know everything's a mess right now, but I swear, if you want to stay here, I'll make it legal and get custody of you. I'll protect you and I'll do the best I can for you."

Even in the dark, tears glistened in her eyes, but footsteps on the porch made me twist to glance out the window. Johnny's shadow was unmistakable. He came inside carrying a box. I relaxed back into my place. "You don't have to decide now," I said to Beverley. "Think about it. For as long as you need to."

She launched herself at me, throwing her arms around me, crying. She'd cried so much lately, it was a wonder she had any tears left. I held her until she calmed. Nana's silhouette shuffled through the dining room and into the living room. "Persephone?"

"Yeah?"

Beverley moved away from me.

"You'd better come and have a look at this." Nana blew smoke at the ceiling.

I moved forward. "What is it? Contents of the box?"

"No. I don't think they've opened that. But I think I found something in the Codex. Something that might be useful."

When I entered the kitchen, the wooden box on my counter demanded my attention first. It was the box I'd seen in Vivian's office at the coffee shop. "Just a second, Nana." I went to Vivian. "You're blackmailing the one who marked you. The threat of whatever's in that box is your moneymaker, isn't it?" I jerked down the gag.

She smiled with false sweetness. "A security blanket lined in gold."

"Then explain why a witch with such a lucrative vampire connection takes a job managing a coffee shop?"

She licked her gag-dried lips. "Because of the standards of the Elders Council. Every Elder selected in the last fifty years has been an active member of the community. Being a successful businesswoman is like gold." I reached to replace the gag; she jerked away. "If you're smart, you'll let me go and let me take the book and box with me. Otherwise, you're inviting the wrath of Menessos."

I knew that name: the master vampire who had made Goliath. I forced the gag back up. "What'd you find?" I asked Nana.

"This." She pointed to the open page. It was in Latin, the letters written in old-style script that was more art than anything. Being this close to something this old, something this precious and beautiful filled me with a sense of awe. I recognized some words here and there as I scanned down the page, but not many.

"What is it?"

"A ritual to harness moonlight and earth energy."

I wasn't following. "For what purpose, Nana?"

"We can use it to force your injured friend to change, to fully change."

"But that's magic!" Erik said.

"Nana you know what could—"

"Of course I do! I'm not a novice, Persephone," she croaked.

Unwilling to scold her again, I waited with my expectant expression plastered to my face. We stared at each other, neither willing to give. Her expression was, well, weird. Her mouth formed its usual angry line, but her brows weren't squished down tight together. Instead, they lifted as if in surprise. I wasn't certain if she was as pissed at me right now as I was at her or if she was going to vomit.

"I don't understand," Erik said carefully. "If you know the dangers, then why suggest it?"

"Magic stirs energies into action. It affects the energy field around wæres and causes a reaction, a change. But most magic doesn't stir *enough* energy to cause a full-out reaction. Most witches couldn't handle the amount needed. This spell has plenty, because it's sorcery."

Silence.

"Persephone, this *can* be done, if you are willing."

I took a breath and considered it. "I'm not *un*willing. It's just that we have all lived with knowing these dangers for so long, it's not easy to just disregard them."

"Don't disregard them; rethink them. If you're hungry, a single bite of food won't ease your hunger; it'll make it worse. If a wære is sensitive to certain energy and is near it, it's the same concept: it's not enough, and it makes things worse."

I followed the logic, but— "What makes you think we can handle the energy?" I'd touched the ley for a smidgen, enough to power my wards. It had felt like touching boiling water. Drawing that much energy would be like dropping your entire body into a vat of boiling water. How could anyone maintain focus like that? If I lost my focus, it might cost Theo her life.

"In this spell, you don't have to be Superwoman and carry the energy to save the day; you're the pilot of the plane that's carrying the energy that saves the day."

Her analogies made sense to me. The partial-change instances I knew of had been connected to energy practitioners being in too-close proximity to a wære. If the difference was only in the volume of energy, then this could conceivably work. But I wasn't going to leap without looking. "Okay, I'm following what you're saying, but how do we call and harness that much energy? It's sorcery. How do we control it and focus it and—"

"You learn the spell, prepare, and practice."

So we had a hope of healing Theo. I imagined the Fates backing away from her thread with their scissors.

Johnny cleared his throat. "That is great news—and I'm excited about it—but hey, I'm *dying* to open that." He pointed at the wooden box from Vivian's car.

"Might as well," Nana said.

Johnny grinned at me. "Go ahead. Open it."

"Me?"

"Your house."

I joined him in front of the Codex and paused. I couldn't think about the box. Just standing this close to him made me feel keyed up, yet at ease. I reached out to the box, feeling confident with him there, but footsteps on the stairs stopped us. "Just a minute," I said. "I want to see the doc out."

Meeting Dr. Lincoln and Celia in the hall, I said, "Thanks for coming by so late. People-doctors aren't usually that courteous."

"Well, I gave my word. You are all doing a fine job."

"Feeding tube?"

"In, no problem. New machine I brought in up there. It will regulate the feeding tube. Celia here has instructions for it."

I paused, facing Celia. "Nana found a spell in that book that might enable us to force Theo to change. I want to explain it to all of you wæres. It will be your decision whether to do it or not, but I wanted to ask the doctor something about it before he left."

Dr. Lincoln put his hand up. "Uh, I don't treat the wære-folk that often but, all that magic stuff aside, is that wise?" He pushed his glasses up his nose. "I mean, she's very weak. How can you be certain she'll survive the transformation?"

"That's what I wanted to ask: Can you do anything to make her stronger? Kind of rev her up and make sure her body has the fuel for a spell like this?"

He considered it. "I have some . . ." He started to tell us the technical side of it, then changed his mind. "Well, hmmm. I just did something like that for the mare, to get her heart pumping and warm her up so she didn't slip into hypothermia while we waited for the crane to arrive and lift her out. I could adjust a protein serving for Theo and make, well, a kind of monster energy drink version for her." He scratched his head. "It . . . yeah, it might work."

"Great."

"There's some in my truck. Let me go get it and think this through again." He opened the door and went out.

Ares started barking from the crate in the garage, and it occurred to me that I ought to get the doc to give him his puppy shots so I could at least do some *normal* business with him. I wondered if Nana had asked the previous owners about shots. I turned to ask Dr. Lincoln about Ares and saw him backing through the door, then standing there, staring outside. His jaw opened and closed repeatedly, but no sound came out.

"What?" I asked, advancing toward him.

His hand came up and he pointed outside. "I think I'll wait a while."

I looked out the door.

Standing just beyond the porch rail, directly opposite my open door, stood a man with luminous white skin and pale, pale hair gleaming silver in the waning gibbous moon's light. I'd have sworn he had to be taller than Johnny's six feet plus. On his elongated scarecrow of a body he wore shiny black, from his high collar to his toes. The intensity of his expression, the tight vibration of his very presence, and the faint smell of rotting leaves unmistakably identified him as a vampire. But it was his eyes that named him for me. I could detect the color even at this distance—blue, like summer forget-me-nots. I had seen them before, on a child's picture.

"Goliath," I said.

His mouth broadened slightly into the most condescending smile I'd ever seen. His chin lowered a minute degree in acknowledgment.

I added, "You killed a friend of mine."

"Perhaps."

Beverley stepped into the hall. "Go back to the kitchen," I said.

"Goliath," she whispered, her stunned expression turning into a grin.

I stared at her. "You know him?"

"Yeah."

"Hello, Beverley," Goliath said.

"You don't think *he*'s the vampire that killed my mom, do you?"

I didn't know what to say. She moved toward the door even as I tried to stop her. "Goliath!"

"Beverley!" he called. His expression too had changed.

I pushed between her and the door. "For now, you let me handle this." I was afraid she'd invite him in or something equally dangerous. "Go to the kitchen, now. Please, please."

For a tense second I wondered if she would obey; then she just walked away.

I turned back to the vampire. He kept his tone cool and stated, "I have come for Vivian Diamond and for the book." His voice was deep. Long vocal cords on a body that tall. It startled me, though. I think it was because from one with hair that pale and fine, I'd expected something softer. Shadows appeared under his cheekbones as he spoke.

This made me notice the sharp angles of his face. Such sharpness should have made him harsh and cruel-looking, but instead he was stunning—in an undernourished, Nordic-supermodel way.

My ears detected Celia slipping away down the hall with Beverley. Ares continued barking. Good dog, sensitive to smelly creatures outside. I stood there and concentrated on breathing normally. What was I supposed to do? Stall. Stalling was good. Get information. That was good too. "Why do you want Vivian and the book?" I asked.

"Both belong to my master."

"Oh. So you're a gofer, huh?"

"Miss Alcmedi," Dr. Lincoln whispered as he moved a step farther from the door, "I don't think it's a good idea to be flippant with a vampire."

"He can't come in, Doc. And he's not about to be invited." It was the only reason I could afford to have a bit of an attitude. That and knowing—in the wild, at least—strength respected strength. I hoped a vampire would do the same.

"That's a wives' tale!" The doctor's whisper was panicky.

"No, it's a witches' tale. I'm a witch, and my house has wards."

"Only holy ground can keep them at bay!"

Through gritted teeth I said, "The average person's residence can be invaded because they don't have wards. Churches put up wards by blessing the ground. It's kind of the same thing."

"But he's *on* your grounds."

I should have swept a bigger circle around the house. "He's staying beyond the wards. Now, please, shut up!"

Johnny came into the living room via the dining room and stepped up behind the doctor. Erik followed a few paces behind him. Johnny tapped Dr. Lincoln roughly on the shoulder, and the doc turned to see his stern face and a "get-out-of-the-way" chin jerk. The doctor backed deeper into the living room, but to his credit, he didn't flee. He stood near the end of the couch. The wærewolves moved into a flanking position behind me. It bolstered my courage, and my shoulders squared as I faced the vampire again.

Goliath looked down his elegant nose. "Finished squabbling amongst yourselves?"

I hated vampires. I really hated vampires. Obnoxious snots. "Quite."

"Give me what I ask for, and I will leave. If you don't . . ." He let me see his fangs. "I might have to take offense at all the digging you've been doing lately."

"Your threat is empty. You can't come in."

Even as the last word left my lips, I felt the pull. It slid across my thoughts like a boat on serene water then stabbed an oar into my brain and pushed. *Come. Come to me,* it said.

I was floating, flowing, ebbing. And it was so nice. I put my hand on the screen door and pushed it open.

Something suddenly jerked me under the water and weighed me down. I was sinking fast, and I couldn't breathe. I clawed for the surface. *I couldn't breathe.*

"Persephone!" Johnny's voice. The enchantment broke. His hands, the *something* that had grabbed me, jerked me back and spun me around, breaking the connection between me and the vampire. I gasped.

I couldn't do this. I knew it. I couldn't face a vampire. I was such an idiot for even considering—

The faith in Johnny's eyes, in that Wedjat gaze, was like a buoyant lifesaver. My confidence clung to it, and he pulled me back to myself. "Don't look in his eyes," Johnny whispered, and turned my body back toward the door.

He didn't expect me to run and hide, didn't expect that I needed protecting. And he didn't know my confidence was false, was based on knowing the vampire couldn't get through my wards. But Johnny hadn't laughed at me when I told him about Vivian hiring me as an assassin, he'd called me a—a—what was it again? Lustrata.

I faced Goliath, staring at the top of his head. I hated it when people did that to me, and I hoped it irritated him as much. At least I'd learned something: that old saying that the eyes are the windows of the soul was true. Looking through the glass was good, but if you opened that window or left it unlocked, something ugly was likely to creep inside.

"You cannot keep yourself and everyone you care about behind magic fences forever." Goliath glowered. "If you taunt me again, I'll have them one by one until you're begging me to take you in their place."

"I don't repeat mistakes."

"Perhaps not. But you do make so many of them." He tsk-tsked me. "Your wards are good, but you must not be much of a witch otherwise. You couldn't divine your data or scry for it. You hired a background checker. Ms. Diamond could have told you much if you had used the right *method* to ask."

He meant torture—of that I was certain.

"I commend you for being able to lure Ms. Diamond to your home, along with her most precious objects. I haven't been able to fake her into such stupidity, and I've been trying for years."

I wasn't about to reveal that he had the wrong assumption. He clearly thought I had known about the "precious objects" and had acted purposely to obtain them. I hoped he'd think I could protect myself and keep them too. But damn it! I'd just been enchanted by his eyes—a stupid, stupid mistake. Surely he was wondering now if I could possibly be a lucky bungler.

"At any rate, you have gained my attention, Miss Persephone Isis Alcmedi." He proceeded to tell me my phone number, Social Security number, and credit scores, and then he rattled off a series he claimed was my Avalon's VIN. "Shall I go on?"

My palms were sweaty.

"If your cerebrum is keeping up, you'll understand now that I have also acquired information about you. And I can use my information to make your *life*"—he spat that last word—"a tragedy worthy of your bastardly Greek heritage."

Nana's hand, holding a lit cigarette, pushed me aside. She stepped up beside me, Vivian's box cradled in her left arm. "You better get your rotting ass off the lawn, and I mean now." She put the cigarette to her lips, flipped the box's lid up, and reached inside.

CHAPTER SIXTEEN

From the box, Nana pulled a wooden stake caked with dried mud.

Goliath hissed—not the kind of theatrical vampire hiss that Hollywood directors make actors embarrass themselves with. This was a hiss that took ten full seconds to build and occur. It started deep in his gullet and rose with such force that Goliath's entire body shook in a growing convulsive wave. His mouth barely opened, but the sound was hellish: fear and loathing and vengeance with a voice.

After that, he fled in an otherworldly blur.

"What the hell is that thing?" I asked, pointing at the stake.

"This is the product of a spell from the Codex. Come back to the kitchen."

"Excuse me," Dr. Lincoln said to Johnny. "Would you, uh . . ." he stammered, and finally said, "Is he gone for good?"

"Probably for tonight, anyway. Why?" Johnny asked.

"Oh," I said, getting it. "He needs his stuff to fix up a bag for Theo."

"A bag of what?"

"To help her body have enough energy to change."

He clasped the doctor's shoulder. "I'll fetch it. A real doctor bag, right?"

"Yeah." He squinted apologetically. "But I didn't mean you should fetch, I mean, you're . . . and that would be . . . you know."

"Red, straighten him out, would you?" Johnny went outside.

Nana headed through the dining room.

"C'mon." I motioned to the doctor. "You're a brain with the medical stuff, but you don't talk with people very well."

He shrugged and followed. "With owners of patients it's almost like a script repeating over and over. When it's not a script . . . you know. More so with *him*; he's so . . . intimidating."

"Johnny? I know. I used to think so too." The words came out and made me realize that I truly felt as if I was over that personal hurdle. Then I thought of something and stopped. "He recommended you because you treat wæres. I thought you two knew each other well."

"Not 'well.' I treated him once, a long time ago. He made it hard to refuse him."

I studied the doc. "I think that's a story I'm going to want to hear someday. For now, you helped Theo and you came by at—what?—*four* in the morning. Nobody here is going to hurt you or intentionally let you get hurt."

"That's reassuring."

It didn't sound sarcastic, so I led him on to the kitchen, saying, "We had a break-in, doc. We've tied the culprit up, so don't be too alarmed. We're handling it." Beverley sat beside Nana at the table, with her head on her arms. She yawned. I wondered how she knew Goliath. There was so much going on, though, and I had to focus on the enemies right now.

Nana had the book open before her and a page of very modern notebook paper in her hand. "Vivian modified a spell of protection for the human servant of a vampire, transforming it from increasing the vampire's protection into binding the vampire's own power to use against him," she said.

Johnny entered with the black leather bag. Dr. Lincoln immediately took it to the counter behind me and rummaged through it. "I need one of the cans of protein supplement I gave you to use in the feeding tube," he said.

"I'll get it." Celia left.

Vivian moaned as if she had something important to say. I pushed her gag down. "What?"

"You guys are so stupid. He's not about to let that thing slip away. He'll come back, you know." Vivian glanced at the clock. "It may be too late for action tonight, but he'll be back tomorrow. Menessos will be with him. You can't possibly stand against him." The last comment she aimed at me.

"We have your stake," I reminded her.

"But you're muddling through the motions, guessing. You don't know anything. All he has to do is torch your house. Bye-bye stake, and his buddies suck dry anyone who comes running out and throw the body back in, disposing neatly of all his threats at once."

"This is when you bargain information to stop him from doing that in exchange for our untying you, right?"

Vivian smiled. "What a good idea," she said mockingly.

"Dr. Lincoln?" Johnny said, making Wedjat squints at Vivian. "Do you have any sodium pentothal in that bag?"

"Truth serum?" the doctor asked back with a laugh. "No. I don't usually need to question my patients."

"Well, I don't need science or pharmacology," Nana said. She left the book and shuffled over to stand behind Vivian. "Might be easier this way anyhow." She placed her hand atop Vivian's head, burrowing her fingers through Vivian's hair to touch her scalp. "Now her protection charm won't jolt me. Ask her what you want to know."

"Do you think pulling my hair will make me tell you the truth, you old crone?"

Nana yanked her hair hard. Vivian squealed and shouted, "Bitch!"

Nana smacked Vivian's face with her free hand. "You were told not to use that language in front of the child." She leaned closer to Vivian's ear and said, "And no, I don't think pulling your hair will make you tell the truth, but it would make me very happy to see your bald, bleeding scalp if you don't lose the attitude immediately." She straightened and gave me a firm nod.

Celia returned then with her eyes wide and her expression otherwise surprised but agreeable as she smiled at Nana. I knew her wolf-hearing had picked up what Nana had said. She handed the protein supplement to Dr. Lincoln. He began reading the label and cross-checking it with a book from his bag. I was interested and wanted to watch, but had other, more pressing things to do. "How are you connected to Goliath?" I asked Vivian.

"None of your business."

With two fingers, Nana tapped Vivian's brow in the

area of the forehead chakra or "third eye." "They were lovers," Nana said.

Beverley straightened. Vivian's mouth flew open. She recovered and said, "Lucky guess."

"You think so?" Nana indicated I could proceed.

"How are you connected to Menessos?"

"I used to do divination for him," Vivian said.

Nana tapped her again. "True." Vivian gave me a curt, unpleasant smile. Nana went on. "And they were lovers, as well. For a long, long time."

"At least," Johnny quipped, crossing his arms as he leaned on the counter beside me, "we know how the vamp's condescending manner actually got rubbed off onto her."

"How are you doing that?" our prisoner demanded.

Sounding like Mrs. Claus on a shopping mall's center-court stage, Nana said, "Why, don't you know? With magic, dear."

Vivian sneered at her. In unison, the wæres all *ooooo*'d their approval of Nana's insult like professional Jerry Springer audience members. I had never been as proud of my grandmother as I was just then. And now I knew why she had always wanted to fuss with my hair when I was a teenager and she was upset with me. It was comforting to know I'd never lied to her, but discomforting to know that, in a way, she *was* a mind reader.

"Which of them marked you?"

Vivian clamped her mouth shut. Nana tapped her and said, "Menessos."

I was surprised. If Menessos had stained her, she needed *him* killed, not Goliath.

"Not Goliath?" I asked. "Are you certain?"

Nana said, "Very. She couldn't have been marked by Goliath; she's much, much older than he is. Older than me, even."

Vivian *hmpf*ed. "You don't look half as good, either."

"My insides aren't tarnished, though." The wæres howled approval for Nana again. Beverley giggled. I admit, it was entertaining, in a masochistic kind of way. And that was why it disturbed me for Beverley to be seeing this. I got Celia's attention and gestured toward Beverley. She understood.

"Hey Beverley, why don't you and I take these Oreos and go sit with Theo for a while? She shouldn't be alone too long."

"But—" Beverley looked at me, and I pointed to the ceiling to indicate "upstairs." "Okay," she yawned. "But leave the Oreos unless you want 'em. I'm too sleepy." She hugged me on the way out. "Tell me tomorrow how this went, okay?"

"I promise." When they had gone, I lifted up the stake that had sent Goliath into a hissing conniption. "Explain this."

Vivian bit her lower lip, hesitating.

"If you don't tell them, I will," Nana reminded her.

"Fine. Fine." She drew a breath. "With a knife used for the killing blow to a mortal, a knife that stayed in the man until his body was cold, I cut a branch from an ash tree inside of a graveyard—a tree whose roots fed, basically, on the dead. I bored holes into its thickest, strongest parts. I empowered that branch in the full light of the sun and blooded it from my own veins. I stole dirt from Menessos's pillow, mixed it with blessed water, and coated the stake with it, then set it in the light of the sun again and again to dry the mud."

"Explain the significance," I pressed.

"Stoker's nice little tale said you could release someone who hadn't yet died from the curse of Dracula by killing Dracula. That's bullshit. Killing the maker doesn't release the spawn. Through connections, there would be pain—the greater the bond, the greater the pain—but death or release from the curse would not happen. However, this, with its blessed water and sun empowerment, is a tool every vampire would fear. When you're inoculated against something, they inject you with a weakened form of whatever disease they're saving you from, right? Similar idea. With my blood and his home earth mixed with holy water, it's a tool designed to kill Menessos with great suffering."

My thoughts ran to Samson Kline and how much he would love to get his hands on this thing. "Because of your blood?"

"It would be reintroducing a diseased part of him into him—connected through his home earth and my blood, which is bound to him, and diseased in that it is mixed with holy water and infused with sunlight. He could not reject it or fight it, because it *is* him."

Johnny shifted, and my attention went to him. He smiled at me, his focus flicking between my face and the stake in my hands. "Lustrata," he said.

"Lustrata," Nana repeated, breathlessly. "Yes. Sweet crone, yes!" She stared at me like she was seeing me for the first time ever. It creeped me out.

"Okay, everybody wait." I put my hands up, the stake

too, and looked directly at Johnny. "You have to explain this word to me right now."

He hesitated, and it was the doctor who said, "Latin *lustro,* 'purify.' The nominative singular feminine form would be *lustrate.* The ancient Romans had the *lustrum,* a purification of the people . . ."

"Getting close, Doc," Johnny said. "More precisely, in this case it's a woman who cleanses by sacrifice, as in purifying the vampire body by sacrificing it."

"You mean vampire assassin?" I said flatly. "Thanks, but the regular English words will work for me. I don't need to candy-coat things with archaic Latin terms. Besides, my conscience won't be tricked into thinking it's okay." When I finished, Johnny and Nana shared a telling glance. I didn't like it.

She said, "Not 'a' Lustrata, Persephone. 'The' Lustrata. It's not a candy-coated term; it is a *title.*"

"Oh, you guys are so full of shit," Vivian said. "She can*not* be the Lustrata."

Nana flipped the gag back into Vivian's mouth.

Everybody knew what we were talking about but me. "More information, please!" The note of panic in my voice bugged me, but I was sure it was only there because of the lack of sleep and fading adrenaline. I hadn't gotten much coffee either.

Johnny let his crossed arms drop, and he stopped leaning on the counter. "I wrote a song about her. The lyrics are:

A pure-blood witch, a caster of spells
An element master and ringer of bells.

As impurity rises from under the world
The dead above ground, diseases unfurled.
Call upon her, upon the witch of old,
Delivering justice, voicing truths untold,
Fauna and flora's mighty daughter
The Purifier! The Lustrata!"

Hearing Johnny saying the words, sincere as any poet reciting his own work, was beautiful. It touched me. But . . . "So, *the* Lustrata is some kind of glorified vampire killer?"

"There are legends . . . aren't there always?" Nana said quietly, the croak of her voice softer than usual. "Legends about the beginning of time, the ending of it. Every culture, every religion has their stories about it—ours is no different. And there are always secret societies, keepers of knowledge hidden from the general populace. There are enemies. There are heroes. The pendulum of power swings." Her focus sharpened on me, and I felt it like a cold blade at my throat. Nana stubbed out her cigarette in the ashtray. "She who can maintain the balance despite the swinging is the Lustrata."

I didn't know what to say. I felt buried under all the responsibility I already had: a live-in Nana, a growing puppy, a terribly injured friend, a grieving little girl, and a newspaper column with a weekly deadline. Add maintaining the balance of the world, and whose knees *wouldn't* be knocking? It seemed an alarm went off in my head, one more substantial than the triggered wards had been.

"Dr. Lincoln!" Celia cried from the top of the stairs. "The EKG monitor's alarming!"

CHAPTER SEVENTEEN

It had not been an alarm in my head warning about the news I'd just been given, but a real warning that Theo's life was in danger. The doctor scooped up his bag and hurried off before Celia had finished shouting. Johnny followed him. My focus stayed on Nana, but the question in my eyes changed. She understood, but said, "No. You need time to prepare to do this spell."

"Then let's do it! What do we need?"

"Persephone, this isn't elementary witchcraft; it's *sorcery.*"

I fled from her, angry that there was nothing I could do to help Theo right then. I took the steps two at a time. I had to do *something.* Standing in the doorway, I scoped out the scene.

Theo was wheezing and sweating, and her skin looked ashen. The doc was listening to her chest with his stethoscope. It seemed so rudimentary what he was doing, so *passive.* My panic rose. I wanted him to act, since I could not. "What's happening?" I demanded.

"Pulmonary embolism," he said calmly, "if I had to

guess." He dug into his bag, pulled a hard-shell case out, opened it, removed a vial, and started prepping a syringe.

"What does that mean? What are you doing?"

"She must have had a thrombus—a blood clot—because of her fractured leg or pelvis. It's come loose and hit her lung." He pushed the syringe into the IV. "This should break it up."

"Should?"

Celia wrung her hands and shifted her weight over and over. Behind her, Beverley stood stock-still, face pale, staring at Theo as tears flooded silently down her cheeks.

"Beverley," I said, maneuvering myself behind her and guiding her with firm hands on her shoulders. "This way."

In the hall, I turned her toward the room we were to share and shut the door behind us. She took a few steps more after I released her shoulders. With hardly any sound at all she said, "She's going to die, isn't she?"

"I don't know," I said. "We're doing everything we can for her."

Goliath had done all this, caused so much pain. How did Beverley know him? I wanted to ask, but this wasn't the right time. "You better get some sleep." It sounded stupid: *Someone in the next room is dying, but you just shut your eyes and sleep. Dream something nice while you're at it.* I couldn't be that condescending to Beverley. "I'm sorry. I know this isn't a time for sleep. I just . . . I don't know."

Beverley sat beside her box and started pushing things around inside of it. "Why do you think Goliath hurt Theo?"

"On the trip from the hospital, Theo woke up enough

to tell me he ran her off the road. Vivian claims he killed your mom too."

She stiffened. "No. He wouldn't do that. None of that."

"Theo saw him, Beverley. She identified him."

"He wouldn't do that!"

I sat in the middle of the room. Maybe now *was* as good a time as any. "How do you know him?"

She turned away and pulled a pair of sweatpants and a sweatshirt out of the box. "He was dating my mom."

It was a good thing she wasn't looking at me. I winced hard enough to give myself whiplash. "What?" I just barely managed not to sound as stunned as I felt.

"Whenever he came to the apartment, he was always nice to me. He actually talked to me like I mattered. Always brought me something too. Not like he was trying to buy me off or anything like that, but like he was thoughtful."

Every fiber of me said that was impossible, but at the same time, I didn't think Beverley would lie.

"He told me once he loved my mom and asked me if I was okay with that. Only a guy who really cares about a woman would bother to ask her kid something like that. He wouldn't have killed her. I know it. I don't believe that he and Vivian were lovers either. I like your nana, but she's got to be wrong about that. Vivian is so mean, and she's just saying mean things."

"I don't understand so much of this, Beverley." We sat in silence for a few minutes.

"I'm going to change into these." Beverley moved for the door.

"I'll step out," I said. I didn't want her to go to the bathroom to change, it'd mean she would have to walk past the room where Theo was.

"Okay. But don't leave."

"I won't."

In the hall, I heard Celia say, "Blood pressure's still dropping!"

Dr. Lincoln responded tersely, "I know!"

My eyes squeezed shut and I whispered another prayer. Finally, the door opened and Beverley said, "I'm done."

I stepped back into the room with her. She now wore the sweat suit as pajamas, and she sank down onto her inflatable mattress with pink flannel sheets and a quilt. The stuffed animal, still wearing her mother's shirt, was lying on her pillow.

"Did he come over a lot?" *Don't think about Theo. Don't fall apart in front of Beverley.*

She shrugged. "About once a week, I think. But he might have come over more after my bedtime."

"What kinds of things did he bring you?"

"Goliath always brought Mom flowers, and he always brought me a little bouquet of colored daisies or tiger lilies for my room. He gave me some books, helped me with homework, and played video games with me. Once he brought me a glass figurine of a unicorn with gold etched into the spiral of the horn. He always had a goofy joke to tell me, and he even gave me an iPod already loaded with a bunch of neat music and super-good earbuds, but that was just to—" She stopped and bit her lip.

I just couldn't picture Goliath, or any vampire, being so considerate of a human's needs and wants. Theo had identified him as the one that had run her off the road; to me, that only reinforced his guilt in Lorrie's murder. "Just to what?"

Beverley blushed. "To keep me from hearing them. But I took the earbuds out sometimes and listened to them. See, he couldn't be Vivian's lover, 'cause he was my mom's lover. He made her so happy. She said she couldn't date human men anymore because she'd hurt them, but she didn't have to worry about hurting Goliath. He wouldn't have killed her. I know it!" She grabbed the stuffed cat and pushed her face into her mother's shirt. Her shoulders jumped as she cried.

I reached out and rubbed her back, fighting the urge to rush down and question Vivian again, but she wasn't going anywhere, so I had time for that later. Vivian had said Lorrie had been killed as a warning from some out-of-control Council enforcement agent. But Goliath was a vampire, not an Elder, and the idea that he worked for anyone besides Menessos was ludicrous. Would Menessos have sent Goliath as a favor for some Elder? What would a vampire want from an Elder? Maybe he was trying to get Vivian on the Council despite her stained status. Maybe the Council was politically in bed with the vampires more than I wanted to believe.

There was another possibility—well, okay, there were probably lots of other possibilities, but this one was bright on my radar. What if Beverley was right and Goliath *hadn't* killed Lorrie? I had taken Vivian's word as proof. Now I knew her word was worthless.

But if Goliath wasn't the murderer, then who was? I didn't even know where to start if I needed other suspects.

What if Vivian had just used this awful situation to her advantage because she could? Because I was that naive?

"Persephone?"

I realized I'd stopped rubbing Beverley's back. She'd stopped crying, at least.

"Sorry. I'm trying to figure this all out." I stood. "It's so . . . frustrating."

"Promise me you'll tell me everything you find out."

"I promise. I won't hide anything from you." At the door, I reached for the light.

"Leave it on. Please."

Theo's heart monitor showed a fast but regular rhythm. Dr. Lincoln and Johnny were talking in hushed tones, but stopped when I stepped into the room. Nana was coming up the stairs and followed me in. Celia sat on the edge of the bed holding Theo's hand. "What do we know?" I asked.

"She had a blood clot; it's common with leg or pelvis injuries. She 'threw' it; it hit her lung. We need an ambulance to get her to the State Shelter where they can perform the emergency surgery she needs."

"No," Johnny said. "They have a spell." He gestured at Nana and me.

"How soon can you do this forced-change ritual?" the doctor asked.

I glanced at Nana. She went to the window seat, leaned and looked up, then stepped back and looked out through the skylights, positioned herself by Theo's bed, calculating. "About twenty hours from now, the waning moon will be shining through those skylights again. Or we could move her to where the rising moon shines on her."

"No. Don't move her." Dr. Lincoln pursed his lips, and his fingers twitched as he figured in his head. "Look, you have to understand. Without proper radiological testing—" He stopped himself, obviously remembering his audience wasn't savvy with medical terms. "Without an X-ray or scan, I can't begin to guess the size of the clot. I can guess at the location because I can hear the obstruction, but . . ." He took a deep breath, then said, "Best case: this thing breaks up on its own in the next few hours, but I know for a fact the chances of that are slim."

"How can you be so sure that's a fact?" Johnny pressed.

"A pulmonary embolism killed my wife." His tone was bitter. "The right ventricle of the heart pumps blood to the lungs to get oxygen, and with the clot there, the ventricle will start to fail as it tries to push blood past the blockage. This kind of scenario has a ninety percent mortality rate. Or she could keep throwing clots." He rubbed his brow.

Johnny took the doc's biceps in his hand and stared down at him. "What can you do to give her twenty hours?"

The doc considered it. "She needs surgery, but I can't perform it. Short of that, she needs oxygen. I have tanks, and I think the nasal cannula for a large dog will work for her." He looked at me. "I'll stay here and try to buy her a day."

"But should we wait," I asked, "until she's a little stronger?"

"She's not going to get any stronger."

Johnny released the doc and took me by the shoulders. "Either she makes it or she dies trying, Red. She'd risk it, and you know it. All or nothing—that's how Theo has lived her life." He released me. "And that's how she'd want to die."

I looked at Theo's face, my eyes burning. "I don't know if—"

"You have to try," he whispered. "She'll die for sure if you don't."

Did we have what it took to turn away death?

I woke around ten, but I didn't feel rested. That sucked, because there was so much work to do.

Downstairs, Dr. Lincoln snored loudly in my cozy chair, and Johnny lay stretched over the ends of my couch. Vivian's chair had been moved to the living room and lowered to its side; one of my worn tan pillows was under her head. She smelled vaguely of valerian. I'd told Johnny about the bottle, and he'd spritzed her with it.

Nana was sitting in the kitchen studying the Codex. A cigarette rested in an ashtray beside her, and the whole of it was one continuous piece of ash. She'd found something so interesting that she'd forgotten the Marlboro.

The aroma of coffee enticed me immediately. As I fixed a bowl of microwave oatmeal, I saw the valerian bottle sitting by the stove. I opened a drawer, took out a marker, and wrote *40 Winks* on the bottle. Didn't want anyone drinking that. With my favorite coffee mug (with Waterhouse's "Lady of Shalott" on it) and my oatmeal, I sat across from Nana. "Find something interesting?"

Nana reached for her cigarette and swore when she saw

it was wasted. "Did I find something interesting," she repeated slowly, sitting back in her chair in a way that said she was stiff from hours hovering over the book. I don't think she'd returned to bed. "You don't appreciate what this book is," she added angrily. Her leg had started bouncing in irritation; I guessed it was an action I was genetically engineered to copy.

She hadn't slept and she was grumpy, so I made an extra effort to stay calm. "I don't *understand* what it is. Explain it to me."

Nana put her hands on the pages reverently. "In layman's terms, this book is, to witches, the equivalent of the Holy Grail or the Cauldron of Annwfn." She overpronounced the funnily-spelled Celtic word: *An-OO-ven.*

Okay, that impressed me. *That* I understood; I mean, Arthur and his men had sought the powerful pearl-edged cauldron, and he had considered the Grail one of the holiest of holy relics. "But I've never heard of the Trivium Codex." Or the Lustrata, for that matter.

"That's my fault, I suppose."

"I didn't say that."

"No. I mean it. I never told you our legends and fables, witches' lore."

"Why not?"

She sighed heavily, and I could feel her anger dispersing with the sigh. "That was your mother's job." She put her hand on mine. Nana wasn't a touchy-feely kind of person. Not that she never hugged me; she did. She'd just never been overly physical with her affections. So the simple gesture meant a lot. "I did the best I could by you, y'know."

"I know, Nana." But I hadn't known she resented my mother's leaving as much as I did.

"If I'd known . . . if I'd seen then what you could become, I'd have prepared you better." She pulled away and carefully took another cigarette out of her case.

"I'm not sure I believe this whole Lustrata thing anyway."

She stared at me as she lit the cigarette. The angry bounce of her leg had returned. "I can only take so much guilt, you know." She blew smoke at the ceiling. "If I'd told you the stories, you'd be proud to step into the role, but as it is—you're blind." She paused. "The Elders Council will never believe it. The Codex and the Lustrata in the same day."

At the mention of the Council, my appetite disappeared. "You haven't called anyone, have you?"

"Not yet."

"Don't." I stood and took my bowl to the sink.

"But Seph—"

"Don't, Nana. I mean it. Just don't. Swear to me."

"But why not?"

"The last thing I need right now is more people staring at me like I just sprouted tentacles and they're not sure if they should be fascinated or horrified. And Vivian indicated that there were less-than-honest members among the Elders, that they were involved in Lorrie's murder. I don't need to blatantly identify myself to them."

"I don't believe a word she says."

"Just keep it to yourself. All right?" Without waiting for an answer, I walked away. I might have felt better if Nana had at least scolded me for accepting the contract on

Goliath. Did being the Lustrata nullify the need for guilt? If so, that was proof that I wasn't the Lustrata. And if not, then the Lustrata must learn not to feel anything. *If that's the case, count me out.*

Nana followed me. "What is wrong with you?"

"I feel like I'm playing some nightmarish game of tag. Everyone keeps telling me I'm *it* and nothing can undo the fact. I don't want to be it. Being it scares me." As a kid, playing that game, I'd always hated being it. When running after the others and trying to tag them, I always felt like we were running from some monster and I was in the back, the first one the monster was going to get.

"Why does that scare you?"

"I don't know." It sounded weak because I did know: I didn't want the responsibility. "Even in my ignorance, I know there's a lot that comes with that title." I shouldn't have said it—I mean, on some level I knew what saying it would lead to—but my totems had me in the habit of being honest.

"Like what?"

"Like responsibility. I don't know if I'm ready for—"

Nana interrupted me with abrupt laughter. "If you were voted the class clown, it would be because you already were the clown. This is no different, Persephone. You already were you. You already took justice into your own hands with Lorrie's stalker and were prepared to do it again to avenge her. You know that if you do something once, it's a mistake, but do it twice and it's either a habit—" She took another drag from the cigarette.

I rolled my eyes. I really hated that old saying.

"—or a vocation," she finished.

My head shook back and forth.

"Why are you doubting yourself now? You agreed to the contract. You—"

"I screwed up! Theo may die because of it!"

"You have already taken on the responsibility for that mistake, and you have learned from it. I'm confident you'll perform the ritual accurately and save her."

That stunned me. "Me? But I thought you would lead and I would support you—" I stopped when she smiled.

Johnny had told me this, had said I had to do it. I'd thought he meant "you have to do it" as in "you witches have to perform the ritual." But they all expected me to run the circle, and it had been obvious to everyone *but* me until just now.

CHAPTER EIGHTEEN

I sat with Theo while Johnny made some breakfast for himself. While I waited, I changed out of my pajamas and ripped robe into a button-up linen vest that had a trim-but-comfortable fit and old jeans. I combed out my hair, put it up, let it back down, put it back up with a different clip. Aggravated, I took the clip out again. What was I thinking? I never messed with my hair, and here I was messing with my hair, because Johnny was going to be back in a few minutes.

Dr. Lincoln came in first, though. "I was wondering about Vivian. I heard the others talking about your kennels in the cellar. Should we put her in one of those or something?"

"No," I said flatly.

"But she's been in that chair for how long? And, well . . ."

"I appreciate your concern, but I don't trust her. She's a witch, and she's marked by a vampire. She might be able to chant the locks open, maybe even bend the bars. I want her in the middle of things so she can be observed, to be sure she's not doing anything we don't want her doing.

And if she's uncomfortable, I'm sure I can show her my baseball bat and explain that she'll be even more uncomfortable with broken bones."

"Okay then," he said, mollified, and left.

I began studying Nana's translation of the ritual, but I didn't get far. Beverley awoke and pelted me with a dozen questions. After I'd given her a rundown on what she'd missed, which wasn't much, she went downstairs to get some breakfast. I turned back to the pages but before I could read more than two words, Johnny walked in with a heaping bowl of Lucky Charms. It wasn't even in a cereal bowl, but a small mixing bowl. "Hungry?" I asked.

He smiled, crunching. "Second bowl," he said.

"I hope you bought a case of that stuff." I smoothed a hand over my hair. If I'd gotten up earlier, I could have showered and washed it by now. I could have done that much. "You did leave some for Beverley, didn't you?"

"Of course. How are you this morning?"

"Tired. Confused. Worried."

He grinned. "Oh, good, so all's normal."

I grinned back. "You?"

"I'm having breakfast with you—well, in your company, anyway. I couldn't be better." He munched another bite, saw my spell notes. "You're absolutely certain this is safe?"

"According to these notes and Nana, it all makes sense, so I want to say yes, but truthfully, I've never done anything on this scale before." I stood and handed him the papers to look at.

"Why is Nana translating this into English?"

"Because I don't know much Latin." Just as she'd

neglected to teach me witchcraft lore, Nana had been lax when it came to my instruction in ancient languages. "It's important that I understand each nuance of the spell and be comfortable with every word."

Johnny's look still held questions.

"Nana's a careful translator; she'll get it right." I went to Theo's bedside. "If it's any consolation, what we're doing is more like sorcery and less like witchcraft."

"And the difference is . . . ?"

"I'm sure the council members have a high-blown and wordy technical answer for that, but in less archaic terms, think of witchcraft as the sand on the beach."

"I like this analogy already," he said, letting his voice deepen.

I didn't scold him. I went on: "The sand touches the sea and the air and stretches along the coast and inland to the soil. Witchcraft is like that: it receives the waves of power—the gods and goddesses of the various pantheons—and touches the energy of nature, influences it, to shape witches' will through rituals and spells. But sorcery digs through witchcraft, burrowing deep into places you cannot see to find the treasure—the power—below the surface. It consumes that power, directly creating an immediate change, not just influencing a future one."

"Witchcraft is sand. Sorcery is buried treasure. Got it." He turned up the bowl and drank some of the milk.

I laughed softly. "Male oversimplification strikes again."

He lowered the bowl and wiped his mouth. "*X* marks the spot." He scanned over the page. "So what do the rest of us have to do during the ritual?"

"Decide if you want to witness it or stay the hell away, I guess."

"What about Beverley?"

"If we're successful, Theo will *change.* I'd rather Beverley didn't see that. Not yet, anyway. Lorrie wanted to shelter her from the visual until she was a little older. We should honor her wishes."

He held another bite ready and I noticed he was not using a regular spoon, but one of my big serving spoons. "Yeah. She *is* a bit young to see something that gruesome, I guess." He took the bite, munched happily.

His phone rang and he mouthed the word "Lycanthropia." I knew it was band business. I took the papers back from Johnny and strolled to the window and read them over again while he talked.

The rite was more intricate and involved than anything I'd ever done before. That alone didn't intimidate me—all rituals follow a logical sequence, and this was just like doing everything I usually did, just fancier and with more flair. But this spell called for a full-scale ceremony with visualization and chanting and the searing ley-line energy. That did intimidate me. I absolutely *had* to focus and get this spell right the first time. In the next few hours, I had to memorize it and rehearse it in my mind. I had to see it perfectly in my mind over and over, the way athletes visualize themselves making all the right moves of their sport.

The life of a friend was on the line. If I didn't act, she'd die. So I was going to take action. My doubt was about the level of energy I'd be drawing from the ley. What if I couldn't maintain my focus? How would I know what *enough* was? If it wasn't enough for a full transformation, we'd have to put her down. Having to actively take her life like that would be so much worse than watching her life slipping from her.

Johnny closed his cell phone. "Sorry about that, Red."

"Don't worry. I still can't believe you get a signal out here."

"Aw, my magnetic personality just pulls the signal in."

"And I expected you to brag about having your own relay tower."

"Oooo. That's a good one."

I got up and headed for the door. "Hey, by the way, thanks."

"For what?"

"For believing in me." He gave me the guy-nod that men make at other men. I started out, then stopped. "Wait. You never told me what beholders are."

"Oh. They're vamp wannabes who've made it to the next level. They're marked humans, lackeys who think they're gonna earn the kiss. They're usually tough and athletic, and the vamps use them as spies. As far as I know, they use beholders hard—like they say about racehorses, 'ridden hard and put away wet.' Vamps don't seem to feel the same allegiance to the beholders—who are doing everything they can to prove themselves worthy—as they feel to the beautiful offerlings."

"Offerlings?" I was learning a lot about vampires.

"The ones who have been approached by the vamps because of their looks or their intelligence. It's supposed to be a huge honor to be sought by the vamp elite. Offerlings get marked twice at the start and, even if their mark is only days old, they have more authority than a beholder with a decade of faithful service."

"Bet that goes over real well with the beholders." My sarcasm won me a smile.

"The beholders usually end up killed in the line of service. It's rare for a beholder to be turned, as I understand it."

"Their chosen ones are offerlings, and their spies and muscle are beholders. How perfectly beatific."

"Of course. They can't be called something mundane."

Pompous vampires wouldn't name something using ordinary words. But, according to Beverley, Goliath wasn't a conceited snot. That whole haughty vampire persona couldn't be a PR scam like the fairies glamouring up wings and acting all benevolent, sweet, and giggly in public—could it? Was I putting more faith in vampirical stereotypes than in facts?

"Johnny." Gentle words weren't coming to me, so I just blurted it out straight. "This Lustrata thing. I don't want to play Atlas, with the world on my shoulders."

His satisfied expression dissipated as he sobered into a blankness that left only the stern and imposing Wedjat gaze. I felt small. "The world can't afford for you to think that way, Persephone."

"I think we should do something in addition to the wards, to increase the protection of the house," I said.

Nana looked up from the Codex. "I'm already working on that," she said as she patted her Book of Shadows and the Codex simultaneously.

"But I can help."

"You should take a nap or go for a walk and get some air. Or meditate or something, to get away from here for a bit. The distance will give you clarity." Nana was formidable in her spell-work, and her expression warned against any thought of further questioning.

Duly rejected, I chose to go out on the porch for some air. The crisp wind felt good. I wanted to walk, but with beholders on the loose, how did I dare to go for a carefree walk ever again? And I knew that my comfortable days of anonymous security from the likes of vampires were over. That hurt.

Could I ever leave Nana alone? I mean, she couldn't go into a nursing home ever again, even if her personality didn't cause problems. She'd be exposed there, open to harm. And Beverley. Poor Beverley. She knew Goliath! Knew a softer side, it seemed. Or an act. How could a killer of his nature even care about a woman like Lorrie and her daughter?

How could I get distance and clarity when my worries never rested?

I stepped off the front porch, determined not to be a prisoner inside my saltbox. I strode purposely around the house taking long, slow paces and studying the fields. Middle of nowhere. Just as well. In the middle of society, neighbors would turn away, shut their eyes, and lock their doors. At least out here I didn't have a false sense of security. Everyone who would come to my aid was already here and seemed to put some value in my honesty, even if it had come late.

By the time I arrived at the cellar, it seemed like an

inviting distraction. Throwing back the door, I stepped down and in as if I had a purpose.

It smelled like cold darkness should smell: empty and damp. Winter smelled like this, when wet snow lay like white blankets on the resting world. The last two years of my life had been a winter. The surface was an organized routine building up buffering white layers, while below dormant issues, emotions, and thoughts waited. Ironically, just as winter was settling in on the geographical world where I lived, the thawing of my frozen life had unavoidably come. Myriad roots within me stirred, stretched. The complications piling up were all the sprouts.

One word echoed in my head: *Lustrata.*

There, beyond the golden beam of light from the open doors, I stepped into Johnny's regular cage. The hay crunched under my shoes, and it gave a grassy hint of spring to the otherwise wintry cellar. I wanted more of that fresh growth, to think about the earth and not myself. I lay down in the hay, breathed deeply of the aroma, and closed my eyes.

"Red?"

I opened my eyes. The beam had stretched with the setting sun and was shining drowsy warmth on me. Presently a shadow fell across the light from the doorway, leaving me cold without the beam. "Red?"

I sat up. "Here."

Johnny came down the steps and stopped at the door to his cage. "Demeter's looking for you." His silhouette was all I could see. He was so tall and lanky. Nana would have said he was cut like a clothespin. Dust floated in the beam around him, creating the illusion of something magical about him. Magical, yet dark, his expression hidden, his face shrouded by strong backlighting. "Red?"

I realized I was staring. "Yeah." I stood up, brushed hay from my backside. I headed toward him. "Sorry. Did Nana get scared?"

He didn't make the polite step to get out of my way. He stood rooted in that spot, facing me. This close, I could see his expression now. He said, "*I* got scared."

I couldn't believe he'd just admitted that. Weren't there strict rules against that in the guy-code rule book? "Johnny. I'm sorry. I didn't mean to disappear."

I waited for him to say something lewd, but he didn't, and the silence thickened, woolen and warm, getting heavier and heavier as if a flood were rising around me, weighting me down and threatening to drown me. Suddenly, he grabbed my arms and pulled me close. For an instant he hesitated; then he kissed me.

I didn't fight against it, but I wasn't prepared for it either. My back stiffened defensively. I'm just not the kind of girl to collapse into a sudden kiss. Did that mean I'd never make a good Guinevere?

Johnny must've read the worst into my body language, because his lips went absent just as I thought to wonder how they tasted. "Forgive me," he whispered.

He had taken my reaction as rejection, but I hadn't pushed him away. It had just happened so fast. I wasn't keeping up. His grip loosened, and he started to release me.

"No," I said, my hands grappling for a hold, one coming up with his shirt, the other clinging to his side. He stilled under my touch. "Forgive *me,*" I whispered, a bit breathless. I swallowed down my fear and said, "Once more?" *Please.*

"No," he said softly, eyes glinting. "It's a hundred kisses, or none."

How could I deny that low, confident yet needful tone? "A hundred it is."

He leaned down and, this time, I was ready. I wanted his kiss. I wanted to know the taste of him. I shut my eyes.

Just before our lips met, he paused and hovered there as if these seconds could last an eternity. Desire mounted in me; anticipation filled every nerve. I inhaled deeply, taking the cedar and sage scent of him into me as if I could pull him that fraction more, so his lips would meet mine.

But it was his will holding him there, for whatever reason.

I opened my eyes. He gave a quick, lopsided grin; then he gave in.

His lips were soft, yet firm, as they pressed to mine. I trembled, and his arms encircled me. Heat brimmed within me. My eyes had shut again, and I thought of the motorcycle ride, of swaying to the hum of the engine. But this, this was face-to-face, this was our bodies pressed together—Goddess, I held him tight—and the roaring music was my heart pounding in my ears.

His arms were so strong around my waist and when he broke the kiss he didn't loosen his hold. We stood, foreheads pressed together, catching our breath. "That's one," he said. "Ninety-nine to go."

"And when those ninety-nine are all gone?"

He straightened. "Then I'm going to ask you for the promise of another hundred."

The look I gave him was teasingly skeptical, but he became serious. "Don't you know that I would give my life to protect yours?" he asked. His warm hands left my waist to take my wrists and pull my palms to his face. "To protect the Lustrata." He kissed each palm in turn. "I've looked for you for so long."

Looked for me?

"The first time I saw you, I knew." He squeezed my hands. "I felt it. And I knew in time, you would know it too." He caressed my cheek. "I'm not wrong."

Even if I didn't believe it, he did. The convinced fierceness in his eyes wasn't scary at all.

"Johnny? Did you find her?" Nana's voice trickled in from outside.

We both turned as she stepped into view atop the cellar steps.

"Yeah. I found her," he said.

Nana put her hands on her hips and scowled at us, but it wasn't a very convincing scowl.

CHAPTER NINETEEN

For further protection, Nana placed empowered sage in each window, with a sprinkling of salt on the sills. She even had Johnny hammer two nails into the wall above my front door and then wired my broom to the nails. For my part, I moved Vivian's *40 Winks* bottle and my baseball bat to the corner closest to the front door.

Beverley wanted to sit with Theo, so she was taking my turn for a while. This was a good thing, because I was too anxious to sit still. I showered and debated over what to wear for the ritual. I sifted through my closet for several minutes, searching. My first thought was to dress formally, to show respect for the religious ceremony I was about to lead. The more the thought rolled around inside my head, however, I realized that would be furthering a witchy stereotype. So, since I didn't have any flowing and billowing gowns or hooded capes, and since I didn't need to impress the attendees with such things anyway, I chose clothing that would simply be comfortable: faded old jeans, sneakers, and, for fun, a girly black T-shirt with the Superman symbol on it in blood red. If they wanted to think of me as the Lustrata, then I could wear a hero's pentagonal symbol to the ritual.

Still filled with nervous energy, I decided to run the sweeper. The floor didn't need it, but I had to do *something.* That's what I was doing when the sun slipped under the horizon. I felt it go, felt its protection leave me, felt the threat of vampires waking up. My imagination, to be sure, but my stress level rose again nonetheless.

After putting the sweeper away, wiping out the sink in the bathroom, and making sure there were clean towels, I was going to check on Theo when, from the living room, I heard Celia ask Nana, "Demeter, would you tell me about the author of that book? I'm curious about her story and the wære she loved."

There was a pause; then I heard Nana say, "Come. Sit." I couldn't see her expression, but it didn't sound like she was being derogatory. I sat on the top step and listened.

"This story is in this book along with the spells, but I learned it long ago. . . . At the dawn of civilization, in Uruk, one of the most ancient of cities, the high priestess Una performed her sacred duties with great devotion and was favored by the goddess Ishtar."

Nana was obviously reciting from memory more than telling the story in her own words.

"One day a foreign magician, Ezreniel, came to Uruk. He served a god previously unknown to its people. A man of great physical stature, strong of eye and voice, he came to the high priestess and she looked upon him with pleasure.

"But Ezreniel insisted the strange and solitary god he worshipped was the only god and that Una must forsake her goddess and all gods. It was customary to honor the gods of other lands, but to insist she reject her own was beyond toleration.

"Una refused to allow Ezreniel further access to her person.

"Ezreniel, however, was not so easily deterred. He bribed his way into the temple where Una lived and served. There, in secret, he watched her. Like his god, he was of an intemperate and jealous nature. He was angered that Una looked upon other men with the favor he had been denied.

"One night when two priests, both her lovers, came to Una, Ezreniel could contain himself no longer. He burst into her chambers, where the three were engaged in full and intimate worship of Ishtar. Both men leapt to defend and protect Una, but they were no match for Ezreniel. One he beat back until the man lay broken and bloody on the floor, whimpering like a starving street mongrel. The other he held in his crushing grasp. Unable to wrench his arms free, the man bit at Ezreniel's neck, drawing blood before he, too, was cast aside, limp and unconscious.

"Una came to the aid of her lovers as they battled and, with a desperate prayer to Ishtar, she plunged a dagger deep into Ezreniel's chest.

"For an instant he stilled. Then he looked at his hands—covered with the blood of both men—and laughed. Stunned, unable to move, Una watched as he pulled the dagger from his chest and, wiping it across his palm, cleaned his own blood from its blade. Rubbing his hands together, he mixed the three bloods together, chanting in his foreign tongue.

"He flung his right hand outward at the first man, splattering the red fluid on his brow, saying, 'I curse thee by the sun.' He thrust his left hand at the second man. Drops of blood splashed across the man's chest. 'I curse thee by the moon.' He turned to Una, lurched forward, and grabbed her face in his hands. 'And I curse thee for loving them both and thereby sealing your doom.'

"Ezreniel then collapsed, smearing blood down Una's face and naked body, saying, 'The curse of three, sealed by me, by my blood and by my death. The curse of three, sealed by me, the reward of my last breath.'

"In that moment, as the curse was realized, lightning struck the temple, shattering it into falling shards of mud-brick. And although none could know at the time, the fate of the world changed. Ezreniel's god would gain power and wield it. Ishtar, her temple in ruins and her beloved priestess—"

"There's a group pulling into the drive," Erik interrupted. I hadn't known he was listening too but as I moved down the steps, I realized he had been standing near the opening to the dining room and had a clear view out the front window.

I hurried to the front door and saw an entourage flowing into my driveway. A limousine that—despite the fading light—I'd have guessed to be silver, escorted by four motorcycles, two each at the front and the rear. The motorcyclists cut their engines and put down kickstands, but none removed their helmets or got off their bikes. The limousine's far rear door opened, and Goliath slid out. His pale hair shimmered; he shot a look toward the house and grinned. The driver, in a neat black suit and cap, jumped out and hurried back to open the door on the near side of the limo. The man who emerged very literally stole my breath.

Longish wavy hair, the color of shelled walnuts, fell around his square face with careless perfection. His beard, trimmed thin on the sides, accented every angle, and he wore it a bit thicker on his pointed chin to balance the squareness of his jaw. A narrow nose above thin lips added to the austere quality of his face. Broad shoulders and a tailored suit enhanced his lean, masculine image.

I was speechless as he approached. But for the modern clothes, he was my Arthur, exactly as I had dreamed him for all the years I'd been enthralled with Camelot.

Closer now, I could see that his eyes—stern and gray like cold, cold steel—were eyes that had seen more horror than happiness. His shirt, open to the fourth button, showed the curve of a muscular chest. As my attention returned to his extraordinary face, I realized he'd seen me counting the open buttonholes. It seemed to please him.

"Persephone Alcmedi." I expected his voice to have an [illegible] when he spoke, but he said my name without any telltale inflections. He even got the pronunciation right.

"Menessos." Saying his name forced me to remember he was a vampire, not Arthur.

He made a show of appraising the area. "What a . . . rural . . . place you have here." I wasn't certain if he was insulting the simplicity of my location and my unpaved driveway or if he was just pointing out that there was no one around for miles to hear our screaming.

I smiled agreeably. "My little piece of the planet."

With his posture and stance set for intimidating perfection, he said, "You will surrender Vivian Diamond, the book, and the weapon. Do not make yourself a part of our quarrels. Relinquish them now and I give you my solemn word, I will leave you in peace."

How much was the word of a vampire worth? Less than any other hustler's word, as far as I was concerned. My expression didn't feel as hard as I wanted it to be, and I glanced away as I changed it. Goliath, who'd obviously seen me ogling his master, was smirking at me. "I absolutely do not want to interfere in your quarrel—" I began.

"I hear a 'but' coming." Goliath snickered.

"But"—I glared at him—"I need the book." I didn't want to call it the Codex. It might make a difference if he knew that I knew what it was. "At least temporarily."

Menessos sauntered forward until he was only a few feet away, just beyond my porch rail and at the edge of my ward. His expression said clearly that he found my refusal as utterly predictable as Goliath did. "That book does not belong to you."

"I know. And I *will* give it to you, but first I have to undo the damage Goliath caused my friend."

Menessos squinted. "What do you mean?"

There was no reason I could see not to tell him, so I did. "I'm going to perform a ritual from the book to save her life."

He cocked an eyebrow. "Which ritual?"

"Enhancing moonlight with elemental energy. A complete transformation is the only thing that can save Theo's life right now. She won't last until the full moon."

He considered it. "I know this ritual . . . are you witch enough to succeed?"

Convincing him was a basic safety requirement, like a hard hat at a construction site, but his challenge to my witchhood was a blow that sent my metaphorical hard hat rolling. *Am I witch enough?*

Smart-ass comebacks came to me easily, but telling others what I truly thought of *myself*—and that was what Menessos was really asking—was much harder. Maybe I didn't think that much of myself. Maybe that was why the whole Lustrata thing made me uneasy.

I hoped Menessos didn't see the frailty I suddenly felt. I mustered the sound of confidence and firmly said, "We're going to find out."

Luckily, that seemed to satisfy him. "I will take you at your word, Persephone. I think we can wait to claim the book in a peaceful manner when you are through."

"We can't start until at least three-thirty A.M., when the moon shines through the skylights of her room. We can't risk moving her."

He checked his watch and then the sky. I noted his profile. "I've heard much about—" He was assessing me and stopped, his eyes lingering on the Superman symbol on my chest. Or maybe he was just staring at my chest because I'd stared at his. He shifted. "You. We will wait, because it is a rare thing for a person to astonish me," Menessos said. "Very rare."

"And anyone who does finds themselves on the endangered list, right?"

"Yes," he answered, expression flat. "But you possess

a unique potential. You could leap onto my short list of allies."

I smiled. "Not sure I want to be in that kind of company."

He smiled too, a smile as without mirth as my own.

Goliath, who stood flanking his master, glared past me to Johnny. "It's better than the company you currently keep," he snarled.

Johnny sneered. I didn't see it, but I knew it was there by the deep growl I heard. "At least my friends aren't limited to dark hours."

"Enough!" Menessos said, surging forward despite my wards and gripping the railing. I could feel the alarms prickling my skin, and my head throbbed like the siren was inside my skull. "Do not threaten me, witch," he spat. His eyes had gone black and pitiless like a shark's. "Waiting for you is a courtesy I extend because it amuses me that you would attempt to conduct a ritual from my book. But have no doubt that, should I change my mind—and you're teetering on the disrespectful edge of forcing me to action right now—I *will* come into your house despite your paltry wards, the presence of the stake, and your jumentous friends . . . and I *will* bring with me destruction such as you have never known."

I blinked stupidly. Eloquent intimidation has that effect on me.

"I'm hungry," Menessos muttered as he turned and walked away. "You!" he called to one of the motorcyclists. "What is your name? Vance, is it?"

One of the beholders stepped away from his bike and removed his helmet. "I'm Vinny."

"Vincent, then. Lower the collar of your jacket."

The beholder immediately exposed his neck. "How long's this pain gonna last?"

Menessos didn't answer, but took a position behind the man and prepared to do what vampires do.

Confused by the beholder's words, I turned away. "Back to the kitchen," I said, mostly to Beverley. "We don't need to see this."

CHAPTER TWENTY

"You're going to wear a rut in the floor," Nana said from the dinette table in the kitchen.

It was twelve-forty. Time was snailing by, and my nervous energy found an outlet in pacing the long hallway from the kitchen, past the steps, and to the front door and back. Moving not only kept me busy, but it kept my mind off my rumbling stomach. I had to fast until the ritual was over.

The vampires had retreated to the interior of the limo, but it remained idling in my drive. Dr. Lincoln—who had left, gotten some more sleep, checked some animal patients, and returned—was monitoring Theo, preparing to feed her through the tube in anticipation of her coming transformation. Johnny sat on my couch, calmly engrossed in something on the Food Channel. Beverley was dozing on the opposite end of the couch. Nana was just rousing from a nap.

Presently, Celia and Erik returned from giving Vivian a bathroom break. Celia, like the doc, had expressed concern for Vivian, so we switched out the soppy dishcloth gag for a fresh and dry bandanna. I even conceded to putting a pillow on the seat of her chair. I thought that was big of me, but Celia showed me the "burns" Vivian had on her wrists from the clothesline, so I added some padding and had the guys reposition her in the chair. As far as I was concerned, that was as comfortable as Vivian needed to get.

Wondering what it said about me that I was less appalled by Vivian's torturous restraints than the wæres were, I paced to the door and peered out at the limo.

Johnny rose from the couch and came to the doorway. "What is it?"

"If all goes well and Theo's transformed, then I *am* going to give Vivian over to the vampires."

"So?"

"So if the others are worried about her being uncomfortable here, they definitely won't like that."

I paced back to the kitchen. He followed. I said, "The way I figure it, she messed with them first. They'd have caught her eventually anyway."

"You're probably right."

My mouth opened, ready to say something else, but I suddenly felt . . . *something* . . . and stopped.

"Red?"

I didn't answer, trying to figure out what it was. Similar to the alarm in my head, it was something, but not a break-in or trespassing.

"What is it?" he asked again.

I glanced about the room. Everyone was here except the doc, Theo and—

"Beverley."

I ran down the hall. From the doorway, I saw that my

living room window was open. "No!" If the vampires had lured her out—

With Johnny at my heels, I flung open the door. In the dim light from the open car door, Beverley stood before Goliath, who leaned against the rear quarter panel of the limo.

I bolted without considering that I was leaving the safety of my home and its perimeter wards behind.

"Red!" Johnny called after me. He'd stopped on the edge of the porch. "Red!"

"Beverley!"

She faced me. If she had been bespelled, she wouldn't have been able to do that. "Seph, I have to know," she said as I neared and slowed.

Menessos slid from the seat, but left his door open. I stopped a few paces away, glad to hear Johnny coming up behind me. "Know what?"

Beverley turned back to Goliath. "Did you? Did you kill my mother?"

The vampire lowered himself to one knee before her and took her hands in his. It was such a gentle and humble and caring human gesture; I could hardly believe my eyes.

"Why would you think that?" he asked. He faced me, and I saw anger rising hot and swift. He stood, releasing her hands. "You told her this?"

Johnny caught up to us, and Erik was swiftly running to join us also. I stood firm. "Vivian claims that you are the murderer."

Goliath and Menessos exchanged a look. It wasn't an "oh-no-they-know" look. It was the "she's-such-a-bitch" look that had—in reference to Vivian—passed over the faces of everyone in my house at one time or another in the last twenty-four hours, so I recognized it well.

"Red?" Johnny prompted.

"That's why you were checking my background," Goliath snapped.

Before I could respond, Beverley blurted, "Vivian hired her to kill you."

Goliath laughed. "Hired you to get yourself killed."

Beverley grabbed his coat in both hands. "Did you kill my mother?" Her voice was taut, her eyes glistening with tears about to fall.

He turned back to her and again wrapped his hands over hers. "Of course not. I loved your mother. You know that."

Seeing Goliath being downright parental gave me a chill. Menessos stepped closer to me; Johnny and Erik countered, growling, but the vampire was unaffected by them. "You've been conned into the middle of a fight that isn't yours, Persephone," Menessos said. Though I was keeping my eyes from his, I knew he was staring at me, his expression one of someone admiring a painting or ancient vase. It creeped me out.

"I don't understand."

"Lorrie was killed for nothing more than petty jealousy." His tone was neutral. "Over Goliath. In order to shame Lorrie's memory with media coverage and hysteria and to further slur the wæres of the world, the killer left those symbols on the wall."

Of course they were going to point the finger elsewhere.

Then it hit me.

"Jealousy?" I repeated. All my blood dropped to the soles of my feet. "Then you know who killed Lorrie?" If the motive had been jealousy, it could only have been one person. It had been in front of me the whole time. *The newspaper said symbols were drawn on Lorrie's walls . . . but she said "occult symbols" at the coffee shop. She'd only know that if she drew them . . .*

"I do," he said. "She must have believed you would be able to surprise Goliath enough to distract him, and thereby injure him or get a fortunate shot," Menessos muttered.

"Never," Goliath affirmed with sinister quiet.

"But if she was jealous, why hire me to kill the one she was jealous over?"

"An offering," Goliath said, then added with disquieting calm: "She would send you to me as a make-up gift, and once I had had you, bled you, and knew why you had come, I would have to thank her."

I wasn't buying that. She'd spent too much money and [illegible]-hungry

Beverley said, "Who did it? Who?" She left Goliath and grabbed Menessos's arm. "Who?"

"Can you prove it?" I asked. I didn't want to be duped twice, even if their claim and my recollection made it logical.

"I do not have to," Menessos said.

I squared my shoulders and met his gaze. "Yes, you do."

He smiled smugly. "Ask her. Confront her. She will not deny it. She's too proud of her work to not claim the credit for it once the ruse is revealed."

"Who?" Beverley pleaded and tugged at his arm.

Menessos faced her after a mildly distasteful glance at her hand on his arm. "Vivian. Vivian murdered your mother, child."

Beverley became utterly still. I wanted to touch her, comfort her, but she looked so fragile, it seemed any touch might shatter her. She whispered, "They gave me to her. My mom trusted her!" She turned slowly to the house.

Johnny and I shared a look. We didn't know what to say or do. Were the vampires lying? Maybe. But if not, I wanted to turn Vivian over to them now and be done with it. Beverley couldn't be expected to stay in the same house as her mother's killer—

Beverley had slipped away from us and was already halfway to the house. "Beverley, no!" I shouted. Johnny ran after her, but even with his long legs and speed, he couldn't get to her before she dashed inside.

I followed, Erik behind me. It wasn't that I was faster than he, just that he kept himself between me and the vampires. Inside, I stopped in the kitchen beside Johnny. Beverley was standing before Vivian, hands clenched at her sides as she glowered at our prisoner. Slowly she reached up and took down the gag.

"I know what you did," the little girl whispered. "*You* murdered my mother." As she spoke, she wrenched the bandanna-gag in her hand, tightening it around Vivian's neck. I moved to step in, but Johnny put an arm out to stop me. Nana and Celia had stopped what they were doing when the girl had run in. They now sat staring, shocked silent at what she just said.

"I was sleeping in the next room while you painted the wall with her blood!" Beverley continued. Vivian's mouth worked soundlessly; she was turning purple. "You were supposed to be her *friend*!" She let go of the bandanna and hit Vivian hard with a balled-up fist. "And you took *me* in! Why? Why would you bother to take me in if you hated my mother so much?"

Wheezing, Vivian slowly brought her head around. For a second I thought of *The Exorcist* and wondered if that evil-looking face was going to go all the way around. Vivian said, "It would have been suspicious not to."

Beverley slowly backed away, then turned and ran.

Even after Menessos's claim, I had expected Vivian to deny it. She started laughing.

I stalked over, put the gag back, and left. Upstairs, I went to Dr. Lincoln. "Fix me a dose of morphine, enough to knock Vivian out and keep her out."

He gaped at me, dumbfounded.

"Now," I said, teeth clenched.

He moved into action, started filling a syringe. "I'm not sure of the dose."

"Your best guess, Doctor."

"Here." He handed me a syringe with triple what we gave Theo.

"Thank you." In the kitchen, I jerked the safety cap off and threw it. Taking a handful of Vivian's hair, I steadied her head and jabbed the needle viciously into the vein in her neck.

"Shit, Seph!" Celia whispered.

Vivian sucked air sharply through her nose.

"I thought you'd be used to having sharp, pointy things in your neck," I snarled as I depressed the plunger slowly.

She'd revealed to everyone that I'd taken her money to assassinate a vampire. Now everyone knew *she* was the killer.

"I agreed to kill for justice—there's at least some merit in that. But you—you killed for jealousy and spite. Now I can't wait to give you to them."

Vivian's eyes went wide and she tried to complain or plead or something, but her head just dropped forward.

I threw the empty syringe into the trash and turned to leave.

"You'd better empty out your room," Nana said. "So there's space to make the circle."

Her words made my stomping steps halt. One life had already been taken, and justice would be served one way or another. But a second life waited. I'd forgotten that. "Yeah," I agreed, anger washing out of me. "I want to check on Beverley first; then I'll see to it the room's ready."

"I'll check on the girl," she said, rising stiffly from the table. "You tend to your room."

Johnny put a hand on my shoulder. "Let us move the furniture—you just supervise," he said. A mere mortal with substandard strength, I would only be in a wærewolf's way. And since I couldn't eat until after the ritual, I was feeling sleepy and low. A glance at the clock told me we had about an hour and fifteen minutes to go. Johnny and Erik followed me to my room and asked, "Where do you want everything?"

"Everything" included a dresser and side tables. "In Nana's room or the hallway."

They moved the dresser out into the far end of the upstairs hall. Then they came back and Erik went for the far bedside table while Johnny unplugged the lamp on the nearer one. He picked up my side table with everything on it.

"Hey. Be careful with that picture. The hinge is loose on the back."

"Right," he said, assessing it. "Who is it?"

"My dad."

He started to say something but stopped. Nana came in. "The child is resting."

"Goddess, she's been through so much."

Nana patted my arm. "Don't worry so much for her. Children often cope better than adults." She paused as Erik excused himself around her. "They have the ability to accept things more easily because they're growing and learning and everything is always changing with them anyway. It's when we stop growing and stop learning that we start forgetting how to ride with the changes."

"I understand what you're saying, Nana, but she lost her mother. It's not like she's just changing schools or some individual thing is changing. It's *everything*."

Her hand withdrew slowly. "I suppose you know what that's like."

Focusing on her steadily, I said, "I do."

"I can see inner strength burning bright in that young girl's eyes. She's going to be just fine."

"I hope so."

"I'm sorry I missed it in your eyes. I'm sure the evidence of your strength was there, I just . . . I wasn't looking."

I didn't know what to say.

Nana smiled. "I better get back to my own preparations."

I strolled to Theo's right side, where I would stand for the ritual, and looked up through the skylights. Not yet. My attention turned to Theo, and I took her hand. "I'll do all I can," I whispered.

Erik and Johnny came back in.

"You're sure this won't make the rest of us change too?" Erik asked.

"I'm sure." My voice sounded weary.

"It's not that I don't trust you, Seph. I do. We all do, or we wouldn't be doing this. It's just that I can't seem to wrap my head around how witches do what they do."

"It's not any different from how you guys change back and forth. I mean, the light of the sun shines on the whole surface of an orbiting heavenly body, which reflects that light, triggering something inside of you, and your entire physical body changes. Not because of a Jekyll-and-Hyde potion, not because of technology or a spoken power word. Because of the *volume* of sunlight reflected into the darkness. It *is* magic."

"I gotta write that down," Johnny whispered. "I can make lyrics out of that."

"Why doesn't it initiate partial changes, then, when it's not full but still shining?" Erik asked.

"Because it's not the whole surface, it's not magic. Moonshine isn't enough to change you or even start a change. But there is a universal reaction, an elemental and magical reaction, when the entire face of the lunar surface is reflecting. It's like it amplifies a hundredfold because everything is in place to allow it."

"When you put it like that, I do kind of get it," he said.

"Persephone," Nana called from the bottom of the stairs.

"Yeah?" I went into the hall, my thoughts for her knees. I hoped she wasn't climbing the stairs again, especially this late. We were all so tired.

"We have a problem. You better come down here."

It didn't surprise me when Johnny followed me. Nana returned to the kitchen dinette and sat before the book. Her finger traced over a section and she said, "I was going through the ritual one last time to determine everyone's position. There are differences depending on what the change is meant for—defense, offense, other purposes. In this instance, as it is meant to heal, I thought this said"—she followed the lines with her fingertips—" 'The one who is familiar with the situation asks the injury to be given favor.' But your veterinarian walks through as I'm talking to myself, and he says I'm wrong. I asked him to look over the passage and he interprets it as—" She gestured for Dr. Lincoln to take over.

"The root word is *pecco,* so that is 'to do wrong' here, then here: *venia,* 'pardon' or 'forgive'—"

"Hey Doc, hold the Latin and try it in plain English," Johnny said.

"It means," the doctor said, "that Goliath must be present during the ritual and ask Theo to forgive him."

The emotion in the room sank in the silence that followed. My heart and my hope for Theo sank with it.

"You're saying in order to save Theo, we have to get the vamp asshole who did this to her to participate in the ritual to heal her," Johnny grumbled.

"That's how I read it," the doc shrugged.

"My Latin is rusty," said Nana. "He minored in Latin at OSU. Trust his interpretation." She looked at me like she was going to be sick.

"I thank you for that, Demeter," Dr. Lincoln said, "but my education didn't cover local dialects and distinctions that witch Latin or even medieval Latin might be laden with."

"You're all missing the point," I stressed. "We can't move Theo. To do this means I have to ask the vampire to enter my home." Damn! That was, literally, a violating thought.

The collective sigh that followed thickened the gloom. Silence followed. Celia ventured, "Well, that's stupid."

"What?"

"You can't have a vampire in your ritual anyway. They're dead."

"Actually," Nana said, "they are not."

"What?" Johnny, Erik, and I said it almost simultaneously.

"For the night hours, they're alive," Nana stated.

"They're just reanimated," I said. "It's not the same thing."

"Isn't it?" Nana said.

Tension suddenly replaced the defeated feeling in the room. "Explain."

"The *living* dead, Persephone. You saw how Goliath treated the girl. He's a conscious creature for the night hours. At the very least, a vampire's brain stem functions. Maybe we all need to look at them differently, if just for tonight. See them as the cursed people they are." She gestured at the book. "Cursed by the sun—cursed to die every single day, to lose the reassurance of the warmth of sunlight on their faces. Cursed people, but people nonetheless."

"People who eat other people," I insisted.

"No," Johnny said softly. "It's wæres who will actually eat other people. Vamps only drink the blood."

I rubbed my forehead. Getting the vampires to help was not what I wanted to do. But I had no time. Theo had no time. "The problem," I said, "is this: I'll have to give up the very thing defending us. I'll have to ask them to enter."

"Only Goliath," Johnny said.

"And once he's in, all he has to do is invite his master, so I might as well ask them both and hope that my courtesy wins me some brownie points." No one argued with that. "And once I've uttered those powerful words, once I ask them into my home, there's nothing stopping them from simply coming in, taking Vivian and the book, and leaving."

CHAPTER TWENTY-ONE

I sat on the edge of the bed, Theo's hand in mine. My bedroom was empty save for the bed, Theo, the medical monitors, and me—Dr. Lincoln had stepped out. Directly across from me, cobwebs frosted the wall where my dresser had been, and a layer of dust coated the floor in patches where the dresser and bedside tables had sat. An injured patient should be in a clean room. I'd thought it was clean.

I put Theo's hand down and stood up. Taking a clean cotton shirt from the closet, I began wiping away the cobwebs and dust, wishing I could wipe all the hurt and turmoil from the lives of the people in my house.

I didn't want Theo to die. I didn't want anyone to die, and if the vampires went postal in my home, we all would. Actually, "going postal" would be too mild a term for what they'd do, not to mention sounding insultingly mortal to them. They'd go "nuclear" or "nova" or something that sounded impressive, but it would really just mean something much more intensely bloody and horribly painful than a mere mentally disturbed human with a loaded gun could accomplish.

The steps squeaked, and I knew someone was coming

to warn me of the time. I expected Nana because the steps were slow, but it was Johnny's face that appeared in the doorway. "What have you decided?"

"I've decided that no matter what happens, I'm screwed."

"Can I apply for that job?"

I smiled. "Johnny."

"If you can still smile, then all's not bad, Red. Have faith."

"Faith. In what? Myself? Fate?"

"Yes."

I thought of Nancy. Her faith hadn't kept her friendships from crashing, hadn't kept her out of the dark valleys of human experience.

But it kept her to her purpose.

It was almost like hearing Amenemhab's voice in my head.

My attention strayed to Theo. I had a purpose too. My lungs filled up, and I let them empty again. *Goddess guide me,* I thought.

"I'm ready."

I walked out into the hall and to the darkened guest room, I left the door open so the light from the hall could shine in. I eased down onto the floor beside the air mattress and touched Beverley's shoulder. She didn't immediately rouse. It made me feel guilty to be waking such a tired, tormented child who'd found some release in her sleep. I shook her again. "Beverley."

"Mmmm. Seph?"

"Beverley, I need your help. I wouldn't wake you otherwise."

"What is it?" She rubbed at her eyes.

"I know Goliath has treated you well, but he's also done some bad things in the past, and . . ." There was no way around this. "I'm going to have to ask Menessos and Goliath to come inside my home."

"Really?" She sat up, eyes wide.

"Really. I thought I should tell you that, in case the ritual woke you, so you wouldn't be alarmed. And . . . honestly, I had wanted to keep you away from the spell, since Theo will change, but now—now I'm hoping you'll agree to be a witness to it. Goliath seems to genuinely care about you and, this is crappy of me, I know, but I think if you're there, he'll be less inclined to let any of his bad qualities from the past creep into this situation. Do you understand?"

"Yeah. It's like his gift of the iPod. It kept me from seeing or hearing things that wouldn't have happened if I'd been watching or listening. If I'm there, watching and listening . . . then he'll behave."

She was so awesome. "Yeah. That's exactly right. Are you okay with that?"

Beverley grinned. "You were going to go out and take on a vampire for my mom. And for me. If I can help you out by simply showing up . . . that's easy."

I hugged her.

"Theo will change," I said again, pulling back. "I don't want you to be freaked out by it—"

"Mom didn't want me to see her change, but I always wanted to."

"It *is* scary, Beverley."

"I'll do it, Seph. I want to help." She kicked her feet from under the covers, ready to go, just like that. "I think it'll be cool."

I couldn't help but admire her. "It's very serious in a circle. No giggling, okay?"

"Right." Her face was earnest. "I get to stand in a circle with witches, wærewolves, and vampires? Wow. Cool." Then she hesitated. "What about . . . *her*?"

She meant Vivian. I said, "When this is over, the vampires will be taking her with them. She's going to get what she deserves for what she's done."

Beverley's spine straightened slowly. "Okay."

I went downstairs. Everyone was in the hall or the living room, but my focus remained on my purpose. I stepped out onto the front porch. The night air was swirling and cold, like my thoughts. But the chill I felt was deeper, in the marrow of my bones and down in the core of me that was so deep it was in another world beyond the boundaries of physics.

"Menessos." I didn't shout. I didn't have to. He was already watching me through the open window of his vehicle. The door opened, and he slid out smoothly and came striding toward the house. He clearly didn't like being "summoned" as such, but we both understood why I wasn't going out there again. Before, I'd left my safety to rescue Beverley because I had thought they had taken her. Now I had what he wanted. Goliath was, of course, following—the expression on his face was guarded, but not guarded enough. I had the distinct feeling that they had been talking about me.

I shifted my weight. There was no time for dancing around the subject. I met Menessos's eyes and asked, "Would you and Goliath stand in my circle?"

An infinitesimal change to the tilt of his head signaled surprise. His perfectly proportioned features suddenly displayed a wonder that was altogether foreign to his face. "You're serious."

"I don't want Theo to die."

"But are you prepared to invite Goliath and myself into your home?"

"That's what I came out here to do."

Amazement silenced him.

Goliath said, "Why?"

"Ritual says you, Goliath, have to ask her to forgive you during the rite."

He grinned. "Oh, so you need me? I thought you wanted to kill me."

"Theo needs you." I wasn't giving him the satisfaction. "If I hadn't screwed up in the first place—and if you weren't such an arrogant, murdering bastard—we wouldn't be here. Either of us. So how about we play nice for just a little bit, and then everybody goes away happy?"

"I'm not sure you're qualified to understand what will make me happy."

"I have the stake, Vivian, and the book. I can figure out what will make you *un*happy. The forgoing of that should, if you're wise, make you happy."

"Fine. What's in it for us? Our assistance has a cost."

"I already said that Vivian, the stake, and the book are yours once the ritual is complete, but if I invite you in, you have the guarantee of knowing there will be no way for me to block you from taking them and that I intend no double-cross."

"You're not offering me anything new."

"I'll be giving up the safety of my home's inherent protection. That's the price I'm willing to pay to save Theo." I faced Menessos. The decision would be his. "The things you fear the most are all inside my house, and despite your intimidation tactic of calling my wards petty—"

"I believe I referred to them as *paltry,*" Menessos corrected.

"Paltry. Nevertheless, the things you desire are ultimately out of your reach, unless I bring them out or I invite you in."

"The stake is inside. Being uncertain of who may pop out of a hiding spot and stake us does not inspire our cooperation."

If I was inviting him inside, it made little difference if his beholder buddies had the opportunity to grab the stake from a location outside. "Then the stake will leave the wards. I'll take it out into the cornfield."

He considered it.

Before he could speak, I added, "But in exchange for that guarantee from me, I want a guarantee from you. A guarantee that no one in my house will be harmed." I paused. "That includes Vivian—at least, until she's off my property. Do what you want to her, but not here. Not where Beverley can see or hear it."

Menessos repeated it all back to me. "We participate and help your friend recover. Then you'll surrender freely these things I fear most, as you put it. Vivian, the book—which I am sure you must be loath to part with—and you'll place the stake outside?"

Parting with my ward-defenses was more loathsome to me than parting with the Codex, but Nana wouldn't have agreed with me. "That's acceptable."

"I will send an envoy for the stake tomorrow."

I bobbed my head in agreement.

"Very well. I promise no one inside will be harmed—"

"Promise no one here will be harmed in any way, inside of the house or outside of it," I pressed.

"I will make oath to that, you will make invitation, and we will wait on the porch, not entering your home until after the stake is removed." He rubbed his hands together. "This agreement seems more equitable than the siege I had expected this evening."

What the hell had he been planning?

He raised his right hand, palm up, and slid his sleeve up halfway to his elbow. With the nail of his left-hand forefinger, he made a slice over the vein in his forearm. Blood welled up instantly, dark and syrupy, pouring in a thick stream over his skin. He pushed through my ward, setting off the alarm in my head. I deactivated it with a thought. He wiped his left hand over the blood and smeared it over the posts holding up my porch roof and across the tread of the first step. "By my blood, then, no one in your house will be harmed, either by me or Goliath or any other under my control or influence."

Behind me, at the screen door, I heard Nana gasp.

"Agreed." I swallowed, hard, knowing what I had to do next.

CHAPTER TWENTY-TWO

"Menessos, Goliath. Please . . . come inside."

Menessos put his foot onto the first tread, unhurriedly, then stepped up onto my porch. I wanted to retreat, to backpedal to the door and inside. I shouted at myself mentally: *Do not show him fear! Even if you are afraid, you'll fight it with every breath, every beat of your heart! Fear isn't weakness, but giving in to it is.* My feet were planted between the vampire and my front door.

He stood there expectantly, gazing into my eyes, though I stared at his lightly bearded square chin. In a fluid motion, Menessos glided right up to me, invading my personal space. I retreated, and he moved with me at the same speed and distance, as if we were dancing. Then my back was against the porch roof support post.

In that instant, I learned something: people's fears are odd things. Some people won't go boating or swimming because of a fear of the water. Some people won't wear turtlenecks or anything tight at their throats. Some people avoid big dogs. I'd always attributed these kinds of things to past-life events, like drowning, hanging, being attacked by animals—whatever would account for the fear. I'd never discovered a specific fear of my own like that—until now, as I stood with my back pinned against a solid post. I wondered if a past life of mine had ended with a post at my back and kindling under my feet.

"Thank you, Miss Alcmedi, for having faith in my word."

"You're welcome." It sounded a lot more confident than I felt.

"You're an uncommon woman."

"What does that mean?" It sounded like praise, but a vampire's praise was a worrisome thing.

"People generally reside in one of two categories. Either the group who think vampires are . . . *cool*"—he made it sound like an expletive—"and offer up thoughtless invitations incessantly, or those with a terror of vampires so intense they offer only intolerance and hate. Most of both categories are imbeciles, and we would never seek their companionship." He touched me, lightly, to smooth my hair. I could not tell if his touch was cold or calloused, but I wondered. "But you . . . Persephone." He whispered my name, and I felt the warmth of a summer breeze on my bare skin. "You are intelligent and brave. If only there were more like you . . ."

From the doorway, Johnny cleared his throat, a sound that ended with a prolonged low growl. I was suddenly embarrassed, angry with myself, and angry that Menessos would try seduction while my friend lay dying for our help. "There is little time," I said, gesturing toward the door.

Menessos whispered, "Vampires have forever."

"Theo doesn't."

He made a gracious gesture of capitulation. "Remove the stake from your home, out the back egress, please."

"Wait here." I could have given Johnny a signal and he would have seen that it got done, but I wanted to get away from Menessos. "Excuse me." I slipped past him and went inside, forcing Nana to back up to allow me through. Johnny moved only enough to be out of the way, surely to keep an eye on the vampires.

In the kitchen, I lifted the lid on the stake's storage box to be sure it was still inside. Such a remarkably common-looking thing; a muddy stick. The sharpened tip gave it an ominous flair, though. And it was pale, the wood's tip, like a fang. Nana touched my shoulder, and I jumped. My muscles were so tight. "When this leaves the house, we have no defense against him," I said.

"And we'll need none."

I looked at Nana; something strange in her expression told me that her words were not simply stating her hopes as if they were pep-talk facts. She must have seen my confusion on my face. "He made a blood oath to you."

"He *what?*" Celia nearly shrieked.

They shared a long look that I couldn't read. Then Nana explained, "He drew his own blood, marked your porch with it, and swore to our safety."

Celia watched me, expression curious. "What?" I asked.

"What did you say to him?" Celia asked back.

Had I done something wrong? "That I'd remove the stake from the house and, after we do the ritual, I'd let him take Vivian and the book away. He'll send someone for the stake tomorrow."

"Rudimentary deal-making. What else?" Celia pressed.

"I asked him for a guarantee. He didn't offer it."

"Well." She put her hands on her hips. "Whatever it was, you impressed him enough to make him draw his own blood. They don't give up their precious fluid for any common reason."

"Such an oath is more binding than any legal contract ever written," Nana added. "And, so long as you hold up your end, more enforceable."

"Enforceable how?"

"Later," Nana said. "We haven't much time."

"Right." So he was impressed. That explained why he had flirted with me. "I have to get this off the property. I'll be right back." After closing its lid, I lifted the box and slipped into the garage, then outside through what my Realtor had called the "man-door" in the rear of the garage. In the yard, my shoes made a *shush*ing sound in the grass. There was little light, but I knew my way, knew every little hill and dip of the yard, so my steps remained firm and confident. The box was much heavier than the object it held, and I switched hands halfway through the yard. At the end of the grass, where the cornfield began, I sat the box down and slid it in between the stalks. I turned back to the house. It seemed so far, so small and bright with all the lights on. Everyone inside was waiting for me.

If I wanted to flee, now was the time.

The sound of a stick snapping caught my attention. Beholders in the field.

It was a good thing I didn't want to flee.

Still, the thought that people were out there, dangerous people, made my back feel exposed—like I was it—so I jogged back to the house.

That was almost funny: beholders were dangerous enough to send me jogging back into the house where their masters were waiting for me.

Everyone was starting to assemble upstairs when I returned. Dr. Lincoln was with Theo, as were Celia, Erik, and Beverley. Nana was climbing the steps. Johnny motioned me on through the hall, and I joined him at the bottom of the steps. Menessos and Goliath remained on the porch.

I opened the screen door. "It's time."

Menessos eased toward me like water flowing to the shore. The metaphysical barrier that restrained his kind from places into which they were not invited seemed like a thick, transparent membrane that I could see stretching as he pressed his hand to it. I'd already said the magic words. The porch wasn't technically "inside." Now all he had to do was push.

His eyes met mine with the confidence of a king. Of Arthur. Too late, my brain screamed at me that I had met his gaze. But there was no power to it, no call in it. Just a man looking at me, into me, as if he'd just found what he'd been searching for. He was entering my home. The vampire was breaking the seal to my private space. Suddenly, this seemed very sexual.

He hesitated, the barrier stretched to the point of bursting. I felt it, felt it like it was part of me pressed intimately against the contours of his body. A hairbreadth more, and it would be gone. . . .

People are sure air exists; we breathe it. We fill balloons with it. We feel it on our faces when the wind blows. We can't see it, but we know it is there. In that instant, I was certain barriers existed—protections unseen, magical and mysterious, remarkable and real. I felt this barrier burst like a soap bubble, felt the tingly flick of its particles fading as the protective shield's integrity evaporated.

Once the unseen dam was breached, everything it had held back came flooding in. Dread, like thick and velvety foam, poured across my floor and drifted against my leg. It would take a full weekend of witchy cleansings to be rid of it.

"Theo is upstairs," I said as Goliath stepped in, his entrance lacking his master's ceremony.

"I want to see Vivian." Menessos strode toward my kitchen.

I didn't like this. "No. After."

He didn't stop. I followed him. Menessos turned the corner and vanished from my view. "Awaken," I heard him say. My pace increased. But I stopped short when I too turned the corner. It felt as though the air, that thick velvet dread, were being slowly crammed down my throat to suffocate me.

Menessos stood before her. I could not see his expression. Vivian's face was white. Her eyes were as wide as half-dollar coins. Trembling claimed her arms, and her chest heaved with fast, shallow breaths. "Vivian," he whispered. His index finger slid under her chin, and his touch jolted her like an electric shock. "Vivian." This time the whisper sounded sad. He grabbed her chin roughly. She tried to pull away but couldn't. "Betrayer!"

Tears showered from her eyes.

Whatever he did to her, I figured she deserved. She'd betrayed him. She'd murdered Lorrie. But his punishment wasn't going to be doled out here. "Menessos," I said.

He turned swiftly, as if he hadn't known I was there. A single bloody tear had fallen from his eye.

I retreated two steps. He mourned this vengeance?

He turned back to Vivian and ripped easily through the clothesline cord. His motions were fierce and violent, yet gentle, like those of a lover who rips your clothes off but caresses your skin with soft adoration. We'd tied her arms down at her sides and then roped her to the chair separately, so I knew she wouldn't be immediately free. "You took an oath—" I began.

He wheeled around. "One I will keep, Miss Alcmedi. But Vivian will not leave my sight. She may not be in the circle, but she will be near me." He turned to her. "Won't you?" He lifted her to standing position, and her weak limbs faltered as he embraced her in his arms. Her eyes above the gag remained wide, pleading with me.

I shook my head at her.

Vivian crumbled, sobbing. Menessos caught and lifted her, then faced me. "Let us go."

"Wait a minute—"

"Vivian will remain thusly bound and outside your circle. And"—he fixed her with a stern expression—"she will behave. She will witness a real witch at work for once."

I hesitated. Vivian *was* a real witch. He was insulting her. The mixed love and loathing he displayed for her confused me, but I'd have to sort it out later. In the hallway, I led him back to where Johnny and Goliath stood glowering at each other. It wouldn't have surprised me to find two puddles on the floor, proof of a pissing contest.

I said, "C'mon." They followed me. At the squeaky step, Goliath—bringing up the rear—stopped and bounced on it. I turned back at the top of the steps and looked daggers at him. He grinned.

Now was not the time to let him distract me. I hoped that in the circle, with Beverley participating, he would behave himself.

"Okay. Beverley, I need you to leave for just a second, while I cleanse the space." She'd been sitting with Theo and obediently left.

Nana came to me at the doorway and produced a necklace from her pocket, which she offered to me. "Wear this," she said.

Feeling the easy vibration of the charged gemstones in the palm of my hand, I lifted the necklace up. It was like a three-row choker of pearls, but the round stones weren't pearls. "It's moonstone."

"Yes." She smiled happily that I'd recognized it. "May I?" She put it on me. "I've empowered it for protection," she whispered.

It covered the parts of my neck that a vampire would most like. That made me happy enough to forget that it was much too fancy to wear with a Superman T-shirt.

"Everything you need is on the tray," Nana gestured, "or at the foot of the bed."

She'd made a makeshift altar out of a bed tray and wedged it against the foot of Theo's bed, which had been pulled far enough from the wall to allow me to circle

Theo, and someone had been brilliant enough to duct-tape the monitor cords to the floor. The book sat open to the proper page, with the translation page atop it. Various altar items were placed around it. Practical, my nana. "Thanks."

Dr. Lincoln had removed Theo's oxygen and feeding tubes and cut the temporary casts down the front. Everything had been removed except the IV, which he'd said he wanted to leave in to continue giving Theo fluids.

Aware that the others were intently watching me, I lit a tall white pillar candle. Nana reached in and flipped off the electric switch. I took up the pentacle incense holder and, lighting the incense, I began blessing the space with the elements. First with the incense representing the element of air. Next, a red candle representing fire, and then a bowl of crystal-water—water that has sat out under the light of a full moon with a charged crystal in it—to represent the element of water. Last, I sprinkled grains from a bowl of sea salt to represent earth. I circled the room in a manner that witches call "deosil"—pronounced *jes-sil*—which simply means clockwise or sun-wise. I walked the circle once with each representation of an element to cleanse the area, then faced the door. "Enter now this sacred space. Let all who enter here bring with them only harmony and peace."

The doctor entered first and took a position just to the right side of the head of the bed. Nana and Beverley came next, leaving a space where the moonlight was shining through the skylights.

Celia and Erik headed toward the stairs. "Where are you going?" Menessos asked.

"She's going to call the quarters next. We have to avoid the energy," replied Celia.

"If you want your friend restored, you need to stay here." Menessos shifted his weight and blocked them from the stairs with Vivian's body.

"It won't do any good to save Theo if it costs the rest of us our lives," Celia pleaded.

"I have already promised Miss Alcmedi that no one will be harmed. I would not negate that now."

"But the energy—"

"I know this spell, dear, skittish wolf. You will not be harmed."

Celia and Erik stepped into the bedroom and backed into the corner nearest the door. Johnny stayed with them.

My room was rectangular, longer than it was wide, so Menessos had room to lay Vivian down beside the closet. "Move not and make no sound," he said to her in a voice so kind and loving that the words that followed—"or your suffering will triple"—seemed even more terrifying. He stood and stepped nearer the bed. Behind him, Vivian turned her face to the carpet.

Goliath moved to his master's side.

Three deep breaths to ground and center. It's like taking a minute to check a map of the universe and find out exactly where your soul lives, and then feeling yourself connected to every molecule of matter and antimatter filling up that enormous universe.

With everyone in place, I lit two white taper candles in gargoyle candleholders placed on either side of the book. Then, with my old ritual broom in hand—the newer one now hung above my front door—I chanted and swept a tight deosil circle just around Theo's bed, containing all of us in the room except the wærewolves and Vivian. My sweeping became faster when I moved between the vampires and Vivian. When I returned to my starting position, I said, "As above, so below, this circle is sealed, so mote it be."

Nana repeated the last part: "So mote it be!" Menessos repeated it after her.

After I drew an equal-armed cross in the air to further seal the circle, my eyes closed. I called up the sub-alpha state.

This was the point in the ritual where things became truly magical.

CHAPTER TWENTY-THREE

I took the first of four saucers from the tray. The saucers were prepared for the element invocations, each complete with an appropriately colored candle ringed in small stones. Each element had its own reaction, an undeniable physical presence that confirmed it was with me. This first saucer represented the element of earth and had a green candle and hematite stones. I lit the candle and held the saucer carefully aloft.

"Hail and welcome, element of earth!
Bring your [illegible] strength and witness this rite.
Protect us and aid us as much as you might."

Immediately I felt a tingle, as if glitter were raining onto my skin. The elements never seemed affected by my clothing; they could pass right through. Flexing my aura with a mental command, I embraced the energy to me, keeping it from drifting over Theo; it had a gritty, rooted feeling to it, and I knew earth was present. I placed the saucer opposite me, in the northernmost position of my circle.

The second saucer bore a yellow candle and green aventurine stones.

"Hail and welcome, element of air!
Bring your experience and witness this rite.
Protect us and aid us as much as you might."

This time, a warm breath swirled around me, exploring. A breeze lifted my hair, but no one else's. With air present, I placed the saucer to the east.

The red candle ringed in bloodstones was next.

"Hail and welcome, element of fire!
Bring your transformability and witness this rite.
Protect us and aid us as much as you might."

Fire touched me in nips and little gnawing bites. It could be painful, but it wasn't angry with me. It understood my respect, and I understood its volatile, consuming nature. I placed this saucer to the south, behind me.

Last was a blue candle ringed in coral.

"Hail and welcome, element of water!
Bring your life-giving womb and witness this rite.
Protect us and aid us as much as you might."

Feeling pressure and current flowing against me, I stood firm until water's greeting was done, then placed the saucer to the west. I remained there and combined my statement of purpose and deity invocation, saying:

"Persephone and Isis, goddesses whose names I bear,
Artemis, Inanna, and Ishtar, your lunar purpose I share.
Hathor and Hera, come to me, be present here tonight,
Hecate! Come to me now, give credence to my rite.
Encourage the elements to participate
And return Theo's life from the Summerland's gate."

The wolves watched with interest and a healthy amount of wariness, but they didn't really know what I was doing, so I didn't feel judged. Neither Nana's nor Beverley's observance bothered me. Their approval surrounded me like a bath of warm light. But Menessos stared coldly, evaluating the ceremony and the reverence I gave to the ritual. He studied every gesture, considered every inflection, surely creating a mental critique. I had the distinct impression that he was gauging my performance of the ritual against that of someone else he'd seen perform it. I regretted letting my sweeping speed up when I had been near him. Maybe he didn't like my statement of purpose or the fact that I called on eight goddesses, but to my thinking, it fit perfectly. eight is the number of transformation.

Lifting my hands above my head, I put my index fingers together and my thumbs underneath, forming an open triangle. Keeping my arms straight, I lowered them before me. I imagined the light of the moon shining through that triangle and onto the third-eye area of my forehead. I wanted Theo to live. I wanted to undo the damage done because of me. I focused on those goals, seeing my will like a blue spiral and my emotion like a red spiral; they slithered, entwining and undulating, joining and forming, until I had one purple spiral.

Straightening the spiral into a glowing violet rod, with the force of my mind I shot it like an arrow at the lunar surface, visualizing it landing in the presence of the goddesses I called on, being passed hand-to-hand as each aspect of the Goddess examined it and considered my plea.

As I held on to perfect trust in divine will, the violet arrow shot back to me, through my triangulated fingers and into my third eye.

Suddenly my body vibrated from within. My throat opened. My mouth opened. I began to sing.

The words weren't mine, weren't even my language, but they came in my voice and the melody rose and fell in crescendos along musical scales that were foreign to my ears, yet beautiful.

In some religions, people speak in tongues—glossolalia, mystical unintelligible utterances that sound like fluent speech—and this singing must have been something akin to that. But how was I going to conduct the ritual if I couldn't stop singing?

After struggling with this, I decided to trust in the goddesses I'd invoked. The song felt good and right. Maybe the odd words were Akkadian—a gift, conducting the spell in its original language.

Turning to face the group and letting my voice fill the room, I continued with the ritual as if this were how it was supposed to be. Though I stepped closer to Theo in preparation to release the moon-energy, I channeled it upward to flow deosil at the ceiling. Drawing a hexagram in the air above Theo, I invoked all the elements at once.

The gritty earth energy scrubbed abrasively over my body like a sand bath to join with the moon energy. The heated breath of air rose next, followed by the churning, nibbling fire energy and, finally, the buoyant current of water.

Menessos suddenly commanded, “Imagine what energy you will offer to this rite, imagine it forming like an orb between your hands!” He glanced at Goliath, who readily took a deep breath. He focused next on Beverley and the doctor. Both looked to Nana. She signaled her approval of this with a single nod.

“Rub your hands together to warm them,” Menessos demonstrated. “Feel the tingle and imagine it growing with the energy you're releasing.”

In sub-alpha, I could see golden sparkles emanating from between Nana's hands and smaller sputters of light as the doctor and Beverley summoned energy. Goliath formed a nice round sphere as if he did this every day. The vampire's orbs were a brassier color. Beverley's orb—pure white—grew suddenly.

Menessos instructed, “Now, everyone, lift your hands up.”

It was awe-inspiring, seeing the alpha-enkindled glow of these energies.

I pushed my offered energy out like fireworks trailing from my fingers, while still holding the triangle shape. Then the flow began to pull on me. It was as if my energy was a kite caught in a wind current, tearing more and more string from the spindle. Fighting against it, the flow from me slowed.

“More, Persephone. For a full transformation, you must give more,” Menessos whispered.

His words drew out of me a sum of energy that I knew was unwise, but I could not deny the spell or Theo's need.

Arms of light shot out of the swirling mass above our heads, capturing the energy offered up and pulling it into the mix, blending and kneading it until the top swirled and deepened to form a spiraling funnel, an upside-down tornado. This cone of power, unlike any other I'd ever raised, appeared like a galaxy of shining solar systems spinning. Every imaginable color flashed sporadically within that cone. I couldn't tear my eyes from it.

"More."

I resisted.

"More!"

My focus wavered. The flow of my energy sputtered.

"You need more to turn her! You know where it is! You must call to it! Take it!"

Mentally, I reached out to the wards surrounding my home. The energy, once set, reawakened. It leapt to my spirit hand, and the strange heat erupted inside my arm. Immediately, I yanked this energy up into the room. It rose through me and out with my voice, swirling into the flow. The tingling-burning overwhelmed me for a fraction of a second, but now it faded.

The energy above sang back to me, a sustained high note, beckoning, daring me to sing that note with it. But I wouldn't. I couldn't. It would surely call to the ley line again, and I wanted no more power searing through me, no more risk of losing my focus.

But that insistent call carried on, slipping beyond me

anyway, beyond the circle. I felt it reaching, crying, begging for more.

Beyond the cornfield, in the little grove . . . the ley line answered.

The ley pulsed and fell into a steady thrumming beat. Enticed, it reached across the field toward me as I had reached for it to power my wards. With each pulse it drew nearer. I could feel the enormity of it, crackling all along the line and arcing forward. I tensed.

I'd dared touch it with my fingertips, and—out of dire fear and need for safety—I'd dared to dip my hand into it. That handful had given me a taste of the immense power and the rush that mortals are rightly meant to fear . . . but this was searching me out, answering the need of the ritual, the need inherent in my song. And I could not stop it from finding me.

"Now!" Menessos whispered.

The energy of the ley line leapfrogged. A bolt jumped to the ward-circle, then into me. It wanted to fling itself outward through my voice, to fill the room and spill beyond as I sang that note . . . but it couldn't filter through fast enough. I sang an octave too low.

In that instant, my body numbed. I could feel nothing—not the vibration of my vocal cords, not the floor under my feet. It felt as if I didn't exist. The energy took me and became tangible—touching, running, roiling inside of me, searching for its purpose so it could have a task and a form. But I could not speak, could not command it; my voice was taken by the song, and I could not keep from singing; I fought to no avail.

Through it all I heard Menessos whisper, "Give in, Persephone. Now!"

I stopped fighting it. My voice rose higher, a flurry of notes rising soprano-high. When the peak tone was hit, when I matched the note my swirling wards had created, it held.

Finally unblocked, the ley-line energy shot out of me and joined with the energy we'd each given.

Menessos stepped forward, hand lifted, and shouted the command:

"Partake of this energy, elements four,
Swallow it down and return to us more!"

The swirling mass split into four arms reaching from the center. The arms reached down, blue and red, yellow and green, touching the candle placed at each compass point. The arms swirled and lowered, stretching until the circle was a cage of colored energy being consumed by tiny candle flames.

Above us, the center exploded. The colored arms shot into the candles like the length of a metal measuring tape recoiling with a snap. But my note did not end.

Menessos said, "Goliath."

Goliath lowered his head some, extended his open arms imploringly, and said, "Theodora Hennessey . . . forgive me."

Energy bolted from the candles like lightning, arcing in crackling jolts until they met over our heads where the center had once been. It scoured my skin as well as the others'. Beverley cried out and hugged Nana tight.

Menessos said:

> *"Rise, cone of power! Rise to our call!*
> *Deliver lunar energies to one and all!"*

With that command, I knew he'd betrayed us.

In my mind, I screamed, *NO!* but my single note continued uninterrupted.

He added something in Latin. I only understood *lux et tenebris,* "light from darkness."

The candle flames sank down to minimal embers, and the room darkened. Light burst around me like a spotlight held at my back. The final note of my song tapered off, and my knees gave way. Moonlight, like a sharply focused sunbeam, shone through the skylight and encompassed my circle.

Menessos continued:

> *"Search for the wolves, caress these beasts,*
> *Loose them now, moonlight increased!"*

Celia stared at the darkening hair on her arms. "No! Persephone, no! I'm changing! Stop this!"

"Feel your wolf inside you," Nana called to her. "Stroke it, pet it, keep it calm, and turn it away!"

It sounded like good advice, but it didn't work. Celia grabbed Erik and buried her face in his chest. He held her tight, sharing an angry look with Johnny. Johnny turned to Menessos and started forward, then stopped. His eyes had gone yellow, and his skin rippled as if a wave were crashing around underneath.

All the wærewolves began to change. Skin split like thin fabric as bones elongated, snapping like dry sticks. Brought to their knees by the power and pain of the transformation, the wæres emitted anguished cries that were piteous half-howls. Beverley screamed. Nana turned Beverley away and covered the girl's eyes with her old hands.

"Come. Come to me, Persephone." When Menessos said my name, I faced him squarely, looking him dangerously in the eye. He extended his hand. "Come to me."

Unlike the time just before, his power flashed forth and imprisoned me. My conscious anger was like a smaller me locked inside a Mason jar. I heard my own thoughts distantly, as if from a radio playing in another room. They were separate from me, distanced and muffled. Though I was seething, my fury at his betrayal could not affect me or get through the bondage confining my will to Menessos.

Unable to refuse, I stood and took his offered hand. His other hand lifted before me, an elegant gesture an expert magician might use before pulling a bouquet of roses from within his sleeve. But Menessos's intentions were not traditionally romantic. Instead, he removed my hand from his and positioned my arms so they were outstretched to either side. He fingered the bottom edges of my Superman shirt, rolling the fabric up. He bared my waist, pausing to touch my skin approvingly, before rolling the shirt up until my bra was exposed. With a word, he made me raise my arms up to allow him to pull the shirt free.

Physically, I complied without question. Mentally, inside my sealed Mason jar, I screamed to no avail.

My neatly rolled shirt dropped to the floor. His fingers glided over the lacy edge of the black bra before deftly unfastening the front clasp. Menessos removed and discarded my bra.

The exposure both horrified and thrilled me. Energy fluttered along my skin, stronger than ever before. My hands, still outstretched, turned palms up.

"Fire," he whispered.

The biting power of fire raced over me, focusing on intimate places. I had an inkling now as to why some witches did their rituals naked—sky-clad, as they called it. It felt good.

Menessos sliced the tip of his finger open with his fang in a motion that looked more like he was dabbing at something at the corner of his mouth. Blood welled up. He licked the first drops away, savoring them, then reached out to me.

My body flowed forward, spine bowing to arch toward him—if I took an actual step, I could not tell. His index finger touched my sternum between my breasts and sank lower, leaving a smear of his blood.

Nana's voice joined that of my bottled anger, shouting at me, calling through the fog, insistent but ineffectual.

Beverley ran at Menessos, but Goliath grabbed her and restrained her gently but firmly.

Menessos added an oblong loop above the first mark and connected them with a crossbar under the loop. He spoke. I didn't understand the words, but the rhythm and cadence complemented his masculine tone and mimicked the melody I'd been forced to sing.

Somehow, that melody connected us.

His powerful, dark eyes met mine and bored into me, reading my thoughts. And I knew his: he would not deny what he had done. *Why should I?* he seemed to ask.

He knew I was disgusted and horrified.

His answering expression could have been that of a warrior demanding information from me and warning me of the means of torture he could employ, or he could even have been Arthur ensconced in the passion that led to his fathering Mordred. I began to yield.

As his chant ended, the ankh he'd drawn on my skin began to glow.

It itched.

It burned.

It felt as if every cell of my skin under his bloody mark called to intangible pieces of my soul, pieces that answered readily only to be bound tight in the thick syrup of his blood. Retreating, those little pieces took the essence of him, sinking deep inside of me to hide in places even post-mortem medical examiners wouldn't find.

Still the energy of fire nibbled at my bare skin, and sandy earth-energy scraped my flesh sore. Water offered buoyancy, but only in waves that left me feeling heavy as they ebbed. Air, the breath of life, seemed only to enhance the heat of fire and make it hotter.

I wanted to be naked. I wanted him to see me and touch me. I wanted to feel those elements caressing other parts of me.

A new chant met my ears, words I should know but didn't. Nana shouted at Menessos and commanded him to stop.

Suddenly the bright spotlight of moonlight waned.

The howls of four fully formed wolves overpowered all the other voices.

But I couldn't look around, couldn't respond to what was happening. My whole world had become focused on the vampire before me, on matching the beat of my heart exactly to his. I could feel each contraction of his heart like a lover's caressing hand squeezing me. It was quixotic, eager, and indulgent. It was blessedly comforting.

Menessos cupped my face in both of his cold hands and drew me adoringly closer, as if I were the first bloom from a seed he'd planted himself and therefore deserved his loving scrutiny. The kiss I was surprised to find I wanted was a breath away when he spoke: "Tomorrow someone will come for the stake." His voice resonated inside my head, whispered syllables heard distinctly despite the cacophony around us. "I have honored my oath to you, Persephone Alcmedi." His hands slid around me as if he would dance with me, and mine conceded to hold him as well. He smelled like hot cinnamon and campfires; his body flowed against mine like a hot, urgent current of fresh magma.

He put his lips to mine in a kiss as fragile as the edge of a toasted marshmallow. I thought of that sticky, melted sweetness thick on my tongue—

My mouth opened to Menessos, and I discovered a new flavor. The savory tang was unlike anything I had known. It was the taste of orgasm, of falling in love, of finding El Dorado in your own backyard.

The sudden coldness of my lips made me realize that Menessos had pulled away. The expression he wore was a complex one. Mystified. Satisfied. Not smug—no, not smug. Yearning.

I touched his cheek. I felt an instant of sadness—the kind of deep, welling misery that brings sobs of grief in choking bouts rising from your throat in tight, painful gasps.

He jerked from my touch, effectively slamming the door on me. In that instant, his surprise was clear. He turned his back on me and stepped to the edge of the circle. With his bloody finger, he traced a rectangle in the air and said, "Open now the door." He pushed the circle of energy open and passed through.

Goliath neatly stepped to the end of the bed and picked up the book. He slammed it shut with the translation page still inside. He paused only to assess my breasts, then followed Menessos through. Menessos made a move as if shutting the energy door and said, "Sealed again is the door." He lifted Vivian, and the three of them left.

CHAPTER TWENTY-FOUR

I felt drunk, but without the cheerful buzz.

I must have stumbled, because suddenly I was in Nana's arms. "I've got you," she said.

Nana quoted the barest of quarter releases: "Thank you, elements of earth, air, fire, and water! We release you now. Go and be free. Come willingly if we call upon you again." She stroked my hair. "If ever we dare to call again. This circle is open. Now slowly," she said, "Beverley, ease toward the door. No sudden movements. Nice and slow."

A silvery gray wolf leapt to the doorway and snarled a deep, primal, guttural sound. Beverley stopped dead; to her credit, she did not scream. The wolf was bigger than Ares would ever be. Its muzzle turned slightly upward at us, nostrils flaring and all those gleaming white canines revealed. Slowly, the animal hunched down, preparing to leap—

A larger black wolf leapt onto the gray wolf, snapping and growling vehemently at it. The gray sank onto the floor, head and tail low. It growled low. The black wolf stayed standing over the gray, and clamped the back of its neck with his jaws. He continued snarling viciously until the gray rolled over and showed its belly in submission. Then the black wolf released the other and turned, keeping itself between us and the gray wolf. With one bark he commanded the tawny amber-colored beast to join the gray. With the amber down beside the gray, the black wolf barked to the remaining black-and-gray on the bed—though to this one, the barks were softer.

The black-and-gray's ears pricked forward, and it crawled to the edge of the mattress, pulling a length of IV tubing with it. It paused and sniffed at the tubing and whimpered. "Dr. Lincoln," I said softly.

The doctor inched forward. He reached out to the slender foreleg, and the black-and-gray wolf snapped at him, sending him backpedaling with a shout of alarm. He hit the wall hard, and his glasses went crooked. The black wolf leapt a pace forward and growled at the black-and-gray, until the black-and-gray whined and put her head down. The black wolf looked at me.

"Did she get you, Doctor?" I asked.

With a jerk and sudden realization of the danger he was in, the doctor righted his spectacles and checked himself over. "No. No, she didn't."

"I think she's ready to let you remove it now."

He pressed himself against the wall. "I'm not ready to risk being a wærewolf. . . ." He swallowed so hard it must've hurt. "I mean, well . . . you know."

I did know, but somebody had to do it. I pulled out of Nana's grip and staggered to the bed.

Bracing myself against the side of the bed with slightly bent knees, I reached slowly to the wolf's foreleg. When I gently gripped it, the black-and-gray wolf turned and looked at me steadily. There was no look of friendship or familiarity in those dark eyes, but I realized this was Theo. We'd succeeded! She'd fully transformed. If things had been normal, I might have cried from relief. I was so weary, though, I was too tired even to make tears. I pulled gently on the tape. It had been stuck to her human skin, but that flesh had split away and left the tape not exactly securing the IV anyway. Sliding the needle out was easier than I'd expected it to be. I dropped it onto the bed. Using the footboard as support, I put my weight on my feet again and stepped back.

The black wolf started making short, quiet howls again. The black-and-gray eased her forelegs down, then slid her haunches down as if it hurt.

The wolves needed to be safely kenneled in the cellar, and I had the thought the stairs were going to be difficult for the black-and-gray wolf. I inched forward. Nana grabbed my arms, thinking I was falling. "It's okay," I said. I moved along the footboard. I held my hand out to the black-and-gray wolf and said, "I can help you down the stairs." She sniffed at my hand.

The black wolf came closer and put his shoulder against me and pushed me back. He turned to the other wolves then and barked an order. The gray and the amber stood and exited; the black-and-gray followed. The black one went last. I followed them to the door, grabbed my robe, and slipped clumsily into it as I watched them descend the steps. The black-and-gray wolf was steadied by the other two.

At the bottom, the front door stood open—thanks to a hurried exit by the vampires—and the wolves went out.

Feeling certain that the black wolf would herd the others to the cellar, I moved into the hall and started down the steps, grateful for the sturdy rail. Outside, the house supported me as I crossed the porch and went around the corner. There, three of the wolves lay in a row just beyond the cellar doors. The big black wolf stood before them, tail wagging.

I opened the door, and they all proceeded down and inside. I followed, wishing I could just stop and rest on the steps. If I stopped, I knew I wouldn't get up again. Menessos had called too much energy out of me, left me so weak. But surely that had been the whole idea.

The black wolf put the gray and amber together in the first kennel. I shuffled over, shut the door, and clicked the lock shut. The black-and-gray went tiredly into the next kennel, lay down on the hay, and curled up. I stumbled, caught myself on the cage bars, then let my weak legs bend. On my knees, I shut and locked that door too. I turned to the black wolf. He stood resolutely at the far end, watching me. Head high, his weight distributed on all legs, he seemed like he was posing. He backed into his cage without taking his eyes from me.

I felt so drained. Darkness pushed at the edges of my vision. My limbs didn't want to move. "I can't," I said.

The black wolf lowered his head, whimpered once. With a big paw, he reached out and pulled the door shut. He glaced at the lock, then back to me. Summoning what energy I had left, I rose to my feet and slowly made it to the last cage and secured the lock. He had not moved, even to lie down. He just kept watching me intently.

My knees gave. Grappling for a bar to hold, I managed

to not fall, but I did crack my forehead on a bar. The wolf was suddenly right there, licking my hand and my head. He whimpered again and looked past me to the cellar doors and back to me. No one was there; he just wanted me to go. I began crawling across the cold concrete floor.

At the base of the steps I looked up—only eight of them, but I knew I couldn't do it. *One at a time,* I told myself. *If it takes all night, just climb one at a time.* I worked my hands up to the third step and put my knee on the first. The last thing I remembered was hearing the lonely howl of a wolf.

Amenemhab sat on my couch in the living room. He looked around, panting, but seemed to like what he saw. I lay on the floor, watching him. "Well?" I said. "What do you think of my home?"

"This isn't your home," he said. "This is just where you live."

I laughed. "Same thing."

"No."

My eyes shot open and I sat up all at once, the dream fading.

I was on the couch in my living room. Nana lay sprawled in the chair with an afghan over her, snoring loudly. Something hurt, but I couldn't tell exactly what. My head did hurt, but there was something else too. Something that wasn't my back or my feet, or anything like that. It was weird.

I swung my feet around to the floor and the movement flaked the dried blood on my chest. I realized I was in my robe and jeans still, and with that knowledge, flashbacks to being in the circle hit me hard.

That was what hurt—my soul.

Angry and afraid, I got up and started upstairs to the bathroom. I had to shower this blood—this vampire's blood—off of me. *Right now.*

Stripping off the robe in the bathroom, I noticed the moonstone necklace was gone. I hoped I hadn't lost it or broken it. I would worry about that later. Now, the shower.

The warm water felt so good, like I'd just noticed how good a shower could be. But I didn't want to scrub the blood off me, I didn't want to touch it. So, I stood there and let the steamy water loosen it and wash it away. Only then did I use the soap and scrub, and only then did I begin to feel like myself.

That asshole! I should've known better than to trust a vampire. *I have honored my oath to you, Persephone Alcmedi.* Yeah, right. A shiver coursed through me as I remembered his words, his voice, the feel of his breath on my skin. Angry, I squeezed the soap hard enough to leave marks in it. How dare he use me like that, play me for a fool. Hadn't I been played enough by Vivian?

I wondered what he'd done to her, but decided I was probably better off not knowing.

At least Theo would be all right.

Wrapped in a towel, I tiptoed to my room so as not to disturb Beverley—I could hear her soft snore in the other bedroom. I wondered if the doc had stayed. I hadn't seen him, but I assumed he had been the one to bring me inside.

The mess in my room devastated me. Clothes the wolves had been wearing lay in ripped and distorted piles. My bed was a complete disaster.

Turning my back on the wrecked room, I went to the closet and picked a navy blue sweat suit with loose ankles and stripes down the legs that matched the stripes on the long sleeves. With a white tank top under the jacket and the hood adjusted flat, I was set. I grabbed a second sweat suit for Theo and carried it up the steps to the attic. There, I took clothes from Celia's and Erik's suitcases and returned to the first floor, where I set the clothes aside and unzipped Johnny's suitcase. The smell of him hit me hard. I held his shirt up to my face and inhaled the cedar and sage scent of him and Gain detergent. I added the shirt to the pile, rummaged for a pair of underwear, didn't find any, and took a pair of jeans anyway. It didn't seem that Johnny owned any undies. I blushed at the thought.

Leaving the living room where Nana was still snoring, I went to the kitchen and started a pot of coffee while I grabbed up all the cookies and doughnuts I could find—and it wasn't many. We hadn't planned on four wærewolves transforming. Breakfast might get ugly.

Carrying all this and the set of keys for the locks, I went outside and headed for the storm cellar. After shuffling everything into one arm, I opened the cellar doors and quietly descended. I left the light off; I wanted wæres to sleep all they wished, but to find their things ready for them when they woke.

I put everything on the floor and sorted it out. I unlocked the first cage, the one I could see clearly in the ambient light. Celia and Erik were sweetly spooned together, naked on the hay. I put their clothes and a baggie containing some doughnuts and a biscotto on top. Erik loved biscotti.

Before unlocking the second cage, I stood staring at Theo. She was curled into the fetal position, her shoulder rising and falling with regular breaths. She was alive, and I thanked the Goddess for it.

I left her the sweat suit and a baggie containing some cookies. She didn't like biscotti, but I knew she did like nuts, so I set a half-filled can of salted peanuts atop the suit. They were Nana's, but I'd buy Nana some more.

As I turned to Johnny's cage, I couldn't help lifting his shirt to my face again and taking in the scent of him.

"I didn't know you could sing, Red."

I dropped the cage keys with a jerk. It was darker back here in the mornings; the light just wasn't strong enough. I'd expected him to be sleeping too, and I'd just been caught sniffing his shirt. I blinked into the darkness, willing my eyes to adjust. He was sitting in the corner closest to the cage door, one knee bent up to be modest. There was a tattoo on his thigh, but I couldn't tell what it was.

"You weren't all supposed to change," I whispered. "I'm so sorry."

"You don't have to apologize."

"Yes, I do." I passed the clothes through the bars, a baggie of Oreos on top. He set them to the side. "Menessos manipulated the ritual and took over. He wielded power a vampire just shouldn't possess, and I couldn't stop him."

Johnny stayed quiet and just watched me, like the wolf had last night. Then he said, "He marked you."

"I know." My voice trembled. Tears welled in my eyes.

To deny them, I snorted and tried to be cool about it. "He lied. Fucker." I glanced toward Theo. "At least she's alive." If Johnny was going to see me cry—me who he was convinced was this tough Lustrata—then I wanted him to think I was crying because Theo was okay.

When I turned back, Johnny was chewing a cookie. He put the shirt and the Oreo baggie aside and grabbed the jeans. He stood to put them on, and I hurriedly looked away again. But my rebellious eyes slid upward just before the denim slid up to cover his buttocks. I got another look at the Celtic knot-work armband tattoos and the Chinese lion-dog and dragon battling on his back.

Across the way, Celia roused and groaned happily as she stretched and made a grab for the goodies. I heard the smack of kissing followed by giggles and "Quit it or I won't give you the biscotto."

"Biscotto?"

Johnny reached through the bars, took up the keys, and unlocked his cage himself, but he didn't say anything else. He just leaned in the open door, shirt thrown over his shoulder like a towel, and munched his Oreos with a deeply thoughtful expression. Apparently, Oreos were the philosophical food of choice.

I, however, felt trapped. I couldn't just dart out or saunter out past naked people waking and getting dressed. I wasn't usually down here when they woke up. I opened cages, left doughnuts, and departed ASAP. But they deserved their privacy, and even if they didn't care about it, I did—so I waited where I was.

Celia came out of her cage and saw me. She started to speak, but Theo roused, moaning and moving very slowly.

Then she took the cookies. Celia and I shared a smile. After eating a few cookies, Theo sat up and lifted the sweat suit. The can of nuts rolled into the hay. "This . . . this isn't mine," she said.

"It's mine," I said. "I didn't have anything of yours."

"Seph? What are you doing down here? Wait—I didn't change here."

"No, you didn't."

Standing and jerking clothes on, she demanded, "What the hell happened?"

Everybody was dressed now. Erik came out and joined us. We passed looks around like hot potatoes.

In the doorway of her cage, Theo said, "I remember . . ." She shut her eyes. "My car. I remember tearing it apart." She looked at me. "I remember . . . Goliath!"

"It's my fault, Theo."

Her expression hardened, and her words came harsh and full of attitude. "You mean that jerk ran me off the road because I took a peek into his *public* history?"

"He tried to kill you because I asked questions. When I asked for your help, I didn't realize how dangerous he was. I'm sorry."

Theodora Hennessey was not a frail woman. She had lean limbs and moved with the in-your-face kind of grace reserved for Paris runway models. When she approached me with smooth, slow steps, her bare feet making no sound on the concrete floor, I knew something bad was about to happen. A slap, a punch, a slash of nails. I didn't care. Whatever she deemed necessary, I'd take it. I deserved it. Her arm moved, coiling for the strike, and snaked out. I resolved not to wince; I wouldn't even shut my eyes.

Another hand shot into my view, restraining her.

Theo gave a squeal of pain as Johnny squeezed her wrist.

"Let go," she growled.

"You would have died in a State Shelter," he growled back, "if not for her."

"And I apparently wouldn't have been hurt if not for her."

"That's true. And she could have said nothing and let you go to the shelter and die. Instead, she signed for custody and took responsibility for all the hospital and ambulance fees. She volunteered her home, her own bed, to be your personal hospital. A doctor I know has been tending you since the accident, but not even his skills could save your life."

Suspicion replaced her anger. "Then why am I alive?"

I knew Johnny wanted me to say it, but I couldn't. I just stared at the floor.

"*Her* skills saved you—at considerable risk."

"Considerable risk? That means what?"

"It means she had to enlist help," Celia said in a voice meant for easing jumpers off of high rooftops. "Vampires had to be involved."

"Vampires?"

"She managed to get the very one that injured you to participate in healing you, Theo. It was no light task to gain that service. And it was no light risk to throw aside the barrier of her home protection," Celia added.

"You asked them inside?" Theo said, focusing on me again.

"I did."

"Damn stupid thing to do."

"We couldn't risk moving you."

The anger and tension were fading. "So I guess we're square, then?"

"No. I owe you, still. A vehicle. And repairs to your business and apartment."

"What happened to Revelations?" Her concern returned.

"Goliath sacked your business and home looking for info on who hired you." I could see the worries flashing across her face.

"No, you two are square," Johnny said.

We both looked at him.

"Seph took a vamp's mark, Theo. She took it to save your life."

CHAPTER TWENTY-FIVE

My unused dining room furniture was getting used. Johnny cooked up everything breakfast-y in the house. Omelets with peppers and onions, blueberry pancakes, biscuits. I hadn't known I had bacon and sausage. They must've gotten them at the store before. Since I had fasted and the wæres had transformed, it was like a feeding frenzy. Theo ate more than Erik did, I noticed, but she deserved it. Beverley and Johnny shared a box of Lucky Charms and giggled and spoke with Irish accents.

Everyone was here except Nana and Dr. Lincoln. The doc had apparently gone home. I didn't blame him, but I did wonder how much his circle participation would cost me and how he'd word it on his bill. Nana was in the shower; I assumed she was avoiding me. I wanted to ask her about being stained, find out if she knew anything about it, if she'd seen anything in the Codex to erase it. It made me think she didn't want to be the one to have to tell me I was seriously screwed.

Beverley said, "So, Johnny, last night you herded the other wolves around. Are you, like, the pack leader?"

"Nah. No leaders here."

"But you did seem to retain an uncanny amount of human sensibility," I added.

"Yeah." He shrugged. "Weird, huh?" He focused hard on his food.

It was the kind of answer that agreed without offering anything, the kind that said he didn't want to discuss it. I wouldn't have pushed him, because I believed that he'd share information if it was relevant. However, Erik, leaning in the doorway to the kitchen and holding a mug of coffee and an omelet-and-buttered-biscuit sandwich, didn't seem to share my hesitation. He said, "Do you always retain your human sensibilities?"

"Yep." Johnny kept eating his cereal and staring at the back of the cereal box, as if by sheer will he could force the subject to something else. But it wasn't working. The tension level rose, though that might have had something to do with Celia and Theo adding their energy to it. Everyone had stopped eating, and the others openly stared at him.

No wonder Johnny had known I'd been stained. I hadn't considered the oddness of that before. Did he also know Menessos had kissed me? Instantly, I pictured Menessos's face and could feel his—

Damn it!

Could Menessos use the mark to create approval and desire for him in my thoughts? Like bespelling me with his eyes, only from a distance? He was a *vampire.* I shouldn't have any contemplations about him that weren't derogatory . . . so why was I thinking of him admiringly? Why was I thinking about him doing things that I hadn't thought about doing in a long time—at least, until a few days ago when I started imagining doing those things with Johnny?

I scolded myself. My thoughts were about as nonsensical as those of a smitten teenage girl.

But I couldn't put that thought away. Menessos had Vivian back. She had cause for a serious grudge against me. She would offer up anything she had that might spare her the pain and torment Menessos clearly had planned for her.

"How's that possible?" Theo demanded, bringing me back to the situation at present.

Johnny, still not looking at anyone, poured more cereal into his bowl. "Don't know," he said, his tone a little sharper. His sore spot had been found.

Theo rested her arm casually on the back of Beverley's chair. I knew this wasn't over yet. "Those are interesting tattoos you have," she said brightly, as if changing the subject. "I've always wanted to ask you about them."

Johnny's expression darkened, however, suggesting that the subject hadn't changed at all.

Theo sipped her coffee. "How long have you had them?"

"Long enough." He put down his spoon and focused his Wedjat gaze on her steadily, trying for the intimidating look that worked on me without effort.

If I had been Theo, I'd have stopped pushing right there, because poking around on a wild animal's injury would get you mauled. But Theo was clearly not intimidated by Johnny, and frankly the nature of her business was asking questions. "Why did you choose the Egyptian Wedjat, the Chinese power-animals, and the Celtic knot-work on your arms, may I ask? It's certainly an interesting mix of artwork and cultures."

He said nothing.

"Do you perhaps have ancestral ties to them?" she pressed.

"Not that I know of."

Theo cocked her head. "I don't understand."

"I didn't choose any of my tattoos."

Theo didn't seem as surprised as the rest of us were. In fact, she seemed more like a cat watching a mouse walk into a carefully laid trap. "You let someone else choose the designs to be forever on your body?"

Johnny scooted his chair back as he pushed the half-full bowl away. He stood. "I remember being attacked." He ran a hand through his dark hair. "And I remember waking, naked, in a park. I had the tattoos then. It was later that I learned I'd become a wærewolf."

He looked so tough, so formidable standing there, spine stiff and muscles taut. Yet a vulnerability swam in his eyes and seemed to be begging for answers to questions he'd carried too long.

I glanced at Theo to see her reaction to this, but the only thing about her that seemed out of place was how pale her knuckles were, her fingers grasping the mug very tightly as she said calmly, "And what of your life before the attack?"

Johnny shrugged. "A blank."

All of this stunned me, but I wasn't alone. Clearly, the other wærewolves hadn't known any of it either.

Johnny put his hands on his hips. "What does this tell you, Theo?"

"Don't know. I've just always wondered." She faced me. "Remind you of anything witchy?"

"No."

Nana shuffled in, wearing a matching top and pants of pale lavender and sage and her fuzzy pink slippers. I hadn't heard her come down the steps, and I wondered if she'd heard any of our conversation. Her cigarette case was in her hand. Since she had fasted for the ritual, she was probably as hungry as I had been. She seemed tired, more tired than I'd ever seen her, and she didn't so much as look at anyone, let alone greet them. Nana set the cigarette case on the table, slid into a chair, picked up a biscuit, split it open, and smeared jelly across it. "Okay, then, so what now?" she asked.

"Wait for the vampire's errand boy to come for the stake," I answered. "There aren't any options."

Johnny crossed his arms. "I don't think we should just hand over the weapon of the millennium. I mean, it's the one thing that can bring him down," he said. "It's the weapon *you* should have."

I knew he was referring to the Lustrata thing again. I didn't want to talk about it. "I gave my word."

"So did he. It meant nothing, so why hold yourself to yours?"

The attention of all the room's occupants now focused on me. I understood why Johnny had seemed so sour when it had been him in the spotlight. "I'm better than that."

"And what price are you willing to pay to be better?"

"You have a good point. In fact, it's a great point. But, no. My security here is compromised. If I don't give the stake to him, he'll just send his lackeys out to come and take it."

"I disagree, Red. With your security gone, that stake is the only thing that will keep him at bay."

I groaned. "I just want to wash my hands of this mess! Keeping the stake will only keep this nasty wound open."

His eyes pleaded with me. "If *wanting* the bogeyman to go away were enough, Vivian wouldn't have needed to make it in the first place."

The mood fell from tense to dismal. I rubbed at my brow. There wasn't enough coffee in the world for a headache and soul-ache like this.

Nana took a second biscuit and put it on the serving plate with what little remained of the omelets. "Menessos is a vampire-wizard, in case you didn't notice." Nana's sarcasm was thick. "And he won't be restrained by a chant. Not even a full-out spell. Only that stake can stop him."

Johnny gave me an "I-told-you-so" look.

"I did notice," I responded irritably. "When I couldn't stop him from staining me."

Nana faced me, and all her tiredness had transformed. She was mad. So she was also able to take all her emotions and force them into anger as it suited her. I had a lot of traits like hers. But one I didn't have: Nana fully pissed off was frightening. She said, "It is a mark you must have."

"Must have?" Celia choked. "It's a vampire's filthy stain, Demeter!"

I winced. *Filthy.* True, but it still hurt.

Nana said, "If Persephone is the Lustrata, she must have it."

Now I really, really didn't want to be the Lustrata.

"Ummm . . . what's a 'lostraduh'?" Theo asked.

"Lus-TRA-ta," Nana corrected. "She is the one destined to erase the lines drawn between humans and wærewolves, vampires, and witches. The one whose word will be law to the benefit of all."

"Okay, that's new," I mumbled.

"Wait a minute, I'm not following you," Johnny said. "Why does the Lustrata have to be marked?"

Nana poked at the eggs on her plate. "You know, Persephone, you were named for a goddess."

I'd been patient with her rambling up until now, but now she was bringing up the meaning of my name? "What does that have to do with being stained?"

"The original Persephone walked in three worlds: the world of the gods, that of humans, and the underworld of the dead. As Lustrata, it is *you* who must be able to walk between worlds. You are a human and a witch, so you live in this world. You already have a presence in the wæreworld through your friends and your column. But you need a mark to have a presence in the vampires' world. It's like . . . like a bus pass."

My words came slowly, trembling with anger and fear. "I don't want a presence in their world."

Hard as nails, the Nana I remembered from my youth said, "What you want has become irrelevant."

Johnny looked at me as if I had a new horrible disfigurement that revolted him. He left the dining room and stomped through the living room and out my front door. His shadow passed the window as he strode off the porch.

My phone rang. I slid from the seat with coffee mug in hand and went to answer it, fearing it would be the errand boy confirming a time for pickup. The voice on the other end of the line wasn't one I'd expected. "Hey, Seph. You're never going to guess what I'm calling about."

It was Jimmy Martin, my contact at the syndicate that had agreed to try to sell my column. Suddenly, I wondered if he was the errand boy, if he had ties to Menessos, if—wait. He sounded happy; he'd *never* sounded happy. "What's up?"

"I just got word that your column has been picked up for syndication by ten major newspapers, including the *New York Times,* the *Washington Post,* the *LA Times,* and the *Minneapolis Star-Tribune,* among others. I didn't even know they were sniffing around. We've never had anything like this happen before!"

I felt a cold shiver go through me. "That's . . . that's great, Jimmy."

"Oh, yeah, and there was a message, too. Where'd it go?"

"Message?"

"Yeah. Here it is. Says, 'You have nothing to fear.' Cryptic, huh? Like a fortune cookie or something. Just don't start thinking you're set, hotshot. Not yet. You do this right, and you can write your own ticket to television. Columns can turn into news segments and then into half-hour shows. And you don't even blog! This is crazy . . ."

Nothing to fear. Nothing to fear. "That's great, Jimmy."

"You don't sound too happy about it."

"No, I am. I am. Just surprised. Stunned. Like you said, we didn't even know they were interested. And right now, I've got company here. . . ."

"Oh, sorry. Go share your good news. I got to get back to work myself. Bye."

"Bye." I clicked the button on the receiver, but kept hold of it.

Nothing to fear. That was what I'd told Menessos. What was that obviously well-connected jerk up to? Showing me how great he could make my life, only to use that as a means to tighten the screws of control and threaten me with ruining my career? Hell, he could do it, apparently. Without the column, I'd be delivering papers just to support Nana and Beverley.

I hung the phone up. Through the window, I saw Johnny in the backyard, staring out across the stubbly cornfield. His hands in his jeans pockets, his back to the house; his weight was evenly distributed on both legs, and it reminded me of the stance of the black wolf. I left my empty mug by the coffeepot and went out through the garage to the backyard.

That ache remained with me; I was aware of it most when nothing else was distracting me from it. Then Johnny's body provided an adequate distraction. He made no move to indicate he heard me coming, but being a wære, he couldn't have *not* known.

"Johnny."

"Yeah."

"I just got an interesting phone call from my syndicate."

That surprised him enough that he faced me. "What about?"

"Seems my column was just picked up by most every major newspaper in the U.S."

One brow arched. "Funny timing, that."

"Yeah. The news came to him with a note for me. Said, 'You have nothing to fear.' That's what I told Menessos: if he helped me with Theo, he'd have nothing to fear because I'd give him Vivian, the book, and the stake."

At the mention of the stake, Johnny shifted back to face the field.

"He's telling me the rewards for turning over the stake and forgetting about him will be better than trying anything stupid."

"It's an intimidation tactic."

"I agree. He could pull the plug on my whole career, and I can't afford that with Nana and Beverley to support now. I bet Goliath made sure to point that out to him and . . ." I left the argument there. "I just *know* that we have to give him the stake."

"Maybe the stain is influencing you to that end."

I clamped my jaw shut. Could it be? Maybe, but I'd intended to keep my word from the start. "Can't you just trust me on this?"

"I trust *you.* I don't trust *him.*"

I let my head tip forward and stared at my feet. "I admit I don't know much about vampires. Can you tell me something that will convince me? I mean, why are you so adamantly against trusting him?" I paused. "Is it because he kissed me?"

"I think the better question would be: Does that kiss have anything to do with why you want to . . . comply?"

What was I supposed to say? I'd brought it up. "He made a blood oath on the steps, he hurt no one, and—"

"Hurt no one?" Johnny spun and gripped my arms. "Shit, Red! He marked you! He claimed you! Like a dog pissing on a fire hydrant to mark his territory that god-damned vamp marked *you*!"

He released me and turned away.

"I'm sorry," I whispered. "I was very wrong. Menessos did hurt someone: he hurt *you*." I half expected Johnny to deny it, but he didn't. "That was all it was probably meant to do, too. Menessos doesn't want me—why would he? I'm nothing but—"

"The Lustrata." He turned back. "Controlling you would be a very beneficial arrangement."

That sounded horrible. But I wasn't convinced I was what he and Nana seemed to want me to be. "Does he know that you guys think that's what I am?"

"Say it! Say the word. Stop tiptoeing around it."

"Do you think he knows that you guys think I'm . . . the Lustrata?"

Johnny grabbed my arms again and stepped closer even as he pulled me to him. "Damn it, Persephone! You are! *You are!*" His hands were trembling despite his tight grip. It hurt. If he could have fed me the passion of his words and made me believe it, he would have.

Johnny searched for words and apparently found none. He released me. My arms stung. "Does Menessos know?"

"I don't know." He turned away and ran a hand through his hair. "If he doesn't, then it's something you need to hide from him. But with the mark, I don't know how or even if you'll be able to do that."

"Vivian knew. I'm sure she's told him. And, Johnny—Nana says the stain is *part* of being the Lustrata. That it is necessary. If she's right . . ."

We stood there, warmed by the sunlight and cooled by

the breeze, for a long time, silent, side by side. I didn't want to go back into the house. I wanted to run into the field and just keep running.

Beverley bounded up between us. "Demeter sent me out," she said. "She wants to talk to you, Johnny. Something about her Tarot cards."

He looked askance at me.

I said, "I'm not the only one who doesn't want to be more than they appear, am I?"

Johnny walked toward the house. "C'mon."

CHAPTER TWENTY-SIX

The living room seemed dark after our time in the sunshine, and my eyes adjusted slowly. I'd held back in the kitchen, but Johnny motioned me to follow, and I knew he wanted me with him for this.

Nana sat to one side of the couch and indicated the other end to Johnny. "Good, Persephone. I'm glad you came too. You should see this."

I sat on the floor opposite them. The cards were upside down to me, but I knew them well enough that it made no difference. Nana's deck was pretty, but worn.

"In light of everything that's happened, I thought doing a reading might give me some insight. I didn't get answers, but it seems very clear this reading is about you, Johnny, so I thought you should see it." She paused. "Have you ever had your cards read before?"

"Nope."

Nana gestured over the cards spread across a Tarot cloth on my coffee table. "This is a Celtic Cross spread. The first position represents you. As you can see, the card is the King of Cups." She lifted the card and handed it to Johnny. "My deck is a Mythic deck, with the populace of Greek mythology adorning the cards. The king here is Orpheus, who was the son of the muse Calliope and was known as the greatest musician ever. I understand you have a band and have written many songs, so I think this card suits you well." She smiled genuinely. "Since the cards in the suit of cups are concerned with emotions, the King of Cups is described as a man who values relationships and human experience above all else. Also, he is a man who influences others with his words, so, again, I believe this is a good match for you.

"The next card, the card that's lying across your king"—she replaced the card—"is the card that identifies the problem. And the problem here is the King of Wands, represented by Theseus. Your current problem is with another man of heated enthusiasm, a man of some strength and nobility of character. He is an impatient man, though, and selfish too. Do you know whom this card represents?"

Johnny studied it. "I think so."

Sounded like a vampire-wizard to me.

"Now the third card . . ." She suddenly sat straighter. "I'm not boring you with the overexplaining, am I?"

"No. Please, go on."

"The third card crowns you and reveals the surface of the issue. You'll see that it is the Judgment card, and the figure on it is Hermes, messenger of the gods. See these pillars here? One black and one white? Remember them. I think you're looking at your past and seeing the patterns for the first time and realizing there is a certain intelligence in it."

"I don't know most of my past."

"But what you do know," I said, "is that there is a pattern to it, a pattern guiding you toward your destiny."

Johnny smirked. "Yeah. I guess."

Nana smirked back. "After all that's happened in the last twelve hours, you 'guess'?"

"All right. All right. I see it."

"The fourth card is the base of the problem, the motivation that drives you, as such." She lifted the card and held it up for both Johnny and me to see. "It is the High Priestess."

"Intuition," I said.

She pointed. "Here are those black-and-white pillars again, see? The secret pattern of your purpose, your particular destiny, is something you already know, but you might be looking for some other future when the one you're meant for is already here."

"I think I know what I'm meant to do already. And I'm not looking for a substitute." Johnny took the card from her, examining it. "Who is she?"

Nana offered me a secretive smile while he examined the card, then faced him to answer. "She is the Queen of the Underworld. She is Persephone."

My chin dropped to my chest. Peripherally, I could tell that Johnny stilled, fingered the card, then replaced it on the table. His voice was deeper than usual when he said, "Go on."

"Fifth is the position of past influences. The card Strength shows Heracles struggling with a lion that represents the beastly side of his own character. I think we all know what this refers to. Sixth is the Hanged Man, Prometheus. This is the position of future influences and suggests that in the future you will have to sacrifice something to gain something else of greater value."

"Like what?" Johnny asked.

"I honestly don't know."

"Any clues? Hints?"

"Only that it will not likely be easy. It could be something physical you must relinquish—or maybe something intangible, like a certain belief or attitude. Seventh here is the Chariot." She held it up. "Notice Ares is driving a chariot with a black horse and a white horse—rather like the black-and-white pillars, don't you think? And the two horses are trying to go in opposite directions."

"I see that."

Nana smiled wryly. "He's not going to get where he needs to be if his motivations aren't working in unison, is he?"

"No." He frowned at the card. "What does this one's position indicate?"

"The position refers to how you see yourself. This card tells me things have been neither wholly good nor wholly bad, that you have learned to accept the consequences of being a wærewolf, but perhaps you have not embraced the fact of being one and you still harbor anger about it as if something was taken from you, when perhaps you need to see it as 'something was given to you.'" She paused. "You're going somewhere, but you can't get there if you don't get your motivations to work together. Even if you want to, even if you *need* to, you cannot be in two places at once." She tapped the corner of the next card. "The eighth position—which refers to how others see you—you'll notice even the title of the card leaves no room for misunderstanding."

"The Hermit."

"Yes."

"The scythe makes him look like the Grim Reaper, though."

"Cronos was the youngest Titan and father of Zeus. The lamp he holds represents the patience and understanding he acquired in his loneliness. It is, perhaps, a great thing to have the understanding, but is that knowledge worth the hardship of being alone?"

Johnny looked at her steadily. "Can you be less cryptic?"

"I think this is tied to the last card, so be patient. The ninth card represents your hopes and fears and can be either one or the other, or both in one. The card here is the Devil, represented by Pan, who is an icon of the bonds all people feel with the instinctive animals that they are. Pan is part man and part beast. Pan is an untamed god of nature"—she regarded Johnny earnestly—"but he is also a musician."

Johnny smirked again. It was almost adorable.

"So is this my hope or my fear?" Johnny asked.

"Both, I believe. You hope to accept fully what you have become and what you will become, yet you fear what doing that will mean."

"You're losing me again."

"Just remember the things I tell you. It'll all make sense eventually."

Johnny turned to me as if asking for proof.

"It will," I said. "It always does. The cards are like that."

"What about the last one?"

"The future outcome. The Magician. Hermes again.

Here, he is the ruler of magic and master of the four elements. He has before him a caduceus with two snakes, one black and one white, representing every opposite you can imagine. Darkness and light, male and female, and so forth. And I think"—she tapped the Hermit—"it is no accident that this card, this lonely patience, brings the reward of being able to see and understand both light and dark, both good and evil. Hermes is the inner guide, and he may guide you to perilous and wearisome places, but only to point out the potential you have and make you choose whether to develop it or leave it uncultivated." She leaned forward. "I've always found Hermes to be an exciting card. I do hope you pursue what he shows you."

"You're not suggesting magic?"

"No. No. I would never. Much too dangerous."

"Then what? How will he show me what to pursue?"

"A dream. A book you stumble on. Anything spontaneous and intuitive at the same time." She tapped the High Priestess card. "Intuitive."

"It's all connected, huh?"

"Oh, yes. You already know that. And what's more, you have two kings and eight Major Arcana cards. It's splendid. Hermes is here twice, once in the underworld where he guided Orpheus"—she pointed to the King of Cups—"and where Persephone"—she touched the High Priestess card—"is Queen. Hermes carried the infant Pan"—she tapped the Devil card—"to Olympus when his mother fled in fright after seeing what she'd given birth to. There is definitely a linking of the underworld through these cards. Heracles, seen here in the Strength card wearing the color of Ares—the god on the Chariot card—

Heracles rescued Prometheus"—she tapped the Hanged Man—"a Titan and brother of Cronos." She tapped the Hermit card. "In fact, the only one who does not have deeper connections on this reading is Theseus, the King of Wands, and, him being the problem here, I'm not at all surprised by that." She studied the cards again, then looked up. "Eight Major Arcana is wildly powerful."

"Why?"

"The Major Arcana are the cards of the gods, the influence of deities. You're definitely unique, Johnny. And they know it."

CHAPTER TWENTY-SEVEN

Johnny and Erik were in the process of moving the furniture back into my room when Celia cornered me. "Look, Seph . . . the past few days have been all over the emotional map and"—she paused—"we've been friends a long time. I thought I knew you—I had you compartmentalized nicely in my mind, labeled safe, dependable, and sweet."

"What are you saying?" I felt my shoulders tighten.

"I had moments these last few days when I wondered about you. I wondered when you'd become this other person and why I hadn't seen it. I mean, we talked about Johnny, and next thing I know you're jabbing needles into Vivian's neck and then . . ." She sucked in a breath and put her hands on my shoulders. "Then you were facing down vampires, saving a life the only way you knew how."

My tension faded.

"You're still safe, dependable, and sweet. I'm just going to have to add brave, tough, and relentless to the list." She smiled.

I hugged her.

"We're leaving the air mattress upstairs for Johnny."

"Thanks."

"I'm glad he's sticking around for a few days just to see that all is well."

"Yeah. I am too." Celia and Erik were going to take Theo home and help with the cleanup there and at her office. I hadn't told them about the call from my editor. It would've just kept their suspicions up. I wanted this thing over. "You know, I wouldn't mind at all tagging along and helping with the cleanup at Theo's and at Revelations."

Putting a hand on my shoulder, Celia said softly, "Oh, Seph. Don't bother. We'll have it done in no time."

Sure, it was a polite way of reminding me that I was a comparative weakling. Plus I knew they were going to talk about me. I wasn't worried about it because of insecurity; it was just that I'd never been like them because I wasn't a wære. I was now even less like them because I was stained. It made me feel like a bizarre outcast, while they seemed like the normal ones all of a sudden. That was weird.

Theo came and hugged me as they were going out. "I'm so sorry for all the pain and loss I've caused you, Theo," I said. I broke out of the embrace and pulled a thick envelope from my pocket. "Take this."

"What?" She opened it. "Persephone—"

"It's for a new vehicle and repair or replacement of whatever was damaged. If you need more, let me know." She pushed the envelope back at me, shaking her head, and started to say something. I cut her off. "Vivian gave me money, and this is out of that. She blackmailed it out of Menessos, so it's kind of like him paying for it. Since his guy did it—seems fair."

"Persephone, you keep me safe every full moon. I know your name and where your house is, but I never felt like I really knew you. Still, I don't feel like I *know* you. I was surprised as hell to find out you're an Arthurian fan." She smiled. "I wouldn't have guessed that, y'know?" She shifted the envelope and took my hand. "But I knew from the start that I felt safe kenneling at your place. Instinctively, I trusted you with my safety. That's not going to change. A dozen times you could have ducked your head and run, you could have given up because things looked hard or hopeless. But you dared to go onward." Her shoulders squared. "Even with your carrying a vampire's stain, I'd put my life in your hands again, knowingly, and feel secure about it. The kind of character you have isn't learned, isn't . . . isn't even a choice. It's inborn, and inescapable."

I squeezed her hand, my eyes were stinging with tears.

"Okay, speech over," she said brightly, and hugged me again. "See you soon."

Theo walked out of my house. Her ankles and one leg had been broken just days ago. My heart felt so big knowing I had helped, truly helped. But my conscience wouldn't let my ego swell much. It whispered, "Saviors don't set up the disaster they're praised for rising above."

A little over an hour later, as I was finishing cleaning up the bedroom, the phone rang. Picking up the cordless from my room, I answered. "Hello."

"Seph, it's Celia."

"Make it okay?"

"Yeah. That rat drummer of theirs, Feral, was already here cleaning up. Said he didn't want us to be overwhelmed."

I carried the phone with me as I carried my cleaning supplies downstairs. "He's a good guy."

"He is. I just wanted to let you know that we made it and that things are gonna be fine. The door will be fixed quick, and she'll have a place to sleep and working locks back on her doors. I figured you'd want to hear that."

"I did. Thanks, Celia."

"Sure. Bye."

I clicked the phone off and laid it on the counter. Beverley had started the dishes. "You didn't have to do that," I said.

She shrugged. "I needed something to do. I'm not in school."

"Well, I appreciate your help. Oh, crap!" It was Monday. "I have to call and get you excused from school!" I was going to have to contact the authorities and somehow get the matter of custody settled. I couldn't even get her enrolled in school here until I had that straightened out.

"It's okay. I mean, the school knows about my mother and all. Then there was all that . . . stuff with the reporters and all. I don't think they expect me back in class right away. Besides, I deserve a break."

"Yes, you do."

She washed on in silence. I put the cleaning supplies away in the laundry room. When I came back through, she said, "Seph?"

"Yeah?"

"When the wolves changed in the circle, was it . . ." She kept her attention focused on the plate she was rubbing a rag over. "Was it like that for my mom too?"

I sat down at the table. "Yeah."

"So that wasn't different because of the circle or the magic?"

"No." Staying matter-of-fact about it would keep me from over- or underrating the experience of being a wære.

She let the plate and the rag drop back into the soapy water and faced me. "Looked like it hurt."

"I think it does hurt. A lot."

Beverley shifted her weight, then turned back to the sink.

"What's wrong?"

"I've *seen* it, Seph. I think I can handle the verbal details."

She sounded so much older than nine; well, she was almost ten. Her birthday was in the first part of November, making her a Scorpio.

I got up and went to her. If she'd turned to me, I would have hugged her, but she didn't, so I grabbed a dish towel and started drying the dishes and putting them away. She wouldn't know where they all went anyway. "I'm not holding back, Beverley. I just don't know more than that."

"But you write a column about them."

"Yeah, I do. But that's social stuff. This is more specific individual experience stuff." I looked around. "Where's Johnny? I'm sure he would answer your questions. He knows it because he lives it; I just observe it."

"I think he went out to get the stake and have it ready for the pickup." She paused. "What if he doesn't think I'm ready to hear the answers?"

"If you're able to ask the questions, I guess you are able to hear the answers."

I thought that satisfied her, but a minute later I realized there were long streaks on her face. I put the rag down. "Beverley?"

With her hands in the water, she dropped her head to her chest and the sobs came out.

I touched her shoulder. "What is it?"

"Me and Mom used to do dishes like this and talk."

"Oh, honey." Regardless of her dripping hands, I turned her and took her into my arms and hugged her tight.

"I miss her so much."

"Of course you do." I stroked her hair. However many times she needed to cry, I vowed to myself I'd embrace her and let her do so.

When her grief subsided enough that she could pull away and wipe her eyes, she said, "Sorry."

"You have nothing to be sorry for or ashamed of."

She nodded, but she still looked miserable.

"I should teach you to meditate."

"Meditate?"

"Yeah. It's a great way to clear your mind or get your thoughts in order. If you're feeling scattered or lost, it can help. It helps me, anyway."

"Maybe." She bit her lip. "I'll try."

The door from the garage opened, and Johnny stepped

inside. Ares bounded in with him. Beverley backed up from me, embarrassed. "Find it?" I asked Johnny.

"Yep," he said with a quick smile. He tapped his nose. "Followed your tracks." He put the wooden box against the wall just inside the door.

That he would be back to himself and not hold a grudge about having to give up the stake reassured me.

"I have a surprise for you," he said.

Apprehensive, I asked, "What is it?"

"Let's go see." He took my arm and led me into the dining room and to my desk.

"What?" I said, fearing a joke of some kind coming.

He bent down and slid my binder marked *Research* from the shelf.

"My notebook?"

He held it out to me. "Open it."

"I already know what's in it." Had he looked through it and corrected passages or added information? Had he found something he didn't like?

"Do you?" he asked.

Now I was really curious, and concerned.

He wagged the notebook at me. I took it and opened it. It felt much heavier than I remembered, but the first page was just as it should be, a handwritten table of contents. Nothing new listed. I tilted it to the side. The index tabs were all marked as they should be: *Historical, Medical, Social, Shelters, Laws Enacted, Laws Proposed, Local,* and *National.* The last two had clippings of articles and lists of governmental and citizen sympathizers, support groups, and anti-wære groups.

There was a new tab at the back, blank. I put my finger on it; glanced at Johnny, who was grinning; and flipped to that section. I couldn't believe my eyes. Flipping the pages quickly, I realized what it was. "The Codex?" Every page, copied, from the ancient book Menessos had taken. "How did you—?" I looked up.

"Your scanner, duh. You really need to catch up with the times, tech-wise. Although you do have one non-techy thing I like."

"And that is?" I had an idea of what he might say.

"That three-hole-punch thing. It *is* handy."

I didn't get to enjoy the surprise for long. When Nana found out, she took the notebook from me and started translating. "I'll have Dr. Lincoln look these over, of course."

I turned my attention to dinner. My cupboards were nearly empty. I mumbled, "Old Mother Hubbard's cupboards are bare."

"Don't tell me this poor dog's gonna get none."

Johnny could put temptation into his voice so easily. I smiled. "Dinner's gonna be slight."

"Slight? You've got pasta and tomato sauce. I can work with this." He reached and turned the oven on.

"Seph?" Beverley called from atop the steps.

"Coming." I started for the hall.

She added, "Someone's coming up the drive real slow-like."

I stopped in my tracks and shot a look at Johnny. He stopped midway through pulling a skillet out of the cupboard and slid it back into place. He straightened and turned the oven off. With a dramatic gesture, one that revealed some of his still-remaining irritation with my decision about the stake, we headed for the front door.

"Beverley, you stay up there. Nana—"

"I'm not moving!" The sound of her lighter flicking followed her shout.

Johnny took up a position just out of sight beside the door as I started unlocking it. The steps of whomever Menessos had sent to collect the stake thudded purposefully onto my porch. When he came into view, I couldn't believe it. And then—then it made perfect sense.

"Samson D. Kline."

"Miss Alcmedi." He grinned at me. "Didn't expect me, did ya?" he said with a laugh. "Well I didn't expect what I've heard that you've done, either."

"What have you heard?"

His grin turned sly. "Gossip on the front porch. How very white-trash. I expected better of the great Persephone Alcmedi, the witch who tempted Menessos back into a circle."

"What do you mean 'back'?"

He made a mock show of sympathy. "It's girls like you who end up disappeared and on the alarmist, scandal-mongering media better known as the evening news. Girls like you who don't find out enough about the boys they're playing with."

"Since background searching led to a near-fatal accident for a friend of mine, why don't you save me the risk and fill me in yourself, so I can stay off the evening news? I mean, I'd hate to think of you watching those awful shows waiting to hear of my gory end and being infected by the lust-indulging breaks better known as commercials."

Samson leered. "Fine."

I opened the door and gestured for him to enter, but didn't say the inviting words.

He made a show of wiping his boots on my welcome mat, then stepped in, came up beside Johnny, and jerked, startled. As he took in the long line of Johnny's tall body and his tattooed and pierced face, the preacher seemed to wilt in his blue polyester suit like a kid who has just realized that rope he's been yanking on is attached to a rather ominous-looking monster.

He recovered himself enough to proceed hurriedly into the living room. "Waterhouse," he grumbled. "Suits you."

"I'm surprised you know the artist's name. I had you pegged as one of those people who decorated with paintings of Jesus on black velvet and considered it high art."

In the dining room, Nana sniggered but didn't look up from the notebook.

Samson flopped down onto my couch without having been invited to take a seat. He spread his arms across the back as he put one ankle up on the opposite knee, trying for a pose of comfort and indifference. The position, however, made his pant legs rise up to show that he wore old-man short boots that zipped up the inside. He followed my gaze and slipped out of the position. "Got anything to drink? Like Scotch?"

Beside me, Johnny crossed his arms and took up a mean-bouncer expression.

"I don't keep liquor, Mr. Kline. How about some water?"

He waved the suggestion off with a sneer like he'd just tasted something very bad. "Well, then, let's get on with this. Where's the stake?"

"I thought you were going to tell me about Menessos getting back in the circle."

"Oh," he said. "Yes." He sat forward. "A glass of Scotch would make this a lot easier, though."

"I still have only water."

"Not even beer?" He looked Johnny over. "Don't tell me you don't keep any beer here."

Enunciating slowly and loudly, Johnny said, "Waaaa—terrrrrr."

"Right. Right." Samson frowned. "It's simple. Menessos gave up magic when Vivian bested him by creating the stake and keeping it secret from him. He vowed never to use magic again until the stake was destroyed."

"He broke that oath."

"Exactly." Samson grinned lasciviously at me. "Broke it for *you.*" He sounded like a fifth grader at the lunch table.

"You sure have a way of making people uncomfortable, Mr. Kline."

"My messages aren't ever meant to put people at ease. I'm a fire-and-brimstone kind of preacher."

"I've noticed."

He seemed to take that as a compliment, though I hadn't meant it that way.

"I'm curious," I said. "How did you find out about this sensitive subject?"

"That thing that used to be my brother."

I should have guessed. "Our last talk left me with the impression that you didn't speak with him anymore."

"*It* has its uses." He glanced around. "Now . . . that stake?"

I turned for the kitchen and heard Johnny ask, "So what do you get out of this deal?"

Samson must have paused to gauge the wærewolf before answering, because he was just starting to answer as I came back down the hall.

"Do you have any idea who I happen to be?"

Johnny said, "You're that prick on TV."

Samson leaned forward, putting his forearms on his knees. His hands rubbed together. "I guess you do."

"So why are you playing errand boy for a vampire? Isn't this a new low in your life of hypocrisy?"

"This is my out, son. My—"

"*Don't* call me 'son.'" The darkness in Johnny's tone sent a shiver down my spine. Made me glad he was on my side.

"My deal is to pick up the stake and destroy it. In return, that bastard Menessos will call off those freaks and wannabes who show up to my every studio sermon." He grunted. "He sends them down there on purpose with orders that the more fervent and freakish they look, the more they damage my credibility, the more they prove themselves to him. He uses me as a test of loyalty for those wretched jerk-offs."

"Maybe he's testing you," I said from the doorway.

"What?" He straightened. "You don't mean the Lord—you mean the vampire?"

"Yeah. Maybe if you had the power to get through to those wannabes and change their minds, he would see you as a threat instead of a toy." I grinned. "Bet you don't even try, do you? You believe in saving people so much—but just worthy people, right?"

Face flushed, Samson stood, finger wagging and ready to deliver a sermon in my living room. Johnny took a half step forward, a low growl in his throat. "She has a point."

Samson's hand fell to his side; his fists were balled tight and his chubby knuckles were white. "You don't know anything!" he shouted. "You're filth. You're all filth." He gestured to Nana, who hadn't said anything to him. "And you'll all rot in Hell."

"Cut the bullshit," Nana snapped, rising from the table and coming at him. "Do you think your sparkling life merits any rewards? You're pathetic."

"You think I don't know what you are, you old crone? I've suffered too many of you for too damn long!" He held his hand out to me. "Just give me the stake and let me get out of here."

"I'm glad I don't have any Scotch," I said, starting forward. "If I did, you wouldn't be in a hurry."

"I can't expect you to understand my sacred mission. You're already tainted. Bit into that apple, I hear. Got your mark. You're well on your way, aren't you? I knew you wanted to be one of them." His pious "you-can't-judge-me" expression—the one that was a cross between an idiot's blankness and rapture—was set in his wrinkled skin. "The first time I met you, I recognized that gleam in your eyes. It's the same one worn by all those fools he sends to my studio."

"I know you're accustomed to forcing your opinions on others, but save it for the studio, Sam. Everyone here knows what a fraud you are." I shoved the box at him. "Take it and get out."

He wrapped his arms lovingly around the box, rubbed his cheek over its upper surface. It was unsettling. "Mark my words, little girl, Menessos is a deceiver. More than any other black-hearted creature ever to walk the creation. But then, we don't suffer him to live, do we? He's already dead. And we suffer him yet."

The door had barely shut when the phone rang.

I jogged to answer it. "Hello?"

"Seph. It's Nancy. Please don't hang up."

She sounded like she was in tears. "Okay. What's wrong?"

"Would you please, please meet me somewhere? Like in Mansfield? I just *have* to talk to you."

I didn't know what to say.

"Persephone?"

"I'm here."

"Please."

"About what, Nance?" She sniffled in answer, so I added, "I mean, I didn't like how things went last weekend either, but it kind of felt like it'd been coming for a long time."

"I didn't want it to."

I let her have the silence this time, and I didn't put in a pathetic sniffle for dramatic effect. Meeting with her would just stir up all the dying-friendship pain again. I understood that she was giving me—her favorite from the group—a second chance, but I didn't want it. Nancy was good at distorting things; she did it without even thinking. It was second nature for her. Instead of her walking out on us with her head and morals high and leaving it at that, she was feeling guilty and wanted the opportunity to blame me for everything being wrong and to forgive me at the same time.

"What did Olivia and Betsy have to say?"

"I don't know. I left shortly after you did." I knew better than to let her wring any gossip out of me. "I think we should just let everything go, Nance. We've all grown apart, and those friendships feel like obligations now. That's not good."

"Obligations?" Now she sounded hurt. "How long have I been an obligation to you?"

Well, if I was going to be the ruination of it all, I could do that from here and save the gas money and the time. "We've grown apart," I repeated. "Gone separate ways. Only Olivia and Betsy have anything in common anymore."

"Bar stools and second shift at the factory."

"Right. If they didn't have that, they'd have forgotten each other by now."

"We haven't forgotten each other."

"Maybe it's time to."

"I have some of your things. I can't mail them to you. Mr. Jarrod cut my hours and my funds just don't have any room."

"What things?"

"A sweater, a few cassette tapes. A book."

"Keep them."

"No. Meet me. I'll give them to you."

"Now's not a good time."

"You have plans?"

"No. I'm just really tired."

"I see. Too tired for obligations. I'll bring them all the way to you, then."

I was sure when I responded that she would know she'd won. "Where do you want to meet?"

"Take 71 South to 30 toward Crestline or Bucyrus. I don't remember the name of the street, but there's an exit by a big Meijer grocery store. In the plaza outside it is a coffee shop. We'll meet there at seven. Thanks, Seph."

CHAPTER TWENTY-EIGHT

Nana threw a fit. Not because she didn't want me to go, but because Johnny said he'd go with me—and that meant he wasn't going to cook dinner. He whipped up a few sandwiches for her and Beverley and promised he'd go to the big grocery while I chatted with my friend. Then he leaned in and whispered something to Nana and then all was well. I made a mental note to ask him what his magic words had been.

The sun was dipping toward the horizon and, since Mansfield was southwest of my home, I had to contend with its glare in my eyes. Even with sunglasses on, I continued squinting, and it was bringing on a headache. I wasn't feeling very chatty. Johnny ruled the radio, but about forty minutes into the trip, he'd had enough. The local stations didn't play much that he deemed suitable for human ears. "So . . ." he said, drawing out the sound and ending it with a slap on his thighs. "What's up with this friend that you gotta drive an hour to meet her?"

Pursing my lips, I tried to decide how to word it. Johnny wouldn't want or need to hear all the details. Girl stuff would probably bore him. "Our friendship is over. It could end on terms that aren't exactly bad, but she won't stop till things get ugly."

"Why aren't you still friends?"

"We've just grown so far apart and become so different since high school that it's a chore. Any relationship that feels like work isn't working. Every relationship has to be worked at, I know, but—"

"Can I put in here that I think you might be watching too much Dr. Phil?"

"Shut up. I don't even watch TV that much. What I'm saying is that a friendship shouldn't be so hard."

His voice sank low and turned yummy. "Some things are at their best when they're hard."

"Johnny," I said exasperatedly. After signaling my annoyance by shaking my head for an appropriate amount of time, I continued: "I don't remember her birthday anymore, but every New Year when I put up the new calendar, I feel obligated to reference the old calendar and write it—and other things—on the right date and send a card and some flowers to her work."

"Lots of people need reminding, Red."

"Okay, fine." He clearly wouldn't stop until he had the whole messy story. "She found Jesus recently—"

"Was he lost?"

"Oh stop it. She's very connected to religion, which isn't a bad thing, but it means that we don't do any of the old stuff we used to do or talk about any of the old stuff we used to talk about because she's 'not allowed.' It all just seems pointless. She doesn't know I'm a witch. I never told her or the others because I knew they'd think I was a freak. Now I *really* can't tell her. She doesn't even know what column, exactly, I write, or she'd be on my case about that because she's very anti-wære." I sighed. "I have to be so careful around her. It's tedious keeping secrets like that. And I know she wouldn't want to be my friend anymore if she knew the truth."

He was quiet, then pointed out the big red-and-yellow Meijer sign in the distance, indicating that the next exit was the one I wanted. "Sounds to me like the truth will set you free."

I dropped Johnny off outside the store and said I'd be watching for him in an hour. I drove off to the little plaza then and realized that the coffee shop Nancy expected to meet in was a Starbucks.

I didn't see her Cavalier anywhere, but I went on inside. I ordered a hot apple cider from a very congenial employee and chose a seat away from the window and the nearly retired sun. I thought about picking up the complimentary local paper to flip through, but my eyes needed to rest.

Backing my chair against the wall, I let my head fall back, shut my eyes, and reflected upon my last visit to a coffee shop. Despite their different franchised names and color schemes, the environments inside the two shops were pretty much the same, and the aroma was definitely the same. It took me back.

Vivian had suckered me and started this whole mess. I wondered if Vivian was dead. Wondered if her flesh was cold and gray, her eyes wide and sightless. It surprised me how strongly I hoped that was the case. For what she had done to Lorrie, for the manipulation of so many, and to bury the info she held and keep it from getting to Menessos.

Leaning on the table, I stirred the hot cider, watching the amber liquid swirl. The strong sense of justice that had embraced me all my life seemed to be gripping me tighter lately, strengthened by the accompanying urge to personally dole justice out in hefty doses to those who required it—but only to those who either admitted their guilt or had it otherwise proven. Sounded like top-of-the-list requirements for a Lustrata.

"You hate me, don't you?"

Nancy stood there with a little box in her arms. Her red-rimmed and puffy eyes were wide and uncertain. Her mousy brown hair was coiled up into a bun, with wisps of shorter, loose hair sticking out. It created a slight wildness about her. I noticed the little doily pinned atop her head. She'd worn it to our brunch too. I realized Nancy had chosen a strict denomination of Christianity, Apostolic. I felt like a bug some kid had just dropped into a jar as she studied me. "No. I don't hate you," I said.

"You look so . . . serious and angry," she said.

"Sorry. Just deep in thought." Nancy didn't look convinced. The kid was going to start shaking the jar and might even poke around with a stick. "I told you it was a bad time."

"Well, here." She set the box on the table. "I'll go get a coffee."

Peering into the box, I saw a bright yellow V-neck sweater neatly folded, and under it was a hardcover copy of *The Mists of Avalon.* An introduction, for me, to Arthur. Fallen to the side of the book were three cassette tapes, rock 'n' roll from my rebellious youth. I couldn't help but smile to myself.

"That's much better," Nancy said, slipping into the chair across from me.

"What?"

"You, smiling."

I sipped my cider. "I just remembered that concert in Cleveland when Olivia won the front row tickets from WMMS and you and Betsy flashed the singer your—"

"I remember," she said quickly, smothering any further such reminiscences. Her faith was such a controlling belief that to show my consideration of it in her presence meant I had to alter myself. It wasn't right. The core of our drifting friendship had became a surge in the opposite direction when she found religion.

We sat, stirring our drinks in silence. My leg bounced with impatience.

The bruising silence lasted a minute, then two.

I looked up from my drink. Nancy was sitting perfectly still. The cross on her necklace glittered delicately in the cozy ambient light. I caught myself wondering if the symbol was anathema to vampires like in the stories.

I *had* to stop thinking about vampires.

Nancy's fingers were curled tight around the cardboard sleeve meant to make holding the hot drink more comfortable. She seemed crushed, as if someone just told her a car had hit her dog. "It's gone," she said. "That feeling of being free. Free of parents—or grandparents, in your case. Just hanging out with friends who won't tell on you or hate you for being young and naive because they are too."

I agreed. For me, that feeling had gone away in college when the bills started coming. Maybe religion was, for Nancy, the ultimate bill with payment due.

"Why is it gone?" she asked.

"I think it has something to do with maturity, responsibility."

"That would explain Olivia and Betsy." She could have made a joke of it, but instead she made it sound depressing.

"Probably."

"Why us?"

"We accept what we have to do and do it." I thought again of being the Lustrata.

"You'd think that maturity and responsibility would leave a mark."

Involuntarily, I touched my chest where Menessos had left his mark, his stain. It was mine because I was responsible for Theo. "It does," I said. "It's an interior stain, spilled over you by failure and pain."

Nancy had picked up on the inadvertent rhyme of my spoken words. "Maybe you should start putting poetry in that column of yours. Or branch out."

I finished my apple cider and put the cup on the table. This suffocating encounter had gone on long enough. "Nancy."

"Don't, Seph. I know what you're going to say and I beg you, don't say it."

"But—"

Nancy leaned forward and put her fingers on my forearm and implored me, "Even if we never talk again, we're friends in our hearts if we don't say that kind of good-bye. If we say that kind of good-bye, if we shut the door on this friendship, we can't open that door again." Her fingers were hot from holding the coffee cup.

"Shutting it might be best."

She sat back, her hot hand drifting from my arm. "Have I been a bad friend?"

I stared at her, choking on the truth. "No. I have."

"No you haven't—"

"I've kept secrets from you. Secrets that would change everything."

She gauged me, and I could feel her pulling away from me. It was as if her aura retreated and took its stifling oppression with it. I could breathe more easily. "What do you mean?" she asked.

"Just trust me when I say that if you knew me, really knew *me,* you wouldn't want to be my friend. You'd run screaming in the other direction and . . ." I'd gotten loud and emphatic enough to widen her eyes, so I toned it down to continue. "I'm so tired of trying to keep up the pretenses to make you happy."

"Pretenses? Whatever do you mean?"

I didn't answer.

"Oh my Lord . . . you're not a wære, are you?"

I stood and picked up the box. "Thanks for returning these." I didn't have to straighten out her thoughts.

"Seph, no. No! You're the only friend I have!"

"My nana says that to have a friend, you need to be a friend. So I suggest you try being a friend to those like-minded souls traveling the same road you're on, because my path isn't anywhere near yours. They can support you.

No matter what I do, I can't. I wish you the best, Nancy. I really do. Enjoy the life you've chosen for yourself, but enjoy it without me in it."

My hour wasn't up yet, so I parked at Meijer and went in. I spotted Johnny just starting down the cookie aisle. In response to the stares, he said a polite hello to the older ladies he passed and gave a friendly guy-nod to the men. He rolled his cart up beside a mother with two little ones strapped into an extra-long cart with a special seat built for containing them. The mother didn't notice Johnny, as she was intently studying the labels on Keebler cookies. Her older son watched Johnny put four bags of Oreos into the cart and said, "Is your momma gonna be mad that you drew all over yourself?"

The mother turned around, stunned silent when she saw Johnny. "Naw," Johnny said to the little boy. "I didn't do it. One night when I was little, I didn't put my markers away like my momma told me to. The bogeyman drew on me, and it's never washed off. So you better listen to your momma."

Cradling two packages of cookies in the crook of one arm, the mother shoved hard against the cart handles and hurried her little brood safely away around the corner of the aisle. I heard the younger boy say, "Wow! Look, Joshua! We get *two* kinds of cookies this time!"

I'd been easing up on Johnny's position, and I was ready to stop and tap my foot and ask if he always scared young mothers, but he sniffed the air and turned suddenly to see me. "Red!"

"I wish I had a camera."

"Why?"

"Seeing you pushing a cart full of Oreos"—I peered into the cart—"steaks, and . . ."—I raised a dubious brow at him—"every spice known to man."

"No point in eating if you don't make it taste good. Just wait till we hit the produce aisle. Some herbs are fine dried and bottled like this, but for some, fresh is the only way."

"Well, if anyone knows all about fresh, it's got to be you."

After I followed him through the produce section and we went through the checkout, Johnny pushed the bag-laden cart across the bumpy parking lot and started putting the bags into the trunk of the Avalon. I watched him sort the bags to keep the cold stuff together and put the fresh vegetables, bread, and doughnuts in a squash-proof area with boxes of cereal acting like a fence to secure them. It scared me. Not because it was terribly obsessive/compulsive, but because it was an act of terrible domestication. And it was what I'd have done.

Goddess, how my life had changed. My home's magical defenses were gone and my personal fences were eroding under the relentless influence of Johnny. Nothing was ever going to be the same again.

I was still standing there staring at him when he shut the trunk. I hadn't helped him at all. "Red?"

"What?"

"Something wrong?"

"No."

"Okay. You can get in the car. I'll put the cart away."

"Right."

Johnny turned to the cart. I grabbed him and I kissed him there in the parking lot, under the glow of the lot lights. My fingers ran through his hair. He recovered from his surprise and slipped his hands to my waist, grip tightening. Parts of me tightened too. He held me close and his fingers strayed around to brush the skin over my spine and push just under the waistband of my jeans. I slipped him some tongue.

"Wow," he breathed as our lips parted. "Apple cider."

CHAPTER TWENTY-NINE

We headed home.

Forcing my shoulders to loosen, a task made more difficult because I was driving, I was just finding a measure of success when Johnny said, “How’d it go with your friend?”

Those resistant muscles clenched back into their taut position. “It’s over.”

“Sounds like a couple thing. You two didn’t ever—”

“Stop it.”

“Well, some girlfriends do—”

“I said *stop*.” Damn it. How was I ever going to relax?

“Okay, okay. Just trying to lighten the mood.” Johnny turned on the radio and maneuvered the dial to the left for the classical station. He adjusted his seat to recline and went to sleep.

“Johnny, wake up. We’re . . . here.” I was not about to say, “We’re home.”

He stretched and said, “Okay.”

After hitting the trunk-opening button, I got out.

The living room lights were off, which I thought was odd because I figured Nana and Beverley would be watching TV, but the upstairs and kitchen lights were on. Nana was probably still translating the copy of the book. I started to gather up the bags. The next thing I knew, Johnny was beside me taking the bags from my hands.

"I can get it," I said, and closed my fingers around the plastic handles.

"I can help." Ever so gently, he again tried to take the bags. His expression was playful as he watched my face while he touched my hands.

"Get your own bags," I said, teasing, but soft and unsure. I'd snapped at him over the girlfriend remark, and he shouldn't be acting like nothing had happened. Men let snippy words roll off of them more easily than women did.

"But I want those."

"Why?"

"To lighten your load."

"You're not a servant."

He stilled, searching my face slowly, making one big counterclockwise circuit, taking in everything. His hands, big and warm, touched either side of my neck. His thumbs rubbed along my jaw. It was nice, sensual, and if he had applied any pressure, it would have been dangerously close to strangling. But he just touched me and let me feel how warm and gentle he was. Cedar and sage filled the air.

Johnny put his lips against mine. Warm and soft and quivering deep down with adrenaline.

While the kiss was still chaste, he pulled away. "I will

serve the Lustrata in all things." He flashed a one-sided smile before walking away with the grocery bags that had been in my hands. I stood there beside the trunk for a minute, dumbfounded. I hadn't registered when he had removed his hands from my neck or when he had taken the bags from me.

In all things echoed in my mind. Happy and thrilled and irritated all at once, I grabbed more bags from the trunk. In the garage, Ares was in his cage barking like mad. "Just a minute, boy," I said. "I'll let you out in a second." I headed for the light falling from the open door. Johnny slipped past me to get the remaining bags, and I set the ones I'd brought in on the table beside the others. I put my coat on the back of a chair and began sorting through the bags. "Nana! Beverley! We're back."

Over my head, the floor creaked.

I found the milk and carried it to the refrigerator. But what I saw when I opened the door made the gallon jug slip from my grasp. Fear stilled me rigid, unable to move. A scream clawed at my throat like that of a caged animal desperate for freedom, but my throat had closed. My mind grappled for understanding.

As soon as I fully recognized what I was looking at, my throat opened. Air was sucked into my waiting lungs, and I screamed.

In an instant, Johnny was there, staring at the silver platter in my refrigerator where the head of Samson D. Kline sat, eyes open wide—as was his mouth, tongue thick and pushed to one side.

Johnny kicked the door shut, and I collapsed into his arms.

The squeak of a step brought me out of the shock. "Nana!" I pushed past Johnny, but he caught me again and restrained me. "No. I've got to go." I pushed against him.

"No." He sniffed. "It's not Demeter."

The footsteps came louder, nearing the bottom and no longer trying to hide anything. A shadow cast by light upstairs shone across my door, and I knew who it was before I saw him. I could feel it like heat inside my spine. "No," I said.

Menessos came into view. "Yes."

"Where are Nana and Beverley?"

He walked toward us, grinning wickedly.

"Bastard!" I tried to get around Johnny, and though I had nothing compared to wære strength, I had desperate strength and I was almost loose. "If you've done anything to them, anything at all, I'll—"

Menessos laughed, cutting me off.

I wasn't finished. "You made a blood oath on my porch! Does that kind of thing expire in twenty-four hours?"

"It expires when the one the oath was made to fails to keep her part of the deal!"

"I gave Samson the stake!"

Menessos stopped about six feet away. Far enough that a single lunge would avail me nothing. Even if I had a weapon, it'd take two steps to reach him and he only needed the advance notice of one—if that—to move out of the way. "Where is it?" His words were soft, but the intensity underneath added a tremulous note to them. If he wanted me to think he was about to lose control, he'd succeeded.

"Where's what?"

Johnny jerked me back. "She doesn't know."

I went still. My stomach felt like I'd just gulped down a twenty-four-ounce Slurpee. Over my shoulder, I asked, "I don't know what?"

Johnny maneuvered me behind him. "I did it," he said.

Panic rising, I demanded, "Did what? What did you do?"

"I exchanged Vivian's stake for a fake."

"How?"

"You were busy, Red. I found a similar stick, carved it a little, rolled it in a layer of thick mud I made. I thought it would work. I thought you should have the real one to protect yourself with, since you'd ruined your protection by inviting him in."

"Oh, Johnny!" He'd done this, and now Nana and Beverley—

"Samson was supposed to destroy it and report the deed done. Nobody would have known!"

Menessos made a derisive sound. "A splendid plan . . . for a mongrel like you. Did you come up with that all by yourself?"

Johnny launched himself forward, ready to fight. In a blur, Menessos shot forward, hit Johnny once in the face, and pushed him so hard that Johnny backpedaled to keep from falling. He growled and snarled, and I heard the popping of bones. Looking down, I saw his hand darkening, changing. Claws sprouted from his fingertips.

My mouth fell open. Johnny could transform *at will*?

"I seriously suggest you quell the notion that your bestial form will fare any better." Menessos laughed condescendingly. "And while you're at it, perhaps you should consider the obvious: she carries my mark. For her to even be near the stake will cause her pain."

It all suddenly made sense: the beholder on the motorcycle asking about the pain, and the ache I'd felt since waking after he'd stained me. "That was the ache I felt all morning?"

"Surely."

"That's why you marked me! To make sure I wouldn't be able to keep it even if I wanted to!"

The vampire smiled in a refined, self-assured, and highly exasperating way. His face was made for that sort of expression. "In truth, that was not the reason, but merely a convenient side effect."

"You bastard!"

"My parentage is no concern of yours, my dear. Now, mongrel"—he gestured toward the door—"go fetch the stake while I"—his focus shifted to me—". . . *entertain* the lady."

Of course, he made "entertainment" sound about as much fun as riding a splintered broom, naked, in a hurricane.

Resolutely, Johnny said, "No."

"Then the old woman and the girl will die."

"Johnny," I said, teeth clenched.

Johnny turned to me; his eye was already swelling where Menessos had hit him. One of his eyebrow rings had been torn out, and blood ran down his face. "Red—"

"Just do it," I said. If anything happened to Nana and Beverley because of him—I wouldn't let myself think about that.

He studied me, then without another word backed toward the door. For each step he took away from me, Menessos took one closer to me. Johnny paused at the garage door; his hands had returned to normal. Ares was still out there, barking wildly from his cage.

Menessos slipped behind me, hands gripping my shoulders, and his lips came close to my ear. "I see from the glimmer in his mongrel glare that your doggie is contemplating something irresponsible. See, Persephone, the dog-like way his nose wrinkles and he bares his teeth and snarls? I wouldn't be surprised if, next, excess saliva began dripping from his uncouth jowls. Of course this show of reverting to his baser instincts substantiates my theory. I will repeat myself, lest you forget, puppy: the lady is my hostage. Your actions will dictate how this unfolds. Do you understand me, whelp?"

"Yeah," Johnny answered, looking at me.

With a gentle touch, Menessos turned my face toward him. "I will witness—at long last—the destruction of Vivian's stake. And you, Persephone, will be with me, at my side, as I triumph."

Johnny started forward. "If you hurt her—"

"You'll find it much harder to finish the task with a broken leg, but I promise you, that's what I'll do to you next." When Johnny didn't move or speak, Menessos added, "Fetch the stake, boy."

Johnny hurried across the yard in the pale light of the waning moon. Watching through the kitchen window, I ached for him. Menessos had released me, confident that

I wasn't stupid enough to try anything, well, stupid. "You're cruel," I said.

He sauntered closer, looking as if I were a silly child he was about to admonish. "He is a dog, and you cannot ever expect him to be anything but a dog."

Defiant, I said, "He is a wolf."

In answer, Menessos faked a yawn.

"Add 'rude' to the list."

"Were we making a list, dear Persephone?"

"I am. Cruel. Rude. And an oath breaker."

"I am not an oath breaker."

"Yes, you are." Johnny disappeared into the night. I was partially afraid that beholders could be waiting for him, but they would feel the pain of the stake too, wouldn't they? I looked away from the window. Menessos accepted my glare without offense. In fact, I think it pleased him to see it. Maybe that was because I felt defeated and it showed. Seeing me beaten would be something that would surely make him happy. "You swore to never step into a circle again until the stake was destroyed. But you entered my circle."

His expression sharpened as he tried to figure out who could have told me. I think he wanted to ask, but he restrained himself. "I thought you were referring to the blood oath again." He whispered, "So many troubled thoughts."

I wasn't sure if the stain would allow him to read my mind or not, but that comment made me wonder. I didn't want him to read the answer in my thoughts, so I guarded them.

"Come, witch. Build me a fire in your hearth."

He gestured for me to precede him. My feet moved before I had a chance to think about whether or not I wanted to comply. There on the table was the notebook with the printouts from the ancient book. Thank goodness Nana had shut it. The label on it read *Research* so it looked like nothing Menessos would be interested in. I didn't touch it.

After checking the flue, I knelt before the hearth. From the basket that held old newspapers, I grabbed a piece and crumpled it, dropping it on the grate. I took a few other sheets and did the same. Before I crumpled the last piece I intended to use, I realized I was holding the front page with the picture of Beverley crying and the headline about her mother. Her grief was so fresh. Only five days ago—it seemed like so much longer than that.

Would Beverley want a copy of this or not? It was hard to say. It was gruesome, but maybe later it would be important to her. I folded it nicely and set it aside, took another sheet of newspaper to crumple, then started placing the smaller pieces of kindling in the iron grate and finally, topped the kindling with two quarter-logs. I struck the match and held it to the newspaper.

Menessos made himself comfortable on my couch, striking the same pose that Samson had tried and failed at. Thinking of Samson made my mind flash on the image of his head in my refrigerator; a wave of nausea hit me. I scooted back from the heat of the fire but continued watching the flames lick and dance. "Will you . . ." I had to swallow down bitter bile. "Will you remove Samson's head from my house?"

Menessos waited before saying, "Perhaps. If I am . . .

satisfied . . . when I leave." The predator in him observed me for a long time; I could feel his gaze on me as surely as I felt the high temperature of the fire before me. "You know, if the whelp hadn't confessed to betraying you, I would have killed you once the stake was destroyed."

"Are you saying that now you won't?" I twisted to look at him. I caught a glimpse of my bat and the *40 Winks* bottle still in the corner.

He checked his fingers as if inspecting the state of his manicure. "Yes. You thought all was as it should be."

Though he said words I wanted to hear, I couldn't trust him and be relieved. I turned back to the hearth. Would the water make *him* sleep? He was very powerful; probably not. "What about Johnny? And Nana and Beverley?"

"Your spirited grandmother and the girl will be returned to you. They are as yet unharmed, though their individual fear limits may have been exposed."

"What does that mean?"

"They are not physically harmed, Persephone, but I cannot account for their ability to mentally deal with being held hostage."

I waited until it was clear that he did not intend to say more. "What about Johnny?" I pressed, letting him know with my tone that I was irritated that he kept avoiding this answer.

"As for the whelp—"

"Cool it with the dog references already. His name is Johnny."

Menessos laughed out loud. I didn't see anything funny about the comment. He sat forward, rubbing his slender fingers together. "Persephone, you're an interesting woman, and because of that I will allow you a measure of patience. I believe laypeople would call it a 'learning curve.' But that measure will evaporate swiftly if you do not address me with more respect."

He was a liar and a murderer. He'd probably kill every one of us. I had nothing to lose. "You're not a guest here. You can deal with the sarcasm."

"I don't believe you fully comprehend the situation."

That sounded like a threat, so I stood up and faced him. "Sure I do. My house, my rules." My arms crossed, and I threw my hip out in a perfect attitude-alert pose. "Anybody who commits breaking and entering, puts a dead man's head in my refrigerator, and kidnaps my family can kiss my ass if they don't like the words I use."

"I would be ever so delighted to do exactly that."

My face flushed crimson, but I mimicked him as I said, "I don't believe you fully comprehend the point of flirting, because *this* is no time for it." I considered going for the bat and bottle and finding out whether they would work, but—

He stood in a lithe, liquid motion and sauntered forward. "I assure you, Persephone, I understand perfectly the art of seduction." He spoke my name like it was a cherry atop a hot fudge sundae, a single bite with sweet and potent flavor. "You are eligible to receive the benefit of my experience, now that you have become my servant."

"Eligible" made me uneasy in an awkward, high-school kind of way. But "servant" was one of those "stand-up-and-take-notice" words. Preceded by "my," it demanded attention. I sidestepped out of reach. "What did you just say?"

He sighed. "Do you not know?"

"I am *not* your servant."

"My mark is upon you . . . within you. Your words of denial can change nothing." He eased a step closer.

"What am I, then? Just a servant to use? A one-mark beholder?" I put my hand up, palm out. "And don't take that as a request for a second stain. I don't want the 'honor' of being an offerling."

"Interesting. You seem to know nothing about vampires, and then you show that you understand unexpected things. Beholders are not so lovely as you." He eased another step closer.

I retreated a step. "Stay away from me!"

In a flash, his vise-like hands held me. "Yet offerlings are not so difficult!" I struggled, though I knew escape was hopeless. When I realized he was not squeezing tighter, not fighting back, not moving at all, simply restraining—no, he was just *holding* me—I stopped. In my ear he whispered, "Bliss does not have to be a difficult thing to find, Persephone."

"I don't want your damned stain upon me. I never wanted it."

He thrust me back, incredulous. "You asked for it!"

"The hell I did!"

"You asked for a guarantee!"

My mind raced, trying to fathom what that meant. "What part of 'I want a guarantee' means 'I want to bear your everlasting stain'?"

Matter-of-factly, he replied, "My mark is the only means by which I could guarantee the safety you requested."

"You didn't tell me that."

He waved his hand dismissively. "At the time, I did not know you were so ignorant of our ways."

"Liar! You just said a minute ago that you were *surprised* at how much I know!"

"All your arguments are pointless. My blood now marks your home and you. It tells every vampire who might happen past that I have laid claim to this place and nothing can be done against you without my consent. To ignore this is to cross me, and all who cross me know great torment before they cease to exist."

"I wanted protection from *you*!" I growled, irritated that my words still didn't convey what I meant. "Protection from the threat that you personally are to me." Miserably, I added, "Besides, I don't think I need protection from any other vampires."

"There are many eager for a place in the echelons of the vampire hierarchy. Many have been rejected. There are a few who appraise my every step in pursuit of some means to avenge their wounded pride. Had I come here and neither ruined your domicile nor laid claim to it, someone *would* have taken an interest in seeing what was here that had briefly held my interest, and then labored at discovering how it could be exploited. Would you care to know how many of my casual acquaintances have expired within a fortnight of a meeting with me?"

"No." I sat before the fire, rubbing my arms. Turning my back to him may have been unwise, but I didn't care—I wanted to feel warm. The quarter-logs were blazing earnestly, and the heat felt good, but it couldn't reach the chill set into my bones. By association I knew wærewolves well enough to write a column about them. But vampires—the filthy, rotten things—the less I knew about them, the better. Yet it was my ignorance that had gotten me into this. I knew so very little. If I was supposed to walk between worlds, I needed to get a handbook or something.

"Are your thoughts always this troubled, Persephone?"

"You're not giving me any cause to have happy thoughts."

Softly he said, "You wouldn't need them to fly in *my* Neverland."

I hadn't expected him to know literature. I mean, I know vampires are supposed to be knowledgeable. Their extended life spans give them every opportunity to become snotty, overeducated know-it-alls. I just hadn't expected him to speak of it softly, to share those words as if sharing a secret.

I asked over my shoulder, "Can you read my mind?"

He smiled in a small and unassuming way. "No, Persephone. With the first mark, a master becomes empathetic to his servant. Exact subjects remain hidden, but with familiarity they may become more obvious. Admitting this to you is surely dangerous, but I want you to trust me. We could have a bountiful future. You could become everything your name implies—the Queen of the Underworld."

CHAPTER THIRTY

When I thought that you had betrayed me," Menessos said, "my anger bested me. But now, now that I know it was the whelp—I mean, now that I know it was *Johnny* who betrayed us both, I am determined to prove to you that I am infinitely more worthy of your trust than he." He added softly, "And I sincerely hope that you will find yourself liking me."

Focusing on the blaze before me because I didn't want to see his expression, I asked, "You never really answered me about Johnny."

Fabric rustled, and easy footsteps brought him beside me, where he sat, imitating my position before the fire. A glance told me the flames lent color to his skin, color that suited him well. I could almost have thought him human.

"I hope you can acknowledge his mistake and understand that a punishment is in order. Consider it a lesson in how unreliable and capricious wæres can be. Placing trust, or responsibility, in them is an incautious decision with an often disastrous result."

I thought of Nana's predilection, "Witches and wæres weren't meant to mingle." The last few days had chiseled the sharp edge off that belief for her. I wondered what it would take to change the vampire's mind. "Trusting *you* was an incautious decision."

Menessos seemed offended. "Have I not done everything I said I would?"

I snorted. "That and more! You made the wærewolves change, all of them, during the spell. Not just Theo."

He held up a finger. "Ah, I said they would not be harmed, and they were not. I never said they would not transform. Perhaps you told them they would not, but I made no such assurances."

I glared at him. "If there hadn't been enough power to change them fully—"

"Persephone, I owned that book a long, long time and I know it well. And I know that if I had let the wærewolf transform without her alpha also in wolf form to guide her and communicate with her, she would have been disoriented and lashed out. I do not make oaths lightly, or without thinking them through to the end."

I faced the fire again. Part of me wanted to demand how he had known her alpha was among them, but another part of me was aware that I was simply arguing because that kept the vampire comfortably at arm's length. Peripherally, I was aware that Menessos had arched his neck to glance down at his chest. "Admittedly, I had not considered *this* possibility."

"What?"

He shifted his torso and opened his shirt. There, inches above his heart, was a deep gash, coated with drying blood, dark and thick. A sickening flap of wasted skin with a piece of muscle still attached lay on his chest, exposing the depth of the cruel stroke that had made it.

"Samson endeavored to use the stake to strike me down. He had learned of this weapon through rumors, so his information was questionable and lacking. For instance, he was unaware that if he carried the true stake on his person, he would not be able to tread within a hundred yards of me or any of my people without us knowing it. Unaware of this limitation, he boldly brought the fake to our meeting place under his coat. He was able to enter with it because we felt nothing of the pain that heralded the true weapon." He stared at the burning logs, words coming faster, posture rigid and hands fisted. "In order to deliver the details of how he had destroyed it privately, I required him to be in close proximity to me . . . and he used the short distance to his gain. He distracted me and struck. I raged and slew him. Too quickly. But it was done. My temper has never been mild." He paused, unclenching his hands and relaxing his position. "I reasoned that you had deceived me. I came here immediately." He paused. "*This* is why the wærewolf has not yet been punished enough."

I looked away. What could I do? Nothing. Nothing to stop him, nothing to change his mind. And where was Johnny? Were beholders beating him up while I warmed myself by the fire?

"Do something for me, Persephone, and perhaps I will feel more kindly toward your Johnny."

"Let me guess—you want to put a second mark on me?"

"I could be devious and say yes, because I think you just might take it to save the wære. But as I said, I want your trust." He paused. "No, Persephone. It does not involve a second mark."

"What do you want me to do for you, then?"

"Tend my wound."

The thought of tending something as awful and deep as that gash on his chest was not one that sat well with me, but for Johnny's sake, I agreed. "Fine. This way." In the kitchen, I retrieved my first aid kit and stared down into the plastic box of supplies. "I don't even know what's appropriate to use on a vampire."

"Proceed with whatever you would use on your own wound." He stripped out of the shirt. The ugly wound marred the beauty of him: swells of masculine strength in his chest and shoulders proportioned perfectly under pale, smooth skin.

"But you're a vampire. It's dead flesh. It seems ridiculous to apply healing cream to the wound of a dead man. Won't that just fester during the daylight hours and make everything worse? It'll stink and—" I realized that Menessos didn't smell like the bottom of a leaf pile. "Why don't you smell?"

"What?"

"Most vampires smell rotten. You don't."

"I am not like other vampires."

"That's pretty much what I just said. Why?"

He caressed my hand. "Perhaps, someday, I will tell you." He paused. "Please tend my wound."

I laid out the gauze, tape, and antibiotic cream atop the kitchen counter and focused my attention on the horrible gash. Taking clean dishcloths from the drawer, I dampened one under the sink faucet and gave him the other. "To wipe with," I said. After adding a disinfectant from the kit to the wet cloth, I squeezed the solution over the gash. Menessos sucked air through his teeth as pink water ran down his chest. "It hurts?"

He wiped the rivulets from his abdomen. "Of course it hurts. Do you think I don't feel?"

"I guess I did." I made certain to not make a disgusted face as I dabbed at the flecks of dirt and mud clinging to the torn skin. If he could bear the physical pain of this, then I could bear looking at it. "There's dirt in there, and some splinters that'll have to come out." Now I understood how the true stake could have destroyed him, leaving pieces like these behind.

I rinsed the wound again. After pouring disinfectant over the tweezers, I used them to pick out the dirt and wood. Blood welled up anew, and I rinsed a third and fourth time to be sure I'd gotten all of the pieces out. "The skin where the splinters were is all gray now."

"It will rejuvenate."

I blotted it dry, as much as I could, and picked up the antibiotic cream. "Yes or no?"

"Yes."

"You're certain?"

"If I feel pain, then I cannot be entirely dead, can I?"

I squirted the cream into the gash, way more than I thought was necessary, and held the flap in place, securing the parted flesh with three bandage-sutures and then covering it with gauze and tape.

When I finished, Menessos gently lifted my chin until I met his dangerous gaze. He said:

"Only when the sun's light has fled
is my life lived and my hungers fed,

but I will live on and on, forever
if you will but swear to leave me never."

He leaned in and put his lips to mine.

The mouth of a vampire is a dangerous, deadly weapon. But when used for pleasure . . . that weapon transforms into a sensual tool. Deep within me, my core shivered and sighed, yet an undercurrent of exquisite pain razored the edges of my tattered soul. I clung to him, as if we could become one and make this bliss last forever.

The smell of cedar and sage drifted to my nostrils and I woke as if from a dream.

"Johnny." He stood in the doorway from the garage, stake in hand.

His posture was a rictus of pain; his expression was agonized. It was more than the blood drying on his face or his blackened eye, which was now nearly swollen shut. He was hurt. Emotionally. It was killing him to see me in Menessos's arms and enjoying it. I thrust myself away from Menessos, but as soon as our contact broke, all the ease and comfort evaporated.

Pain overwhelmed my every nerve, contracting every muscle. My body rebelled against living. Anguish swallowed me. I crumbled to the floor, writhing, unable to speak.

"Destroy it now!" Menessos commanded, pointing to the living room. "The hearth is already aflame."

Johnny tossed the stake up in the air and caught it repeatedly. My pain continued, but the pinpoint of it rolled back and forth with the stake's movement. "I've been thinking," he said.

"It is a dangerous time for you to try to change this situation. There is but one outcome here: the destruction of the stake."

"See, that's what I've been thinking about. Maybe I shouldn't destroy it after all," Johnny said.

"Look at her! She will die if you do not act quickly!"

"Oh, I doubt that. Though if she did, it would spare her from the horrors of the . . . *affection* you'll force on her."

"You care for her so little? Her death would mean nothing to you? Not hers, or her grandmother's and the child's?"

Johnny paused to consider that. "To rid the world of you, it might be worth it." He stepped forward. Menessos retreated. I screamed in wordless agony.

"You're killing her!" Menessos shouted.

Johnny took another step, and another. *"I'm* killing her? *I* am?" With each step, my torture increased threefold. I was burning. I was freezing. My skin was being torn off. My brain was buzzing as every nerve in my body sent contradicting messages of the kinds of torment I could experience. Death would be a welcome release. I started praying to the Goddess, begging her to grant me that outcome.

"Why, I wonder, are you not the one writhing on the floor?" Johnny asked Menessos as he stopped beside me.

I managed to roll my head enough to see Menessos where he had retreated. "She is mortal yet," he said. "That is why her pain is greater."

"Really?" Johnny knelt beside me. He laid the stake on the floor only inches from me. I screamed and choked, and my eyes welled up and tears blurred everything.

"You are killing her!" Menessos shouted, each word emphasized.

"No," Johnny shouted back. "You are!" Softer, to me, he said, "He's using you, Red. And only you can stop it."

Menessos stomped a trio of steps closer, but Johnny grabbed the stake and held it before him. "C'mon!" he shouted. "C'mon! Let's see what happens. Let's see which of us wins."

I blinked away the tears. Johnny was on his knees, rigid and trembling, but not backing down from the vampire.

"He's using you, Red. Using the mark. He's transferring his pain onto you, to keep himself able to act. This pussy is putting twice the pain onto the mortal woman and taking but a small, unavoidable dose of it himself." He cracked the stake on the floor beside me again. "You have the power now. Right now. Not him. You do. Use it, Red. Use it. Take the stake in your hand—"

"No! It will kill her!" Menessos insisted.

"No, Red. It will set you free. It will burn away the mark he put upon you."

"That's a lie! The whelp is lying, Persephone! He is willing to sacrifice you and those you care about! He said it already. And if you touch that stake, you *will* die."

"He just doesn't want to feel the pain, Red. He knows he'll be overcome like you are overcome now. He knows he'll be weak. He knows I'll stake him through."

"Do not listen to this nonsense, Persephone. He cares nothing for you! He has proven himself a devious plotter and a backstabber. Do not listen to him!"

"Take it," Johnny whispered. "Take it."

I moved my hand, only a little. It was like reaching blistered fingers into boiling water. A whine left my lips. "Hhhhhurts. I can't!"

"Do it, Red. Just do it. It'll all go away."

Menessos shouted, "No! It is your life that will go away!"

I turned my back on Menessos and rolled to my side, coming inches closer to the stake. "Persephone, no!" the vampire wailed behind me. "No!"

I looked into those Wedjat eyes.

All I could think was that I had asked for a release and the Goddess had provided one. I sucked in all the air my lungs could hold and summoned all my strength, all my resolve. I seized the stake and, clutching it to my chest, I screamed my last breath.

CHAPTER THIRTY-ONE

Thirst.

I stood before my grove of ash trees, sweating and weary. The sun overhead shone down unnaturally bright and hot. The once lush foliage of my ever-springtime meditation place was now wilted and dying in the heat. I dropped to my knees at the edge of the stream, cupped my hands together, and lifted handful after handful up to my mouth. At least the water was still cold. Rivulets poured down my throat and over my skin, and I was so grateful for the small relief they gave. I drank for many minutes before I'd had enough. I splashed a handful over my face. That was when I saw Her.

The buckskin mustang stood at the opposite side of the stream, head down, drinking also. The hot sun cast a bluish sheen on Her black mane, but Her dun-colored hide looked soft and sleek. I stilled and watched as if She were a wild animal I did not want to alarm or frighten away.

She drank and drank as I had done, and I relished this nearness. I yearned to touch Her, but knew that I could not. So I studied Her and memorized Her image, even the blurry part reflected in the water. It stunned me to see that the reflection was not that of a horse, but that of a woman kneeling and drinking with both hands, as I had.

I remembered that Amenemhab had told me this was the Goddess. He had said She appeared to me in the color of mild tarnish. If that color represented tarnish, then such a taint was acceptable—She was beautiful. Her presence comforted me, for surely I was dying and She had not abandoned me.

Suddenly the stream was drinking the mustang, slurping it up in a swirl of colors.

"No!" I shouted. "No! Don't leave me . . ."

The woman of the reflection rose up from the water. Her hair was black like the horse's mane, glistening and wet. Her copper skin radiated a soft glow. I realized it was the sun, which had traveled swiftly into a setting position, shining at Her back. She wore no clothing, but Her dark hair covered Her breasts, and Her stance was such that Her body was slightly angled away from me. One leg, raised enough to allow Her foot to rest on a rock so it was slightly higher than the other, protected Her modesty.

Her chin tilted slightly down, darkening Her eyes and expression. I wanted Her to look at me, to see me and be happy, but She did not face me directly. She gazed past me, to the east. Carefully I turned, curious as to what so fixedly held Her attention.

I saw smoke. Black smoke, rising past a grove of oaks.

Movement caught my attention. The Goddess pointed toward the smoke. I looked at it again and when I turned back to Her, She was gone.

I stood and walked toward the darkening eastern sky. Time passed so quickly! I began to run. I passed the oaks and stepped into a clearing where red-cloaked figures stood in a circle around a high, tapering pole. Firewood had been piled high and wide around the base of the pole, and a black-clad figure was bound to it. The fire had nearly reached the figure.

I hurried around the circle to the front of the bound figure. I could not tell who it was; the hood of the cape was pulled down low. But the figure struggled, the heat rising and smoke billowing chokingly upward. "What is happening here?" I asked. None of the red-cloaked figures acknowledged me. This wasn't right. "What's happening?" I shouted.

"Help! Help me!" the dark figure called.

I turned sideways and slipped between two of the red-cloaked figures. Both turned to me then and held me back. "What are you doing?" I demanded.

"Please! Please help me!" The figure in black struggled more as the flames neared. The hood fell away, and I beheld my own face.

I backed away.

"No! No! Help me!"

The bound me began screaming as the flames caught her black robe. She struggled harder, more desperately. The chest of the cloak opened and revealed a bloody ankh on her chest. This was me, burning at the stake, a stake that I now realized was shaped like the one Vivian had created as a weapon against Menessos. That was me up there, the stained part of myself, the shadowed part of me, being destroyed.

I watched, numb, aghast at the barbaric execution. That people had once done this, brought their children and came to the town squares to watch someone be burnt alive as *entertainment,* horrified me.

The black robe burned in earnest now, and the other me's hair was smoking. Her head whipped back and forth as if she could put out the flames, but she couldn't. The exposed ankh on her chest turned to ash. The flames burned her feet directly, blackening her skin. The weakening screams of the other me became a renewed frenzy of shrieks. The stench of burning hair and flesh wafted toward me, and I gagged.

If only I could blot out the pitiful sound of her! Even as I thought it, her voice weakened, her throat becoming raw and her voice hoarse. I knew the flames were eating the air, leaving nothing but smoke for her to breathe.

I was witnessing the death of a part of me that I loathed and wanted gone. But not like this. No, not so cruelly as this.

She, the one bound there, was more than Menessos's mark. She was the part of me that had slain a stalker. The part of me that kept a baseball bat for defense and smarted off to people who deserved it. She was the part of me that had agreed to kill Goliath. Together, we were one. I was not complete without her.

I would not let the stake take more of me than I was willing to give. I would not let it destroy all the parts of me that Menessos had attached himself to.

I am Persephone Isis Alcmedi. And I am all that my roots have made me.

I yanked down the hood of the nearest red-cloaked figure. Again, I saw myself. I punched this me in the face and kicked her feet from under her. As another me turned to stop the assault, I faked to the right and rushed past her and leapt up onto the burning timbers. The flames died. The ropes binding the dying me turned to dust in my hands. I took this other me into my arms and fled.

The red-cloaked me's did not try to stop our retreat. I cradled my other self to my chest and returned to the stream, thinking the Goddess would be there and would know what to do.

By the time I arrived, the night was full and only the soft glow of the moon provided any light. I eased down at the edge of the water. "Where are you?" I called across the stream. "I need you!"

I looked at the horribly burned me now shivering in my arms. She was unrecognizable. So pitiful. Her hair gone, her skin a mass of blisters and blackness. She breathed shallow, wheezing breaths, and I knew I'd acted too late. I'd hesitated too long. I'd stopped and thought when I should have acted! I knew it was wrong.

"I'm so sorry." Tears filled my eyes. "I didn't know. I didn't know." I reached to the water and let drops from my hand moisten her lips.

The other me moved—fingers only, but she touched my arm. The swollen blisters that were her fingers dragged sickeningly across my skin. "You know now," she whispered.

"I do. I know now. I know I need you." And I knew what I had to do. "I won't let you go."

My palm rested lightly on her chest where the ankh had been. "Come," I said. "Come back to me." Our blood surged. Our bodies trembled.

She melted into me—slowly, weakly. I took her burns into me, unafraid, for they had always been mine. *"You are mine."*

An inner glowing overtook me, but it was not like the pompous rays of the sun. This was a cooling, luminous light, the moon's light. This light filled me from the inside out—cool, soothing, and healing, like aloe. I marveled to know that it was no accident, the names given me at birth. Both Persephone and Isis are lunar goddesses, and tonight the Moon embraced me and healed me and told me I was Her own.

CHAPTER THIRTY-TWO

I heard screaming.

I sat up, turning to the sound and thinking, *Not again.*

Menessos writhed on my floor, folding in and out of the fetal position.

"Red?"

I turned around. Johnny grinned at me. Even with the swollen eye and dried rivulets of blood on his face, he was charming. I reached up to where the eyebrow ring had been torn out.

"It'll be fine," he said. "You okay?"

Though I felt pain distantly, as I had that morning, I grinned. "Never better."

He stood and extended his hand to me. "Then let's finish this." He helped me up and eased nearer to the agonized vampire. I moved forward, and Menessos rolled away from me. He crawled from my advance like a worm. I followed him through the dining room and into the living room, where he rolled up against my couch. He could retreat no farther. I stopped.

"What's wrong?" Johnny asked.

"Nothing."

"Go on, then. Stake him!"

I twisted the stake in my grip. Spun it between my fingers and stopped with the pointed end in a downward position. My grip tightened.

Menessos continued to moan and scream and writhe. I understood his pain; I'd felt it. He could not even beg for his existence. For the first time he was suffering everything he deserved.

I watched him, wondering if anything he'd said to me tonight had been sincere. Yes, probably some of it had been. The problem was time. What he meant sincerely tonight might be entirely different under the next moon.

Women, especially witches, didn't let things like that slide. I smiled to myself. Menessos was feeling the wrath of a witch whose scorn he'd earned.

I wondered if he'd killed Vivian. I didn't care if he had; she'd killed Lorrie. But I thought I could understand how Vivian had become the seriously unhinged person she was. Menessos could be charming, could be delightful, but he could drive even a devoted partner away with the hoops he expected them to jump through, the orders he expected to be obeyed.

"Red," Johnny urged. "Do it."

"No."

"What? We've come too far not to kill him now!"

I strode straight to the living room hearth.

"Red! Red, no." Johnny followed me. "I beg you! Think about what you're doing! This is *the* weapon. Stake him, and then you can wear it on your belt and be a threat to every other vamp on the planet. It's the weapon *you* should wield."

I looked him in the eye and tossed the stake into the flames.

Immediately, Menessos's moans ceased.

Johnny crouched before the hearth, hand poised to snatch the stake from the flames, but it had caught fire as if it were paper. The orange flames licked over it, devouring it like a child with a delicious candy. Johnny gave up on rescuing it. He stood and grabbed my shoulders. "Why did you do that, Red? Why?"

I jerked out of his grasp, but didn't retreat.

"I'm the Lustrata," I whispered. "If I wanted him all the way dead, I wouldn't need that to kill him."

CHAPTER THIRTY-THREE

Menessos made a call instructing that Nana and Beverley were to be immediately returned to the house. Then I made him leave, sent him walking down the road before they arrived.

We watched him stroll down my driveway from the porch. "You're just letting him walk away?" Johnny asked, incredulous.

"When was the last time you think he was forced to take a good, long walk?"

Johnny snorted.

"With no one he knows to talk to or command, no one to make this easy, his thoughts are his own right now. And he has a lot to think about."

"Yeah—like revenge, retaliation, and retribution."

"Or options, opportunities, and open doors."

Johnny turned and leaned on the railing, facing me. "He marked you. He has forever to manipulate you to do his will."

My eyes left the vampire reluctantly, but when I focused on Johnny, my gaze was unyielding. "Your time frame for explaining how you managed to start and then suppress an at-will, uncyclical partial transformation is much shorter."

"Maybe we should go inside. . . ."

I allowed him to hold the door for me and wasn't surprised when he found something else to talk about in order to stall. So he wanted it to be a conversation for another day. I was tired and he was, literally, beat. It could wait.

Besides, Nana and Beverley would be home soon.

The following day a truckload of flowers arrived, and I do mean a truckload. Every room in the house had three different vases, even the bathrooms. Hundred-dollar gift cards to every store imaginable arrived in a FedEx package. A big-screen TV and all new appliances arrived. A limousine drove in at dusk, and I was afraid that it was Menessos. When the driver opened the back door, however, he removed a large, flat package. He brought it to the door, bid me a polite "good day," and promptly left. When I opened the package, I cried. It was an original painting—not a poster—by John William Waterhouse. Menessos's overwhelming way of saying "Thank you; please forgive me" might just obligate me to forgive him. Damn it.

Ares spent the day bounding around the yard with Beverley. I think they'll be good for each other. Nana found a spell in the Codex copy that reinstates the house protections that were broken when I asked the vampires inside. I guess Menessos will get a surprise if he ever comes back, but I don't look for him to show up.

And Johnny. The swelling around his eye is down, but his ego is in a world of hurt. He growls every time he passes a vase of flowers, and he stares resentfully at the painting. I know he's jealous, but it's not like I'm making a big deal of the stuff sent to me. There's anger brewing around him, I feel it. At least part of it is at me, because I burned the stake and let the vampire go. Let him be mad. He lied to me, and it could have cost us all our lives. His lie *did* cost Samson D. Kline his life.

He hasn't offered to explain the partial change yet. I'm going to have to push for that info. And I know he thinks the stain is gone, burned away like the stake. But it isn't. I can *feel* it. I don't know how to tell him that I chose to keep it because I realized that giving it up meant giving up myself. I can't even explain how I kept the stain and fed Menessos back his pain.

Though I still have questions, I've learned a lot in the last week. Like the power of words, of intentions, and of friendships. And how the death of a friend—and the death of friendships—can change you. Most people let something like that change them in sad ways, bad ways. They retreat inside themselves and hide from pain and conflict. But that's a weak response. It hurt like hell, physically and emotionally, but I faced the pain straight on. It changed me, for the better—and I earned that.

But, if I'm going to walk between worlds, I still have much to learn.